The Reckoning

Legacy of the King's Pirates 5

The Reckoning
Legacy of the King's Pirates 5
by MaryLu Tyndall

All Scripture quotations are taken from the King James Version of the Bible.

Library of Congress Cataloging-in-Publication Data is on file at the Library of Congress, Washington, DC.

ISBN-13: 978-0-9908723-5-1
E-Version ISBN: 978-0-9908723-4-4

Cover Design by Ravv at raven.com
Edits by Relz Author Support Services
     Lora Doncea, EditsbyLora.com

Acknowledgements

During the process of writing every book, God never fails to send people into my life to help me along the way. Sometimes it's the same people who are always there for me, people such as Debbie Mitchell, friend and confident, and Michelle Griep, friend and outstanding author—both of whom read over this manuscript in its raw form and offered suggestions for improvement. Sometimes it's just a kind word of encouragement from long time author friends such as Louise M. Gouge, Laurie Alice Eakes, Ramona Cecil, Debbie Lynne Costello, Susanne Lakin, and Julie Lessman. Often it's my crew of friends and readers online who bless me with their kind words and excitement over my next book. There are too many to list here, but I love you all dearly! You have no idea how your kindness keeps me going on days I want to give up on this crazy career!

Special mention goes to Sarah Venable, Diana Flowers, Jessica Pifer, Stacey Dale, Liz Riggs, and Elizabeth Campbell, who helped me choose pictures that best matched my hero and heroine. Great job! Thank you, Ravv, once again for the gorgeous cover! And thank you, Rel and Lora, for your fabulous editing. But most of all, thank you, Father in Heaven, for giving me this story and allowing me to share it with others. May your name be glorified.

Out of Time

Chapter 1

San Diego, California, August, 2015

"**D**id you hear me? I have cancer." Morgan Shaw repeated the dreaded words to her boyfriend Jason, who sat beside her on the sticky metal bench. From the look on his face, she supposed the middle of San Diego's crowded annual Tall Ship Festival was not the best place to convey the horrid news. She'd been trying to tell him for two weeks, but he'd always been too busy with his job tending bar, too distracted with memorizing lines for one of his many auditions … or just too plain drunk.

No doubt the condition he'd soon be in if he didn't stop gulping down the Mojito he held so fondly in his hands. He took another swig and stared at her again, his baby blues pools of shock and … dismay? Not sorrow, not horror … not even concern.

He squeezed the plastic cup holding his precious alcohol. It made a crackling sound even above the chatter and buzz of people passing by, the lap of waves, and the bells ringing from boats in San Diego Bay.

"Are you going to die?" he finally asked, pressing fingers to his perfectly-moussed dark hair while nodding at an attractive woman who smiled at him as she passed by.

A sharp pain stabbed Morgan at his callous tone. Even the doctor had been more tactful. Hepatocellular carcinoma, he had said. Liver cancer, Stage 3C. With chemo and radiation, she had a good chance of surviving. But she'd spotted the pity in his eyes, and when she arrived home, the Internet provided the true survival rate—less than thirty percent.

"Everyone's going to die," she returned, shifting out of the hot sun.

"Are you gonna have to go through chemo and lose your hair?" He studied her as if assessing how ugly she would be.

"Maybe." She dabbed the perspiration on her neck. "Yes, I guess. I go for my first session on Tuesday."

Why, oh why, had she allowed him to talk her into coming to this stupid festival? She hated these old boats anyway. And she didn't much care for the sea either. Last year when she'd gone whale watching, she'd spent the entire four hours puking her guts over the side of the boat. But Jason loved historical sailing boats and had bought tickets to this weekend event two months in advance. So, they'd grabbed Morgan's roommate, Tiffany, and her boyfriend, Brad, and made a day of it.

Speaking of … where was Tiffany anyway? She and Brad had gone off to the nearest bar for take-out drinks forty minutes ago. Though her roommate's cheerleader-type exuberance normally grated on Morgan, she sure could use her help now with Jason. If only to untie the knot of tension forming between them.

By the way he was chewing his lip and glancing around, Morgan thought he might bolt. She'd expected shock. She'd expected it would take time for the news to sink in. But she'd also expected a speck of care, of concern, and perhaps even a willingness to help. After all, they'd been "dating" for nearly six months now. She still had to pinch herself to believe that the coolest, best-looking guy in San Diego had chosen her— plain, nerdy, control-freak Morgan. He'd said he'd grown tired of the model types and wanted a woman with intellect, someone like her—the lead software engineer at Qualcomm Holographic Industries. Morgan couldn't have been more thrilled. Jason was good-looking, smart, and going places. He had a way about him that made her feel special, cherished, something she'd never felt before. Yes, being his girlfriend definitely hiked her confidence up a notch and made it worth dealing with some not-so-pleasant aspects of their relationship. As in not seeing him the past two weeks due to his job at the FLUXX, and his insistence that flirting with patrons was just part of his job. "How can you expect other women not to notice my good looks?" he had said to her. Those good looks, along with his talent, were going to make him a fortune when Hollywood discovered him. And she'd be right by his side when that happened. Or so he said.

Yet as he gulped down the rest of his Mojito and avoided her eyes, Morgan feared his promises were as fleeting as the hot wind blasting over her.

A man dressed like a pirate walked by and winked at her. Across the popcorn-strewn path, a vendor selling cotton candy handed a sticky pink glob to a small boy, who immediately dove in with his entire face, much to his mother's dismay. Behind Morgan, the creak of an old boat—the *Star of India*, if she remembered correctly—mimicked the ache in her heart.

She suddenly felt so terribly alone.

Tossing his empty cup into a garbage can, Jason finally faced her, and she thought she saw a glimmer of care in his eyes. "But you look so healthy. Maybe the doc was wrong, got someone else's MRI or whatever mixed up with yours. I mean, you've even lost weight and look great." He flashed his straight white teeth and took her hands in his.

As usual, his touch sent a thrill spiraling through her. His fingers stroked her palm … gently, lovingly—finally offering her a lifeline. He'd been so proud of the way she looked in her bikini that she hadn't had the heart to tell him that shedding pounds was part of the disease.

"No, they got it right," she said. "Listen, Jason, I'm going to need you. To help me through this."

"What about your parents?"

She ignored the pang in her heart. "You know my father. He just wants to throw money at it and pretend it doesn't exist. And Mom. She's hysterical, of course. She has every prayer chain in the country praying for me while she ups her meds and remains dazed, unable to deal."

Jason released her hands and began twirling the class ring on his finger. "What can I possibly do to help? Will you still be able to go out and have fun?"

Was he kidding? "I'm going to be pretty sick." She leaned toward him and grabbed his hand again, desperate for the care in his eyes to return. "I don't want to go through this alone. I'm scared, Jason."

His hand felt limp in her grasp as he stared out over the bay. Sunlight highlighted his strong smooth jaw and wavered over lashes that were the envy of every woman.

"I can't do this." Tugging his hand from hers, he swallowed, a look of panic on his face. "Sorry, Morg. I can't do this."

"*You* can't do this?" Anger simmered in her gut.

"Cancer, man." He shook his head. "That really sucks. But I'm not your guy. This kind of stuff scares the crap out of me. I wouldn't be much use to you. Can you see me hanging around some hospital? Geez, I'm only twenty-three." His eyes flashed with an emotion foreign to him—shame. "I'm too young for this heavy stuff. I can't handle it. I'll only bring you down. I'm sorry, Morg. It's been fun." He stood and brushed off his designer jeans as if he could as easily brush away any remembrance of her. "Let me know how you're doing." Then turning, he strode away, drawing the gaze of every female in the vicinity.

Two men dressed in British Naval uniforms cut him from her view.

She wanted to cry. But the tears raising havoc behind her eyes refused to flow. Instead, a numbness pervaded her senses. And her mind.

A drop of sweat slid down her back beneath the cute purple T-shirt she'd worn just for Jason—the one that flattered her rather small chest. The sun seemed to halt right on top of her and engulf her in a sauna. A bell clanged down the walkway as a man called, "All aboard!" for a sailing tour of the bay.

"Honey, you look like you need this more than me." Tiffany's voice preceded a set of manicured nails surrounding a lime-colored drink decorated with an umbrella.

Morgan stared at the way the sun sparkled over the ice cubes floating on top. She never drank alcohol. Hated the stuff. She saw what it did to her father and her friends when they acted like fools. Socializing was difficult enough without becoming a slurring imbecile. Besides, the Bible said it was wrong to drink, didn't it? At least that's what her mother had hammered into her. Though the same rule didn't seem to apply to the handfuls of anti-anxiety and anti-depressants her mother downed every day.

Morgan took the drink. Rules or not, she needed it at the moment.

Yanking her Prada handbag higher on her shoulder, Tiffany sat beside her. "What happened? I've never seen you drink. Where's that hunk of a boyfriend of yours?" She swept a narrowed gaze over the crowd.

Brad strolled up in his muscle shirt and khaki surfer shorts, a plastic cup in each hand.

Morgan sipped her drink and cringed at the strong, biting taste. "Jason broke up with me," she managed to choke out as the liquor sped down her throat in a heated blast.

Tiffany splayed her designer nails over her mouth and gasped.

"Dude, that sucks," Brad chimed in with his usual enlightened comment, though his tone held more concern than Jason had expressed over her impending death.

Morgan took another gulp, wondering when the buzz would start numbing the pain. *You'd think she'd be used to being dumped by now.* This was the fifth time in the six years since her mother had allowed her to date at eighteen. "I'm going home." She stood.

"No way. Not letting you." Tiffany threaded her arm through hers and smiled. "We're here, so we might as well enjoy the festival. On Jason's dime, I might add. A bit of revenge, eh?" She winked, and Morgan could swear she felt a breeze from Tiffany's lash extensions.

"I don't see how touring a bunch of old boats will get back at …" Morgan couldn't say his name. Didn't want to say his name. *Had he really just broken up with her?* Those tears began pooling behind her eyes again.

"The slime bucket?" Tiffany interjected, grabbing her drink from Brad.

Brad chuckled and ran a hand through his long sun-bleached hair. "How 'bout puke-worm?"

Tiffany giggled. "You did tell us to clean up our language and use more imaginative words."

Morgan had. But at the moment she wouldn't mind hearing Jason called some really nasty things. She took another swig of her drink. The umbrella jabbed her eye. *Great.* Plucking out the silly decoration, she tossed it in the garbage and felt the world spin.

Tiffany dragged her along, the heels of her Gucci pumps clapping over the pavement. "I know just what you need, girl. A pirate ship battle."

What did she say?

"Yeah, dude." Brad eased beside Tiffany, downed his drink, and tossed the cup. "Maybe they'll let you fire the cannons. You could pretend you're shooting at Ja—I mean puke-worm."

"I don't want to go on a boat. Pirates stink, and I don't want to run into … what's his name. This is *his* festival." Morgan tugged from Tiffany's grip.

Tiffany was having none of it. Instead, she halted, and force-fed Morgan the rest of her drink. "There. The perfect cure for a broken heart. I guarantee you'll feel better soon."

As the liquor burned her tongue and heated a puddle in her stomach, Morgan couldn't help but wonder what her religious mother would think. Oddly, the thought brought a smile to her lips. But that was surely the alcohol. Morgan was a good girl. A perfect girl. She didn't drink or do drugs or lie or cheat or steal. She went to church every Sunday and volunteered alongside her mother at the children's shelter. Then why had God sentenced her to death? That singular thought had been floating through the recesses of her mind since she'd learned about her cancer, but she'd been too afraid to latch onto it—too afraid of what it meant about her—or worse, about God.

Wait … why did she suddenly not care? What a marvelous feeling!

"See, I told you." Tiffany's perfectly made-up face began to sway in Morgan's vision.

She glanced around at the vendor booths selling ocean-themed candles, watercolor seascapes, ship models, pirate clothing … all fuzzy and distant. The stench of hot dogs, Chinese food, and funnel cakes threatened to turn Morgan's stomach.

Brad appeared out of nowhere, waving three tickets. When had he left? "Guess who's going on a pirate battle. On some old pirate dude's ship." He stared at the tickets and squinted. "The *Reckoning*. Belonged to the famous pirate, Rowan Dutton from 1694. Whoa. That's totally ancient, dude." He gazed toward the wharf. "That's like over three hundred years. Wonder how it lasted so long?"

Tiffany swatted him. "It's a replica, dummy."

"Oh." He chuckled and flipped hair from his face. "C'mon. They're boarding."

Boarding? Morgan tugged from Tiffany's still-firm grip. "I'll stay here. Me and boats don't get along."

"Nonsense." Tiffany yanked her down the wharf. "It will be an adventure. And believe me, girl, you need an adventure right now."

Would her friend be so anxious to drag Morgan to an adventure if she knew Morgan was dying? Morgan hadn't had the heart to tell her yet. She wasn't ready to hear Tiffany's positive platitudes. But that was Tiffany. Always cheerful, always optimistic, the type who loved to experience new things, who feared nothing, who was always leaping from one adventure to the next.

So unlike Morgan.

"Welcome to the pirate ship *Reckoning*!" A man dressed like a pirate announced when the tourists were assembled on the main deck. Morgan leaned against a post and held her stomach. Tiffany and Brad had rediscovered each other and were smooching at the edge of the crowd. Maybe this wasn't such a good idea, after all.

"Just a bit of history before we set sail," the man continued, marching before the tourists, the fake sword at his side blinking in the sun. "Rowan Dutton was one of the most notorious and vicious pirates to ever sail the Caribbean. But he didn't start off that way. He started as a privateer for the British with permission granted in what they called a letter of marque to capture and plunder French ships." He stopped and hooked his thumbs in a belt strung across his chest.

Half the people listened; the other half chatted or wandered around. A group of teens texted on their phones. Two young boys started climbing a rope ladder until their father dragged them down. A seagull screeched overhead. She should leave. She was never much for history. Or pirates. But the boat was rocking, and the crowd blocked the way to the dock.

"But something happened to Captain Dutton," the man continued as he winked at an attractive woman in her twenties, then swept his gaze to a young boy standing before his parents. Scrunching his face, the guide gripped the handle of his sword and uttered, "He turned pirate! Argh!" making the boy laugh.

"Not only pirate, he turned mean, attacking any ship that crossed his path, torturing, maiming his victims. His crew was terrified of him. He even sailed with Blackbeard for a time!"

Gasps filtered among the tourists.

A little girl with blond curls approached the man and tugged on his vest. "What happened to him, mister?"

The pirate smiled down at her. "Well, little lady, like the fate of most pirates back then, Captain Dutton died before his time. In 1714." He glanced over the crowd and laid a hand beside his mouth, lowering his voice. "Killed in a duel with a jealous husband."

Figures. Morgan grimaced. *Men.* She searched for Tiffany and Brad, but the swarm of people wouldn't stay still. There. She caught a glimpse of them by the far railing, their faces glued together. Great. Just what she needed after her heart had been put through a shredder. Pushing from the post, she started forward, weaving through the throng.

The pirate announcer grabbed onto a thick rope leading to the sails above. "Now this magnificent ship is just a replica of the *Reckoning*. But there are some original pieces on board—behind glass, of course—recovered from the real ship discovered five years ago off the coast of Antigua. She was a real beauty. A three-masted British merchantman, housing twenty guns and ..." But Morgan wasn't listening anymore.

Her stomach felt like someone had flipped it upside down and was trampling on it. She needed to get off this stupid boat. Fast.

"As we set sail, feel free to roam about. There are signs explaining the different parts of the ship. In the captain's cabin, you'll find a copy of a painting by the famous pirate artist, LM. Nobody knows the true identity of the artist, but his paintings of various Caribbean pirates are renowned throughout the world. Worth millions. This one is of Captain Dutton. They say 'tis a good rendering of the man."

"Are we gonna shoot the cannons?" one little boy asked.

"We are at that, little pirate. See that sloop?" He pointed to another boat just raising sail. "That's Captain Jenkins, the fiercest pirate in these waters. It's our job to catch him and bring him to justice."

"Cool." The little boy's grin couldn't be wider.

Wonderful. A ship battle. Just what Morgan needed.

The crowd began to disperse as she wobbled to the dockside where Tiffany and Brad seemed oblivious to anyone around them. Maybe she could sneak away. After tripping over a lady's foot and apologizing, she was nearly at the ladder when a flash of a FLUXX nightclub t-shirt, a prideful gait, and a familiar chuckle turned her head to see Jason strolling down the wharf, a woman on each arm.

Morgan ducked behind a rather large man arguing with his wife. *No, no, no! Oh, God, if you're up there, please make Jason go to another boat.* She couldn't stand seeing him again so soon. How could he dump her one minute and be laughing with two women the next? Even the alcohol couldn't numb the new pain scraping across her heart. Had she meant nothing to him at all?

He strolled over the plank, leapt onto the deck, then turned to assist the giggling airheads. Great. Normally she would just confront the idiot, but the alcohol was torching her vulnerable emotions and bringing tears to her eyes. And she wouldn't give him the satisfaction of seeing her pain. There must be another way off this boat. She followed a group of people down a hatch on extremely narrow steps and into a dimly lit room. Signs hung about, labeling various sections of the boat: Bulkhead, Hatchway, Ship Lantern, Pursers Office, Gunroom, Gunport. Shoving through the throng, she rose up another hatch and wandered down a long hall.

A thundering sound snapped her gaze above. The boat jerked and started to move. *No!* Visions of her retching over the railing while Jason and his women laughed at her, prompted her to rush to the end of the hall into another room. Windows! There were large windows. She dashed around a desk and leapt onto the window seat, then pried, pounded, and cursed at the latches.

They wouldn't budge.

In a panic, she spun and surveyed the room. No other exit. Just a plain desk with a leather chair, shelves housing various trinkets, a four-poster bed, an old cannon, a large empty chest that smelled of moth balls. And a painting. Or a print.

Encased in glass, something about it called to her. Perhaps it was the artist in her—her many classes in oils, proven by half-finished paintings scattered about her apartment. Or maybe it was the subject. A man, a good-looking man she determined as she came closer. Light, windswept hair was tied behind him, a dark goatee covered his chin, and a jagged scar—no, a fresh wound—etched across his right cheek. He sat on a chair, arms crossed over an ivory shirt and a leather vest strapped with silver-buckled belts into which a gun was stuffed. A gold earring dangled from his right ear while a sword hung from his hip. But it was the look in his stark blue eyes that mesmerized her. One that defied his prideful stance and frightening pirate garb.

A look of complete adoration.

And in that moment, she would have given anything to be the object of that look. She dropped her gaze to the bottom of the painting, searching for the artist's name, but found only LM scrolled there in dark paint.

The floor tilted and her stomach roiled. *Drat*! Holding her belly, she scrambled out the door and down the hall, then back into the gunroom, where only a few people remained at the exhibits. Stumbling past them, she was about to climb the ladder to the main deck when Jason's voice tumbled down upon her like a ton of bricks. She dared a peek above to see him standing right beside the hatch with the two women. Now what was she to do?

She had no choice but to stay out of sight until the tour was over. Someplace dark where she could quietly vomit and pray for relief from a God who was obviously not on her side.

She found another hatch with a rope strung across it, displaying a "Do Not Enter" sign, but that didn't stop her from descending deeper into the bowels of the wretched boat. At least it would keep Jason and his new girlfriends out and give her some peace.

Voices shouted above, followed by a rumbling noise. The boat teetered. She slipped off the last rung of the ladder and landed on the hard wooden floor. Splinters jabbed her palms as a shard of pain etched up her tailbone. *Great, just great.* Struggling to rise, she glanced around at the boxes, crates, tools, and various equipment that filled the storage area beneath the dim light of a single overhead bulb. Such mayhem. You'd think the sailors would store their supplies in a more orderly fashion. And the dirt! Ugh. A layer of grime draped over everything. Feeling lower than she'd felt in years, Morgan found a small space to crawl into between an object covered with a cloth and a stack of ropes. Leaning back on the wooden hull, she prayed for her head to stop swimming and her stomach to stop flipping.

How did a twenty-four year old software engineer, wanna-be artist, end up tipsy in the stinky hold of an old pirate replica? A boat that was now sailing out to sea—or at least into San Diego Bay.

Minutes passed as the boat tilted back and forth … back and forth … back and forth. Morgan puked onto the stack of ropes, but it didn't help her feel better. How long were these silly pirate battles anyway? Surely not more than an hour. She could last an hour. Right?

The tears finally came. Maybe it was being alone in the shadows. Maybe it was the numbness of her drink starting to diminish. Maybe it was because she finally had time to absorb the events of the past few weeks.

She was dying. And she was all alone in the world.

Muffled shouts and voices drifted from above, but they only made her feel more alone. The floor tilted, and she grabbed onto the cloth to keep from sliding. It fell away, revealing an old brass lantern sitting atop a crate. Picking it up, she set it in her lap. Old wasn't the word for it. It was downright antique, so rust-ridden she feared it would crumble beneath her touch. Maybe if she found some matches, she could light it and chase away her pity party. But how did these things work? Blowing away cobwebs, she discovered a small sliding door, no doubt where the oil went. Opening it, she tipped the lantern, and a chain dangled out. One tug and a tarnished amulet in the shape of a heart appeared. Odd. Flipping it over, she rubbed away the grime, revealing two raised crosses on either side of a red stone that was also in the shape of a heart. With a little TLC, this would be a beautiful piece again. But what was it doing here? She squeezed her eyes, still brimming with tears, and a single tear slid down her cheek and dropped off her chin.

Straight onto the amulet.

It began to glow. *Glow?* She blinked. The alcohol was making her see things.

The roar of water sounded from outside, and the boat suddenly jerked upward. Morgan tumbled over the deck and struck her head on a barrel. Pain speared through her.

Boom!

A massive explosion quivered her bones. The boat leapt. Water roared against the hull. What was going on? Were they supposed to be going this fast? And what was that *smell*?

Looping the amulet around her neck, Morgan made her way to the ladder, where a stream of light filtered from above. The galloping boat knocked her this way and that, shoving her into crates, barrels, and stacks of rope and sails she didn't remember seeing before. She also didn't remember the layer of slimy water that coated the floor and caused her to slip more than once.

The sea continued pounding against the hull as the boat rose and dropped like a roller coaster. Was the crew crazy? They were putting all these tourists in danger going this fast! And that cannon sounded real. Too real.

She finally reached the ladder and climbed up one level, then started up the next, struggling against the heaving boat. Distant thunder bellowed. She didn't remember storm clouds. The hull crashed open. A cannonball sped past her. Water gushed inside.

They'd been hit!

The torrent knocked her off her feet. She gripped the ladder, legs flailing in the rushing water. Her arms burned. Her breath crimped in her throat. But she finally managed to hoist herself up and crawl up the remaining rungs. When they'd advertised that the pirate battle was realistic, they weren't kidding. Two men dressed like pirates—and smelling like them too—flew past her, giving her odd looks, but not slowing in their task.

Mind reeling, Morgan reached the top deck and dared to pop her head above. She didn't want to risk seeing Jason, but obviously with a hole blown into the boat, the danger outweighed her pride.

Sailors dressed like pirates dashed everywhere. Each of them wore pistols, swords, and axes. The boat tilted again, and she climbed above and grabbed ahold of a post, scanning the scene for the man in charge of this ridiculous pirate battle. In the distance, another boat, smoke pouring from its back end, turned away from them.

Foul language spewed from the sailors' mouths.

She would speak to the captain about that, too. There were children aboard, after all.

Wait. Where *were* the tourists? She searched the boat again but saw only people dressed like pirates. Above her, sails flapped in the wind while men lined the yards sticking out from three masts. Shielding her eyes from the sun, she searched for San Diego's North Embarcadero where the festival was taking place.

She saw nothing but sea.

"Starboard guns fire as you bear!" A voice resounded above her—a booming voice, an authoritative voice.

Craning her neck, she peered at the upper deck, seeking its owner. A man appeared and gripped the railing.

Morgan's heart seized in her chest. It was the pirate in the painting, Captain Rowan Dutton.

Chapter 2

January 1694, South of Puerto Rico, Caribbean

Rowan Dutton struck the quarterdeck railing with his fist and let out a foul curse. "To the Devil with these French dogs!" Grinding his teeth together, he raised his spyglass for another glance at their prey, smoke curling from her stern. At least he'd done her *some* damage.

"Cap'n, we're takin' on water!" a pirate yelled from below, water dripping from his hair and coat.

"Patch the hole and tend to the pumps!" Rowan bellowed, then gestured to two men nearby. "Assist them!"

If they couldn't slow the sea from pouring into the hold, Rowan would lose the chance to finally gain the fortune he'd been seeking the past two years—the fortune that would change his life. Rarely did a French merchantman—especially one reportedly loaded with over five tons of silver bars, two tons of gold doubloons, and a chest full of rare pearls—land in Rowan's open arms. Even rarer did she sail without the protection of at least two French warships. But Rowan had heard about her precious cargo on the good authority of a French sailor on Martinique, who'd also told him that she hoped to avoid detection by sailing without escort.

Now, thanks to his master gunner's skill, they'd crippled the French ship, giving Rowan one more chance to level her masts and take her as prize before she slipped away.

"Ready the bow chasers!" he yelled down to Terrin, the man in charge of relaying his orders to Cudney—his deaf master gunner. "Fire on my order!"

With a nod, Terrin quickly interpreted the order to Cudney with signs and signals they'd worked out between them, sending the two men, along with the rest of the gun crew, speeding to the bow.

"We'll rake her stern. That'll teach her," Rowan said to no one in particular. "Hard aport!" he ordered his helmsman before shouting for his first mate to raise every scrap of canvas to the wind.

Kerr brayed further orders, and men leapt up the ratlines to task. Sails flapped as the ship veered to port, creaking and groaning beneath the weight of added seawater in the hold.

Nick, Rowan's quartermaster and friend, gave him a look of concern. "She's sluggish."

"Aye." Rowan could feel it as well. "But we're nearly upon the Frenchman, and I'm confident in Cudney's skill to demast the strumpet and bring her begging to my side."

Nick adjusted the plaid tartan at his throat and chuckled. "Och, now. She's no' one of yer married leddies, Captain."

The ship bucked over a wave. Rowan braced himself as seaspray showered him. "Is she not? Both have sleek lines and beauty, both like to play chase, and both have treasures found within."

As if on cue, whistles and catcalls rose on the wind, jerking Rowan's attention below. A woman emerged onto the main deck. Scantily dressed in odd men's attire, she wore a look that bore none of the fear one would expect from a lady on a pirate ship. Especially a ship in the midst of battle. Quite the opposite, in fact. She placed fists on her small waist and scoured his men with an angry gaze.

Rowan growled. Who had defied the articles his men signed that forbade bringing women aboard the ship, especially harlots?

"Back to your posts!" he shouted, but the deck tilted and the woman tripped, luring every available man within reach to come to her aid.

"Lud!" He hadn't time for this. Another second and they'd be within firing range of the merchantman. One glance toward Cudney told him the entire gun crew was focused on the wench as well. In fact, pirates gathered around her, mewling and pawing like a pack of wild cats. The woman slapped them away and stormed across the deck, all eyes following her.

"Fire as you bear!" Rowan yelled to Terrin standing beside Cudney, but both men's gazes remained locked on the woman as she climbed the ladder to the quarterdeck in breeches so tight, little was left to the imagination.

"Kerr!" Rowan sought his first mate. The man quickly faced his captain, nodded his understanding, then leapt onto the foredeck and shouted for the gun crew's attention.

Jerked from their stupor, they swung about and lowered matchsticks to two swivels that quickly belched their chain shot in a thunderous roar. The ship trembled. The woman screamed, fell to the deck, and covered her ears as smoke tickled Rowan's nose. He batted it away and raised his glass to assess the damage.

The shots splashed harmlessly into the sea just yards behind the merchantman's stern. *Just yards!* And now, with all sails raised to the favoring wind, she sped away, spitting foam at him in defiance.

"Blast it all!" A stiff breeze tossed his hair, and he doffed his tricorn and ran an arm over his sweaty forehead.

Below him, a pair of intelligent eyes the color of sea moss latched onto him and narrowed.

"You …" Rowan ground out. "You …" He grabbed the woman's arm and jerked her to her feet. "You caused me to lose my prize!"

"What are you talking about?" She had the audacity to wrench her arm free and glower at him. "This is abuse. I'm going to report you to the festival authorities!"

Rowan took a step toward her, desperate to clutch that delicate neck and strangle the life from her. He raised his hands to do just that, when Nick stepped between them. "Let the lass be. She didna mean t' stop yer plundering an' raping."

"She stopped far more than that." Rowan backed away with a snort and glanced toward the merchantman, now just a spot on the horizon.

Wind sifted through Nick's short red hair as the older man squinted into the sun. "There'll be more prizes."

"Not like that one." Rowan glared around Nick's burly body at the woman. "You'll pay for this, wench!"

To her credit, the woman didn't flinch, didn't cower, nor did a speck of fear appear in her eyes. Instead, she cocked her head, released a heavy sigh, and said, "Stop this ridiculous act and take me back to San Diego at once."

He started for her again, but Nick held him back and ordered two pirates to take her below.

"To my cabin," Rowan added. He would deal with her later.

The woman kicked and clawed at the men—spitting out words Rowan had never heard before—as they all but carried her down the ladder to the companionway.

He turned to the crew, some still staring after the woman, others grumbling and cursing over their lost prize. "Mark my words, gentlemen, whoever brought the wench aboard will suffer the cat! And worse, if my temper remains. Now back to work!" He nodded toward Kerr, who began ordering the men to adjust sail, scattering the mob like cockroaches before sunlight.

Unfolding his clenched fists, Rowan gripped the railing and hung his head, still unwilling to believe he'd had such treasure in his grasp only to see it slip away.

"Perhaps 'tis for the best, Captain." Nick slid beside him. "Maybe they would ha' defeated us wi' blade an' pistol when we boarded."

"When have you ever seen me defeated with cutlass in hand?"

Sunlight glistened in the green sapphire broach Nick always wore pinned to his doublet—from his Viking ancestors, he liked to brag. "Perhaps 'tis a lesson in humility tha' the great Captain Dutton doesna always get his prize."

Rowan snorted. "'Tis a fool's ambition to gloat over lost treasure, Nick. Think of the charities that will suffer from your empty pockets."

"Think of the games tha' will suffer from yers, eh?" he countered and smiled.

"Indeed. Precisely why 'tis such a tragedy. All those wasted winnings."

"But if ye'd invest the fortune from yer raids, instead of losing it at the tables, maybe ye'd ha' acquired this illusive fortune ye deem necessary t' repay yer sister."

Rowan frowned and raised a brow. "Alack, do I possess the brains of an investor?"

"Och, aye. More brains than required for piracy, I'll grant ye." Nick gave a sly smile.

The deck canted to starboard as a fist of wind struck Rowan, increasing his fury.

"Where to, Cap'n?" Scratch, the helmsman asked, a lithe fellow with long pointy fingernails and a mustache that hung to his chin.

Rowan sighed and gazed over the sea, sparkling like a turquoise diamond in the afternoon sun. He'd prefer to set sail for a port where he could mollify his misfortune with rum and cards, but the nearest one was Bridgetown, and it was too far away to risk getting caught with a hole in his hull. He'd never be able to evade a Spanish or French warship in this condition.

"Set course for that small island we saw yestereve," he ordered. "We can patch up the ship before we make way for New Providence."

"Aye, aye, Cap'n."

The ship bucked, and Nick grabbed the binnacle. "Charles Town? Why visit tha' den of—"

"I have business there," Rowan interrupted, tired of Nick's pious intervention.

"An' what d'ye intend t' do wi' the lass below?"

"Make her pay, of course." Rowan smiled for the first time all day. "She caused me to lose a grand fortune, and I intend to make her work off every shilling."

Morgan could think of only one explanation for the insanity surrounding her. At first she'd thought she was dreaming, but the painful grips of the smelly men assured her she was quite conscious. No, this was her father's doing. It had to be. When she'd informed him of her cancer, he'd leaned back in his leather chair in his office and put on his *I-can-fix-your-problem* business expression that surely was one of the reasons he'd risen to CEO of Dynamics, Inc.

"We will fix this, honey. Nothing to worry about. If I have to spend every dime I own to get you the best doctors, by God I will. Nothing harms the daughter of Macon Shaw. Nothing and nobody!"

Why did the man always speak of himself in the third person? He punched numbers on his phone, and soon two admins filed in and jotted notes as he droned on with instructions about locating specialists and hospitals, etc. Morgan had stopped listening. All she'd really come for was a hug—a rare gift from a man who'd always been too busy and too standoffish to engage in *unnecessary displays of affection*, as he called them.

When he was done, he sent the admins out with a wave of his hand and led Morgan to the door with the excuse he had an important meeting to attend.

"Now don't you worry about a thing, honey. I'll take care of everything. I'll even send something your way to keep your mind off your troubles." And with that, he gave her a peck on the cheek and ushered her off, already speaking to someone on his Bluetooth before he shut the door.

Now, as she glanced around the most authentic pirate ship she'd ever seen, felt the salty spray on her face, smelled the unwashed bodies of men who could easily be on the set of one of the Pirates of the Caribbean movies, she realized her father had spared no expense to keep her mind off her troubles. He'd done this before, of course. When she'd suffered her first broken heart at thirteen, he'd paid for an entire Western town, complete with horses, Indians, cowboys, and saloon girls. He'd staged drunken brawls, a gunfight in the street, an Indian raid, and a handsome son of a rancher who took a shine to her.

By the end of the week, she'd forgotten all about the boy who had broken her heart.

But cancer was different. You couldn't run from cancer. Or pretend it doesn't exist. And no amount of fun or role-playing would cure it or take away its pain.

Regardless, she had to admit her father had done a good job finding an actor who looked just like the painting she saw of Rowan Dutton. Still, the man took his role a little too seriously.

"Ouch! You're hurting me." She struggled in the men's grips as they dragged her past the captain. One final glance over the sea revealed no coastline was in sight. Surely they hadn't gone too far from San Diego.

The pirates shoved her down a ladder into a dark hallway where the smell of moist wood and smoke joined other yucky odors that curled her nose. Her head began to pound again as one of the men opened a door and shoved her inside, mumbling something about how the captain gets all the wenches.

"Hey, watch it!" She rubbed her arm and glared at him. "My father won't be happy to hear how you manhandled me."

He answered with a snort and a belch before he and his friend ambled away.

The floor tilted, and she ran to grab the desk for support—a completely different desk from the one that had been there just an hour ago. This desk was solid wood and sturdy and had etchings of waves and dolphins along the bottom. Maps, old papers, a quill pen, lanterns, and several strange instruments were scattered in a cluttered mess around three open bottles of some type of alcohol. In fact, everything in the room was different, she noted, as she looked around, searching for a phone or a computer—something she could use to contact her father and call off this charade. The four-poster bed had transformed into a cot attached to the wall. Sheets and covers were tossed haphazardly over it as if the owner had just risen. The chest was replaced by a tall closet. The shelves had become bookcases filled with books lying in disarray and barricaded by a wooden rail. Beside them, an assortment of hideous-looking weapons hung on the wall. Flies hovered over a tray of dirty plates perched on a leather chair, while an assortment of clothes littered the floor. How could they have staged this so quickly?

Had Tiffany put something in her drink to knock her out?

Behind the desk, the horizon dipped in and out of sight through a wide span of colored windows. Morgan's stomach vaulted. Didn't her father know she got seasick? Of course not. He'd never spent enough time with her to know such a thing.

Well, if pirates were supposed to be slobs, they'd done a good job creating the captain's cabin. Sifting through the mess on the desk for a phone, Morgan gathered the documents and placed them in neat piles, then lined up the bottles and instruments.

Pounding boot steps alerted her, and she glanced up to see the man posing as Captain Dutton march into the room, followed by two men. He seemed larger … taller than he had above deck. Maybe it was the low ceilings, which barely allowed him to stand at full height. Windswept light hair fell to his shoulders as he sauntered past her without a glance. She backed away from the desk. The second man appeared to be forty or so with short red hair, a trimmed beard, and kind hazel eyes that smiled at her as he stepped inside, while the third man was young, dark-haired, and looked like a typical handsome pirate from the cover of some swashbuckling romance. *Seriously?*

The captain removed his sword and laid it across his desk. Brow darkening, he stared at the orderly piles with a bewildered look, then raised his gaze to a paper she still held in her hands. "You'll find nothing of value here, wench."

Morgan set down the document. "Listen, guys. Bravo, bravo"—she clapped—"Great acting. Well done. I'm totally impressed. But I'm really tired, and I want to go home now. I'm sure my father will pay you for the entire week or however long he booked you but I—"

"Silence!" The actor-captain's eyes flamed. The tone and volume of his voice would certainly have scared her if he were a real pirate. His gaze lowered to her chest, and his mouth twisted like a pretzel. He stormed toward her.

Instinctively, Morgan backed away.

Clutching the amulet, he tore it from her neck, then held it up before her. "Where did you get this?"

She'd forgotten all about it. "Below in some old lantern. Hey, if it's yours, keep it." As he dangled the chain, she noticed how rough and callused his hands were. "Sorry. I got distracted when you fired a cannon. A little too real, don't you think? And the return shot with all the water? Yeah, very cool. But my father asked you to distract me, not give me a heart attack."

The three men eyed her as if she'd said she was from Mars. Water roared a mad dash against the hull, mimicking the pounding in her head.

"'Twas my mother's," the captain said, his tone filled with sorrow, before his anger returned and he shoved it in her face again. "You stole it!"

Morgan swallowed at the rage in his eyes. This guy deserved an Emmy. "I did no such thing!"

"How did you come to be on my ship, wench?" He scanned her with contempt. "And why are you attired thus?"

"No doubt she slipped on board at Antigua." The handsome pirate plopped into one of the chairs and spread his feet before him. "To entertain the crew." He winked at her.

"What?" Morgan shrieked. "That's disgusting!"

"Antigua was two weeks ago," the captain said. "Where has she been this entire time?"

"One of the men must ha' brought the lass aboard, Captain." The red-haired man with the kind eyes spoke.

The captain growled. "Forsooth! They know I suffer no women aboard, save Edith. I'll keelhaul the man who disobeyed me!" He laid the amulet on the desk with a gentleness that defied his angry tone, then faced her and fisted hands at his waist. Two leather belts, studded with silver buckles, crisscrossed his white shirt and brown vest. The dark stubble lining his jaw matched the goatee on his chin, while sunlight glimmered on a gold earring hanging from his right ear. Her compliments to the costume director.

"Okay. Okay." She held up a hand. "The archaic language. Nice touch. Really good. But I'm done, okay? Please call my father."

"I know nothing of your father, wench." Confusion rode on the captain's brow. "Alack, what I *do* know"—he strolled toward her, the thump of his boots heavy on the floor—"is that since you refuse to answer how you came aboard my ship, I must conclude you are naught but a thief."

She laughed. "Good one."

"Forsooth, the wench admits it!" He glanced at his friends.

Morgan huffed and shoved past him. "Where is your cell? I'll call my dad myself." She didn't make it two steps before the actor-captain clutched her arm and held her fast. Then snatching the pile of fly-infested plates, he tossed them to his desk in a clatter, and shoved her into the empty chair.

"Gross!" Imagining the rotten food beneath her, she squirmed to get up, but he held her down. "My father will hear of this!"

Impervious to her threat, he merely rubbed the stubble on his chin as if pondering what to do with her.

"Captain," the red-haired man spoke up as he leaned back against the desk. "The lass isna a thief. Why would a woman steal from pirates? She'd haveta be daft t' even try."

"Humph. Daft or not, she is clearly a woman." His eyes roved over her. "A bit lacking in the chest, but the rest of her curves are in the right places."

That was it! "You pig!" She stood and swung at him, but he leapt back with a laugh. "I daresay, the sprite has some bite."

His chauvinistic friends chuckled.

She thrust hands on her hips. "Weren't men more chivalrous back in pirate days? Perhaps you should read your script more carefully."

Again his expression twisted. "How now? I find myself in agreement with you, Nick." His chuckle faded as he studied her, his blue eyes like ice. "More devil than daft, I make bold to say. You lost me my prize, wench! And you'll pay for that, I assure you." Grabbing a bottle from his desk, he drew it to his lips and gulped down several swallows of the amber liquid. Probably tea or Kool-Aid. Surely, her father wouldn't let them drink on the job.

The boat leapt like a cat, tossing her back into the chair. She drew a deep breath to settle her stomach, then slowly rose and lifted her chin. "You have insulted me enough. I insist you turn this boat around and take me back to San Diego."

"Ship, if you please. And I know no San Diego. Though now"—the captain's eyes narrowed—"the name makes me wonder if you aren't a papist pig."

What the heck was a papist? "Listen I'm done here. K? I'm done." Frustration at a boiling point, she began searching the room. There must be cameras somewhere. Her father— no, most likely one of his admins—was probably watching to make sure the actors did a good job. Maybe a Hollywood producer or two as well, which would explain the grand performances.

She circled the room, brushing hands over the rough wooden walls and peering into the dark corners. Nothing. She curled her fingers around the edges of the desk, swept a gaze over the window ledge, and straightened a sword hanging askew on the wall.

The men seemed to find this amusing as each one poured more Kool-Aid into tiny pewter mugs and sipped while watching her.

She leapt atop the chair, peered above the closet, and scanned the beams across the ceiling. A cockroach scrambled across one and she cringed. *Nice touch.*

Pleasurable moans sounded, and she turned to see their gazes on her behind. *Men*! Huffing, she jumped down to search the bed. What a hard, lumpy mattress. And the sheets were none too clean.

"If it's to bed you wish to take me," the infuriating captain drawled, "I'm happy to oblige. 'Twas to be part of your payment anyway."

She scowled at him and opened his closet. Shirts, pants, vests, and coats came tumbling down upon her, smelling musty and reeking with body odor. Apparently pretend pirates-of-old never washed their clothes either. Without thought, she began folding the garments and hanging the shirts on hooks.

"For what are you searching, my little minx?" her captor asked.

The man called Nick pointed his cup at her. "T' tend yer disastrous wardrobe, 'twould seem."

"Mayhap she seeks your hidden treasure, Captain," the handsome man offered as he poured himself another drink.

"Right in front of me?" Rowan laughed and crossed arms over his chest. "Faith now, she's either a pretty fool or more fearless than most men."

Bristling, Morgan only then noticed she was folding the ridiculous costumes. What the heck was wrong with her? She left the clothes on the floor and slammed the closet shut. The boat creaked and moaned as if sympathizing with her plight. "Where are the cameras?" she demanded as the floor tilted to the left. Stumbling, she reached for the wall before she fell. But it was her stomach that plummeted, shooting something foul up her throat. She pressed a hand over her mouth.

All the men's brows lifted. "I fear the lady intends to toss her accounts!"

Taking a deep breath, she swallowed, and gathered herself. Enough of this. Moving to the center of the room, she spun and waved her hands through the air. "I know you're watching. Go tell my father I wish to come home. I'm sick and this is not helping!"

"Alas, the lassie speaks t' spirits!" Nick's voice was alarmed.

"A witch, to be sure," the handsome man said nonchalantly as he sipped his drink.

"Mayhap that explains how she got here," the captain added.

Morgan stared at them, anger churning. "I'm outta here." She headed to the door.

"I have not given you my leave." The captain was on her in seconds, his hand cinching around her wrist. "Enough of this foolery. Who are you and why are you here?" A cloud of alcohol enveloped her. So, they *were* drinking.

Though he stood several inches above her, she put on her sternest look and met his gaze. "Listen, I need to go home. This whole thing is staged for my benefit, but I don't want it. Can you get that?" Besides, she needed her meds. For her OCD and anxiety. She'd taken them that morning, but for some reason they seemed to be wearing off. "Stop this insane charade at once!" She tugged from his grip.

"Woman, your impudence tries me sorely."

"And your bad acting tries me sorely!"

Nick chuckled.

Rowan scowled. "I have a mind to give you to my crew. After I'm done with you, that is. Surely that would loosen your tongue."

"Precisely my thinking." The handsome pirate licked his lips as if she were dessert.

"I am not a wench, and I'll thank you to stop calling me that. I am Morgan Shaw, daughter of Macon Shaw," she stated emphatically. "Name ring a bell? The man who is paying your salary?"

"Morgan!" The actor-captain bent over in a howl. "Now 'tis clear from whence this sassy minx hails. One of ol' Henry's discarded offspring, I make bold to say."

"I'll take her off your hands, Captain." The handsome pirate set down his cup, desire glinting in his eyes. "Upon my oath, she'll be no bother to you the rest of the journey."

The boat seesawed again, and Morgan leaned against the wall. "You will do no such thing!"

"Nay." The captain chuckled. "I would not subject even a mad woman to your advances, Kerr."

"I quite agree." Nick nodded toward her. "Either tha' gash ha' stolen her reason, or the lass's mind's been blasted t' bits."

"Indeed. Pity. I admire her spirit." The captain finished his drink and set down the cup.

"A goodly share of pluck for one so slight of figure," Nick added.

The handsome pirate shuffled forward and fingered a lock of her hair. "We could still let the crew have her." He winked at her, and she rolled her eyes at his act—convincing as it was.

"Nay, this madness she suffers might be contagious." The captain fingered his chin. "And the crew is crazy enough as it is."

Morgan huffed. "You know I can hear you. I'm standing right here."

"Kerr," the captain continued. "Find those responsible for bringing this madcap aboard and bring them to me." The handsome pirate nodded and started off. "And get Farley," the captain shouted after him, eyeing her forehead. "I'll have him tend to this wench's wound. Then mayhap she will speak plainly."

Grrr. Morgan could never remember being this angry. While the annoying captain turned to address the red-haired actor, she inched toward the desk, pretending to gaze out the window. Grabbing the handle of the man's sword, she swept it out before her and pointed it at the captain. Good grief, the thing was real. And heavy! Using both hands, she kept it level and poked him in the back.

He slowly turned, a grin lifting his lips.

"You want to play pirate?" Morgan said. "Then I will play too. Take me back to San Diego or I'll slice you in half!"

Chapter 3

Rowan didn't know whether to laugh at the sassy minx, drag her to his bed, or toss her overboard. What a fascinating creature! The weak wench could barely hold up his sword. Even now, her arms shook as she bit her lip and gazed at him with eyes the color of lustrous moss.

"I swear I'll do it! Whatever my father is paying you, I'm sure it's not worth ending up in the hospital."

Nick chuckled behind him. "Ye best do wha' the bonny lass says, Rowan. I'm trembling for my life."

The ship bounded over a wave. In one swift move, Rowan shoved the blade aside with his forearm, knocking it from the mad woman's hand, then caught it by the hilt in midair.

Eyes wide, she backed away—the first evidence of fear he'd seen on her face. But then the panic faded, replaced by her normal shrewish expression.

"So, you're a stunt man too, I suppose. Very impressive."

Stunt man? Rowan shook his head, hoping to evict the woman's nonsensical ramblings from his brain. "From whence do you hail? I make no sense of your speech."

"You know very well from where I *hail,*" she spat back, brushing hair from her face.

The ship rose and plunged over a wave, and the woman held her stomach and lowered into the chair.

He sheathed the sword lest she attempt to grab it again. "Why do you wear men's breeches and an undergarment for a shirt if you did not come aboard to service my men?"

She merely released a heavy sigh as if his question was ridiculous. "I'm wearing jeans and a T-shirt, as well you know."

"Of what material is it sewn?" Rowan had never seen the likes of it before and reached out to touch her breeches.

She slapped him away.

He grabbed her wrist and yanked her to her feet. "You dare strike the man who holds your fate in his hands?"

Nick's hand on Rowan's arm stayed him from giving into his anger. "She doesna know any better. 'Tis mad she is."

He released her with a sigh. He wouldn't have struck her. Alas, he was many things—many vile things—but he was not an abuser of women. Even when they deserved it. He would, however, be happy to frighten her into submission, though he was beginning to wonder if that were possible. Such a shrew! A devilish trifler, to be sure. And no great beauty, either. Hair the color of rich dirt was tied behind her in the most unflattering style. Her oval face did bear some pleasantness, he'd allow: a dainty nose, pink lips, deep-set eyes. But she was too small boned, far too thin, and too deficient in curves for his liking. And though she appeared to lack the modesty of a decent lady, neither did she possess the wantonness of a trollop.

But what was she about? Surely it must be more than to steal his amulet.

Water pounded the hull. The ship creaked and groaned as if sharing his confusion.

He was about to question her further, when Farley waddled in, black satchel in hand. His gaze alighted upon the woman. "Well, what 'ave we 'ere?" he said, his toothless smile spreading wide. Kerr entered behind him and leaned against the door frame.

"'Tis a lady as you can plainly see, man." Rowan turned a hard look her way. "One who refuses to explain her presence here. Mayhap once you fix her wound, her senses will return."

"The only senses in question here are yours!" She pointed a finger at Farley. "And there's no way that beast is touching me!"

The insolence of this woman. "If I have to hold you down myself, I assure you, Farley *is* touching you."

"Allow the man t' tend yer wound, lass," Nick, always the peacemaker, interjected. "He wilna hurt ye."

"What are your qualifications?" The woman backed away until the bulkhead prevented further retreat. She pressed a hand to her wound. "Are you even a real doctor?"

Rowan chuckled at her sudden fear of the surgeon when naught else—being tossed overboard or passed among his crew—had unnerved her. "In truth, ol' Farley was a butcher—weren't you, Farley?—before you joined my crew."

"Aye, Cap'n." His eyes flashed as he slid a thin layer of hair over his bald spot. "Not much difference 'tween butcherin' an' surgeonin', says I."

The woman's face paled. Her breath heightened, but then she huffed and glanced at the deck above her. "Very funny! Ha Ha. Now, go get my father and tell him I wish to go home!"

Kerr chuckled and rubbed the back of his neck. Rowan exchanged a baffled look with Nick before he marched toward her and ushered her to the chair. "Sit down and allow Farley to tend your wound."

She did. Why, she obeyed, he could not say. Mayhap she grew tired of playacting the fool. Mayhap she believed he wouldn't tolerate further defiance. Yet the defeat and sorrow weighing her down was no charade, and he found himself preferring the shrew.

What also wasn't a charade was the courage she displayed while Farley stitched up the gash on her forehead. Aside from a small wince, the lady made neither whimper nor whine as he expected from the weaker sex.

Grabbing a bottle, Rowan poured more rum into his mug. Women had always been easy for him to figure out. He knew exactly what they wanted: what words they longed to hear, what gifts they wished to receive, how to adore and cherish them until they groveled at his feet. But this woman? She intrigued him.

And he had not been intrigued in a long time.

When Farley finished his ministrations, she glanced up at Rowan, stitches on her forehead and the fight gone from her eyes. "Will you take me home now, please?"

For a second, he truly wished he could. But he was a pirate captain, not a milksop fawning over the whims of a female. "To this San Diego—town of Spanish dogs? Nay. Not even if I knew where it was."

"Am I to be your prisoner, then? Your love slave? Is that the game?"

Rowan arched a brow at her brazen talk. "Nay, you are to be my prisoner in the hold where all thieves belong."

She huffed and glanced down.

Farley looked up from packing his things and winked at the lady. "I'd be content wit' that, miss, if I was ye. He usually ties betrayers to the topmast fer a month 'till alls that's left be burnt skin an' dusty bones. One time—"

"That'll be all, Farley." Rowan's harsh tone caused the man to finish packing his satchel and take his leave.

Cudney and Abbot appeared in the doorway. "You called fer us, Cap'n?"

"Aye, take the woman below and lock her in irons."

Lady Minx leapt to her feet. "You can't be serious?" She blinked and started to wobble, and Kerr dashed to grab her arm, but she batted him away.

"Faith now! I'm the captain, and I can be serious whenever I please."

Cudney advanced, grabbed the woman, and dragged her to the door. Her kicking ceased when Abbot took her other arm, and the two of them lifted her from the ground.

"My father will hear of this! You won't get paid a dime! I'll see you never work in Hollywood again and that …" Her voice faded down the companionway.

Nick straightened his blue braided doublet, making Rowan wonder, yet again, how the man's apparel always remained so clean and unwrinkled, whilst the rest of the crew—himself included—wore naught but stained and rumpled attire. "The lass's father sounds mighty powerful."

"If he even exists." Rowan snorted and grabbed his mug.

Kerr grinned. "Spy or not, I wouldn't mind her warming my bed at night."

"She's no trollop," Rowan shot back, wondering why he defended the little thief. But he'd seen the way the man gaped at her, and he allowed no ravishing on board his ship. "And she'll be locked away from your lecherous hands."

Kerr snorted. "Why, you're no fun at all, Captain."

Rowan chuckled and sipped his drink. "Lud, I've been accused of many things, but never of not being fun." Rays of sun from the window swayed over his desk like golden arrows as the sound of flapping sails and shouts drifted from above. "You're dismissed, Kerr. I need you above."

Frowning, Rowan watched the man leave. He was too much like Rowan—a gambler, a rake, and a ruthless brute when need be. And being five years his senior, Kerr's continued slide into debauchery didn't bode well for Rowan's future. Though the ladies still swooned at Kerr's feet, beneath that charm, years of wanton living had stolen the clarity from his eyes and the healthy glow from his skin. Would Rowan still be preying on these seas, drinking and wenching at seven and twenty? And what would another five years of such a life do to him—if he survived?

Which is precisely why he'd needed that prize today. If the rumors of the wealth she carried were true, it would have been enough to buy him out of the trade and into a respectable life. Anger rekindled at the woman's interference.

"Och now, Rowan, why lock up the lass?" Nick's voice jarred him from his thoughts.

"What would you have me do with her? Keep her in here with me?" Rowan set down his empty mug and crossed arms over his chest. "She's far safer below."

"So ye *are* protecting her after all?" A twinkle crossed Nick's eyes.

"I don't know why. I should punish her for causing me to lose my prize. *And* for stealing my amulet." He glanced down at the necklace and swallowed a burst of emotion at the memories it evoked.

"Who do ye think she is?" Nick asked.

"Until she explains herself, a thief."

"Not a verra good one, 'twould seem, eh? How much treasure could such a wee lass carry off this ship?"

"Mayhap she's after the map. She was shuffling about my desk when we came in."

"No one knows ye stole it, save Margaret, and ye said if she told anyone, tha' would mean her death."

Rowan nodded. "Indeed, by her husband's hand. Still, I'll not deny this strange woman has me baffled. Her attire, her speech … this spirit-father she hails. And have you ever heard of San Diego?"

Sunlight reflected off the sapphire broach on Nick's doublet. "Nay. But she hasna a Spanish accent, nor does she look like a papist."

"Or dress like one," Rowan added, remembering the tight breeches and nightshirt she wore. "I do find her entertaining.

And presently, I could use some entertaining. If she won't talk, I might charm her into my bed."

The usual look of disappointment appeared on Nick's face. "Leave the lass be, Rowan. Dinna ye prefer lonely wives? Women who drool over ye while ye are present and pine over ye while ye are away? Ladies who expect naught from ye but the occasional performance in bed when their husbands are gone?"

Rowan snorted. "I'm well aware of your disapproval of my lifestyle. But it suits me. Keeps me warm at night with fond memories and free during the day with no shrew to order me about."

"What of marriage? Family?"

"Lud, man, are you trying to put me in an early grave?" Rowan chuckled.

"Nay, pirating will do tha' quite nicely."

"And yet, I have achieved nothing but success upon these seas. Have I not filled the crew's pockets? Made a name that is feared all over the Spanish Main?"

"Aye." Nick snorted. "But to what purpose?"

Rowan walked to the windows and stared at the glittering sea. "You know my purpose."

"T' repay a debt ye owe yer dear twin sister, Juliana."

Just hearing her name doused Rowan in shame. "I stole one of our family's merchant ships and left her destitute."

"An' went off pirating."

Rowan gave his friend a searing look over his shoulder. "'Twas the only way I could make money. I intended to return once I made my fortune, but by the time I sailed back to Port Royal, the city had fallen into the sea."

Nick rubbed the back of his neck. "A horrible tragedy, tha' earthquake."

"Thank God, my sister survived. I would have never forgiven myself otherwise."

"God? Ha' my ears deceived me? D'ye finally give credit where credit is due?"

Rowan frowned. "'Tis but an expression. Your father may be a vicar, but I'll hear none of your preaching."

"An' ye didna stay t' help her because ye feared for yer own neck."

"I lack no conscience that you need remind me." Nay, Rowan's conscience had reminded him every day since. And he always justified his actions the same. There had been pirate hunters about, in particular Captain Edmund Merrick, the preacher pirate. Rowan already had a bounty on his head, and once he discovered his sister was well cared for, there was naught he could do. Instead, he'd sailed away, intending to capture more prizes and return some day to restart his father's shipping company and provide a lavish living for him and his sister—one which would garner society's admiration and respect.

"Have ye no' acquired enough wealth yet t' pay back this debt?" Nick asked.

Rowan shook his head. "Not enough to ensure Juliana lives like a princess."

"Wha' if she doesna want t' live like a princess?"

"Everyone wants to live like royalty, Nick."

"Wha' if yer sister would rather ha' her brother home instead?"

Circling the desk, Rowan dropped into a chair and stretched out his legs, battling between anger at his friend's impertinence and laughing at the ludicrous notion that his sister would want him home.

"I will not return empty-handed and be a burden to her like I was before. I will return a victor, her champion, someone she can depend on and respect." Respect— something he'd never received from her before. Or from anyone in Port Royal.

Nick let out a deep sigh. "'Tis been nearly two years since ye walked into tha' tavern and recruited me for yer venture."

Rowan smiled. "You would never have signed on with me if you weren't running from Mr. Childers."

The ship creaked over a wave, and Nick glanced out the window. "Indentured servitude was no easy burden t' bear. Not from tha' man."

Rowan only nodded. Word had spread through Port Royal of Childers' cruelty to his servants and slaves.

"Ye did save me from tha', I'll grant ye. Though I fear the news tha' I turned pirate would put my father in an early grave."

"Then we shall not send a post to inform him." Rowan smiled, grabbed the bottle of rum, and saluted his friend. Nay, if he admitted it, Nick was more than a friend. He was like a father to Rowan—one who cared about him—and nothing like the ogre of a man who had sired Rowan and who did naught but berate him and tell him how useless he was.

But he would prove his father wrong. He would prove everybody wrong. He was not a wastrel like all of Port Royal believed him to be. He would return the richest man in Jamaica, and all of society would bow to him and Juliana.

Morgan ended up back where she had started—in the stinky, sweltering cargo hold. Only this time, at least three inches of water that smelled like sewage saturated the Nine West Sandals she'd splurged on for Jason. The sludge seeped between her toes and soaked the hem of her jeans. Bile rose up her throat. Two men, bare-chested and sweating, manned an old wooden pump that filled buckets with the excess water, while a third man tied them to a rope that was then hoisted above. Old sails formed a patch over the hole made by the cannon, though water still seeped from it and dripped onto the floor. She'd appreciate the authenticity of the scene if she wasn't so angry.

The men shoved her into an iron-barred cage that went from floor to ceiling and was no bigger than her walk-in closet at home. She held a hand over her mouth to keep from barfing up what was left in her stomach as the shorter one locked the gate and gaped at her with curiosity—and something else reminiscent of looks she'd received at Jason's nightclub from drunken men.

"My father will hear of this!" She gripped the bars and rattled them. "What are your names again? Abbot and Cudney? Yup, I'll make special mention of you both to him."

Her threats seemed to have no effect on the actors. Rather good actors, she had to admit. Both looked dumber than a box of rocks. Layers of filth covered their skin and leeched onto their baggy pants and shirts, while their hair hung in greasy strands.

The shorter one—the one with the strange shiny eye, a thicket of hair bursting from his shirt, and arms like Popeye on spinach—laughed at her and thumbed toward his friend. "Cudney here can't hear a word yer sayin', Miss. Had his ear blown off by grapeshot. So, goes ahead and threaten all ye wants."

Gnarled pink flesh covered the spot where Cudney's ear should have been. Great makeup job.

Abbot wiped spit from his mouth with his sleeve. "I sure would like t' taste this rare treat." He fingered the key as if contemplating unlocking the gate.

As if understanding his intent, Cudney shoved down Abbot's hand and muttered, "D'ye want the cap'n after ye?"

Grunting—as if unable to form a coherent sentence—they turned and ambled away, taking the lantern with them, the only light except for a distant glimmer near where the men were pumping water.

Darkness suffocated her, forcing her to slosh through the sludge and grope for the crate she'd spotted. Upon finding it, she sat, pulled her sopping feet from the water, and wrapped her arms around her knees. Disgust shivered through her. God only knew what germs, diseases, and bugs were slithering through that water and were now on her feet and jeans. Fear clenched her heart into a ball of panic. She resisted the urge to wipe off the sludge. That would only get it on her hands. But she needed to get clean! She had to get off this boat where all was disorder and chaos and return to her orderly life where she knew what to expect.

Except for the cancer and Jason dumping her.

But at least she had her job, her safe apartment, her reliable Volvo, a daily scheduled routine, and her painting on weekends.

The boat tilted, and she nearly tumbled into the water. Grabbing the edges of the crate, she resisted the urge to cry. She resisted the urge to scream and shout and wail. Instead, she stoked her anger to near boiling.

Just wait until she saw her father. What had he been thinking? It was one thing to send a thirteen-year-old on a wild-West vacation and quite another to send a twenty-four-year-old woman who had OCD and anxiety and stage three cancer to a pirate boat in the middle of the sea. No doubt he'd told the actors to be as authentic as possible, but locking her up in the heat and dark with sewage for a floor was a little too authentic. What was next? Flogging at noon? Walking the plank? No doubt in his self-aggrandizing mind, her father thought putting her in such a horrible situation would take her mind off her cancer.

But nothing could take her mind off the fact that in less than six months she would be dead.

Not even the handsome pirate above—the actor who played Captain Rowan Dutton. A total hunk, as long as he didn't open his mouth. Raw masculinity was another description that came to mind, along with jerk and male chauvinist and self-centered pig! He was obviously more interested in getting paid for his part than making sure she was comfortable. He'd be lucky to be paid at all after she told her father how he'd treated her. He was probably supposed to pretend to fall madly in love with her too, like some cheesy pirate romance novel. She'd laugh if she wasn't so miserable.

The roar of water against the outside of the boat, along with the constant creak and moan of wood, only added to her frayed nerves. Was this boat even safe? It sounded like it would split apart at any moment. Great. Sinking to the bottom of the sea would definitely take her mind off of her cancer.

Maybe it was a better way to go anyway.

Her heart took up a rapid beat, and the familiar tightness in her chest returned. Her anxiety was rising, and she needed her meds. Did her father think every problem could be solved by throwing money at it? No doubt he already had the best oncologists lined up to work on her case as soon as this little weekend adventure was concluded.

Her mother wasn't much help either. Her solution to everything was to go to church and pray. Incessantly. She was forever in the pastor's office, seeking counseling. The poor man was probably sick of her by now. Even her prayer loop grew tired of the constant requests for every petty little thing. If God answered prayer, then why did her mother need medication for anxiety and depression?

Morgan laid her head on her knees and tried to focus on anything but the filth and smell around her—and worse, *on* her. No wonder her parents had divorced. Her father was an alcoholic who worshiped money and power, and her mother was a religious zealot hooked on pills. Of course Morgan had no right to judge on the pill front, though she wondered whether her addiction to them wasn't her mother's fault as well.

Morgan had been sent to counseling at age twelve—trauma from the divorce, her mother had told the psychologist. Though Morgan hadn't felt traumatized.

Whenever Morgan had trouble making friends at school, whenever she was teased and bullied because she was smart and plain, whenever Morgan's heart was broken, or she wasn't picked for the girls' soccer team, her mom sent her to the shrink for more pills.

Pills and prayer, the answer to everything.

But neither had helped her mother. Or Morgan. She was still plain and shy and insecure and nervous. And she still had to keep everything in her life as ordered as possible—tidy and in its place—or she might go off the deep end.

Funny choice of words, seeing as the water seemed to be creeping up the side of the crate instead of retreating. And what was that squealing? Something scampered on a beam overhead. No way. Her father wouldn't have put real rats on the boat.

She shivered and tried to focus on something else. What had she been thinking about? Ah, yes, her miserable life. Despite her crazy upbringing, she'd been able to get through college with a degree in Information Systems. Which landed her a great job at Qualcomm Holographics, along with the ability to finally move out of her mother's house—also known as loony town—and into her own place.

Cussing echoed through the boat, followed by sloshing and stomping, and finally the distant glow of a lantern disappeared. Great. The men had given up on the pumps and left.

"Hello!" she shouted. "Are you going to let me drown down here?"

But her only answer was the creak and groan of the boat as it tipped to the right. She placed a hand on the moist hull to keep from falling from her perch. Wherever this boat was going—and she hoped it was back to San Diego—they better get there fast before they sank. That cannonball and the hole it made were quite real. Another nice touch by her father.

And so she waited in the pitch blackness, serenaded by the slosh of water, the scrape of wood-on-wood, and the squeal of rats, many rats—the sounds of which must be piped in from an MP3 player somewhere.

She supposed her father wanted her to use this time to think about all the good things she had in life, instead of her cancer, but all she could think about was her queasy stomach, the putrid stench that filled her lungs, and the sensation of being roasted alive.

They couldn't leave her down here much longer. Could they?

Yet an eternity passed. Morgan's head bobbed in exhaustion, and more than once, she had to pinch herself to stay awake, fearful she might fall into the sewage.

Finally a pinprick of light appeared in the distance, blossoming like a bud into flower as someone headed toward her. A middle-aged woman with dark skin came into view, holding a lantern and wearing a look of concern.

"Let's get you outta here, child," she said as she inserted a key into the lock, clacked it open, and removed it from the gate. It dropped into the water with a splash, drawing Morgan's gaze to the now four inches of slime covering the floor.

"Tsk, tsk, tsk, I dunno what the Cap'n be thinkin', leavin' you down here like this."

Relief unwound a few of Morgan's nerves. "Finally. Thank God."

The woman swung open the gate, and Morgan slid off her crate into the water. Warm muck saturated her jeans, and she swallowed down another burst of nausea. "Are we almost at San Diego?"

"I dunno 'bout no San Diego, child." The woman led the way through the water, the bottom of her dress sloshing back and forth.

Morgan sighed. Would no one admit to this charade?

"If I'd a known you was down here, I'd a come sooner."

"My father called you?" At least the man has some heart. "That uncouth Neanderthal would have left me down here all night."

The woman looked confused for a moment but then chuckled. "Oh, you mean the captain?"

"Who else?"

"Who d'ya think sent me to git you?"

Chapter 4

Morgan dreamed she was in a wine cellar, one of those damp, dark basements where they kept oak barrels used to age grape juice. She'd visited several of the local wineries around the San Diego area with friends—sipping, sampling, tasting—much to her mother's dismay, and placing another blemish on Morgan's tarnished soul. Now, as she hovered on the brink of consciousness with the scent of aged oak filling her nose, the room rocked like a teeter-totter, and she feared the worst. Had she passed out in a wine cellar? How embarrassing!

She forced her eyes open. Wooden beams stretched overhead where a rope looped through a hook and lowered to a white canvas suspended in mid-air. *What?* Memories crept out from hiding, but not quick enough to stop her from jerking to sit up and flipping over whatever she'd been lying on. She hit the floor. *Hard.* Pain jolted up her arms then etched across her back. Her head began to throb. Moaning, she struggled to rise, only then seeing the hammock swinging back and forth above her.

Great. She was still on the stupid boat. Morgan hoped her father would have rescued her during the night. No doubt he didn't want to waste the money he'd already invested in this insane fantasy. Her stomach soured, and she lowered her gaze to beams of sunlight that oscillated over the floor from a round window behind her. How long had she slept?

"Good, you're awake." The female voice preceded a gust of salty wind from the open door, and the woman who'd rescued her from the sewer came in with a tray she set upon a small table attached to the wall. Turning, she took one step and shut the door, then planted hands on her wide hips and chuckled. "Them canvas bags are hard gitting used to."

"Don't they have beds on this old boat?" The scent of ginger and lemon lured Morgan to stand and approach the tray. "Is this the same tea you brought me last night? It really helped."

"Aye, glad to hear it, child. The cap'n told me to bring you some for your seasickness."

Morgan slid onto one of the two chairs and picked up the steaming mug. She found that hard to believe, unless he had now switched from the role of nasty pirate to would-be-boyfriend.

The tea was lukewarm and tasted bitter, but Morgan gulped it down as if it were a Pepsi. "Are we in San Diego yet?"

"I dunno where this San Diego is, but we's close to some island the cap'n wanted to git to."

Morgan shook her head. "Please … Edith, is it? Please drop the act when it's just you and me? I really can't take it anymore."

Edith stared at Morgan as if she'd told her to transform into a toad. And a pretty toad the middle-aged woman would make too. Barely a few wrinkles were visible around her mouth and eyes, leaving the rest of her skin as smooth as milk chocolate. A few curls sprang loose from shiny black hair that was pinned up in a bun. She was plump in all the right places, and her eyes brimmed with both kindness and wisdom. And, at the moment, concern.

"Child, that bump on your head musta jangled something loose upstairs. Now, don't you worry 'bout nothing. You's in good hands."

Morgan groaned inwardly. Her father had probably told these actors he'd ruin their career—make it so they'd never work in Hollywood again—if they stepped out of character even for a second. Okay, she'd play along. For now. "In good hands? Hardly. I'm on a pirate ship."

"Aye, but the cap'n won't hurt you none. He's not that way."

"Hmm." Morgan set down her mug and picked up a round hard biscuit from the tray.

"Tack," Edith said. "It's not tasty but it's all we's got till we git to land. When your stomach settles, I'm making turtle stew for dinner."

Turtle stew? Morgan wrinkled her nose, not sure that sounded much better. But as she bit off a chunk of tack, she quickly changed her mind. A taste similar to the chalk she'd eaten on a bet in fifth grade filled her mouth, and she gulped her tea to wash it down. Her gaze landed on a dress and some lacy garments hanging on a hook.

"Are you the only woman on board?"

"'Sides you." Edith unclipped the hammock and began rolling it up.

"Why are you here? I thought pirates were notorious for raping every woman they came across."

"Shhh now, child." Edith scolded her, her cheeks flooding maroon. "A proper lady shouldn't say sich things." She paused and folded the hammock, then stuffed it in netting attached to the wall. "Some pirates do, I suppose … but the cap'n don't go for sich things. 'Sides, I help wit' mending sails an' clothing, cooking, an' sometimes doctoring wit' my husband."

"The surgeon is your husband?" Or rather butcher. Morgan absently touched the stitches on her head, surprised they weren't infected.

Edith studied Morgan's wound. "He did a good job, my Farley," she said with pride.

"Ah ha! He's white and you're black. People didn't marry outside of their race back in the day, right? My father should have thought of that!"

Edith's brow wrinkled. "I dunno what you're saying 'bout the day an' your father, but yes, whites and Negros don't wed. But you see, Farley rescued me." She sat across from Morgan. "I was a slave to the apothecary in Port Royal, an' Farley was the butcher down the street. He'd always make an excuse to visit me, some new ailment he had which needed a special potion. But the apothecary was a cruel man, an' Farley couldn't stand to see me beat, so's one day he up an' stole me away." She smiled. "An' we got married an' joined wit' the captain. Been wit' him ever since. Someday, though"—her dark eyes sparkled—"when the world accepts our marriage, we's going to open our own apothecary an' help heal people when they's sick."

Wow. If any of that was true, Morgan would be touched by the romantic story. Good grief. Had her father given everyone on board their own history?

"Was God's doing," Edith continued. "I prayed an' prayed to be free an' God not only freed me, but He sent me a husband—a good man."

Morgan snorted. "Does my father know you're religious? I doubt he'd have hired you if he knew."

"I dunno nothin' 'bout that, child, but I know you seem confused. Do you remember how you come to be here? Seems like you jist appeared out'a nowheres."

Morgan finished the chalk, hoping it would absorb the acid in her stomach. "If you don't know the answer to that, I'm in bigger trouble than I thought."

Edith tilted her head. "I will pray for you, that God makes your path clear."

"You can pray all you want, but God isn't listening." As evidenced by her mother's prayers for Morgan all these years—for prosperity, happiness, and health. None of which had happened.

Edith gave a sad smile but no rebuttal. Instead, she grabbed the gown off the hook and held it up. "Now, child, let's git you cleaned up an' dressed proper."

At first Morgan protested. Not the cleaning part. She was more than thrilled to use the water in the pail Edith brought earlier to wipe off as much muck as she could. The problem was the dress. Morgan hadn't worn one in years—not even to church—and she wasn't about to start now. But there was blood on her t-shirt and sludge on her jeans, and a smell emanated from both that would make a sewage worker faint. She could hardly believe she'd slept in such a condition, but when Edith had brought her to her room instead of the captain's and given her some soothing tea, Morgan's nerves had begun to unwind. And she must have fallen asleep.

"Okay, but I don't suppose you have a clean pair of jeans handy?"

Edith pretended not to understand. So, an hour later, holding her stomach with one hand and the ladder railing with the other—and looking like a stuffed china doll—Morgan followed Edith onto the main deck. She'd begged the older woman to take her above so Morgan could see for herself how far they were from the California coast.

Edith agreed but would only leave her there if the captain was on deck.

He was. Standing one level above them by the tiller. Hair blowing in the wind and earring winking in the sunlight, he raised a scope to view something in the distance.

Morgan didn't have time to see what it was when the boat shifted, and she stumbled forward, nearly tripping over her gown … skirts … whatever they were called. What ridiculous things women had to wear in the past. Something called a chemise that was like her grandmother's old nightgown, then multiple petticoats, stockings, stays, and a bodice so tight Morgan could hardly breathe. At least she'd be safe from any stray bullets, for nothing could penetrate the stiff stays that covered her stomach and chest. On top of all the layers, Edith had flung an emerald green over-skirt embroidered in gold braid.

Edith pointed toward the railing. "Excuse me, child, but I have things to do below." And off she disappeared down the same hatch.

Morgan tripped again, and the actors chuckled. With narrowed eyes, she scanned their filthy faces, only to find all gazes fastened upon her. She wasn't used to having men look at her, but she supposed there wasn't any other woman on deck to slobber over at the moment. When she reached the railing, the sea spit in her face. Groaning, she closed her eyes against the sting of salt but found the water cooled the sweat already forming on her neck and arms from the blaring sun and humidity.

The toe of her brocade shoes—as Edith had called them—struck a coil of rope on the deck, and she noticed the loops weren't aligned correctly. Kneeling, she adjusted the top strand so it fit with the others.

Wait. Hot and humid?

Alarm sent her heart into a frenzy. The northern Pacific wasn't hot and humid. She rose and gazed over the waters. This was a tropical sea, with a tropical island in the distance. She blinked to focus, but the scene remained the same. Had they sailed down by Mexico? They couldn't have gone that far in this old boat. Turning, she scanned the deck. Where were all the ship signs? And the table of souvenirs and chest of soft drinks? The replica boat didn't have a raised deck at the front like this one. Or cannons lining the railing. She gulped. How could they have changed things so quickly?

Morgan must have been unconscious for quite some time. *Tiffany!* Morgan's father had probably paid her off. The girl never could resist a new pair of Pradas, and Morgan's father would have convinced her it was the best thing for Morgan. Yup. That was it. Her loyal friend had slipped something in her drink. The betrayal stung. Was there no one Morgan could trust?

The tightness in her chest returned, along with shortness of breath and the feeling of dread that always accompanied an anxiety attack. She needed her meds. And she needed them now. The boat leapt over a wave, and she gripped the railing. Turquoise waters, capped in creamy foam, spread out as far as the eye could see. Thick cottony clouds, so uncharacteristic of California, rolled like tumbleweeds across the blue sky.

Wherever she was, she wasn't in Kansas anymore.

Whistles and catcalls brought Rowan's gaze to the deck below where the woman stood by the railing in billowing green skirts and a tight gold-colored bodice. The tip of her bound hair flopped over her back in the breeze. She raised her hand to shield her eyes from the sun and turned slightly, giving him a peek at the creamy mounds of a chest he didn't think she possessed. *Lady Minx?* But of course it was her. And from the looks of the crew gaping at her, he *now* had a problem on his hands. They'd been at sea for two weeks, and that was long enough for the men's appetite to grow to desperation. Blast it all! He hadn't thought putting her in proper attire would make her appealing. Now, what was he to do with her?

She stood there, head held high, shoulders back, appearing to harbor no fear of being ravished—in truth, no fear of anything. An admirable quality to be sure. And one that befitted a woman whose wits had abandoned her. Not a thief. Either way, her brazenness would make his job of protecting her all the more difficult.

Wind, ripe with the scent of brine and tropical flowers, blasted over him as he glanced at the island, now just a mile off their larboard beam. It would take a few days to repair the ship. He might as well careen it as well, which meant no one could stay on board. His crew would relish the chance to stretch their legs and feast on fruit and fish. But they would also relish a woman's company. Rowan would have to assign a few trustworthy men to guard the minx. But he had so few he could count on.

She met his gaze then, the usual defiance searing her eyes. And something else. She gave him a curt little smile, a smile of power and independence as if to say *she* was the one in command.

Of all the …! Obviously her time in the hold did little to assuage her pomposity. Forsooth, what a marvel! He turned to Kerr and found him staring at the lady as well. "Lower sails and prepare to navigate the shoals. We'll come in under tops."

With a nod, the first mate leapt onto the main deck and shouted across the ship, "Lay aloft! Haul taut! In main and fore!" Men leapt into the ratlines and scrambled above as Rowan leaned toward Nick and pointed to a curved outcropping that formed a small bay. "Bring her into that cove."

"Aye, Captain."

Rowan rubbed sweat from the back of his neck. "And where's Jorg with the blasted logline?"

Nick scanned the deck and found the man talking with two other pirates. "Jorg, the depth!" Jerking to attention, Jorg sped off, returning within minutes and tossing the line over the railing.

"Braces ease, trim your sheets, trim the bowlines!" Kerr continued shouting as the ship slowed and limp sails flapped in the breeze.

"Twenty fathoms!" Jorg shouted over his shoulder.

Rowan leapt down the quarterdeck ladder, glancing at the woman as he passed her on the main deck. She clung to the railing, her gaze taking in the island, the frothy water, the crew at their various tasks as if she were enthralled with it all—and completely oblivious of the attention she garnered from every man aboard.

Shaking his head, he made his way to the bow to navigate the *Reckoning* through the shoals. He'd never met a woman—except his sister, mayhap—who didn't know precisely how to attract a man's attention and who, once she had him begging for her every favor, didn't revel in the power she had over him. But this woman … this Morgan Shaw was different.

Leaning over the bow, Rowan scanned the water on both sides as the *Reckoning* slipped through the sea, arrows of foam rising up her hull. Shaking off thoughts of the woman, he focused beneath the waves for reefs and shoals that weren't marked on the charts. One mistake and he'd ground his precious ship. But he'd yet to make such an error. Unlike everything else in his life, Rowan had found purpose and a home on the sea. He was good at it—being a captain and a pirate. He only wished it was something his sister could be proud of as well.

Sails were lowered and the ship veered to larboard as Rowan shouted orders to the helmsman to make small adjustments to port or starboard. Once safely within the bay, the ship slowed to a near crawl, and Rowan returned to stand beside Nick.

"When we're at ten fathoms, drop anchor and ready the boats," he ordered as his gaze once again landed on the woman. "I'm taking the lady below to gather some things."

"Aye, Captain." Nick winked. "Behave yerself, now."

"Don't I always?" He grinned as he made his way down the quarterdeck ladder and approached the woman. "I would speak with you in my cabin." Without waiting for one of her caustic replies, he took her arm and dragged her alongside him.

Wincing, she slugged him. Chuckles rose from the crew, prompting him to hoist her over his shoulder to show them who was in charge. Even with all her attire, she was lighter than the wind. The lace from her petticoats tickled his face, and he blew it aside and bunched the fabric against her legs, holding tight against her kicks.

Not that she didn't try. She also pounded his back with both fists, but the action felt good and helped loosen his muscles. Mayhap he should hold her like this a little longer. Besides, he was enjoying her scent. A sweet scent he couldn't place, one that reminded him of flowers, though none he'd ever smelled.

He carried her down the ladder and through the companionway, then kicked open the door and set her down in his cabin. Her face had turned the most charming shade of red.

She blustered, trying to catch her breath. "You could have just asked me to come with you instead of carrying me down here like a sack of potatoes."

"What fun in that, Lady Minx?"

She narrowed those green eyes of hers. "What do you want, *Captain*? This is no way to win my heart. Isn't that your next play?"

He chuckled. "In good sooth, if I wished to win your heart, it would already be mine."

"Is that so?" Her tone mocked. "*In good sooth*, I see your ego exceeds your brains."

"Faith now! Such wit!" He'd never been thus insulted by a common wench. He should be angry. He should lock her up below again or, better yet, stuff a handkerchief in her mouth. But instead, he found himself utterly amused. "Alas, though this lovely gown has formed a lady on the outside, I regret to discover it has had no effect on her tongue."

With a dismissive huff, she walked to the bookcases and began pulling out books and then putting them back. "That's right. How could I forget? Women don't have a mind of their own in your time."

"Most have a mind, I'll grant you, but a sane one."

"Very funny." She stepped back to admire her work, and only then did Rowan notice she was lining up his books in a perfect row from shortest to tallest.

The grating of the anchor chain rumbled, followed by a splash, and the ship came to a halt. She stumbled and gripped the back of a chair. "What is it you wanted to tell me, anyway?"

"We are to go ashore for a few days." He moved to his cabinet and began gathering his weapons—two pistols, a long knife, shot and powder, and an extra cutlass. He would need them to not only defend this woman's purity, but her life as well should she use her biting tongue on one of his crew. "'Twill not be the most comfortable situation for you, but there's naught to be done about it." When he turned around she was moving his backstaff back and forth on his desk, lining it up with his journal. A little shove here, a little shift there, before she stepped back to assess her progress.

"You really are a slob, you know." Her gaze landed on the weapons in his hands, and her brows jerked upward. "Has my father staged a battle?" She started for the windows, but tripped on her skirts. With an unladylike growl, she clutched them and continued, climbing onto the window seat and peering at the island bobbing in and out of view. "Tell me we are at the end of this ridiculous act and there is a boat waiting to take me home."

Rowan stuffed pistols in his baldric and sheaved the blades, not bothering to make sense of the lady's words. "This is the only ship available, and it will take you where I say it will. I am the captain, you are a thief. Ergo, you will do as I say."

"Ergo?" She giggled and glanced over her shoulder, then plopped down on the seat like a little girl, her skirts puffing in a cloud around her.

A rather delectable thief at the moment. Rowan swallowed.

"Very well. Let's get on with it—whatever my father has paid you to do. What day is it anyway? If I was out cold for a day, it's probably Monday, right? Maybe Tuesday." Her face paled. "Father!" she shouted into the air. "You do know that I have a doctor's appointment on Tuesday!"

Nick appeared in the doorway, a chart in hand. "Captain, a minute."

Rowan thanked the fates for the interruption, for he was beginning to question his own sanity. Assuring himself he'd left no weapons lying around, he approached his friend and attempted to pay attention as his quartermaster informed him of their exact location. Movement behind him—shuffling, banging, sighing—caused his frustration to rise, and he spun to find the minx pilfering through his desk drawers. Pilfering and yet straightening his belongings at the same time.

"Are you now to steal my possessions right in front of me?" He charged toward her and stayed her hand.

"Says the pirate." She arched a brow at him.

Nick chuckled. "The lass does ha' a point."

Giving them both a superior look, she shoved hands on her hips. "I'm looking for your phone. Where is it?"

"I know not this word *phone*. Is it some kind of weapon?"

At this she raised her hands and squeezed her temples, uttering a growl that would lift the hairs on a seasoned hunter.

Even Nick shrank from it.

But Rowan stared at her because he could do naught else. He'd like to label her mad and be done with her, but in truth, there was no lunacy in her eyes. Only clarity, wisdom, and a hint of desperation. Shadows hung beneath those same eyes, and her skin was sallow and dry as if she'd been ill for a time. Her hair was uncurled, uncoiffed, and a common brown. And though her attire gave the appearance of curves, he knew better. There was naught to recommend her. At least not to *his* liking. But still … she fascinated him. Her strange words, her ludicrous demands, her astounding courage. And an underlying sorrow and fear that reached out to him from deep within her.

Her tantrum over, she hung her head, her gaze brushing over his desk and fixing on something. Before he could stop her, she spread out the corners and exclaimed, "A treasure map! Of course there would have to be a treasure map. Dad thinks of everything."

Rowan snagged the chart from her grasp and rolled it up. "'Tis none of your concern."

"Oooh, touched a chord, did I?" She smiled. "Where is this great treasure? Does my father want us to go on a hunt?"

"Why don't ye ask him, lass, eh?" Nick remained at the open door. "Since ye seem t' think he's here somewhere."

Rowan backed away from her. "You aren't a witch are you?"

Her lips slanted. "If I were, I would have already turned you into a toad."

Nick chuckled and Rowan couldn't help but smile.

Ignoring them, she picked up one of his discarded shirts from the deck and began folding it. "So, is the treasure here on the island?"

Though her tone bore delight, Rowan could tell she mocked him. Why, he had no idea. He grabbed the shirt from her hands, reassessing his decision about her sanity. "What ails you, woman. Leave my things be."

"Och, Rowan," Nick interjected, "let her clean up a wee bit. Lord knows ye could use some help."

A huge grin appeared on the wench's lips that made her look almost pretty. Rowan had never seen such perfect white teeth. "You don't know where the treasure is, do you? You can't decipher the code on the map. Of course." She tapped her chin. "My father wants to keep me entertained, so he left a code for me to figure out, a treasure hunt, and a handsome pirate." She pointed at him before her gaze found Nick. "And his lively Scottish sidekick. Well done, gentlemen."

Ignoring her nonsensical babbling, Rowan honed in on one word—code. Mayhap she was a spy after all. "How do you know this code?"

"I've seen others like it." She crossed arms over her chest and leaned back against his desk. "I took cryptology in college and was hired to write a decryption program for the NSA if you must know. But I'd have to kill you if I told you any more." Her eyes sparkled playfully.

"Kill me? You?" Rowan snorted. "Should you try, you would find yourself in the hold once again. Or worse."

"Geez. It was a joke." She rolled her eyes. "Lighten up."

He exchanged a glance with Nick, who looked as puzzled as he was.

"You will interpret this code." He lifted the rolled map, still in his hands.

"We don't live in the Stone Ages, Captain, and I'm not part of this charade of a crew. *Ergo*, I don't take orders from you."

Rowan's blood began to boil. He took a step toward her. "That is where you are wrong, Lady Minx. You live or die by my command alone."

Where most men would have lowered their eyes beneath his glare, apologized for their affront, or at the very least exhibited a flicker of fear, she only smiled, feigned a look of fright and said, "Oooh, I'm scared."

Nick's jaw dropped, while shock held Rowan's tongue, along with his reason.

"Tell you what, Captain." The minx continued in her fearless, supercilious tone. "I'll be happy to do as you ask on one condition. As soon as you fix this old boat of yours, you promise to take me back to San Diego."

Rowan growled. "'Tis a ship, not a boat!"

~ 65 ~

Chapter 5

Morgan sat in the wobbly boat, holding a hand to her nose at the stench of unwashed men. With the actor-captain's help, she'd navigated a rope ladder flung over the side of the bigger ship down to this one below. Easily accomplished had she been wearing her jeans, but after getting tangled up in her skirts—twice—and nearly falling into the water, she accepted the hand he offered. Now as she settled in the small craft, her dress ballooning around her and sweat starting to form beneath all the layers, she gained an overwhelming appreciation for what women endured in the past.

With more dexterity than Morgan would have thought she possessed, Edith climbed down the ladder, slapping away pirates' hands reaching to help her, and sat on the seat beside Morgan, offering her a wide smile and a reassuring nod. "A proper lady needs an escort…'specially with sich rakish pirates 'bout."

Morgan smiled at the woman's calm motherly concern, so unlike her own mother who would have been in a nervous twit by now.

The captain, a.k.a rakish pirate, leapt into the boat, sending it jostling, then settled on Morgan's other side, eyeing her with suspicion—and something else. Something playful that made her heart skip. Sun-streaked hair waved about him in abandon, slapping his strong jaw peppered with dark stubble. Man, but he was handsome. Not in Jason's polished metro-sexual way, but in a devil-may-care wild kind of way. Her father had chosen well. Kerr, the other handsome pirate, sat beside his captain and gave her a wink before ordering the crew to start rowing.

Pressing their oars against the hull, the men shoved off from the larger boat and plunged them into water the most beautiful shade of turquoise Morgan had ever seen. She'd never been much for traveling. Too claustrophobic in planes, too sick on boats, and an inability to sleep in strange motels kept her close to home. Regardless, she had gone to Mexico on Spring break once, but she never remembered water this gorgeous.

Reaching over the railing, she allowed the liquid—warm as a bath—to caress her hand as movement beneath the surface drew her gaze to brightly-colored fish darting this way and that just below the surface. Beautiful fish, the likes of which she'd only seen at the San Diego Aquarium. Tropical fish, if she remembered. Which meant she was not anywhere near California. Which also meant she must have been unconscious for quite some time.

Familiar fear began to claw its way through her belly and into her heart, pinching and cinching as it went until her entire body felt coiled tight like one of her mother's balls of yarn.

"What day is it?" she asked Edith.

Wind blew the woman's black curls into her eyes, and she brushed them aside, looking confused.

"You know, Monday, Tuesday, Wednesday …"

Edith waved a hand through the air. "We don't needs to keep track of sich things, child."

"Well, *I* need to. I have an important appointment I cannot miss on Tuesday."

When Edith offered no response, Morgan turned to the captain, but he was in deep conversation with Kerr.

Perhaps once Morgan got Edith alone, she could tell her about the cancer, appeal to her motherly instincts to stop this ridiculous charade.

The small craft leapt in the air, and Morgan gripped the sides, her stomach vaulting. Groans sounded from the men as they heaved the oars through the incoming waves.

Shielding her eyes from the sun, she glanced back over her shoulder and was surprised at the enormity of the boat that had brought them here. The side rose a good twenty-five feet above them, and the length was over twice that long. Three masts as tall as telephone poles stretched into the morning sky. Where had her father found such an authentic ship? It must have cost him a fortune.

When she turned back around, she found the captain staring at her again, a grin curving one side of his lips. "You approve of the *Reckoning*, Lady Minx?"

"I guess it's okay as far as boats go."

His mouth grew tight. "Ship." He gestured toward the craft they rode in. "*This* is a boat."

"Whatever." Morgan looked away as a wave struck them. The boat rocked violently, and she tightened her grip on the edge as seawater splashed over the side, soaking her shoes. Although the ginger tea had helped calm her stomach, queasiness clambered up her throat once again, and she was thankful they'd be on land soon. If her father possessed an ounce of mercy, he would have his people waiting on the island to take her home. Enough was enough.

Pain jabbed her right side just below her ribs—a pain the doctor said would worsen until they could operate to remove the tumor, a pain reminding her that no matter what grand romantic adventure her father had staged for her, she was still going to die.

Especially if she didn't start treatment soon.

Incoming waves punched the small boat, splashing over them and sending the craft speeding toward shore. Morgan nearly fell from her perch twice, but the captain's strong hand came to her rescue. When the boat struck sand, he leapt into the shallow water and swept her up in his arms before she had a chance to protest. With a grin that would melt the staunchest feminist, he waded toward shore, his boots sloshing through the water, causing the strangest sensation to come over her. She'd never been the type of girl to need a man for much of anything. A women's libber all the way, she prided herself on her independence, on her ability to take care of herself. But decked out in this frilly gown, being carried ashore as if she were too precious to get her feet wet by this strong, handsome man, well, it made her feel like a princess from one of those fairy tales she used to read when she was a little girl.

The fairy tales that life had taught her never came true.

And part of her—a small part—wished that all of this were real.

For such a brute of a man, the actor set her down with the gentlest of care before he turned and assisted his men with the supplies. Farley had a bit more trouble carrying Edith. For one thing, the woman made it quite clear she didn't want to be carried. For another, the aged surgeon nearly dropped his wife twice, dragged the bottom of her dress through the waves, and then endured her playful swats as she chided him for his clumsiness. He finally put her down on the sand beside Morgan.

Morgan backed away, expecting them to start yelling and accusing each other, but instead Edith reached up on tiptoes and kissed her husband's cheek. The loving gaze he returned made Morgan swallow a burst of emotion. If that had been her parents, they'd have started World War III by now.

A chorus of birdsong and the buzz of insects added to the gentle lap of waves and shouts of the men as they moved crates, barrels, and sacks from the boat and stacked them on shore. Farley went to help, leaving Morgan and Edith standing in the hot sun.

Morgan swept a gaze over the beach and the jungle beyond, seeking any sign of her father's people—a camera, a flash of modern clothing, anything to let her know this stupid act was at an end. Yet nothing but pearly sand, emerald waters, and lush greenery filled her vision.

Sweat pasted Morgan's underthings to her skin. "How did women stand wearing all these clothes in the old days?" she asked Edith.

"Come, child." Edith led her down the beach. "Let's find some shade while the men settle things."

A breeze wafted over Morgan, cooling her neck and dousing her with the freshest air she'd ever breathed as they lowered to sit beneath a palm tree. She took off her shoes, dumped out the sand, and rubbed her stockinged feet, longing to rip off the confining hose and wade in the surf. But then she'd just get wet and sandy, and with no shower to wash off the saltwater, she'd end up more miserable than she was now.

The captain's deep voice echoed from down shore where he stood, wind tossing his hair, hands on his hips, directing men who obeyed him swiftly and without question. He made a good pirate captain. Perhaps a famous producer was watching, and Rowan—or whatever his real name was—was auditioning for the next *Pirates of the Caribbean* movie. If so, Morgan would definitely cast her vote for him to fill the role—of the villain, of course. She smiled.

No sooner had the men finished unloading the cargo from the ship, than a few of them, with ropes in hand, climbed into the sails and tied the ropes around the masts. She watched with interest as they tossed the other ends of the ropes to men in boats below, who rowed them to shore and tied them to trees. Within minutes, they created a pulley system, which they used to pull the top of the boat toward shore, exposing half of its bottom.

"Why are they tipping the boat?"

"They needs to careen the bottom, you know, from barnacles an' rot and sich. An' then they'll mend the hole in the hull from the shot we took."

Morgan had never heard of such a thing. But then again, she didn't know much about boats. "Wow. My father thought of everything. You guys are really great at this."

Edith studied her with concern. "You don't look well, child. I'll go gets you some water."

Morgan grabbed her hand, stopping her from rising and thanking God for the perfect opening. "I need to talk to you about something, Edith. I have an important doctor's appointment … or I did." She paused and stared into the woman's kind eyes. "Listen, I'm sick." Morgan assumed—no, hoped—her father had an ounce of decency and had not told the actors about her condition. She hated when people knew. She'd learned that lesson early on when she'd made the mistake of telling a few friends at work. One had immediately backed away as if cancer was contagious. The next friend became overly emotional and started acting as if Morgan were already eight feet under. The third friend offered a curt sympathetic phrase like "How horrible" or "I'm so sorry" but then quickly changed the subject. And the last friend—her religious friend—had told her she mustn't worry, that God had a plan, that He would either heal her or help her through it.

Exactly what her mother had said right before she became such a blubbering, sobbing mess that Morgan had to numb her with pills and platitudes … when it had been Morgan who had needed comfort the most.

"You's ill, child?" Edith's voice brought Morgan's thoughts to the present as the woman took her other hand. "I knows some healing. Using herbs an' sich. I learnt it from the apothecary who owned me. Jist tell me what ails you."

"It's nothing you can help with." Morgan snapped hair from her face. "Listen. You seem like a decent person. I'm begging you. I'm not enjoying this adventure my father has staged. I just want to go home. I *need* to go home. Can you please have Rowan, or whoever he is, call my father?"

"Your father?" Edith placed the back of her hand on Morgan's cheek. "You ain't feverish. That be good. I dunno who your papa is, child, but I sure the captain will take you home as soon as he can. Now, don't you be worrying none."

Edith's warm smile made Morgan almost believe her.

But Morgan didn't believe in happy endings.

The chime of metal snapped her gaze down shore where two actors had drawn their swords. Bare-chested and barefooted, they shuffled through the sand, kicking up grains, and slashing their blades through the air.

She breathed out a ragged sigh. "Well, I suppose a good sword fight was to be expected."

Edith must have mistaken her comment for fear because she patted her arm. "They's jist playing, child."

"I have cancer." Morgan blurted out. "My father hired you all to keep my mind off of it, but it's not working. I need to go home and get treatment."

"Goodness be, child." Shock and sorrow poured from Edith's eyes, along with concern—true concern. "No wonder you's so pale and your tummy's bothering you," she continued. "I knows jist the thing." Her voice spiked with hope as she struggled to rise and ambled away before Morgan could stop her.

No doubt to contact Morgan's father. Good.

Laughter that seemed to mock her newfound hope rumbled down the beach where the fight had finished and several men now sat drinking from bottles. Rum, no doubt, for that would be the drink of choice for pirates. Beyond them, other men had rowed out to the ship and were doing something to the hull.

If they were going to stay the night shouldn't someone be setting up tents and folding chairs, or maybe a grill or two? Morgan had always hated camping. Too much dirt, too many bugs, and not enough order and comfort. Instead, these actors sat around drinking and playing swords, while all the crates and barrels they brought ashore remained in a disorderly heap on the sand.

While she sat here sweating like a pig.

Boastful shouts, followed by laughter filled the air and the captain flung off his shirt and drew his sword. Another man did the same, and the two stepped to the center of the drinking mob and began to fight.

Morgan's traitorous eyes landed on Rowan's bare chest, and the air suddenly grew warmer. *Oh my.* Muscular wasn't the right word. Brawny? No. Powerful. Yes, that fit. It wasn't the type of chest she'd seen a thousand times at the beach— the gym-made chest where muscles bulged in weird, awkward places and looked more like balloons inflated beneath skin. No, Rowan's chest was firm and round in all the right spots, as if he actually used his muscles for a living instead of created them with machines. Which affirmed her guess that he was a stunt man.

What also affirmed her assumption was the graceful way he moved—a quick leap here, a dive there, a sudden spin— and the skill he had with his sword, beating back his opponent one minute and swerving to meet his attacker the next. Morgan had only seen sword fights in the movies where camera angles and editing made it look almost real. This sword fight wouldn't need any special tricks to make it appear authentic.

Rowan leapt to the side to avoid the other man's thrust. Laughing, he slashed his opponent's sword away, then ducked to prick his thigh with the tip of his blade. Growling, the man swung madly at his captain, but Rowan met each slash expertly with his blade, muscles rolling across his back as he went. Skillfully and quickly, he struck the man's hand with the hilt of his sword, sending his opponent's blade to the ground.

Grimacing, the man wiped sweat from his brow and picked up his sword. The mob cheered and continued their drinking as Edith returned with a mug half-filled with what looked like sludge.

"Anamu tea." Edith handed her the drink. "I didn't have hot water so's you's gonna have to drink it cold. Go on now," she added when Morgan hesitated at the smell. "Anamu s'pose to cure cancer."

And, apparently, from the smell, it could cure an appetite too. Morgan took a gulp anyway, sure her expression was twisting into a dozen knots. "Thank you, Edith. Did you find a phone to call my father?"

Edith's expression knotted, but her attention was quickly diverted down shore. "The captain comes. You can ask him 'bout your father yourself, child."

Morgan faced the jungle, not wanting to stare at the man and feed his overblown vanity.

His footsteps sounded behind her, and she slowly rose, tea in hand, and took a sip as if she didn't notice his presence.

He cleared his throat. She turned to face him, shocked when his powerful chest filled her vision. She spewed the Anamu tea all over his pants.

"Seems ye have the same effect on all the lasses, eh?" Nick said as he strolled up beside his captain.

Rowan—or whatever his name was—stared at the spray on his pants and the drops glistening over the—*oh, my*—six-pack rippling over his belly.

"Wow, ah … I'm really sorry. I didn't expect to see …" *Such a magnificent chest up close.* "… you … here." Okay, she was mumbling, and she had no idea why. He should be the one apologizing to her for putting her through all of this.

Edith shook her head. "Where be your manners, Captain. Put on a shirt in front of a lady." Taking the mug from Morgan, she sped away. "I'll make some more."

"Beware your tongue, woman," Rowan called after her with a playful tone.

Gathering herself, Morgan backed away and raised her gaze to his. "If you came to ask me to play swords with you, I must say no."

Nick laughed.

Sunlight winked at her from the earring in Rowan's ear as if taunting her. "Alack, the idea is not without merit." He grinned. "However, I've come to tell you my men will build a shelter for you and Edith." He jerked his thumb over his shoulder at a group of men who resembled Hell's Angels heading her way with hammers, saws, and ropes.

"I don't want some crude shelter, and I refuse to sleep in the sand. I am sick, and I demand you stop this insanity and take me home."

They both looked at her as if she'd sprouted horns.

"All right. I'm outta here." Clutching her ridiculous skirts, she turned and started down the beach away from the camp.

"Faith now, and where do you think you're going?" Rowan shouted after her.

"I'm sure there's a resort or hotel or at least a small town on this island, and I intend to find it and call my father." Despite her confident tone, she tripped yet again over her skirts and uttered a curse under her breath.

She heard only groans for replies as she slogged forward and rounded a small bend which led to more beach and more jungle. After a few moments, she glanced over her shoulder and saw nothing but white sand tynd trees. Good. They hadn't followed her.

She started forward again. How big could this island be anyway?

"Let her be." Rowan raised an arm to block Nick's advance.

"But, Captain, the wee lass may get hurt."

"She can't go far, Nick. 'Tis but a small island without much to harm her, save birds and spiders. She can walk around the length of it in three hours." Rowan gazed up at the sun, nearly above them now. "The *lass* needs to be taught a lesson—several, in fact. The first is to respect those in whose hands her safety *and purity* lie. Forsooth, but she irks me with her sharp tongue!"

Nick chuckled. "I'll grant ye, I've never seen ye so vexed by a lass."

"And you won't again. Not after I leave her at Charles Town. Faith, does the woman not realize that in the hands of any other pirate captain, she'd be chained to the bed? On her back?"

Nick gave a half smile and adjusted his plaid cravat. "Then the good Lord put her on the right ship."

"The good Lord has naught to do with that thieving minx," Rowan spat, then waved off the men coming to erect a shelter. If she didn't want privacy and protection, then she would get neither. With a growl, he strode back to camp, suddenly needing a drink.

Nick fell in beside him. "What of the code she claims t' know? Don't ye wish yer precious map deciphered?"

The sun's rays lashed Rowan's back, and he grabbed his shirt from the sand and threw it over his head. "No doubt she'll be in a more cooperative mood when she returns. At which time I will order her to tell me what the code means or pay the price."

"An' if she truly doesna know?"

"Then I know someone in Charles Town who might. Either way, I *will* have my map deciphered and the treasure to which it leads." He smiled. Enough treasure to make up for all his past sins and establish him and his sister in luxury.

"And then I shall quit this roistering, Nick, as you've begged me repeatedly to do, and settle down. Mayhap get a wife and breed a bevy of little pirates."

"Och, now, laying aside yer stealing and pilfering, that would indeed make me verra happy. But ye settle down? Now that I'll hav't' see."

"Quit pirating?" Kerr's incredulous voice sounded behind Rowan before he appeared beside him. "Not you, Captain. Never. Once you taste this freebooter's life, how can you ever go back?"

Nick gave a disdainful chuckle. "So ye'll be stealing an' raping when ye are old an' gray, eh Kerr?"

The pirate shrugged. "I've made it to seven and twenty when most pirates are long since rotting in Davy Jones' locker. When I meet my fate, 'twill be in a blaze of glory with my cutlass in one hand and a buxom wench in the other."

"At the rate ye're drinking and whoring, I wouldna expect you to see thirty."

Kerr snorted in response and glanced toward the ship being careened.

Rowan followed his gaze, noting how hard his men were working in the hot sun. "In an hour, call in those men and replace them with another ten. Then another group two hours after that. Continue until sundown. I want to leave this island as soon as possible." He glanced out to sea, a band of glittering sapphire rolling toward the horizon. Though the *Reckoning* was well hidden behind the arm of the cove, they made easy prey for enemies sailing past.

And Rowan had many enemies.

With a nod, Kerr sauntered away, already shouting orders before he reached the surf.

Nick went off to read one of his many books, leaving Rowan with his thoughts. They unavoidably leapt to the lady who called herself Morgan. The only Morgan that Rowan had known was the aging once-famous pirate Henry Morgan. And this lady was just as fickle, crazy, and fearless as he.

Rowan took to drink. It seemed the logical thing to do instead of traipsing after her like some cowering toady. With bottle in hand, he strolled the beach, kicking up sand, shouting orders to anyone in earshot to unload supplies, build a fire, scavenge for fruit, and catch some fish. Anything to keep his mind off the blasted woman.

But it didn't work. He plunked to the sand, bottle half empty, and gazed at the rainbow of colors swirling on the horizon. It was nearly dark and the lady had not returned.

Mayhap he should not have allowed her to leave. He took another swig and squeezed his eyes shut to stop the world from spinning. Kerr had called in the last shift from the ship, and the men assembled around the fire, roasting the fish they'd caught and passing around jugs of rum. In an hour they'd be fighting, singing, or unconscious.

Movement came from that direction. A barrel emerged from the flames and waddled his way. But it wasn't a barrel. It was Rowan's bosun, Abbot. Shorter than Rowan and built like a cannon, the man always made Rowan nervous. Mayhap 'twas his glass eye that always seemed to be staring at Rowan. Mayhap 'twas that his bulging arms were bigger than his thighs, making him look as though he'd tip over at any minute. Regardless, whatever dire news the man had to tell Rowan, he was not in the mood. Abbot stopped before him, shifting his feet in the sand, his one glass eye pointed out to sea while his other eye stared at Rowan.

"What is it, Abbot?"

"I thought ye should know, Cap'n, Adney and Pax took off after the lady."

"What?" Rowan struggled to his feet, then waited for the ground to stop moving. "When?"

"An hour, mabbe two. They snuck off that way sayin' they was goin' to find her and have some fun."

Chapter 6

Morgan needed her meds. Ever since she was fourteen and diagnosed with Obsessive Compulsive Disorder and acute anxiety, she'd never been without them for more than a day. Now it had been at least that and more. Chaos ran rampant around her, ratcheting up her heartrate and playing havoc with her breathing. She tripped over a root and stumbled down the dirt path. Leaves the size of elephant ears flapped at her as she passed. Bugs as big as coffee mugs—man, could she use one of those iced coffees now, the ones with the whipped cream on top—dove for her. Massive spider webs hung like fish nets between trees, trying to trap her. She shivered, imagining the size of the spiders that must have made them. Trees and vines entwined to form a terrifying labyrinth. Even the path was chaotic, narrow one minute, wide the next, and crisscrossed with dangerous spindly roots. She took to numbering the rocks along the way—anything to add a pinch of structure and keep her from curling up in the fetal position under a bush.

Didn't her father remember that she needed her meds? Probably not. He didn't seem to remember much of anything about Morgan, not even her birthday.

A bird squawked overhead, flapping its wings and strutting back and forth across a branch, where a ray of sunlight illuminated its gorgeous purple and yellow feathers. It stared down at Morgan with one eye as if she were an alien from another planet. Maybe she was, for this island didn't feel like any place on earth she'd ever been. Where the heck was she? She had combed the beach for hours and found no glimpse of civilization—not a restaurant, fishing village, hotel, nothing. Not even a boat dock. Quite odd since it seemed a lovely spot for a secluded spa—maybe a Sandals or even a private resort for rich people.

She knew she was in trouble when she'd come upon the pirate camp again. Realizing she'd circled the entire island, she'd done an about-face and decided to head inland. Maybe some rich guy owned the island and built a vacation home on top of one of the hills that rose from the shore. But now her feet ached, her side hurt, her mouth felt like it was stuffed with sand, and her nerves were wound so tight she feared she might faint at any moment.

To make matters worse, it was growing dark. Something she had not thought of in her desperation to find a way home. Shadows slunk from behind trees and shrubs rose from the dirt like ghouls in a horror film. She hugged herself and continued onward as a chorus of katydids rose to grate on her already frayed nerves.

Wait. Was that the sound of water? Turning toward the bubbling chorus, she plowed through leaves and vines, not caring about anything but cooling her burning tongue. She tripped over a rock, and before she could grab onto anything, lost her balance and fell down an incline. Tree trunks, roots, and rocks rose up to strike her as she tumbled down … down … down… and landed face first in the mud.

Wet slime oozed over her cheeks and crept into her nose with each breath. Every inch of her body ached. Especially her right side where the cancer continued to devour her. Could things get any worse?

Two pairs of footsteps slurped through the mud to stand beside her. "There ye be, sweet flower. We 'ad a 'ard time findin' ye."

Apparently, yes. Shoving her palms into the muck, she pried her cheek from the ooze and sat. The shadowy figures of two of the pirate actors leered at her as if she were their last meal.

"You've got to be kidding me." Growling, she rose and batted mud from her dress. "What do you want?"

The short one spit and then ran a sleeve over his mouth. "We want ye, ye steamy wench. How's about a little love fer yer fellow man?"

"Or men." The other brute of man chuckled. "Aye, she be a rare blossom ready t' be plucked, says I."

Morgan groaned and rubbed her sore arm where she'd rammed into a tree. "Do I look like a flower to you?" The sound of water beckoned, and she started toward it. "I'm not in the mood." She waved them off. "If your captain sent you to fetch me, you can tell him I'm not coming until he stops all this craziness. In fact"—she faced them again—"tell him he'll have to answer to my father if I get hurt, so he best contact him and get me out of here right away. As in *now!*" Her shout had no effect on the morons. They simply stood gaping at her as if she were speaking a foreign language.

Her frustration near boiling, Morgan continued onward, slower this time, peering through the shadows just in case there was another drop-off. She heard the men groan and follow her, and she thought to give them another piece of her mind when one of them grabbed her arm and shoved her to the ground.

"Ye've got a shrewish tongue, I'll give ye that, missy," the short one said as he forced her other arm to the ground and held her fast.

"Aye, a saucy wench that'll sure give us gents a bit o' sorely needed pleasure." The other man hovered over her and began unbuckling the belt that held up his baggy pants.

Morgan struggled against the man's grip. "You're hurting me!" She tried to kick him in the crotch, but he slammed his knees on top of her legs. "Ouch!"

The man on top of her started grunting like a pig.

"Okay, I get it," Morgan said, gasping. "Raping and pillaging. Now, get off of me!"

"Naw, we's jist gettin' started, missy." The man tightened his grip, and she felt his spit spray her face. Totally gross!

The darkness stole their features, but she could make out the shape of the larger man push the shorter one aside and take his place all the while ordering him to hold her arms.

Cursing, the man took a spot above her head and pinned her down again.

"Okay, enough is enough! My father will hear of this!"

Struggling was useless against two of them, and for a split second real fear sliced through her. But then she remembered none of this was real. It was just part of the play her father had staged.

The pirate began slobbering on her face, and she slammed her forehead into his.

"Ow! She 'urt me 'ead."

A booming voice bellowed from the darkness. "I will hurt more than that if you don't release her this instant, Adney!"

Rowan. For some ridiculous reason, relief washed through her.

The man holding her arms leapt from her as if she were on fire. "Aw, Cap'n. We meant 'er no 'arm. We thought ye was done wit' 'er, 'tis all."

Morgan pounded her fists on the other man's chest, but he wouldn't budge.

"Get off her, Pax, or I'll gut you and string you up as fast as you can spit."

Morgan could sense the man's hesitancy … his anger. Such great acting! "Ye let 'er go, Cap'n. I says that means she be free game."

"I told the crew she was not to be touched, and until I say otherwise, that order stands," Rowan answered calmly, but with each word he uttered, his voice grew in volume and intensity. "Now you've gone and upset me. And you know what happens when I'm upset."

The short man must have had an inkling because he bolted through the foliage and disappeared.

"I told you to get off her!" Rowan's growl was enough to frighten Big Foot. He charged forward, but the man released her, leapt to his feet, and drew what looked like a knife—a rather large knife.

If all this weren't a silly act, Morgan would be terrified. As it was, she rose and attempted to once again brush dirt from her clothes. Could she never stay clean in this crazed adventure?

"Get back, woman!" Rowan shouted as he barreled toward the man, nearly knocking her over.

"Hey!" Morgan peered through the shadows to see Rowan slam into the smelly actor and the two of them fall to the ground, grunting and groaning. What happened next, she couldn't say. It was too dark to see much of anything until Rowan dragged the man up by the collar and slugged him across the jaw. His head whipped around and he stumbled backward. Snatching the knife from the ground, Rowan kicked the man in the back then forced him against the trunk of a nearby tree.

"Beware your defiance!" Spinning him around, Rowan pointed the knife at his throat. "Not many have lived who have dared cross me."

The man's breath came hard and fast, and Morgan sensed his terror.

"Apologize to the lady."

"I'll not apologize t' no trollop," the man ground out.

Rowan pressed the knife. A stream of red spilled down the man's neck.

"By all means. Then you'll die right here, and I'll leave your filthy carcass for the beasts to feast on."

"Apologies, miss," he managed to sputter out.

Rowan released him. "Begone!"

The man's shadow raced before Morgan and disappeared. "Wow. That looked totally real. Like you really cut him. Was that one of those fake blood thingys they use in the movies?"

Sheathing the knife, he took a step toward her. Though she couldn't see his features, she sensed him staring at her with his usual look of bewilderment.

The smell of alcohol overwhelmed her. "You're drunk."

"Not quite enough to make sense of your incoherent drivel."

She sighed. "Listen. That was great. Very chivalrous and all. The hero rescues the damsel in distress. Nice touch. I know I'm supposed to swoon in your arms now, but I'm really not in the mood."

He said nothing. Instead, grabbing her hand, he pulled her along, batting leaves and branches out of the way as they went. The sound of trickling water grew louder, and before long they came upon a creek that looked like liquid silver in the moonlight. He ordered her to sit on a boulder, then left. The man had the manners of a hoodlum, but in all honesty, it felt good to sit down. Slipping off her shoes, she rubbed her blistered feet and enjoyed the breeze cooling the sweat on her neck. Even though this had all been staged, Morgan couldn't help the relief she felt at not being alone anymore. Or was she?

Where had Rowan gone? Wasn't he supposed to be flirting with her? Playing the dashing hero? Or maybe her father had told him to play the hard-to-get bad boy. She could care less at this point.

The sounds of the jungle returned—chirps, buzzes, and croaks along with the flutter of leaves—much more haunting at night. Her anxiety returned with it. She hugged herself.

Something dove at her, and she leapt from her perch and swatted the air.

Except for a milky glow slicing the leaves from the moon above, it was pitch dark. Still, she didn't really want to wander through this jungle at night. Nor could she stay here.

She started for the creek to parch her thirst when brush fluttered and boots stomped and Rowan returned with an armful of wood. He dropped it to the ground and began arranging it.

"What are you doing?"

"Making a fire."

"Why?"

"You need ask?" He glanced up at her. "To keep predators at bay for one. To provide warmth and light for my Lady Minx for another."

"But aren't we going back to camp?"

"Nay, 'tis best we stay here."

"Oh, I get it." She huffed. "If you think I'm spending the night here with you, Romeo, you got another thing coming."

"Ah, the lady knows Shakespeare." He chuckled as he finished stacking wood. Then pulling two objects from a satchel swung over his shoulder, he struck them together. "Alas, if you wish me to die for our love, you must pardon me there."

"Very funny." Morgan made her way to the creek. Seeing no other way to get a drink, she knelt in the sand and drew handfuls of the precious liquid to her mouth. Nothing had ever tasted so good.

Leaning back, she drew a deep breath, realizing how heavy her eyelids felt … she let them fall … for just a minute.

When a deep, throaty growl rumbled through the jungle.

Chapter 7

Sparks flew from the flint and steel and landed on the tinder Rowan had collected. Leaning over, he blew lightly, then placed sticks on the small flame until it caught the wood. The woman had gone to the creek for water, but he kept one eye on her lest she attempt to dash off.

He'd put nothing past her, this outlandish lady. He'd never met anyone like her. From what he'd overheard, she hadn't been afraid in the slightest of being ravished. Forsooth, quite the opposite! 'Twas like she believed she was, indeed, in a drama and all of them actors playing their parts. Which would explain her Shakespeare reference. But he didn't want to believe that, for that would mean the lady truly *was* mad. And for some reason, that thought saddened him most of all.

A growl rolled through the jungle, and the lady leapt from her spot by the creek and dashed toward him, eyes wide. "What is that?"

He smiled. So she *was* afraid of something. "Most likely a jaguar, though I'll admit to being surprised at finding one on this island."

"Jaguar?" She stared into the darkness. "Then we aren't safe here."

"Naught to fear, Lady Minx. The fire will keep him at bay."

She stared at him, the growing firelight reflecting both horror and unbelief in her green eyes. But then the shrew returned. "I insist you take me back to camp at once."

He chuckled. "You'll soon discover that rare is the person who insists anything of me. Besides, you'll be safer here."

"With man-eating beasts roaming about? I don't think so."

"Lud, better than the woman-eating beasts back at camp."

At this, she frowned. "I'll be safer when I'm home in bed."

"Ah, is it to bed you wish to go?" He rose and gave her a rakish grin—the kind most women could never resist.

She huffed in disgust. "Touch me and I'll sue you for harassment."

He scratched the growing stubble on his jaw and studied her. "Faith now, but you are a strange little tigress. In good sooth, you'll find I never have need to force myself upon a lady."

"Really? I bet they all fall at your feet just like Jason."

"I know not who this Jason is, but aye, ladies find my charm irresistible." Except this particular one. Nay, where other ladies vied for his attentions, this lady did all in her power to escape him. Not only escape him, but insult and berate him. Extraordinary! He could make no sense of it.

Scanning the small clearing, he found two logs wide enough to sit on and pulled them near the fire. "Have a seat or 'twill be a long night upon your feet."

She glanced down at the log as if it were a brick of horse dung, then stooped and began to move it one way and then the other, an inch here, an inch there, always stepping back to assess her efforts before doing it again. "I don't see why we can't return to camp," she said, still fumbling.

Flames crackled and leapt for the sky, scattering light over the trees at the edge of the clearing. She continued fussing with the log until it lay in a perfect line horizontal to the edge of the fire.

"You may return if you wish." Rowan nodded in the direction his pirates had fled. "I should warn you there are predators along the way and a host more when you arrive on shore, for my men are no doubt well into their cups by now."

"Into their cups?" she asked as if she had no idea what that meant. "Oh, never mind." One brow arched. "Are you saying you can't defend your lady love against a wild beast?"

"Even *I* cannot fight off a hungry jaguar," he retorted.

She placed a hand on her heart. "Forsooth, my hero has a weakness." She gave him a taunting grin before lowering her gaze to once again study the log. Finally happy with its position, she proceeded to furiously brush away dirt and twigs from the surface before lowering to sit upon it. Once settled, she began fluffing out her skirts, but the more she fluffed, the more her face scrunched—in the most adorable way, he might add—as she began shaking dirt from her gown and trying to press out the wrinkles. She continued her ministrations for several minutes until Rowan felt it was *he* who would go mad.

"Leave it be, woman!" he snapped and threw a log on the fire, shooting more sparks into the night. "Edith will find you a clean gown when we return."

"I can't stand to be dirty. And everything is out of place." She looked up and must have seen his perplexed expression. "I need my meds, Rowan. Can't you see I'm going nuts without them."

Nuts? Was she to turn into a pecan next? "Do you refer, perchance, to medicaments?"

"Whatever you want to call them. Yes."

Ah, that would explain her odd behavior. Mayhap she had a brain disease. He'd have to ask Farley if he could use his trephine to bore a hole in her skull and relieve the pressure. "And what is it exactly that ails you?"

A bug flew about her face, and she slapped at it, horrified. Then pressing her right side, she winced and faced him. "I have OCD and anxiety, if you must know."

"Anxiety?" He snorted. "Over what? You are safe here, as I have said." Memories rose of how she'd attempted to sort his things back in his cabin. "Mayhap you would not be anxious if you stopped tinkering with everything and let things be."

"But things are not right." She hugged herself and glanced around their tiny camp. "They must be right"—she rubbed her temples—"or my world falls apart."

"Nothing is right with this world," Rowan returned. Something he'd learned long ago. "If perfection is what you seek, save yourself the trouble and acquit the futile quest."

The eerie shrill of a night bird echoed through the canopy, and she sighed and stared into the fire. "I can't believe my father is making me sleep in the dirt with bugs and wild animals. And a pirate," she added with disgust as if he were worse than the prior two. If he were any other pirate, he would heartedly agree. But he'd been raised the son of a rich merchant and was taught to treat women with respect. All women.

Even impish thieves.

"Alas, perchance this will help." Rowan reached into his sack, pulled out a flask, and handed it to her.

"Rum? You're giving me rum? Alcohol is what got me into this mess in the first place." She ran both hands through her hair—rather beautiful hair, he was forced to admit, as the firelight accentuated ribbons of auburn woven among the brown.

Shrugging, he took a swig.

"Haven't you had enough?" She spat. "How are you going to protect me if you're always drunk?"

He chuckled. "I do my best work when crocked to the gills."

She frowned. "Not that there is anything to really protect me from. I'm sure those animal growls are soundtracks."

As if in defiance of her words, a distant roar resounded, and her wide gaze sped to the surrounding jungle. Finally, she rose, tripped over her skirts, and plunked on the log beside him. She grabbed the flask from his hand. "Since I don't have my meds, perhaps a sip or two will help."

The sip turned into three or four, during which time Rowan watched her shoulders lower a bit and her breathing steady. What had happened to this lady to make her wound so tight? And why would a woman so nervous about everything sneak aboard a pirate ship to steal an amulet? 'Twas an act of bravery—or stupidity—not one belonging to one so skittish.

Yet, she wasn't skittish at all, but brave beyond compare. What an enigma.

The katydids took up a chorus as a breeze stirred the flames and showered them with sparks.

She took another sip and snickered. "If my mother could see me now. Drinking alcohol with a pirate."

"Indeed? Was she opposed to spirits? Or just pirates?"

"Both." She smiled then took a deep breath, the rise and fall of the sun-kissed mounds above her bodice drawing his attention. "She opposed many things," she continued. "Swearing, gambling, drinking, movies, most TV shows and books, and of course dancing."

He had no idea what TV shows and movies were, but the rest he could attest to as favorites of his. "Dancing as well? Faith now, what a tedious life."

"She's one of those religious freaks. Goes to church every time the door is opened, you know the type."

He did. In a way. His sister, Juliana wasn't quite so devout, but she did tend to preach to him overmuch.

Morgan pointed the flask at him so quickly, it startled him. "It's not that I don't believe in God. I do. It's just that for all my mother's churchgoing, she doesn't practice what she preaches, if you know what I mean."

The rum was loosening her tongue, along with her nerves, as he had hoped. Rowan nodded. "Hypocrites. I know many such people."

"I'm surprised you know anyone who goes to church in Hollywood." She took another sip.

He wondered where this Hollywood place was. Sounded a lot like that den of pirates, Charles Town, he was planning on sailing to next.

She stared into the fire, the flames reflecting angst in her eyes. "She preaches trust in God, but then falls apart when something bad happens. She preaches healing but then runs to doctors for every hangnail. She preaches faith and peace and joy, yet she is on more anti-anxiety and anti-depression meds than anyone I know." Morgan eased a lock of hair behind her ear. "The truth is"—she rubbed the flask between her hands—"I can't count on my mother for anything. She literally freaks out at the slightest thing and then calls me for help. Most of the time I feel like I'm her mother instead of the other way around."

Rowan had no idea what this *freaks out* meant, but it didn't sound like Morgan's mother was of much use.

"Do you believe in God, Mr. Actor? Or should I call you Captain? What is your real name, anyway?"

"Rowan will do." He shrugged. "In truth, I don't know whether I believe in a divine Creator. My sister seems to think He exists and He cares. I have yet to see evidence of either."

"I've always believed in God. Always prayed. I suppose going to church since I was a baby gave me no choice. But lately, well … lately, I have doubted whether He's even there."

A sorrow hovered around the lady as if she were deeply burdened by the revelation. Or was it something else? Oddly, it made him long to help her, to take away her pain. Odd because, if he were truthful, Rowan wasn't the type to care much for the problems of others.

"And your father?" he asked, finding himself ever more curious about this woman's past.

"Well, I'm sure you met—no, he probably sent his admins to hire you." A distant roar stiffened her, and she searched the darkness. "He's the president of one of the biggest software companies in the country. Rich, smart, powerful and decisive." She paused and lowered her gaze to the fire. "And distant, cold, and unloving."

So, the poor girl had neither mother or father to raise her properly. At least Rowan's mother had loved him. Though her early death had robbed him of that when he needed it the most.

The warble of a mockingbird accompanied by the distant chatter of monkeys filled the silence between them.

Tears blurred Morgan's eyes, and Rowan swallowed, longing to take her in his arms and comfort her. Comfort himself, in truth, for he knew precisely how she felt— unwanted, unloved, and worthless. Instead, he took a sip of rum. "My father was much like yours. Always too busy with his shipping business to pay me any mind."

"Really?" She wiped away a tear and looked up at him. Red pinked her cheeks and the tip of her nose from the fire— or mayhap the rum. Dirt smudged the right side of her face that, he was sure if she knew about it, would drive her mad. And the stitches Farley had sewn into her forehead stood stark against her creamy skin. But her eyes sparkled like emeralds, and the look of care in them set him aback. In truth, she could almost be called beautiful.

"Then you understand," she said, swatting away smoke from the fire.

He clenched his jaw. "I know what it's like to not be loved by your own father. Mine was even worse than yours.

He spent what little time we had together scolding and upbraiding me."

She laid her hand on him, so small and delicate against his thick forearm. "I'm sorry."

He looked away. "'Twas a long time ago. He's gone now." Buried in land at first, then at sea when most of Port Royal slipped into the bay.

"And your mother?"

"Gone as well."

"So we are both orphans, our parents stolen by death, pills, and power."

He smiled. "Rather philosophic for one so mad."

She saluted him with the flask then brought it to her lips, but he snagged it from her grasp. "Or one so sauced," he added. "I believe you've had enough."

At first she frowned, but then relented. "I *do* feel better," She rested her cheek in her hand and glanced at him. A strand of hair dangled across her forehead, curled at the tip from the humidity. She blew at it, sending it dancing, then smiled at him. He didn't recall her having such thick, dark lashes—a forest of silken black surrounding glistening green pools.

"You are a pretty little minx."

She gave him a slanted smile. "I'm neither a minx nor pretty and you know it. It's the rum talking. I'm plain. I have small breasts and skinny legs and dull straight brown hair. And my toes"—she stared down at her wet, muddy shoes—"well, I've been told that since the second one is longer than the big toe, I'm deformed."

He laughed. First at her unabashed reference to her small chest and then at her uneven toes. "And, pray tell, who told you such a thing?"

"One of my boyfriends."

Boyfriend. Hmm. "Withal, the insult does reek of the immaturity of a lad. Henceforth, I recommend avoiding boys and sticking to men."

"Men like you who pretend they are someone they are not?" she snapped. "And just how old are you, pirate-actor?"

"Two and twenty. And I never pretend."

"Then you are still younger than me by two years. Should I avoid you as well?"

"Some men mature faster than others." He winked.

She huffed and looked away. "I have yet to meet one."

The fire crackled and a breeze stirred the leaves and danced through her hair. Grabbing her skirts, she labored to stand, batting away his efforts to help her, spouting nonsense about something called women's lib and how she didn't need his help. As she headed toward the creek—or rather teetered—light from the moon found its way to her through the canopy, haloing her in a milky glow that made her look like an angel.

Until she looked down and screamed.

Punching to his feet, Rowan dashed to her aid, but she barreled past him and sprang on top of the log they'd been sitting on. Shrieking as if her feet were on fire, she lost her balance, and started to fall, but Rowan caught her in his arms. "What ails you woman? Why such racket?"

Clinging to him for dear life, she pointed to the ground, where a spider skittered away—a large hairy spider.

He chuckled. "He means you no harm, Lady Minx."

"He's gross and filthy and carries diseases." She squirmed against him, and he was surprised when his body reacted.

"Not unlike my pirates, yet you harbor no fear of them." Grabbing her legs, he swept her in his arms and carried her to the creek, where he helped her get a drink, then returned her promptly to a spot on the log.

When he dropped down just inches beside her, she started to move away, but finally releasing a heavy sigh, she leaned her head on his shoulder. "I'm dirty and smelly and my dress is wrinkled, and I cannot possibly sleep in the dirt with all the bugs and wild animals and ..." her mumbling tapered off and soon her breathing deepened, and he felt her body relax.

She was wrong about one thing. Her odor was not unpleasant. She didn't smell like strange flowers anymore. She smelled of sweet honey and woman, and the aroma heightened all his senses. She mumbled again, drawing his gaze to her moist lips. Were they as sweet as her scent? He licked his own, longing to find out, an urge burning within him that he rarely denied. Growling inwardly, he wrapped an arm around her shoulder, put his other behind his head, and leaned back on the log.

He'd spent many a night with many a lady. None at all like this night. This night he'd been more frustrated, confused, and annoyed then he'd ever been. But he'd also been more interested, intrigued, and entertained. And touched, if he were honest—touched somewhere near his heart.

She stirred in her sleep and nestled closer against him.

What was it about this little minx that enthralled him so? He longed to know more about her and was glad for their time here alone. He might even delay their return to camp just for the chance to become better acquainted.

What sort of thief was she? Where did she come from? How had she ended up on his ship and for what purpose? And why were her words so foreign? A dozen questions filled his mind as he drifted off to sleep.

Chapter 8

Someone was twisting Morgan's brain like a wet washrag. She reached up to touch her head, but found her hand was stuck between her cheek and something warm and hard. And hairy! She pried it free. Heart pounding, she remained still, too afraid to open her eyes to discover she'd been trapped in some gargantuan web and the spider was waiting to devour her when she woke.

But then the spider groaned in its sleep. Did spiders groan? No, but men did. She opened her eyes to find her hand on the pirate-actor's chest, her fingers splayed on the hair springing from his open collar, and her head leaning on his shoulder! Even worse, his arm was wrapped around her back—a band of strength, keeping her pressed against him.

Horrified, she pushed away. What had she done? What had *he* done? She glanced down at her filthy gown, then reached underneath her skirts and checked her bloomers—or whatever they were called. Thank God they were still intact, as was her underwear beneath them.

The pirate-actor groaned and his lips twisted as if he tasted something sour. "Come back to bed, love. 'Tis far too early," he mumbled.

Scattered memories returned of drinking rum and telling this impostor far too much about her life. What had he done to her after she'd passed out? "How dare you!" She lifted her hand to slap him, but he caught it by the wrist, his eyes still shut.

"How dare I what?" he replied gruffly.

How had he done that without seeing? Morgan tugged from him and labored to her feet. A relentless ache hammered the back of her eyes, and she rubbed them and glanced about. Remnants of a morning mist slithered away as rays of a rising sun pierced the jungle like a multi-pronged fork, transforming the creek into a river of diamonds. Above her, hundreds of birds sang a chorus that, if her brain weren't being tromped on by a soccer team in cleats, would have been pleasant.

Rowan finally sat up and gaped at her with one eye. "How now, Lady Minx?"

"How dare you feed me rum and then take advantage of me? What did you do to me, anyway?" She hugged herself and took another step back.

He chuckled and rubbed his stubbled chin before standing and stretching as if he hadn't a care in the world.

"I said, what did you do to me?" she demanded, not entirely sure she wanted to know.

He raked his hair back and grinned. "Do you feel pleasantly satisfied this morn, Lady Minx? Mayhap as if you dreamed you were floating on clouds of ecstasy?"

"Of course not! What are you talking about?"

"Then I assure you, I did not steal your purity." He winked then headed toward the creek.

Morgan's insides boiled. "You … you … vain egotistical pig!"

He answered with a chuckle as he knelt to splash water over his head and draw handfuls to his mouth.

She thought to kick him into the creek, but the water looked too refreshing, especially to her sandpaper tongue, so she stooped beside him and cupped her hands. Ah, once again, she'd never tasted water so pure and sweet. Even expensive bottled water from France was like sludge compared to this. She took her fill then sat back on a flat rock and watched Rowan stand to his full height, his shoulder-length hair wet and slicked back, his damp shirt clinging to his chest, his pants tight around his thick thighs. He scanned the surrounding maze of green as if making sure all was safe. And she felt the oddest leap of her heart at the thought of being protected by such a man.

Ridiculous romantic notions. She stood. "We should get back to camp."

He faced her, his blue eyes full of mischief. "Why the hurry?"

"Because I'm hungry. And because now that you've played the part of my knight in shining armor, I'm sure my father is waiting to take me home."

He gave her a cynical look. "The cold-hearted father who ignores you? *That* man is chasing you around the Caribbean, concerned for your welfare?"

She sighed, frustration rising along with the ache in her head.

"Very well, Lady Minx, as you wish," he finally said before strolling back to the fire and kicking dirt onto the embers. Grabbing his empty flask, he filled it with water from the creek, then retrieved his sword and knife from the ground and flung his sack over his shoulder. "Shall we?" He gestured toward the impenetrable wall of green surrounding their camp before he plunged into it, swallowed up by the greenery.

Morgan followed, happy to be on the move again, though her aching feet disagreed.

The chill of morning soon fled beneath a heat that seemed as thick as the jungle around her. She longed to shed some layers—at the very least the stockings that were pasted to her legs—but all these undergarments with their hooks and ties were impossible to discard without assistance. If she asked

Rowan for his help, would he think her immodest? Maybe after last night he already did. She cringed.

"Tell me the truth, Mr. Actor. What happened last night?"

He continued shoving his way through the foliage. "If you must know, you drank overmuch and then fell asleep in my arms." He said it as if it was an everyday occurrence.

Heat blossomed up her cheeks. "So you didn't take advantage of me?"

He slashed through a thick vine blocking their path. "You use me most ungraciously to suggest I would."

"And you claim to be a pirate," she teased.

"Aye, but a gentleman pirate, if you please."

"Well, you're a good actor, I'll give you that." She stepped over a thick root crossing the path and tripped on her skirts. "Uggg!"

He stopped. "That you grace me with any compliment pleases me." He reached up and plucked a yellow-and-red fruit from a tree above them and handed it to her. "I believe you'll find this to your liking."

"It's a real mango!" She bit into it and the sweet nectar filled her mouth and dribbled down her cheek. Embarrassed, she wiped it away.

He stared at her. "'Tis just a fruit, not a nugget of gold."

"But I've never had one fresh from a tree before."

His brow folded. "'Tis unclear to me in what other state one would find them."

She shook her head at his persistent acting. "My father must be paying you a pretty penny."

At this, he laughed and continued onward. "If your father was paying me at all, I'd require a chest full of doubloons from so wealthy a man, not a penny, no matter how shiny it may be."

Morgan struggled to follow his rapid pace while nibbling on her mango. Her stomach welcomed the succulent fruit, but all too soon it began to sour, as it often did lately—the cancer reminding her it had no intention of going away.

The loamy scent of moist earth and life filled her nostrils, and she took in a deep breath—so different from the smog of San Diego. If anything, this adventure her father had staged was giving her an experience she'd not soon forget.

Including the man in front of her. He walked with the confidence and awareness of a predator whose world was his prey. There was an arrogance about him, yes, but also a certainty, a boldness and daring she admired. Sweat matted his shirt to his back, and she could see his muscles bulging and rolling with each heft of his sword. My … my … the sight of him was almost worth battling the stifling heat and onslaught of insects. *Almost*. She batted away a horde of gnats while finding herself suddenly curious about the man. What prompted him to choose acting as a career? How did her father find him? Sadly, he had more than proven he would not answer any question that would give away the charade. So, she decided to play along, perhaps catch him in a lie.

"So, Mr. Actor, tell me how you became a pirate?"

He stopped and ran a sleeve over his brow before continuing. "'Tis a long story."

"I have nothing else to do at the moment." But sweat and suffer. And try to keep her mind off the creepy-crawlies and dirt and the chaos that had become her life the past few days.

He swung his sword and marched forward, branches and leaves crackling beneath his blade. "In truth, I needed money. A fortune. And piracy was the only option open to me."

"There are always other choices besides a life of crime."

"Humph. This from a woman who snuck aboard my ship to steal my amulet."

"I didn—" She sighed. "Why did you need money? Got fired from your job?"

"Job?" His tone was one of outrage. "You mean employment? Bah! Duttons do not perform menial work. We have servants for such tasks."

"I see." Morgan smiled and tossed the remainder of her fruit.

"In truth, I owe my sister a large sum, which I unfortunately lost at cards."

"Ah, so you gamble too, along with pillaging and plundering and pilfering."

He chuckled. "All three mean the same, Lady Minx, though pilfering involves smaller booty, which I rarely bother with." He swung his sword, his breath coming hard. "Alack, you make it sound so nefarious."

To her right, mist glittered over an intricately woven spider web. Beautiful as it was, she cowered around it. "So now stealing isn't bad?"

"I look at it more like draining my enemy's coffers."

"And who is your enemy, Mr. Actor?"

"Mainly the French, since we find ourselves at war with them more often than not. But I do throw in an occasional Spaniard just to liven things up."

Whatever her father was paying this man, it wasn't enough. "I see you prepared by studying the history of the time. What year is it supposed to be anyway?"

He stopped and faced her. "Baffling little goose, aren't you?" Retrieving the flask from his sack, he handed it to her.

"Goose, tigress, or minx, which am I?" The distant sound of waves met her ears as she grabbed the container and greedily gulped down water.

He studied her, his blue eyes intrigued. "I've yet to decide." He took the flask and tipped it to his mouth, reminding her of last night when they'd shared rum—and so much more. Had the story of his childhood been part of the ruse, an effort to woo her by gaining her sympathy?

"Is it true what you told me about your father?" she asked, wondering why she hoped it was. Why she longed to keep that tiny connection that had formed between them. He was just an actor, paid to spend time with her.

Sorrow shadowed his expression. "Aye." He started forward again.

"Tell me about your sister. Where is she now?"

The trail widened and he sheathed his sword. "Alas, I have no idea. Last I heard she had moved to Kingston."

Morgan brushed aside a fern. "Is she a pirate too?" she asked playfully, but he answered in a tone that was surprisingly serious for so carefree a man.

"Juliana is everything I am not. She is good and kind and wise, charitable, honest, and honorable."

Perhaps this man really *did* have a sister.

"She is my twin," he added.

A rather large lizard skittered across the path in front of her, and she leapt out of the way, surprised she was actually getting used to the little creatures. "Your twin? Then you must be close."

"We were once, I suppose. But I haven't seen her in over two years."

"What a shame. If I had a brother or sister, I'd want to see them all the time." As a child, Morgan had longed for an ally, someone who understood, someone to hug when her parents were shouting and throwing things and the house had been filled with misery and tension.

The breeze grew strong and the jungle less dense, and soon the dirt transformed into sand.

"Where are we going?" She tripped again, then clutched her skirts higher.

"To the shore."

"But isn't that the long way back to camp?"

He glanced at her over his shoulders and grinned. "Not enjoying my company, Lady Minx?"

A traitorous smile curved her lips. If she had to admit it, she *was* actually enjoying herself. Despite the heat and bugs.

"I don't know why you aren't in more of a hurry, that's all. What if your crew decides to mutiny and take off without you?"

He swatted aside a final branch and they emerged onto the most beautiful beach Morgan had ever seen. It was one of those beaches you see on the Travel Channel or in a vacation magazine: white, sparkling sand that looked as soft as down, waving palms, and water that was a canvas of swirling turquoise and green gently lapping the shore. A breeze lifted her hair and tossed her skirts, cooling her skin.

Dropping to the sand, Rowan began removing his boots. "'Tis a pleasant day and my crew can handle the careening while I'm gone. Why not rest, enjoy the scenery, have a little fun?" He looked up at her, the gleam in his eye matching the one on his earring. "You concern yourself overmuch with time and tasks and order."

"And you seem to not concern yourself at all with them."

He leapt to his feet and drew a deep breath. The wind frolicked among the strands of his hair. "Faith now, that is the fun of it, is it not? Not to restrict oneself with time or money or place, but to be free to live each moment, never knowing what the next will bring?"

Just the thought of living like that made Morgan's insides coil. Her headache resurrected. She'd met far too many men like this one—careless, reckless, party animals who leapt from thrill to thrill, without a care who they hurt in the process, without a thought for work and paying bills and the responsibilities that most people had to deal with. These were the type of men her mother warned her to stay away from. They made bad boyfriends and even worse husbands. Sure they were good for a few laughs, but they rarely held down a job and were lazy, untrustworthy—and dangerous.

Yet as Rowan made a dash for the water, a small part of Morgan wished she could be so carefree. If even for a day.

"Come, dip your toes in, Lady Minx!" he yelled as he stripped off his shirt and tossed it aside. Yup. She'd been right about his muscles. There they were in the bright sun, rolling across his back in a symphony of magnificence.

She could stare at him all day. But wasn't that what got her into trouble with Jason? His good looks? Why was she so attracted to shallow men?

Rowan dove head first into the foamy waves and disappeared, only to reappear a minute later several feet away. Grinning, he stood waist-deep in the turquoise water, raked back his wet hair, and gestured for her to join him.

The entire scene could have been plucked from some silly romantic movie.

Morgan wanted to remember it, implant it in her mind where she could conjure it up when she was hugging a toilet, throwing up from her chemo.

Maybe she *should* do something crazy. Just this once. With this silly dress plastered to her skin, she'd much rather dip her entire body in the water, not just her toes. In fact, she'd love nothing more than to go frolicking among the waves with this way-too-handsome man and afterward bask in the sun on this private beach that was too close to paradise. But that was just it.

There was no such thing as paradise.

Still … she bit her lip. If the annoying man insisted on staying here awhile, maybe a short swim couldn't hurt. She headed toward the waves, kicked off her shoes, sat to remove her garters, then rolled off her stockings. By the time she stood to remove her outer skirt, Rowan was wading toward her with the oddest expression on his face.

"What, pray tell, are you doing, woman?"

"Taking off this ridiculous outfit so I can swim."

His astonishment transformed into a rather sexy grin. "Should you remove your attire, Lady Minx, I fear we will be here much longer than expected."

She put hands on her hips. "And what does that mean?"

"It means, that I am but a man, *and* a pirate by your own tongue. Ergo, I doubt I could resist so tempting a morsel."

Tempting morsel? She'd never been called such a delightful term before. That and the look in his eye caused an odd sensation in her belly. "I'm not getting naked, you idiot. I'm just taking off a few of these layers."

He rubbed his jaw. "You were terrified I'd stolen your purity last night, yet today, you all but beg me to do so."

"I thought you asked me to join you?" She fumbled with the eyelets in back of her skirt but made no progress. "Here, can you get these?"

"I asked your toes to join me," he returned and reached for the back of her skirt. She could almost feel his hand hesitating over her as if deciding whether to proceed. Finally, she heard him shuffle away.

"You tempt me overmuch, Lady Minx, but alas, a gentleman does not steal favors from a woman whose senses are askew."

"What?" She spun to give him a piece of her mind when something offshore caught her eye. It was a boat. A magnificent boat even larger than the one her father had hired. A flag fluttered in the breeze off one of the masts—a white cross on a blue background with a gold crest in the middle.

Rowan followed her gaze, and without hesitation, darted to his shirt, shouting. "Get your shoes and stockings."

"Why? Who is it?"

"Now!" His tone was so urgent, she could do nothing but obey. Grabbing her things, she followed him back to the jungle where he scooped up his boots, sack, and weapons, then grabbed her hand and dove into the greenery.

"What are you doing?" Her question was immediately silenced by his hand on her mouth as he forced her to crouch behind a bush.

"'Tis the French. A navy frigate."

Yea, right. She huffed silently. What did her father have planned for her now? A run for their lives? A battle at sea?

Rowan lowered his hand. The heat from his body filled the air between them, tainting it with his scent of sweat and salt. Water dripped from his hair onto her shoulders, and she felt moisture seep into her skirts from his wet pants. His hot breath sent a tingle down her neck—a heady feeling that annoyed her with its pleasure.

After the ship sailed out of sight, he cursed and rose to his feet. "Heading east," he said as he sheathed his sword and knife and tugged on his boots. "Put on your shoes, we must get to the *Reckoning* before they do."

She did as he requested, struggling a bit with the stockings and garters, but finally stood and faced him. "Listen actor-man. I'm done. Go battle the French, shoot your cannons, drink your rum, do whatever you want, but tell my father I'm staying right here until he comes to get me." Despite enjoying this man's attention, she couldn't take this charade another minute. For one thing, it wasn't real. For another, she was starting to *want* it to be real. Which only meant she'd be devastated when it ended. And lastly, without her meds, her heart felt encased in barbed wire. She was hungry, thirsty, riddled with bug bites, and if she didn't have a bath in the next few hours, she would scream.

"I haven't time for this, woman. I must warn my crew. If the French come upon us, we will all be captured or worse, executed."

He started for her, but she dashed down the trail, batting leaves and branches and vines, thinking of nothing except ending this cruel play. Ending it because it could never be her life. It was a romantic adventure found only in movies and books and the naive dreams of young girls.

No footsteps followed her. Good. Perhaps Rowan finally got the hint. Halting, she caught her breath and leaned against a tree trunk, dabbing her face with her sleeve.

Something heavy plunked onto her shoulder. Petrified, she tried to move, but her feet wouldn't cooperate. She attempted to swat whatever it was away, but her hands had gone numb as well. The creature slid down her chest. Pulse racing, she lowered her chin and dared a peek. A snake! A snake as wide as a man's arm. It must be an Anaconda or Python or one of those man-eating snakes she'd seen on Animal Planet—the ones that could crush a person to death. It was cold and slippery and continued slithering over her as if she were part of the tree. Maybe if she stayed really still, it would think she was and go away.

Leaves fluttered and the pirate-actor burst onto the scene.

But it was the real terror in his eyes when he saw the snake that caused Morgan to panic. "Rowan … help!" she said as softly and slowly as she could, but the snake coiled around her neck and began to squeeze.

Chapter 9

So this was how Morgan would die. Not by cancer or chemo, but by having every bone in her body crushed by a gargantuan snake. Wait. Her father wouldn't want this. He wouldn't have placed her in danger. The snake must be fake—one of those mechanical things she'd seen at Disneyland. Then why did it feel so clammy and gross? And why was the pressure on her neck halting her breath like a dam does a river?

"Stay still," Rowan said as if she had a choice. Yet the confidence in his tone did much to calm her nerves. He drew his knife and raised his gaze to hers. Fear. For the second time in as many minutes, she saw fear in his blue eyes—real fear. And that frightened her most of all.

The snake continued to tighten its grip until it felt like an elephant sat on her neck. *Okay. A little too realistic, Dad.* She could no longer breathe. Panic spun her mind into chaos. She clawed at the beast.

In one fluid motion, Rowan raised the knife and tossed it at her. What was he thinking? She slammed her eyes shut.

The thud of metal into wood ricocheted through her ear. The pressure on her neck lessened. She gasped for air as the snake relinquished its hold and began thrashing against her legs. She screamed. Which meant she could breathe, thank God! Rowan grabbed her arm and yanked her from beneath the beast.

Raising a hand to her galloping heart, she looked up to see the blade expertly placed between the reptile's eyes, pinning his head to the tree. The rest of its—now that she could see the entire thing—seven-foot body flailed through the air like a deranged whip.

She ran to a nearby bush and threw up what remained of her mango.

Thankfully, Rowan gave her privacy. Once she regained her dignity and wiped her mouth, she turned to find him retrieving his knife and kicking the odious snake aside.

She wanted to thank him. She wanted to run into his arms and find safety there. But then she remembered this had all been staged. And the snake wasn't real. "You could have killed me!"

At first he appeared hurt from her accusation, but then his smile returned. "Nigh impossible, Lady Minx. I'm quite an expert at knives."

"But it *was* a possibility. You're not perfect, you know."

He seemed to ponder this revelation as he wiped the knife on his pants. Wait. Was that blood on the blade? She crept toward the now-still snake to investigate when Rowan took her arm and dragged her back down the trail. "We haven't a moment to waste."

She hadn't any strength left within her to fight, so she followed him, trying to match his heightened pace. Roots and rocks—and her skirts—tripped her. Fronds and ferns slapped her. But he only tightened his grip and all but hefted her off the ground. They didn't talk. Mainly because Morgan's mind was so numb, it couldn't form a coherent thought. Everything that had happened the past few days paraded through her vision like scenes from an adventure movie, each one mocking her sanity. It was as if she'd *really* been transported back in time. But that couldn't be.

Time travel was impossible.

Back at camp, Rowan left the woman with Edith and immediately sent two of his men with a spyglass to the top of a nearby cliff. Thankfully, the *Reckoning* sat upright in the water, the lines latching it to the trees gone.

"How is she?" he asked Nick who approached and stood beside him.

"Careened an' the hole patched, Captain," he said, glancing over his shoulder at Morgan. "An' jist what mischeef have ye been about?"

Rowan followed his gaze. "Not what you think. Unfortunately." He huffed. "But we have bigger problems. A French frigate."

Nick's face crinkled as he scanned the horizon. "Where?"

"Heading our way. Order half the men to load everything back onto the ship and the other half to collect as many palm fronds at they can." His gaze took in the jungle behind them. "Vines, leaves, anything green."

"What are ye thinking?"

"To hide if we can't run." Rowan gave him a look of alarm.

"Och, now, she's that close?"

One of the pirates Rowan had sent as a lookout came barreling toward him. Halting, the man leaned over to catch his breath.

"Report man!" Rowan snapped.

"We spotted 'er, Cap'n. A Frenchie she be. Looks t' be a thirty-two gun frigate."

"Where stands she?"

Tearing off his bandanna, the pirate wiped sweat from his neck. "Driftin' off the coast 'bout two miles to the west."

"Drifting?" Nick asked.

"Aye, she don't seem in a hurry."

Rowan drew a deep breath. "Report again if she moves."

The pirate darted off as Kerr joined them. "That doesn't give us enough time. If we stay here, she'll trap us. We must raise sail, Captain, and be off at once."

Rowan snorted. "And make ourselves bait?"

"He's right, Kerr." Nick frowned. "D'ye want her t' spot us an' give chase? They'll have the weather edge approaching from the east."

"We're pirates, not yellow-livered sissies. I'd rather fight than be trapped like a fish in a net."

Rowan shifted his boots in the sand and gazed at the sun high in the sky. "As would I. But a fair fight. Not one where we are outmatched and outgunned." He rubbed the stubble on his jaw. "Nay, we'll let them pass, and if the fates are with us, they'll go on their merry way without ever knowing we were here."

Kerr gripped the pommel of his sword, one eye twitching. "You've grown soft, Captain, or perhaps 'tis the woman who makes you so."

Insides churning, Rowan glared at the man. "Faith, you make too free with your opinions, Kerr. Mayhap when we are done here, I will show you just how soft I am."

Fisting hands at his side, Kerr shifted his gaze away. Though Rowan knew the pirate longed for his own command, he also knew he didn't wish to die before he acquired it.

"Load up these supplies and get everyone on board," Rowan ordered before turning to Nick. "Get to those leaves and vines. Lots of them. Make haste, we don't know how long we have."

Both men took off, spouting orders.

Rowan kicked ashes into the fire and scattered the logs, his gaze landing on Edith and Morgan sitting on a crate. Wind flapped his shirt, showering him with the lady's scent from where she'd laid her head during the night. He smiled. 'Twas the first night he'd ever spent with a woman fully clothed. Odd, but where he should feel naught but frustration, he felt only satisfaction. The lady had given him a peek at her heart last night, and he'd found in her a kindred spirit. 'Twould seem they were both wounded orphans, lost and alone. Yet there was so much more to this little minx, so much she kept hidden. She baffled him—so full of spitfire and pluck, it brought a smile to his lips even now. Lud, she'd been about to disrobe at the beach! One minute she behaved the chaste maiden, the next the wanton wench.

Mayhap her presence *had* affected his decision to hide from the French Frigate. He rarely ran from a good fight. But he also rarely harbored such precious cargo.

He stopped one of his topmen and ordered him to take the women back to the ship. Then he went in search of Cudney. He had a very important task for the master gunner. One upon which—if things didn't go as planned—would mean the difference between life and death for them all.

Her kingdom for a pair of jeans. Morgan would love to see any of these men try to climb a rope ladder in three petticoats and a ballooning skirt. *And* with the wind blowing all of the above into her face. Which is probably why they were not only gawking at her from below in the boat but laughing at her as well.

"Come now, child, you pay them no mind." Edith helped her over the railing and led her toward a hatch. "Lemme git you a clean gown. Mabbe I can start the stove an' heat water for a bath."

"That sounds heavenly, Edith." Morgan had never perspired so much in her life. With the aid of the sea breeze on the beach, her sweat-soaked underthings had finally dried, but as she and Edith wove around men darting across the deck, the material now rubbed against her legs like sandpaper. What was everyone so freaked out about? And why did the men form an assembly line hoisting all sorts of leaves and branches from the boats below up into the masts?

The sound of hammering brought her gaze up to other men nailing the shrubbery to those same masts and also to the yards that crossed them.

"What's going on?" she asked Edith.

Shielding her eyes from the sun, the woman glanced above. "Jist one of the Captain's ploys, I 'spect. Hiding us from the French."

Incredible, the lengths these actors went to in order to make all this seem real. "What happens if they spot us?"

"Don't you worry, none, child. I sure the captain's got a plan for that too."

To her left, several men erected a pulley system over the yards above, while others flung ropes around two cannons. It would all be very interesting. If it wasn't staged. "I suppose my father has an exciting sea battle planned."

Edith's eyes widened. "Lord have mercy, I pray not. Nothing exciting 'bout gitting blown to bits."

Morgan let out a long sigh as Edith led her below. Yet one thought gave her hope. Maybe this battle would be the grand finale, and her father was on that French ship waiting to take her home, or—knowing him—whisk her away to France or Switzerland where he'd procured the best cancer specialists money could buy.

Against all logic and reason, the thought brought an unexpected sorrow. She shook her head, hoping to knock some sense into her flighty mind. Had she gone as crazy as these pirates claimed she was? She couldn't live in a fantasy forever. If her anxiety didn't kill her, without treatment, the cancer certainly would.

Edith erected a curtain across her cabin in case Farley came in unannounced. Though she couldn't manage warm water, she did fetch several basins of fresh water, which Morgan used to wash the salt and grime from her body and hair. She could honestly say that she'd never enjoyed a bath more, nor felt more refreshed afterward. And though she begged Edith for her jeans and t-shirt, the woman brought her fresh petticoats and a clean gown instead, spouting some nonsense about her man-clothes being gone for good.

The gown was a printed blue calico with gold embroidered flowers threaded throughout, bordered by a lacy ruffle at the hem and cuffs and finished off by a maroon bodice laced about her waist. She surprised herself at how pretty she felt, only confirmed by Edith who, upon standing back to examine her work, declared Morgan to be beautiful.

Rarely had anyone called Morgan beautiful. Well, except her mother and the occasional guy trying to flatter his way into her bed. She twirled around as she'd seen women do in movies and delighted in the way the fabric swooshed and bounced.

"Wish we could do something 'bout that hair of yours." Edith shook her head as Morgan tied her damp hair behind her. "But I got no proper pins."

Footsteps pounded above, along with shouts and commands, some of which were Rowan's. His deep tenor—as soothing as hot cocoa and as powerful as a cannon blast—was unmistakable. Yet now there was an urgent edge to it, and she wondered why they put on a show when she wasn't around to watch. She was about to ask Edith when the woman left, muttering to herself, and returned within moments with a plateful of fruit, salted beef, and a pot of cold tea.

Edith bowed her head and offered a blessing for the food that, even for its brevity, sounded more genuine than any Morgan had ever heard. And she'd heard her share of blessings. When they both sat to enjoy their meal, a strange silence gripped the boat. Not a voice or footstep could be heard, just the gentle lap of waves against the side and the whistle of wind from above …

and a tiny meow.

Morgan set down her cup and glanced in the direction of the sound. "Did you hear that?"

"Sounds like a mouse to me." Edith bit into a banana.

"Mrow, mrow," the squeal repeated, and Morgan followed it to the corner of the small room where an old chest stood, its lid broken and clothes spilling over the edge. Kneeling, she gently peeled aside pieces of clothing, being all the more careful as the squealing grew louder. Finally she lifted what looked to be one of Farley's shirts and there beneath it, was a black kitten shivering from fright. Morgan's heart sank as she lifted the tiny creature into her arms, feeling its bones through its skin. "You poor little dear."

"Ahh, that's what Smoky was doing in there!" Edith smiled. "I kep' tossing her out, not knowing she gots little ones."

Morgan nestled the precious kitten against her cheek, and soon purring filled her ears. "Poor thing is starving. Wonder where her mother ran off to."

Edith shook her head, frowning. "Come to think on it, I haven't seen her lately. Musta gotten herself killed somehows. An' me wit'out milk on board. Wait." Her eyes sparkled. "Coconut milk might work. I'll go git some." Edith popped a slice of fruit in her mouth and ran out the door, leaving it open, as Morgan sat down and cuddled the agitated kitten.

"Now, now, it will be all right, little one." She stroked its fur, trying to stop its nervous shivering, understanding all too well what if felt like to be terrified and alone and at the mercy of others. But the kitten refused to settle, and finally letting out a loud squeal, it leapt off her lap and darted out the door.

"Drat!" Morgan tore after him, fearing the poor thing would be trampled by all the actors. "Kitty, kitty, come back!" She tried to make her voice soft and calm, but the little thing took one glance at her before leaping onto the ladder that led to the deck above.

Clutching her skirts, she burst onto the main deck and spotted the kitten pouncing on a pile of ropes as if they were a bundle of mice. It wasn't until she'd snuck up on him and grabbed him from behind that she noticed the absence of a single sound—not a whisper, word, footstep, or creak. Nothing but wind and waves.

She turned. Dozens of eyes met hers. Why was everyone just standing around?

The kitty leapt from her arms and skittered away. One of the men raised his boot to step on it.

Morgan screamed, "Don't you dare!"

The man held his foot in midair, glaring at her—first with anger, then horror—before slowly lowering his boot.

The kitten thankfully dropped down one of the hatches, and Morgan started after him when a low growl sounded from the deck above where the tiller was housed. She glanced up to see rage knotting Rowan's face and turning his eyes into slits. What was *his* problem?

"They's coming about, Cap'n!" a voice filtered down from the masts above.

The men groaned. Rowan stormed across the deck, shouting, "Raise all sail! Weigh anchor!"

Silence fled for cover as chaos took residence.

A dozen men leapt into the ropes, scrambling above so fast it seemed they were flying. Palm fronds, ferns, and vines fell to the deck as if a hurricane struck, while other men gathered and tossed them overboard. Ten men circled a wheel-thingy, shoved thick rods into its side, and began spinning it round and round, grunting and heaving as they went. The rattle of a large chain sounded.

Wind whipping through canvas brought her gaze up to sails dropping like clouds falling from heaven. Kerr continued shouting orders to the men above while Nick commanded those below—both of them using words and phrases that might as well be Greek to her: "Loose the main! Man the tack and sheet! Haul taut! Sheet home! Hoist away royals and jib!"

Men bumped into her from all sides, pushing her this way and that, until finally, she made her way to the railing. Thank God, because the ship jerked forward, and she would have fallen if she hadn't had anything to cling to.

She found Rowan leaning over the front of the boat, shouting back directions to Nick at the tiller. Morgan dared a glance over the side. Sharp, craggy reefs rose from the deep, threatening to pierce the hull. Where would an actor learn how to navigate an ancient ship through such narrow shoals? She hadn't time to consider it when the boat burst from the bay into the open sea, rising over a wave before crashing down again. Foamy spray showered over her. Gripping the railing, she sought balance on the heaving deck and drew in a deep breath, relishing in the refreshing mist. How exhilarating! Heck, she might even take up sailing when she returned home.

If not for the queasiness in her stomach.

And the fact that she'd be dead in six months.

To her left, the boat she'd seen offshore was making a turn toward them. The French, of course. So, her father *had* arranged a battle at sea. Great. Just great. She pressed a hand to her stomach, praying she didn't lose what little she'd just eaten and embarrass herself even more. She also prayed that this insane adventure would soon come to an end. She needed treatment. Needed her meds. Needed to stop pretending that she actually had an exciting life, that she was on a real adventure, and that this handsome pirate found her interesting … perhaps even enticing.

She needed to get back to reality.

Stuffing the telescope into his belt, Rowan marched back to stand beside Nick, relaying a series of orders as he went, which Nick then shouted to the crew. Above her, sailors lined the yards, adjusting sails, their bare feet clinging to nothing but thin ropes that offered little protection from falling to their deaths. Her head grew light at the thought.

Soon, the boat slowed and turned to hug the coast of the island, and she wondered why they weren't high-tailing it out of there if the French were faster and better gunned … or whatever Rowan had said.

As if reading her thoughts, the handsome pirate Kerr approached Rowan, several grumbling men in tow. "Captain, shouldn't we raise all canvas to the wind and get as far away from them as we can? I thought you didn't want a fight."

Rowan's piercing gaze assessed him. "Do you not trust me, Kerr? Have I ever let you down? Any of you?" He scanned the throng.

"Ye know the Captain ha' all authority in battle, gentlemen," Nick said. "Ye signed the articles, did ye no'?"

Some grumbled, others nodded, while the rest fixed their gaze on the French boat that had completed its turn and, with raised sails, headed toward them at full speed. A mustache of foam arched on its bow as it sped just yards off the island. Morgan didn't have to be a sailor to know that at this rate they'd catch up to them in minutes. Which probably meant her father was on board. And all this would soon come to an end.

The impending battle disbanded the grumbling men. Even Kerr ran off to his duties, but not before Morgan saw him scowl at his captain.

"Cudney!" Rowan's bark blared across the ship, bringing two men to his side. "Load the stern chasers. Fire on my order."

One of the men made gestures to the other before they both dashed off.

Fire the cannons? How exciting! She wondered if Rowan would let her shoot one. She started toward him to ask when his eyes met hers. The warrior-like intensity and determination in them halted her in mid-step.

Tearing his gaze from her, he marched across the boat like a man who knew who he was, knew exactly what he was doing, and answered to no one.

A flash of bright yellow burst from the French ship.

A thunderous boom echoed across the sky.

"All hands down!" Rowan yelled.

Chapter 10

Morgan froze. Most of the men, except Rowan and his officers, had crouched to the deck. Had they actually been fired upon? Her answer came quickly when the sea exploded in a mighty splash just yards from the boat.

"Yer goin' t' get us all killed!" one of the actors yelled. The fright in his voice almost sounded real.

Ignoring him, Rowan studied the oncoming French ship then turned and nodded toward Nick, who sped off to the stern and leapt onto a rope ladder.

A chill coiled around Morgan. Would a fake cannonball have made such a huge splash? Or maybe it was real and they'd simply missed on purpose? She felt the familiar pinch of her heart and tried to remind herself that none of this was real and she was perfectly safe.

"Fire as you bear, Mr. Cudney!" Rowan shouted across the deck to men hovering over two small cannons mounted on swivels at the back of the boat.

Heart thumping in excitement, Morgan clung to the railing and crept closer as the men swung the cannons toward the advancing French.

The explosions trembled the ship like a California earthquake. Smoke slapped Morgan in the face, stinging her eyes and blinding her. She swatted it away, coughing, trying to see if the balls actually struck the boat or if they were only pretend as she suspected.

Yup. The clearing smoke revealed no damage to the oncoming French. None of this was real. Rowan's crew, however, growled and spit like a pack of rabid dogs, their anger making her almost believe otherwise. A mob approached the captain to complain, fingering the hilts of their swords.

"Their next shot will sink us fer sure, Cap'n!" one man yelled.

Shouts of ascent and cursing followed. "We're nothin' but a soused goose waitin' t' be plucked," another man yelled.

Was there to be a mutiny too? A battle *and* a mutiny. Her father had thought of everything. What a grand finale!

Rowan appeared unmoved by their threats. Instead he stood, arms crossed over his chest, hair waving in the breeze, staring at the mast where Nick had raised a purple flag and was heading back down.

Two powerful blasts shook the afternoon sky. Startled, Morgan scanned the scene, seeking their source. Rowan hadn't fired them, and they hadn't come from the French boat or there'd be smoke curling from her cannons.

The sound of a tree splitting pummeled the air—the creak and crack of death as it toppled to the ground, followed by piercing screams and frantic shouts. But there was no tree. It was a mast aboard the French ship—the top half anyway. It teetered back and forth for a few seconds, then in one final snap, crashed to the deck, dragging its sails and ropes down into a web of confusion. The boat nearly tipped over beneath the weight.

"Huzzah! Huzzah!" Cheers rose from the actors. Some leapt into rope ladders and thrust their swords toward their enemy as if they had been the ones who'd defeated them.

Still, she no idea where the cannon shots had come from. Not until she spotted smoke drifting above the trees of the island. So, that's what Rowan had been doing with the cannons and the pulleys. Very clever. He had used the

Reckoning as bait to lure the French close to the island within reach of the cannons he hid in the jungle.

He seemed quite pleased with himself, too, as he grinned and faced his crew, braying orders to raise all canvas to the wind. His men were only too happy to comply. Releasing the railing, Morgan hoisted her skirts and started toward him, but Farley blocked her way.

"Come now, Miss. The cap'n orders ye below t' his cabin."

"Oh, he does, does he? You may tell him I don't want to go below. I wish to see my father."

"Beggin' yer pardon, Miss, but he says ye would say that, an' that I'm t' shoot ye if ye don't comply."

Morgan ground her teeth together and glanced up at Rowan standing at the helm, but he refused to meet her gaze.

"Oh, never mind, Farley, I'll go." Besides, she was exhausted and her stomach hurt and she was sure Rowan was taking her to her father now anyway.

"I'll ask the cap'n if Edith can bring ye some food, Miss," Farley said as he headed out the door of Rowan's cabin. "An' I'll check on those stitches soon." He gestured toward her head.

The kitty raced through the door just before he shut it and circled Morgan's feet.

"There you are, you little troublemaker." She scooped him in her arms and took up a pace across Rowan's messy cabin—resisting the urge to straighten it—for what seemed like an hour. During that time the boat sped, slowed, and even stopped for a while. Night dropped a curtain on the windows as if it were the intermission of a play. And she began to wonder if it *was* only the intermission of what her father had planned for her. After all, she'd spent a week at the Western Town, and from what she could tell, she'd only been here three days.

The thought only increased her annoyance. Which increased her OCD and anxiety. Which forced her to set down the kitty and start cleaning and organizing papers and trinkets on Rowan's desk once again. She set the documents in a neat stack, rolled up the charts, lined up the quill pens beside them, set the two lanterns at the right and left corners in an artistic display, and lined up the weird nautical instruments in two rows. All in the light of the moon sifting through the windows. Then she corked the open bottles of rum and set them on a shelf.

The kitty leapt onto the stack of papers and started cleaning himself.

Grabbing him, she stood back and surveyed her progress. Much better. Now, to arrange the chairs in front of the desk.

Without warning, the door crashed open and Rowan marched in, a gust of salty air in his wake and a lantern in his hand. He ran one hand through his windswept hair and hooked the lantern on the ceiling as his gaze latched upon her—blue icy eyes that sent an unexpected shiver through her. His presence filled the room, and she couldn't help the tiny leap of her heart.

"Forsooth, here stands the little minx who nearly got us killed."

Morgan refused to allow this actor the reward of his grand performance. She settled into a chair, the kitten in her lap, and pretended nonchalance. "Killed? How could one little woman do that?"

He huffed. "By alerting our enemy to our hiding place. And for what?"—His gaze dropped to the kitten—"that hairy beast!?"

She lifted up the precious cat and stared into his slit-like eyes. Blue like Rowan's. "You mean Blackbeard?"

Rowan only stared at her.

"Blackbeard. You know, the famous pirate? Smoking hair, tortures his crew … that guy?" She sighed. "Must be after your time."

Rowan rubbed his eyes, his lips drawn into a stiff line. "I will not have you risking my life and the life of my crew, Lady Minx." Turning, he slammed the door shut.

Morgan jumped, every nerve tensing. "There's no need to shout. Even if all this is real, you set a trap for the French anyway."

"Aye, contingent on too many factors to be assured of its success. The main one of which was whether the French would come about close enough to the land for a strike."

"Well, your plan worked, pirate-actor, so what's the big deal?"

"The big deal?" He scrubbed his temples with his thumbs. "You twist my mind into knots with your words!" He dropped his hands. "I would not have lost two perfectly good cannons!"

She stroked beneath the kitten's chin. "Can't you go pick them up?"

He waved his arm toward the window. "Aye, and get blasted from the water by the French frigate still anchored there?"

"I thought you were a pirate. Why aren't you plundering them, anyway?"

He closed his eyes as if he had a headache. "Because they are a navy frigate filled with marines and weapons and nothing of value a pirate would want."

He withdrew his sword, the grinding sound etching down her spine. For a moment she thought he intended to stab her, but he approached his desk and set it down. "What's this?" His tone raged. "Alack, what curse has come upon my things?"

"The curse is called tidiness and organization, and you'll find they will make your life much easier," Morgan replied with smugness. "Why don't you ever make your bed and pick up your clothes? Didn't your mother teach you anything?"

He roared so loud, Morgan felt his hot breath on her face. In one swoop of his muscular arm, he brushed everything on his desk to the floor. "Where is my rum?"

Despite the fact Morgan knew it was an act, she leapt in her seat. So did Blackbeard, who scrambled from her lap and disappeared under the bed.

"Now, look what you've done." She got up then dropped to her hands and knees and peered beneath the bed. "You really should watch that temper of yours. I know a good anger management counselor back in San Diego I could recommend. Here, kitty, kitty."

Before she could retrieve the cat, she was lifted from the floor as if she weighed no more than the kitten. Strong arms forced her back against the wall and set her down on her feet, while a face twisting with rage filled her vision.

"Why are you not frightened of me? Men cower before my anger yet you do naught but mock me."

His eyes shifted between hers, sparking in anger. His hot breath, smelling of smoke and salt, saturated the air. And her heart felt as though a Taser had zapped it. Settling her breath, she replied simply, "Because you aren't real."

"Truly, you must be mad." Pushing from the wall, he retreated as if she had a disease. The look in his eyes wounded her more than it should.

Blackbeard crept out from beneath the bed and began pouncing on Rowan's things on the floor, swatting the feathers of the quill pen and leaping on the papers.

Minutes passed while Rowan searched for something. Finally he grabbed the bottle of rum from his shelf, uncorked it, and took a swig. "Where did this infernal cat come from?" He pointed the bottle at Blackbeard.

His stern tone sent the kitty leaping into her arms. "Takes a big man to frighten a little kitten. You must be so proud." She stroked Blackbeard's fur, trying to settle him.

Growling, Rowan stepped over the mess on the floor as if it didn't exist, opened a drawer of his desk, pulled out a scroll and spread it on top.

"You will make up for your error today by decoding this map."

"If you want someone to do something for you, you should be kinder to them. Not manhandle them and yell and scream like a madman."

He stared at her, strands of hair hanging in his face, making him look more wild then he already did. She feared he'd throw another temper tantrum when a knock on the door brought a reprieve.

His shout of "Enter" brought in Nick and Kerr. Both men's gazes shifted from her to Rowan to the mess on the floor.

"As I told you before," she said, feeling more courageous now that she wasn't alone with him. "I won't decode your precious map until you bring me to my father."

Kerr took a step forward, his glance taking in the chart sprawled across Rowan's desk. "Captain, we picked up Carter and Tate."

Circling his desk, Rowan stood before the map, blocking its view from Kerr.

"Very good. Plot a course for New Providence immediately."

Kerr nodded and started away.

"And give the men an extra ration of rum," Rowan yelled after him.

Kerr winked at Morgan before he left.

Nick straightened his vest and glanced at the mess on the floor. "Did a storm come through I didna know aboot?"

"Aye, the minx storm." Rowan leaned back against his desk and nodded toward Morgan.

Blackbeard skittered across the room, chasing a dust ball, and Nick leaned over and scooped him up. "Now where did this wee beastie hail from?"

"'Tis the wench's demon cat."

Nick chuckled and handed the kitten to Morgan.

"Lady Minx," Rowan began, obviously restraining his anger. "I am the captain aboard this ship and you are but a thief. By the laws of the sea, I could hang you from the yardarm, yet I have been naught but kind. Ergo, you will decipher this map or suffer the consequences."

She lifted her nose in the air. "I have given you my conditions, Captain."

Nick's brows rose along with the tension in the room. And for a moment, Morgan thought Rowan would follow through with his hanging by the yardarm threat—or at least pretend to. But instead, he heaved a huge sigh and turned to Nick.

"Lock her in the sailing master's cabin. We'll see if that will loosen her tongue."

Rowan hadn't been kidding about locking her up. Nick escorted her to a room smaller than her walk-in closet at home, containing a cot, a mite-infested blanket, a small table and chair, and a lantern which she had no idea how to light. After giving her a look of sympathy, he shut the door. The clank of the lock slammed across her heart with its finality. Since then, no amount of pounding or screaming had set her free. How dare Rowan do this to the daughter of the man who was paying him!

At least she had Blackbeard for comfort and a small porthole to help gauge the passage of time. The first day Edith came twice to bring her food and empty her chamber pot.

Which was totally gross—the chamber pot, not the food, though that wasn't much better. Still, using it—and being in the same room with it—made her incredibly thankful for indoor plumbing, and she vowed never to complain about scrubbing her toilet again.

She also vowed never to complain about heat again. San Diego on its hottest day had nothing on this wooden coffin of a sauna. Sweat plastered her hair to her head and her clothes to her skin, and the air was so heavy she struggled to fill her lungs. But no matter what, she would not give in to Rowan's request to decode his stupid map. The joke would be on him when her father ruined his acting career for torturing her.

Morgan tried to tell Edith as much, and though the woman was always kind and sympathetic, she refused Morgan's pleas for freedom.

"No, child. I can't be disobeying the captain. If I do, he might put Farley an' me ashore somewheres. An' I sure the authorities are still looking for us."

Morgan broke off a piece of the fish Edith had brought and gave it to Blackbeard, then poured water into a saucer and set it on the floor. "What would be so bad about that? Surely living on a boat gets old after a while."

Edith shook her head and laughed. "Why, child. I'm a Negro an' Farley's as white as coconut milk. We never be allowed t' stay married. An' I probably be sold off as a slave agin or taken back to my owner."

Morgan hadn't thought of that. Sorrow swept through her at the thought of how people of color had been treated in the past.

"Still, you know as well as I do, that wouldn't happen now." Morgan grabbed Edith's chubby hand and gave it a squeeze. "Please let me out. My father will hear of this, believe me, and I don't think he'll be too pleased." Or maybe he would. He had always told her what a spoiled brat she was. Perhaps this was his way of disciplining her. But even *he* wouldn't be so cruel.

Would he?

Edith patted her hand. "Child, you make no sense t' me sometimes. Now, you must eat. You's shriveling t' nothing but bones."

"I'm not hungry." Morgan sat back with a sigh, though she wasn't sure whether it was the cancer or seasickness that stole her appetite.

Edith lifted a pot and poured hot liquid into a cup. "Here's the tea I gave you before. The one I said might help wit' your cancer. Drink it. I knows you'll feel better."

Morgan smiled, thankful for the woman's kindness and concern, and for not treating Morgan like she had the plague as some people did when they found out she had cancer.

Thanking Edith, she sipped the tea. A little bitter for her tastes, but the warmth spun a trail of comfort down her throat.

The older woman studied her with a smile. "God will heal you, child. I knows it."

Morgan couldn't help but huff. If she had a dollar for every time someone at church had said that same thing, she'd die a rich woman.

"You don't believe me?" Edith asked, still smiling.

"I don't think God cares anymore."

"Ah, now don't you worry 'bout that, child." Edith rose and leaned over to pet Blackbeard, curled in a ball in Morgan's lap. "He can heal you anyways. Now, is there anything else I can git you?"

"You don't happen to have canvas and paints, do you?" Morgan said teasingly. If she was going to be stuck in here for much longer, it would be nice to have something to do. And in lieu of meds, painting always helped calm her nerves.

Surprisingly, Edith didn't laugh at her request. Instead, she grew excited. "You paint, child? How wonderful. Lemme see what I can do." And off she went.

The next day, it was both Farley and Edith who paid her a visit. Edith set a tray of food on the table and then emptied Morgan's chamber pot while Farley removed her stitches and doused the wound once more with rum.

"Healin' nicely, if I do say so meself," he declared, sitting back to examine his work.

Edith kissed him on the cheek. "The best surgeon I ever seen."

If it was possible for the aged man to produce a blush beneath his leathery skin, Morgan was sure she spotted one. He swept a comb of hair over the bald spot on top of his head and folded hands over his chubby belly. "Reminds me o' the time we stitched up that little girl down by the docks at Bridgetown. Poor thin' fell off a boat an' hit her head on the reefs. 'Member that, Darlin'? Turns out she was the daughter of the dread pirate—"

"Now, now Farley, I sure Miss Morgan don't want t' hear your stories," Edith interrupted. "Oh, almost forgot, child." She set a canvas sack on the table. "It ain't paints, but it might help you pass the time."

After they left, Morgan peeked inside the satchel and found two sheets of old, crinkled parchment and a stick of charcoal. It felt like Christmas.

On the third day, the lock jangled, and Nick came in with orders to escort her above for fresh air.

"How kind of the captain." Morgan was being facetious as she ascended onto the main deck and the bright sun slammed her eyes shut.

"Aye, 'tis true, lass. Though ye'll not believe it, Rowan doesna tolerate disobedience on board his ship." Nick led her to the railing.

She gripped the hard wood and blinked as her eyes grew accustomed to the light. "I suppose I should be glad he didn't make me walk the plank." She chuckled.

"I wouldna joke aboot sich a thing, lass. I've seen him do jist that."

She glanced over the deck, seeking the object of their discussion, but he was nowhere in sight. Instead, she found several of the men staring at her, a few even leering. Some attended their tasks, while others loitered about drinking from a bottle they passed among them. A small group circled a barrel, playing cards.

Turning back around, Morgan drew in a deep breath, hoping to force the stale air out of her lungs. Before her, the sea spread to the horizon like turquoise frosting on a cake, decorated with golden sprinkles. She licked her lips. What a beautiful sight. Wind wove cool fingers through her hair and fluttered the folds of her skirt, drying her perspiration. The boat rose and plunged over a wave, and she balanced her feet on the deck and smiled when a cool mist sprayed her.

"Well," she said. "Do thank the captain for not tossing me to the sharks, and for allowing me a moment above. I've never really liked the ocean, but this is stunning."

"Aye, that it is. God's creation always amazes me."

"God? I assumed pirates didn't believe in God, Nick. May I call you Nick? Or is that not proper in … what year are we pretending to be in again?"

"The year of our Lord sixteen hundred and ninety-four, lass. And aye, ye may call me Nick." He leaned his elbows on the railing. "Most pirates believe in God." He squinted toward her and smiled, sunlight turning his hair to burnished bronze. "They jist don't follow Him."

Sounded like some of the people in her church. "And you?"

"Weel, my father was a man of the cloth, as they say, so aye, my faith is strong."

"Just because your father believed?"

"Nay, God ha' revealed himself t' me in many ways, lass."

"Hmm." Sails flapping above brought her gaze up to see men inching across the yards again, clinging to ropes. Kerr shouted an order from the helm, and his eyes met hers briefly. He winked at her as he was prone to do, making her wonder at his motives.

She faced the sea again. "How did you get into acting?"

"How's that, lass?"

"Okay." She sighed. "I'll play along. How did you become a pirate?"

The deck wobbled, but Nick barely moved to keep his balance. "Och, now, that is quite a tale." His hazel eyes sparkled. "I was a lieutenant in the Royal Navy once."

"That's the British navy, right?"

"Aye." He scratched his red beard, giving her a queer look as if everyone should know such a thing.

"Give me a break, I took math in college, not history." Yet his odd look remained. Shaking her head, she stared out to sea. "So why aren't you still in this Royal Navy?"

"I disobeyed a direct order. Something ye canna do in the Royal Navy an' survive. They cashiered me an' sent me t' prison."

She had no idea what this cashiered was, but prison she got. "You? You don't seem the type. You are so obedient to Rowan—even to the point of locking up innocent women." She grinned, and Nick chuckled.

"Rowan's a good man. Captain Hawkins, now there was a monster."

"What order did you disobey?"

"To whip a young midshipmen for a wee infraction. The lad ha' already been punished enough. It would ha' probably killed him."

"They sent you to prison for saving a boy?"

"Aye, but I ended up in Port Royal as an indentured servant." At her look of puzzlement, he continued, "A slave t' serve out my term." He gave her a mischievous grin. "But I got oot, ran away, and met up wi' Rowan recruiting for his crew. 'Twas no' but God's grace. 'Cause jist a few weeks later, an earthquake sank Port Royal into the sea."

"Wow. It must have taken awhile to come up with all these great back stories." And just for her benefit. Perhaps her father really did care for her.

Nick stared at her, confused yet again.

"Never mind." She waved him off, wanting so badly to trap him in some lie that would surely force him to give up this charade. "So, Nick, how do you, a God-fearing man as you say, justify raping and pillaging?" Ah ha, she had him now.

"What a beguiling lass ye be. I can see why he likes ye."

"Who likes me?"

"The captain, of course." He said it as if it were common knowledge. The boat pitched over a wave, and Morgan closed her eyes as cool mist sprayed her again. Good thing, because a hot flush consumed her face.

"But t' yer question," Nick continued. "I stay where the good Lord plants me. An' for some reason, he's planted me here wi' Rowan. It may comfort ye to know, lass, that Rowan ha' papers from Governor Beeston granting him authority t' prey on the French. So, 'tis really no' pirating he does unless he attacks the Spanish. And then I beg off from duty."

Morgan rolled her eyes. "You actually believe God has put you on a pirate ship?"

"Aye." He smiled. "He's full of surprises, no?"

No. She had not witnessed that. To her, God seemed rather staunch and demanding. "But don't you have any goals of your own? Don't you want to go home? Live a normal life?"

He frowned and stared down at the foamy water zipping against the hull. "Aye, more than anything. I suppose I'm free t' go back now tha' the navy thinks me buried along wi' my owner at Port Royal."

"To Scotland?"

"Aye. Aberdeen." He tugged on the red plaid tartan around his neck. "These are my clan colors, an' this"—he fingered the broach pinned to his vest—"'tis a green sapphire handed down from my Viking ancestors."

Sunlight turned the gem into liquid emerald, and she couldn't deny the setting looked quite antique.

"There's a bonny lass waiting for me back home. A' least I hope she's waiting. I intend to marry her an' raise a bevy of bairns."

Even though none of this was likely true, Morgan couldn't help but smile. "So, why don't you?"

"I'll go when God releases me from Rowan. I'm needed here for now. Och, but Rowan may ha' been the reason I was sent here in the first place, no?"

"So you think God had you arrested and enslaved so you could help Rowan?" She snapped hair from her face. "And you're not mad at Him for that?"

"Was no' the good Lord's fault I disobeyed an order. He jist turned it out for good. An' He may ha' something else for me to do before He sends me home."

"How can you live like this? Not knowing where you're going to be next year, next month, or even tomorrow? Not knowing what you'll be doing, who you'll be with, or whether you'll be a slave or a pirate?" She shook her head, just the thought of so frivolous a lifestyle causing her insides to knot. "Trusting a God you can't see or hear?"

"Seems a better way t' live, lass, than trusting yerself, eh? We canna control wha' happens in life. 'Tis best to trust the One who can."

Shouting and cursing turned her head around to see the men who'd been playing cards leap to their feet and shove the barrel over, sending cards flying. One man punched the other across the jaw. He reeled backward into the arms of his fellow crewmen, who tossed him forward again. A fist fight ensued. Both men jabbed and slugged each other while a mob formed around them, shouting both encouragements and insults.

She imagined it was like watching stunt men practicing for a bar-fight scene. Though from the crunch of fist on bone and thud of punches to the gut, it sounded all too real. Finally, Kerr dove into the fray and yanked the men apart, threatening something called keelhauling for the next man who threw a punch.

A gust of wind whipped hair into Morgan's face, and she tossed it aside and turned to the sea once again.

Nick studied her. "Ye're a strange lass, t' be sure. Where other women would be scairt t' death being amongst pirates, ye act like ye've been on a pirate ship yer whole life."

She shook her head, weary of the pretense. "Oooh"—she pasted on a fearful expression—"I suppose I should worry about being raped."

His lips slanted. "Nay. 'Tis in yer favor the men fear their captain more than they wish t' satisfy themselves."

"Lucky me," she replied glibly.

"Ye'd feel even luckier if ye'd do what he asks."

She shot her gaze to his. "So, that's what all this is about. He sent you to convince me."

"No' in so many words, but, aye, I'd recommend it."

"I might have decoded his stupid map it if he had asked nicely. But to be honest with you, Nick, I've been bullied about by so many men in my life, I'm not taking it anymore. If he wants my help, he should first apologize for his rude behavior and then ask politely."

Nick chuckled. "I'm thinking 'twill snow in the Caribbean before tha' happens."

Yes, she'd noticed Rowan's pride as well.

"So, tell me, lass, how did ye end up on this ship?"

She wondered if it would be worth trying to explain yet again. "As I already told you and your captain, I was touring a replica of this boat at the Tall Ship Festival in San Diego. My friend put something in my drink, and I guess I passed out. When I woke, I found that stupid amulet stuck in a lantern down in the hold—as you call it. I hit my head and the next thing I knew I was here. That's the God's honest truth." Balancing on the leaping deck, she met his gaze head on.

He studied her with a look she was very familiar with— the look of a psychiatrist to a patient. A deep assessing look, an inquisitive look, yet ... a caring look. At the end, he glanced over the sea, consternation rolling across his jaw.

She snorted. "So, here's the part where you call me crazy."

"Nay. I fear I canna do tha', lass."

"Why not?"

"Because, I dinna think ye're lying."

Chapter 11

Rowan slid the candle atop the table in Morgan's cabin and lowered into the chair, careful to be quiet. Golden light from the sputtering flame joined silvery moonlight drifting in through the porthole—both shifting over her face with each gentle sway of the ship.

Her deep breathing assured him she had slept through the sound of him unlocking the latch and the creak of the door as it opened and shut. Though the small kitten snuggling against her breast had peeked up at him when he entered, it must have considered him no threat to its mistress, for the little beast quickly went back to sleep.

He smiled at how foolish he felt sneaking into a lady's chamber merely to watch her sleep. The kitten was wrong. There *was* a threat present—one to his heart. For he'd not stopped thinking of Lady Minx for the three days she'd been locked away. He'd oscillated from feeling like a cad for treating her thus, to outrage at her continued insolence toward him in the presence of his crew. What was it about this pert little shrew that had him so captivated?

Was it her courage, her strange speech, her innocence, wit, keen mind? Or mayhap 'twas the wounds she hid deep within her heart—so much like his own.

In the past, he'd always been lured by beauty, full figures, and full purses—unattainable, attached women wherein he could enjoy all the pleasures of their intimate company with none of the responsibility.

Alack, he could hardly remember most of their names! Save for the few whose husbands had called him out to swords. Even those faded into an oblivion of boredom.

But this woman. This skinny cheeky-mouthed slip of a girl had him mesmerized.

He'd instructed Nick to spend time with the minx today in order to discover her true identity—where she hailed from and to what end had she boarded his ship. 'Twas the reason Rowan had stayed below, out of sight so as not to distract her. If anyone could discern the woman's true purpose, it was Nicholas Doran. The man could see past any facade, uncover any lie, and even cause a person to speak of things they wouldn't dare tell anyone else. Nay, 'twas clear Nick had inherited his reverend father's penchant for confession, for with but one look from Nick, every sin Rowan had ever committed dribbled from his lips like foam over a mug of ale.

The ship rolled over a wave, wood creaking and water dashing against its hull. Morgan stirred slightly, letting out a tiny groan before she settled down again.

Rowan rubbed his eyes, exhausted from the day's work, but unable to find rest due to his pestering thoughts—stirred into a cauldron of confusion and angst due to Nick's report. He didn't believe the lady was lying. He believed her confusion was real and that all evidence pointed to the possibility that she hailed from a different place ... a place unknown to them.

And mayhap even a different time.

'Twas the last declaration that blasted a hole through Rowan's sanity.

Yet ... somewhere deep inside, it made sense of her strange speech, her constant insistence that none of this was real. Her fearlessness in the midst of pirates who'd just as soon pleasure themselves with her and toss her overboard than cater to her feminine whims.

Rowan had seen many strange things in his two years at sea. A glimpse of the giant octopus they called the Kraken, fish that flew through the air, a turtle as big as a ship, and even what he'd been sure was a mermaid. He'd also seen his home town of Port Royal sink to the bottom of the sea. Why, then, would traveling through time be so unbelievable?

Still, 'twas too far-fetched for any rational man to believe. Parchment on the table caught his eye, and he grabbed a piece and brought it to the light. 'Twas a drawing of a ship. *His* ship, the *Reckoning*. He stared at it, blinking to clear his vision, shocked at the exquisite detail of each line, sail, railing, and deck, right down to the binnacle and capstan and even the belaying pins. Had the minx drawn this?

He leaned forward, elbows on his knees, and studied the odd lady. Her lips twitched and her breathing grew heavy as if she were dreaming. Dark lashes caressed her cheeks like stormy waves upon the shore, while strands of brown hair lay across her bosom—ribbons of auburn over cream. How he longed to touch her. Not in an improper way, but just to … be near.

What an alarming thought! If word got out, his rakish reputation would be thrown to the wind. Alack, a most daunting tragedy for all the ladies who had yet to enjoy his lovemaking.

He shifted in his seat, an unintentional groan spilling from his lips. The pesky cat mistook it as an invitation, for it squeezed from its mistress' arms and leapt onto Rowan's lap. The movement woke the fair lady. Her eyes suddenly popped open, and she leapt backward in her bed, slamming against the bulkhead.

"'Tis just me, Lady Minx." Rowan tossed the drawing back onto the table, while inadvertently stroking the cat with his other hand.

Several seconds passed as wind whistled against the window and candlelight swayed over the edge of her cot.

"Have you come to steal my cat or my virginity?" she finally asked in a curt tone.

He laughed. "Neither, though the latter has some appeal." He realized he was petting the infernal cat and set it on the floor.

"You may take your appeal, along with yourself, elsewhere."

"It would serve you well to remember upon whose ship you sail."

"It would serve you well to remember who is paying your salary."

"Ah, the illusive father, of course." He chuckled.

The kitten leapt onto the cot and disappeared into the shadows with its mistress.

"What is it you want, Rowan?" she asked. "You lock me in this stifling room for three days for no reason. And now, I've missed my onco—doctor's appointment. I hope you're happy with yourself."

"I find myself nearly always so, Lady Minx."

She huffed. "So I've noticed."

Despite her insult, he found himself wishing he could see the sarcastic quirk of her lips.

Leaning back in the chair, he crossed arms over his chest. "In truth, I have come to make amends for my recent treatment, though you rightly deserved it and more."

She laughed, then uttered one word emphatically. "Fail."

Rowan searched his mind for any possible meaning. "I beg your pardon?"

"When an apology is followed by an insult, it loses its meaning."

He rubbed his temples, seeking to stay the frustration churning there. "Do you wish to be free or not, Lady Minx?"

"Stop calling me that, and of course I do. But that will happen soon enough. Apologize properly or get out."

The ship bucked and Rowan grabbed the candle holder before it slid to the deck. It gave him time to collect his temper, lest he say something he would regret. Still, anger seethed from his tone when he said, "For what offense? Saving you from ravishment, from being crushed to death by snake, or from a French prison?"

"For being rude and trying to bully me into interpreting your silly map."

He growled. "A spoiled little chit, aren't you?"

"You could use some lessons on how to apologize."

"A million pardons, Lady Minx, if I have offended you." That was as good an apology as she was going to get. He'd come here merely to watch her sleep, to ponder what Nick had told him, but the woman had a knack for pricking his ire.

She finally moved to the edge of the cot and swung her feet over the side. Candlelight flickered over features tainted with both fear and fatigue. She looked so thin, so frightfully thin, that his anger fled him.

"Edith informs me you haven't been eating."

"I told you I'm sick."

"Hmm. Very well, I shall gladly take you home if you would but tell me where home is."

She huffed. "San Diego, as you well know."

Rowan had searched his maps and found only one reference to a San Diego Bay, but that could hardly be the place to which she referred. "This San Diego borders the Mal del Sur?"

"The what?"

"The South Sea."

She merely stared at him.

"Nevertheless," he continued, "'tis Spanish territory and you are clearly no papist."

She seemed to sink into the mattress. "I am so tired of all this pretense, Rowan. Can we please stop?"

"I am *trying* to stop this madness," he ground out. "If you would but cooperate."

"There's that temper again." Her voice taunted him.

He jumped to his feet, took the single step toward the porthole, and glanced out, trying to cool said temper.

"Where are we going?" she finally asked.

"New Providence, Charles Town."

"Good. At least a place I recognize. That's an island in the Bahamas, right?

Rowan had never heard of this *Bahamas*.

At his silence, she continued, "I assume my father is waiting there with a plane."

A plane? He spun to face her, his mind jumbling with her words.

"Ah, yes, you wouldn't know what a plane is, would you?" She smirked. "It flies people to different places."

Rowan pondered her statement as he sought her eyes—what he could see of them in the candlelight—for any deception. He found none. Only annoyance and sorrow before she lowered her gaze to the cat perched in her lap and stroked its fur.

"You sketched my ship," he said, hoping to douse the tension rising between them.

Her gaze snapped to the parchment on the table. "I was bored. It helps me relax."

"'Tis quite good."

He finally got a smile out of her. "Thanks. It's sort of a hobby of mine. Actually, oil paints, not charcoal. I wish I was good enough to make a living at it."

Rowan glanced at the drawing. "Odd fancy for a thief," he joked. "But I do believe people would pay highly for such beautiful work."

She smiled again and lowered her lashes. The folds of her pretty blue skirt spread about her legs like waves at sea, and he suddenly wanted more than anything to kiss her—to kiss away her sorrow, her frustration, to kiss away her crazy notions. And his frustration.

He approached and held out his hand. "Truce, Lady Minx?"

At first she stared at him, her eyes questioning. But she finally put her hand in his and allowed him to lift her to her feet. The cat sprang onto the bed.

The deck tilted and he grabbed her waist to steady her. "If I could conjure up your father and a flying machine for you, I would." He brushed his knuckles over her cheek.

Her stunned expression transformed into one of wonder as the air seem to charge between them.

Placing a finger beneath her chin, he lifted her head and placed his lips on hers.

Ah, sweet and madness and thrill! Lips as soft as clouds, her taste of spices—sweet and tangy, her response one of passion as she pressed against him, moaning.

He deepened the kiss, and she pushed from him. He expected a slap, but she merely stood there, chest pumping, her eyes filled with horror, and something else … mayhap a spark of desire?

He smiled. "I shall leave you to your rest." Then dipping his head, he left before he proceeded to do what every cell in his body screamed to do.

Shutting the door, Rowan leaned back against it and listened to make sure he hadn't frightened her overmuch. Or worse, that she wept in disgust at his touch. But no sound emanated from within.

Whether or not the lady was insane or she actually did travel through time, he would not—no could not—set her free in Charles Town. Not in that nest of pirates.

Morgan didn't sleep a wink after Rowan left. She tried pacing, drawing, snuggling with Blackbeard beneath the covers. But nothing stopped the warm excitement buzzing through her at his gentle touch … his kiss.

Why had he done it? When all they ever seemed to do was argue. Even worse, why had she allowed him when the fool couldn't even apologize properly? She was so done with arrogant, vain, alpha males!

Shouts filtered from above, and footsteps pounded the deck as the ship made a sharp turn. Morgan laid a hand on the wall to keep from falling and then moved to the window for a peek. Rays from a mid-morning sun spread a net of jewels over the sea while in the distance, land rose out of the deep. New Providence, the Bahamas. Civilization at last! Soon she'd be home getting the treatment she needed.

And this romantic adventure would come to an end.

She forced down sorrow at the thought. Fairy tales were not for plain, nerdy women with cancer.

Except—she touched her lips—that kiss was like none she'd ever experienced.

Blackbeard circled her feet, and she stooped to pick him up, her anger once again rising at the way her body had responded to Rowan. Yet … something in the way he'd kissed her … tender passion, a whispered promise … almost like he actually cared. But that couldn't be. It wasn't even real. Her father had probably included a kiss in the man's salary.

And she was a complete fool to think otherwise.

During the next few minutes, the boat pitched and tilted, sails flapped and thundered, and commands continually echoed from above. But finally the roar of water against the hull lessened to a soft swish, and details of a city began to form outside Morgan's window.

Weird. Where were the hotels and resorts one would expect to find along the port's shoreline to service the hundreds of tourists on incoming cruise ships? All she could make out before the boat made a sharp turn were clusters of small wooden and brick buildings, sandy streets, and horses and wagons.

Horses and wagons?

She blinked and rubbed her eyes, then flattened her face against the glass again, trying to gain a better view, but the boat must be facing the shore, and all she saw was another dock extending to her right where a smaller boat and a larger one were tied. Both appeared to be ancient sailing ships. Probably here to take tourists out for rides just like they did at the San Diego Tall Ship Festival.

Which would make sense of the quick view she'd had of the city. Maybe they were hosting one of the Renaissance fairs they had back home where everyone dressed up in costumes and pretended to live back in the day. Ridiculous waste of time and money if you asked her.

Cuddling Blackbeard to her chest, she sat on her cot and waited for either her father or Rowan to walk through the door. She'd already made her bed, placed her drawings in a neat pile, set the chair in the right position beside the table, and used a piece from her torn pantaloons to sweep dust into a corner. It was the most she could do to keep order in what had been her world for three days—anything to help keep her anxiety down, though it hadn't helped all that much.

Even now she felt it rising to squeeze her breath at the thought she had nothing to look forward to but surgery and chemo.

More shouts ricocheted from above, and finally the heavy sound of boots thudded outside her door. The latch clanked and Rowan entered, two of his men behind him. He'd changed his normally messy clothes into a cream-colored embroidered shirt with wide sleeves and ruffles that fluttered from the cuffs of his leather coat. Brass buttons lined the lapel and also the belt buckled around his waist, while another one crisscrossed his chest and provided a sheave for the sword hanging at his hip. Brown pants were stuffed in knee-high boots that were also buckled in brass. His hair was combed—for once—and lay neatly at his shoulders, his goatee trimmed, and the earring shone from his right ear.

And the desire—or was it affection—sparking from his blue eyes sent her heart careening in her chest. But then a harsh shield dropped over his expression as he said, "You are to remain on board."

"What?" She jumped to her feet, the motion making her dizzy. "I will not! Where is my father?"

"'Tis for your own protection. Charles Town is no place for a lady."

"Oh, *now* I'm a lady. I thought I was a wench and a thief."

"A thief, I'll grant you, but the wench is yet to be determined." He dropped his gaze to her lips and grinned.

Drat! Was she blushing? She turned away and placed Blackbeard on the cot, then faced Rowan once again. "Whatever I am, I insist on seeing my father at once!"

"When are you to learn that I allow no one to insist anything on board my ship?"

"Then let me get off and I'll gladly stop."

"Alas, in another lifetime, Lady Minx, but not today." With that, he tipped his hat and strode from the room, one of his lackeys locking the door after him.

The Awakening

Chapter 12

R owan slammed the rest of his brandy to the back of his throat and gestured to the barmaid for another.

"Best go easy on the spirits, Captain, or ye wilna make sense of wha' the mapmaker says." Nick sat beside him, looking none too pleased at loitering about in such a nefarious den.

"If the peevish old cur ever makes an appearance." Rowan leaned back in his chair and surveyed the gloomy punch house—so like all the others he'd visited over the years. Men taking to their cups, trollops selling their fleshly wares, barmaids tolerating salacious invitations and wandering hands for an extra coin tossed their way. Foamy ale sloshed over mugs on trays while smaller pewter cups held rum or brandy. Smoke from cigars and pipes joined the smell of unwashed bodies, whale oil, and tallow in a haze that hovered over the boisterous mob like the fog over London.

"He'll come," Nick said, always the optimist, sipping his drink which was naught but water tainted with whiskey.

Following an afternoon of scouring the villainous port, Rowan and Nick had finally found a man who knew the aged mapmaker and swore—by the powers that be—that the man frequented the *Stuffed Goat* most nights, where he sat alone in a corner and drank himself into a stupor before wandering off in the wee hours of the morning to who knew where. No one knew, apparently, for the gray-bearded man appeared and disappeared at will. No one even knew his real name, only that he made the best maps in the West Indies.

Cursing bit the air as an altercation ensued in the far corner—a common occurrence as liquor flowed with the night. Nick cast uneasy eyes that way.

"Have a real drink, Nick," Rowan urged. "It'll make all these luxurious surroundings bearable." He chuckled.

"An' end up a slobbering fool like ye? No thanks."

Elbow on the table, Abbot leaned toward them. "Better a slobberin' fool thans a tea-tottlin' nimbycock." His slurred words preceded drool spilling from his lips.

"Och, aye, I believe I've made my point." Nick smiled at Rowan.

Rowan examined the four of his crew who had accompanied them: Abbot, his bosun, who had now dropped his forehead onto the table; Cudney, his deaf master gunner, who stared blankly into the air; Scratch whose long mustache dangled in his ale like a fishing line, and Jorg singing an off-key ballad. And he was forced to agree with Nick's assessment. Did he appear as doltish as they did when he drank? Nay. He waved off the ludicrous thought as the barmaid brought another round of drinks. Setting his mug on the table, she gave him a suggestive wink, which he would normally find, at the very least, flattering, at the most, inviting. But tonight he had no taste for women. Or at least not for any woman but one.

The thought alarmed him, and he was glad for the drink in hand to drown the sensation. He felt for the sack flung about his neck, ensuring it was close and its contents safe. No one must know he had such a valuable map in his possession or mayhem would unleash in this place. He would have preferred to have left it on board the *Reckoning,* but the eccentricity of the mapmaker did not assure him the man would be willing to return to Rowan's ship.

"Ye surprise me, Captain." Nick fingered the rim of his drink and winked at Rowan. "Ye bought the lass a gift." His gaze dropped to the sack.

"Paints and brushes. 'Twill keep her busy and out of trouble until I can figure out what's to be done with her."

"Weel, still … 'twas uncharacteristically kind o' ye." He smiled that knowing smile that always annoyed Rowan to distraction. "She's good for ye, is she, no?"

"Nay. She drives me mad." Rowan sipped his brandy, wincing at the bitter, cheap taste. Regardless, it was doing the job of numbing his senses—helping him forget the look of desperation on Morgan's face when he'd left her locked in her cabin.

The chink of coin and slap of cards lured his gaze to games commencing around him. He licked his lips. How he'd love to join them, double the doubloons in his pouch, and show these pirates how Faro was meant to be played. But now was not the time. Still, if the mapmaker delayed much longer, Rowan doubted he could resist the temptation all night.

A clamor arose in the corner—cursing, shouts, and the chime of blades being drawn. A mob formed as tables and chairs crashed to the floor and two men crossed swords.

Nick sipped his drink and shifted his shoulders as if trying to shrug off some wicked spirit. But it all bored Rowan to death. He used to seek out fights, enjoyed displaying his skill with sword and fist, but it was such brutish business—so beneath his class—and he grew weary of the resulting aches and pains.

Kerr appeared out of the horde like a ghoul from Hades. He shoved Abbot out of his chair and slid next to Rowan, excitement flickering in his eyes. Unless his news was about Morgan or the mapmaker, Rowan didn't have a care.

"I've been talking to William Bloodmoon," Kerr said.

Bloodmoon. Agitation sparked through Rowan, tightening his nerves. He had no idea the callow scamp was in town. Which made it all the more imperative that Rowan conduct his business and leave forthwith.

"He says there's a Spanish fleet sailing from Nombre de Dios in two weeks, loaded with silver ingots and gold."

Nick laughed. "Bloodmoon? And jist how does tha' bedeviled mongrel know sich a thing?"

Ignoring him, Kerr grabbed Abbot's abandoned drink and took a swig. "He wants us to join him, Captain. Says he needs another ship." He leaned in closer and lowered his voice. "Says the treasure will be more'n we've ever seen. Fifteen tons of silver and one hundred thousand pounds of gold coins. We'll be rich beyond our dreams!" He slammed his fist on the table. Abbot moaned from the floor. "What say you?"

Rowan rubbed his chin, hating to slash the man's enthusiasm to pieces, knowing it would set him off. "I wouldn't sail with Bloodmoon if he were God himself come down for vengeance. He's a vicious, untrustworthy cur, and he'll sooner gut you and toss your carcass to the depths than give you a share of the booty."

Kerr's frown was only heightened by the brewing anger in his eyes.

"The Cap'n's right." Jorg halted his lewd ditty to add. "He 'as ice in 'is veins, that one. Why once 'e tied a man t' the bowsprit fer days an' stuck lit matches in 'is eyes, just fer darin' t' question an order."

Though Kerr tried to hide it, Rowan spotted a shudder coursing down his back.

"Is that the type of man you want to ally with?" Rowan asked. "Is that the type of man you trust to divvy up the plunder fairly?"

Kerr's jaw stiffened. "If he fills my pockets, I don't care if he's the devil himself." He finished Abbot's drink and leaned back in the chair, feet spread apart, and arms banded across his chest. Defiant, arrogant, and greedy.

For the second time in as many weeks, Rowan saw so much of himself in this volatile pirate, it sickened him. Five years hence, when he was Kerr's age, Rowan hoped to be a wealthy respected member of society, not a thieving freebooter. Yet, of late, he wondered if the path he trod led in but one direction alone.

Across the tavern, the fight ended with cheers and groans—one victorious, and one most likely greeting the devil.

Rowan cleared his throat. "I'm working on a plan to stuff your pockets full, Kerr. And we'll do it without the help of a bellicose snok like Bloodmoon."

"What plan? Your unreadable map?" Kerr snarled.

Rowan flinched. He'd done his best to keep the map a secret for reasons of his own. "Let me see to it."

Kerr let out an exasperated snort and shook his head. "You allowed our last prize to escape. The men are starting to complain."

So Rowan had heard. He well knew these men would not blink before they stabbed him in the back and made fish bait out of him. "I've kept you swimming in gold, Kerr, along with the crew. Have I not?"

Kerr's eyes narrowed before he glanced away.

"Trust me. After tonight I'll know exactly where to find more treasure than two Spanish fleets can carry." Then Rowan would retire from this cutthroat business. *And* these cutthroat men.

"Besides," Nick interjected. "We havena papers t' attack the Spanish."

"Blast your papers!" Kerr stood, shoving the chair to the ground and drawing the gaze of more than one man. "And to the devil with your morals. In case you haven't noticed." He swept his hand over the mob. "We're amongst pirates. Which means we are pirates as well. And we should live as pirates, beholden to no man or country."

"Aye, aye!" Abbot, waking up from his rum-induced nap, shouted as he struggled to rise.

Light from the lantern sparked fury in Kerr's eyes. His hand slid precariously close to the hilt of his cutlass.

Beneath the table, Rowan's did the same. The last thing he wanted was to draw swords with his first mate, but he'd have no choice if the man persisted.

The impending altercation seemed to awaken the rest of his men from their stupor as their gazes shifted between Kerr and their captain.

Rowan sighed. "If you're to challenge my authority, Kerr, do it now before I run you through out of sheer boredom."

Morgan knelt by her cot to pray. It was the only thing she could think to do. For the first hour after Rowan had locked her up again, she'd pounded on the walls, demanding to be released. All her outburst achieved were bruised hands, curses from the guard outside, and an hysterical Edith charging in to make sure she hadn't completely lost her mind. Still, no amount of begging and pleading or even tears convinced the lady to release her—so fearful was she of Rowan's retribution. Give Morgan a break. Enough of this insane pirate pageant!

The next two hours she spent trying to decide who she hated more, her father or Rowan. Both men were so full of themselves they should be floating through the air like Goodyear blimps. Both wielded their power like the line of a fly fisherman, not caring who they hooked on the other end. Both men thought they knew what was best for everybody, while they hadn't a clue what was best for themselves.

She finally decided she hated them both equally and sat down to calm her nerves by petting Blackbeard, who had scampered to the corner during her rant. Her chest was tight with anxiety, she was dizzy and tired, and her side hurt where the cancer still ravished her body. And it was so hot! No, not just hot, it was stifling in this cabin. The stupid window wouldn't even open.

That's when she decided to pray. She was filled with nothing but hate and complaints, and if her mother were here, she'd certainly scold her for such sinful behavior. She'd no sooner bowed her head when the stomp of footsteps sounded outside her door, followed by loud voices, a scuffle, a thud, and a scraping noise.

Grabbing Blackbeard, she waited in hopeful anticipation of the end of her trip into pirate la-la land. But it was the pirate, Kerr, who entered, smelling of rum and grinning at her as if she were the gold vault at Fort Knox.

"What do you want?" she asked as he cocked his head and studied her. The man was good-looking, she'd give him that, with his short black hair and dark stubbled chin, his fit physique, covered in sexy pirate attire. But there was something unnerving about him—in his eyes—and Morgan was very good at being unnerved.

His smile failed its climb to those eyes as he spoke. "I've come to fetch you to your father."

At last! Words she'd longed to hear for so long! Yet … coming from this man, they lost their impact. "My father?"

He shifted his stance and gripped the pommel of his sword. "Aye, he's in town and asking for you."

Morgan could only stare at him as a battle brewed within her. She wanted so much to end this mad charade, but she'd grown to mistrust most men, and this one made her feel particularly suspicious.

"Where is Rowan?"

"With your father. Now come along." He turned and gestured for her to follow. "Do you not want your freedom?"

Blackbeard leapt from her arms, hissed at Kerr, and darted beneath the cot.

"Oh, drat! Come here, Blackbeard." She knelt, but Kerr took her hand and tugged her along.

"Leave the cat. Farley's wife will see to it."

But she didn't want to leave Blackbeard, her only true friend on this crazy adventure. When she resisted, Kerr added with a sigh of annoyance, "You'll see the cat again. If you bring him, he'll get lost in town."

She knew he was right, but she still hated herself when she followed Kerr out the door, up the ladder, and onto the deck.

Darkness coated everything in black paint, and she was forced to take his hand as he assisted her from the railing to the wobbly dock. A breeze spun around her, cooling her skin. She drew in a deep breath, happy to be free from the stifling cabin at last. The scent of salt and fish and the spice of rain filled her nose as the lap of waves and distant music and laughter filled her ears.

Kerr grabbed her hand again. "Make all haste, your father awaits."

Tugging from his grip, she followed him. Old barrels and crates and a bucket of fish lined the wharf as the sound of Kerr's boots echoed down the rickety wood. Boats were docked alongside other wharves, while several were anchored offshore. All were old-looking boats like Rowan's. Odd.

"If this pretense is over, why are you still speaking like you came from the seventeenth century?"

He turned to stare at her quizzically, but Morgan no longer cared about the handsome actor, or his speech, or about much of anything when her eyes took in the sight beyond him.

Lanterns flickered from posts, illuminating a street paved in sand and passersby dressed in … well, dressed much like the pirates on board Rowan's boat—embroidered vests that fell to their knees, lace dancing about the cuffs of their shirts, bounteous scarves tied around their necks, three-cornered hats on their heads, and weapons strapped to hips and chests. The few women who strolled about wore long skirts and colorful bodices, much like Morgan's, though theirs were much tighter and pushed up their breasts until there was nothing left to the imagination.

Horses and wagons and a few carriages cluttered the street, beyond which stood a row of buildings, most one to three stories high, some dark and quiet, while music and laughter spilled from others. At the end of the dock, a stone wall rose on either side with two small cannons poking through holes.

Amazing! What had her father done? It was like a scene out of an historic movie, down to the smallest details of lanterns and dress and horses and cannons … even the music sounded archaic. Perhaps it was a movie set for an upcoming film, and her father had rented it for the night. But why the charade if he was ending it and bringing her home? One last adventure maybe?

Kerr entered the set as if nothing were amiss, gesturing her to follow. Gun shots cracked the air. Heart pounding, Morgan nearly leapt out of her shoes. A scream brought her gaze to a man chasing a poor lady across the street. A horse reared up, nearly running the woman down, while the rider let out a string of expletives, most of which Morgan had never heard before.

Two men, arms flung over one another and mugs in their hands, staggered down the street singing—if one could call it that. One rather large man leaned against the brick wall, his hat tipped low over his face, smoking a cigar. She felt, rather than saw, his eyes bore into her, and she hurried along, suddenly feeling unsafe.

Lightning lit the sky. One flash then another, like a light bulb on a camera igniting the scene for a millisecond then dousing it in darkness again. She hugged herself when a pig the size of a German shepherd darted across her path, squealing. *A pig!*

Still staring at the crazed animal, she stepped in something warm and squishy. A stench pricked her nose and caused her stomach to vault. Kerr's laughter brought her gaze up to him as he retraced his steps to stand beside her.

"Not used to walking about town, Miss?"

"Not used to horse poop being on the street." She pried her shoe from the pile.

Another shot fired. Two men barreled down the stairs of one of the buildings, shoving and pushing each other as a mob formed around them.

Kerr grabbed her arm and dragged her along. "Come, 'tis not safe here."

Morgan sighed and allowed him to pull her forward. Besides, this would all be over in a minute. As soon as she saw her father and gave him a piece of her mind, he'd put a stop to this ridiculousness. A tinge of unavoidable sorrow pierced her heart at the thought. Despite the discomfort and frustration, it *had* been a mildly fun adventure. She would miss Rowan most of all, and she wondered what sort of man he really was behind the pirate character he played. Probably not her type, anyway.

Turning a corner, Kerr strode down another street away from the main drag. Following him, she tripped on her skirts, groaned, and clutched the blasted things higher. Now, she would see what the set looked like behind the scenes.

But there was only more of the same—sand covered the road, lanterns lit the way, and crude buildings made of brick and wood lined both sides. Signs hung above doorways, squeaking in the rising wind: *Ye old Swagfish Tavern, Miller's Punch House, Miss Fable's Pleasure Palace*—which, from the looks of the women hanging out the windows, was a whorehouse. They passed a dark building that looked like a shoemaker, and another with a sign depicting a candle and the word Chandler.

Men and a few women roamed the streets, laughing and singing as if it were Mardi Gras. Thunder rumbled, sending a flock of chickens squawking in front of her. Morgan could only stare in awe. She must really be dying because, obviously, her father had spared no expense.

Soon, the lights grew brighter and the music and shouts louder as they entered a section of town humming with activity. And not the reputable kind either. With half-dressed women and nefarious-looking men loitering about, it reminded Morgan of the red light district in San Diego—at least what it would have looked like a hundred years ago.

A man stumbled down the stairs of a bar onto the street and peered at her through glassy eyes. "Hey, sweetheart, hows 'bout sharin' a drink wit' ole Briggs?"

"Tempting"—she gave a wry smile—"but I'd rather boil in oil."

The man's look of shock transformed into fury, and he drew a knife and started for her. "Why, ye ill-bred fishwife!"

Drawing his pistol, Kerr leapt in front of her. "Never mind her. This one's mad." He spun a finger around the side of his head to indicate her state of mind.

The man pondered this for a moment as he teetered in place, his gaze shifting from Kerr to the weapon in his hand. Finally he withdrew his knife. "I'd put a muzzle on 'er if I was ye."

"Splendid idea." Kerr replied as he took her arm once again. When they were out of earshot, he leaned toward her. "You'd do well to keep your shrewish mouth shut."

"You'd do well to remember your place."

"The captain's right. You are a madcap," he grumbled, weaving around horse droppings and more chickens and pigs than she'd seen on a farm.

What was this place? Hiring a boat filled with pirates was one thing, but hiring an entire town? And all these actors! How had her father afforded it?

Unless … panic took root in her gut and began to spin faster and faster. Drawing a deep breath, she attempted to slow it back down. No. Ridiculous. There was no other explanation, and soon everything would make sense.

But things only grew more hazy. Particularly when Kerr hauled her up the stairs of what appeared to be a bar, shoving aside drunken slobs and giggling women, and dragged her to the back corner.

"You're hurting me!" She yanked from his grasp and rubbed her arm, all the while taking in the band of grimy, leering pirates surrounding the table before her. "Where is my father!"

Her answer came in the form of Kerr shoving her into a chair, stuffing a sweaty handkerchief into her mouth, and binding her hands and feet.

That's when the real panic set in.

Chapter 13

"So what did yer yellow-livered captain say?" William Bloodmoon snarled as he sat in the King George Tavern, muscled toadies guarding his flanks, a buxom wench on his lap, and a mug of rum in his hand. His gaze took in Miss Morgan, groaning and struggling, tied to the chair in the corner.

Kerr accepted a drink from the barmaid and frowned. "He refused, of course, being the fatwitted priss he is." He took a gulp of ale and wiped his mouth. "He and his Scottish priest make quite the pair."

Bloodmoon smiled and his men laughed, while the trollop nuzzled the pirate leader's neck—thick and leathery from the sun, a perfect match for the skin on his face. Stubbles of gray sprouted on his shaved head and lined his jaw and chin, surrounding a surly mouth and dark, wicked eyes. The black leather jerkin, breeches and boots—buckled and strapped with more weapons than Kerr thought a man could carry— confirmed the rumors of his violent, cruel nature, and Kerr suddenly regretted returning to deal with the man.

"An' who be this? A gift?" He gestured toward Miss Morgan.

Eyes like flaming moss shifted between him and Bloodmoon as the woman attempted to shout something through the handkerchief stuffed in her mouth.

"Nay. I'm delivering her to someone."

"Rowan tired of her, eh? Or maybe he can't …" Bloodmoon's face scrunched in disgust. "He's not a fluff shirt, is he?"

Kerr smiled. "Nay, but he had some colorful terms for you."

"I bet he did." Bloodmoon gulped down the remainder of his rum then slammed the mug on the table. "I met the man once in Port-de-Paix and it weren't a pleasant experience, I tell ye. He won a chest full of pieces of eight in a game of Faro. Cheated, if ye ask me, an' when I called him on it, he drew a pistol on me." He spit to the side in disgust, then ran a callused finger over the swell of creamy bosoms protruding from the woman's bodice. She giggled and gave him a saucy wink.

Someone took up a fiddle across the tavern, drowning out Morgan's groans.

"Why d'ye still sail wit' him, Kerr?" he asked. "A man wit' yer skill and wit should be in command of his own ship."

Kerr sipped his rum, his chest expanding beneath the compliment. Indeed, he *should* be captain by now. And a good one he'd make, too. Capturing more prizes and acquiring more treasure than Rowan, or even Bloodmoon. Someday . . .

"Unless ye are nothin' but a weak-kneed whiffet like yer cap'n." Bloodmoon snorted.

Grinding his teeth, Kerr forced down his fury. "Let's just say I'm waiting for my opportunity. Thus far, the fair amount of prizes he's won the crew have kept most of them loyal."

"Ah! But if they knew what fortune awaited them, they'd jump at the chance t' follow a man like you."

Kerr's rum-addled mind searched for the reason behind Bloodmoon's flattery. He was sure the man did not oft extend such compliments. Still, Kerr could not deny that the pirate's words settled on a bed of truth in his heart. Settled in and got comfortable. At seven and twenty, he *should* have his own ship—his own fleet of ships—by now.

"Why not steal his ship, this *Reckoning,* and sail wit' me?" Bloodmoon lifted his mug toward Kerr then glanced over his crew, most of whom remained in the shadows. "Mayhap the day o' reckoning has come fer yer nimby-hearted captain."

Chuckles emanated from his men while the trollop giggled and cooed in Bloodmoon's ear.

Exactly what Kerr had hoped Bloodmoon would say. And exactly why he'd brought the woman. Still, he shifted his shoulders beneath a twinge of guilt. Despite Rowan's annoying personality, he'd always been good to Kerr—appointing him first mate after only six months at sea and trusting him with much of the ship's command. Hadn't he just promised Kerr they were on the verge of finding a fortune? What to do? He stared down at the amber liquid swirling in his mug as if the answer were to be found therein, then over to Miss Morgan, hatred firing from her gaze. Smiling, he took a gulp and lifted his gaze to Bloodmoon's malicious waiting eyes.

"Truth be told, he's got some grand plan to gain more treasure then we've ever seen. More than your Spanish ships, he says." Kerr knew he played a dangerous game, but he needed Bloodmoon's help if he was going to steal the *Reckoning* from Rowan.

Moments passed in which all he heard was a fiddle, a ribald ballad, shouts and laughter, and the slosh of ale and cards.

Bloodmoon sipped his drink. "I believe ye'll be tellin' me all ye know 'bout this treasure, lad."

"'Twill be my pleasure. But first, what will you give me in return?"

A snake-like smile twisted Bloodmoon's lips. "How 'bout yer life?"

His men chuckled.

Kerr swallowed and forced a look of nonchalance. "How about my life in addition to your crew's help to subdue Rowan."

Bloodmoon seemed to ponder this, though Kerr knew he had to give him something first before the man grew weary and put a bullet in Kerr's head. Rising, he untied Morgan, yanked the gag from her mouth, and shoved her to Bloodmoon's table. "She knows where the treasure is."

Miss Morgan slapped him away. "What are you talking about?" She faced Bloodmoon. "Listen, I'm finished with this insane act. I demand to see my father at once."

Bloodmoon stared at her as if she asked him to hand over all his treasure. "Ye dare demand anythin' of me, wench?" The woman in his lap cast a smug look toward Morgan.

Kerr leaned toward her. "Tell Bloodmoon what you saw in Rowan's cabin. The chart?"

"You mean that stupid map?"

Bloodmoon jerked in his seat. "A map?" But it was his tone that sent a shiver through Kerr. "What sort o' map?"

"A ridiculous map with a primitive code even a monkey could decode," the madcap woman responded.

At this, Bloodmoon jumped to his feet, dropping the trollop to the floor.

"What'ya do that for?" She struggled to rise, but at one look from him, scampered away, mumbling obscenities.

Bloodmoon's men gripped the handles of the pistols lining their baldrics, ready for their captain's command.

Yet the pirate captain seemed to be having trouble breathing. "A map wit' strange distorted islands on it an' words an' numbers that make no sense?"

What made no sense was how Bloodmoon knew of this map. "Aye, but how do you know of it?" Kerr asked, though he suddenly didn't want to know the answer.

It came in a bellowing roar. "How do I know o' it?" Bloodmoon thrust his reddening face toward Kerr. "'Tis my map, you churlish whoreson! Yer captain stole it from me!" His eyes suddenly widened then narrowed into thin lines as he took up a pace, growling and spitting like some otherworldly dragon. Kerr half-expected fire to come from his mouth.

Nearby patrons scattered, and others stopped to watch, no doubt hoping for a fight.

Amazingly, Miss Morgan plopped into a chair in a huff.

Bloodmoon halted, his eyes crazed in the lantern light. "The only way he coulda gotten that map was from me house. From me wife!" Plucking his pistol from its brace, he waved it about, scattering everyone within range. "That lyin' cheatin' whore! Devil's blood, I knew she'd had someone in her bed! I'll tie her t' me keel an' drag her over the reefs, I will!"

Miss Morgan clapped. "Bravo! Bravo!"

Kerr searched for a way of escape, but Bloodmoon's minions blocked the only path to the door.

Bloodmoon continued his rant, spitting and cursing and calling his wife names even Kerr wouldn't dare call a trollop. "An' yer loutish, flapmouthed clod of a captain!" Bloodmoon pointed the pistol at Kerr. "He will pay fer this!"

Kerr forced down the terror squeezing his throat. One thing he knew about pirates. They fed on fear like ravenous sharks, and he wasn't about to make himself bait.

Mayhap 'twas Miss Morgan's ploy as well, for she started lining up the mugs on the table.

"D'ye know whose map it is?" Bloodmoon continued his rage. "'Tis the map of Roche Braziliano, the pirate they called the Rock of Braziliano, the meanest nastiest sod ye'd ever meet. I sailed wit' him when I was a young lad. He taught me everythin' I knows. He spent years plunderin' every ship that dared cross his waters and amassed a fortune. Which he buried in an unknown location."

"Aye," the man to his right added. "Gold, jewels, silver pearls, enough treasure to last an eternity."

Bloodmoon spit to the side again. "'Cept he coded the map so's no one but him could find it. And then the old sea snake died."

One of Bloodmoon's crew, a wiry fellow with no teeth, spoke up from his seat at the table. "So why d'ye want it back, Cap'n? If ye can't understand what it says? Makes no sense t' me."

Without hesitation, Bloodmoon shot the man in the arm. He toppled to the ground.

"Ye shot me! Ye shot me!" Yet no one dared rush to his aid as he scooted away, pressing a hand over his shoulder.

Shaking her head, Miss Morgan rose and started for the door. "I'm outta here."

"Nay, little one." Kerr caught her by the arm and shoved her back into the seat.

"Where's Rowan? I thought you said he was with my father!" The little chit stood, fisted hands on her waist, and glared at the band of pirates.

Bloodmoon tossed the smoking weapon aside and snatched another one from his belt, and Kerr suddenly found himself staring at the round, dark barrel.

"I should shoot ye jist fer tellin' me. An' the mad wench too!"

"Hey, what did I do?" Morgan shouted. "And you shouldn't point that thing at anyone. Even if it is fake."

Kerr's insides boiled. The crazy woman was going to get them both killed! "You *could* shoot us both," Kerr addressed Bloodmoon, drawing his attention from Miss Morgan, "but then you'd never know how to decipher the map."

Bloodmoon glared at him and cocked his pistol. "Tell me now. Or Lucifer waits t' greet ye."

Miss Morgan retrieved the handkerchief from the floor and began wiping dirt from her arms.

"First, do we have a deal?" Kerr arched a brow.

"Speak an' I'll let ye know."

Kerr gestured toward Miss Morgan. "The woman knows the key."

"Be that true, wench?" Bloodmoon asked.

"Sure." She shrugged. "I can decode the stupid thing." She stared up into the rafters. "Is that what you want, Father? Is that what will get me out of here?"

Bloodmoon's eyes narrowed.

Kerr gave a nervous laugh. "She's a bit mad, but I assure you she can interpret the map."

"Then why hasn't she sent Rowan t' the treasure?"

"Because she refuses his request to decipher it."

Finally, the man chuckled, sweeping away the tension that threatened to ignite the room into hellfire. "Only a feeble want-wit like Rowan would allow such defiance!" He silenced his men's laughter with a snap, his fierce gaze finding Kerr again. "Where be yer cap'n?"

"At the Stuffed Goat last I saw him."

"Bring the wench. I'll take care of Dutton meself. But mark me words, if she can't interpret the map, 'tis yer gizzards I'll be eatin' for lunch."

Kerr attempted to hide the tremble in his legs. "I would expect no less." Yanking Miss Morgan from the chair, he followed Bloodmoon out of the tavern, allowing a smile to form on his lips. If everything worked out as planned, this would be Kerr's lucky day.

Morgan took to pleading. She'd never been much for begging. Not even from God. She simply laid her requests before Him and hoped He'd give her what she asked. But He rarely did. Just like Kerr was doing at the moment—dragging her back onto this crazy pirate movie set, ignoring her demands, her requests, and finally, her tears.

She just wanted to see her father and end all this madness. But apparently he had more adventures planned for her. Maybe she should have deciphered the map back when Rowan had first asked. Maybe that was the key to going home.

Or . . . that panicky feeling stirred in her belly once again. That terrifying sensation that none of this was her father's doing.

Bloodmoon and his men halted in front of a two-story building. Lamplight poured from the windows and front door onto a porch filled with drunken men and women who were wearing too much makeup and showing far too much cleavage. Someone inside banged on an out-of-tune piano while several patrons sang along.

The sign hanging outside read, *The Stuffed Goat.*

Bloodmoon approached Kerr. "Get him out here. Tell him whate'er ye want, but get him t' come out. We'll take it from there."

She thought she saw Kerr swallow nervously before shoving her toward Bloodmoon and mounting the stairs.

"I demand to see my father at once!" Morgan stomped her foot and tugged from the smelly beast of a man. But he only laughed in return and pinched her arm so tight, she cried out again.

"Ye are a mad little flower, aren't ye? Never ye mind, I'll be yer father or whate'er ye want when all this be over."

She shrank from his foul breath. "What kind of name is Bloodmoon anyway? Give me a break."

His tiny eyes sparked fury in the light spilling from the tavern. "I'll show ye some blood, wench! But it'll be yer lover, Dutton's, not mine!" He shoved her toward the man beside him with an order to watch her on pain of death, then commanded his men to retreat into the shadows beside the building.

Her new captor, who smelled worse than the first, pushed her against the brick building and drew his sword. Her "ouch" didn't deter him as the other men also drew their weapons, some pulling out blades, some pistols, others knives—all hefted in air growing thick with tension.

If this were real, she'd be worried for Rowan. As it was, she was just annoyed. Good grief. How much longer was this going to go on?

Lightning flashed an eerie gray over the men and sent an ominous tremble through Morgan. Thunder shook the ground. Drizzle turned into thick rain drops that plopped onto the sand all around her.

Great. Just great. Now, she'd be wet *and* annoyed.

Somewhere in the distance, she heard Rowan's voice, muffled through the slap of rain.

Bloodmoon gestured for his men to follow as he led the charge around the corner. Grabbing her arm, her captor dragged her along, brandishing his sword before him.

They rounded the corner. Thunder roared, and Morgan made out Kerr, Rowan, Nick, and four of his men stomping down the stairs onto the now-muddy street. Well, maybe stomping wasn't the right term. More like wobbling, all except Nick. But where was her father?

Even though it wasn't real, she thought to yell out a warning, but the rain drowned out all sound, including the ten men about to attack Rowan. Ten against six, excluding Kerr. Not good odds, even if Rowan and his men weren't drunk.

What happened next was like a war film in 3-D. Rowan spun around just in time to duck out of the way of the aged pirate's sword. In a flash, his own sword was in his hand and he met the man's next thrust with one of his own. Surprisingly, the rest of his men instantly sobered, grabbed their weapons, and met the advancing pirates.

All except Kerr, who took up arms against one of his fellow crew.

Grunts and groans filled the air, along with the clank of swords and thud of fists, all muffled beneath the pounding rain. Morgan wiped water from her eyes and peered through the downpour, heart cinched tight. A chill seeped through her as she stood watching this mock battle that looked more real than any she'd seen on film. Swords struck with intent, knives appeared to draw blood, and bones cracked beneath iron fists. Faces writhed in exertion and anger, mouths growling and spitting at their enemies.

Nick stabbed one man in the gut and kicked him to the ground, then turned to face another. Rowan, sword in one hand, knife in the other, held off two men who came at him. One of them was Kerr. Another of his crew held a pistol to his attacker, but when it refused to fire, he slammed it hard across his opponent's face. The other three men battled equally well, leaping, slashing, and kicking their opponents until one by one, their enemies dropped to the wet sand.

In the mayhem, her captor had released her arm and now gripped his sword with both hands. Lightning scored the sky. Rain puddled in her lashes. She dabbed them with her sleeve and inched away from him.

A loud curse brought her gaze to Bloodmoon, battling swords with the youngest of Rowan's men. Though Bloodmoon had to be in his late forties, he fought with the strength of one much younger. Clearly the lad was outmatched, and in one swift move, Bloodmoon thrust his sword into his gut. Eyes wide, the man folded to the ground.

Morgan blinked. She could have sworn she'd seen the blade disappear inside him for a moment. But that couldn't be. She screamed anyway. Bloodmoon glanced her way before charging toward Rowan, who had just dispatched two more opponents. Their blades met heavy in the saturated air. Rain dripped from Rowan's hair and plastered his shirt to his chest where muscles toiled and rolled in exertion. Growling, he dove toward his attacker, barely missing his side, then swung about and jumped as the man slashed at his feet.

Her guard finally joined the fray, taking on Nick, who met him with a fist to the gut before he could even swing his sword. Then ramming his boot into the man's head, Nick knocked him out cold and swung to meet Kerr. A bloody gash etched across the traitor's cheek as the two parried like madmen, their boots spitting up water from puddles on the ground.

Lightning flashed, followed by the bellow of thunder, and Morgan spotted Rowan holding a hand to his shoulder. Blood oozed between his fingers. She gasped and unthinkingly started for him when, with a demonic chuckle, Bloodmoon went in for the kill. Rowan didn't flinch, didn't bat an eye. Instead, with the confidence of a seasoned warrior, he knocked the man's blade away with his own and then brought the hilt down on Bloodmoon's hand. The villain's sword landed in a puddle with a splash.

The aged pirate bent to retrieve it, but the muddy ground was littered with at least eight, maybe nine bodies, and still Rowan and four of his men remained.

Breath heaving, Bloodmoon backed away from Rowan. Kerr, hand pressed to his wounded side, took a spot beside him, his face unreadable, while the remaining two of Bloodmoon's pirates looked as if they'd been dragged across the bottom of the sea.

Rowan raked a hand through his wet hair, his hard gaze piercing his first mate. "Curse me for a rogue, Kerr. What devilment is this?"

Kerr shrugged. "Nothing personal, Captain."

Thunder rumbled as Bloodmoon pointed his sword at Rowan. "We shall meet again."

"Unless you wish to finish this now." Rowan started for him, but the man turned and dashed away, his men by his side.

A pervasive numbness crept up Morgan's legs. She scanned the street, once again searching for her father—

All the while knowing deep down he wasn't there.

While Rowan and his men gathered their breath, she inched toward the man from Rowan's crew who had fallen … waiting … desperately hoping that all of the actors who'd been slain would get up and start laughing and congratulating each other for their grand performance. But none did. By the time she stopped before the fallen man they called Jorg, the numbness had reached her waist. Rain fell on his still form. *Plop, plop, plop*, turning red as it streamed from the gash in his belly. A real gash with real intestines spilling forth.

But that couldn't be.

The numbness circled her heart.

She blinked and wiped rain from her eyes. But the image remained. There was no faking this. It was real. And Jorg was dead.

And that meant …

Hands gripped her and turned her away from the sight as Rowan's face filled her vision. "Are you alright, Lady Minx? Are you wounded?"

But she couldn't answer. She couldn't think. Couldn't breathe.

"What's wrong wi' the lass?" Nick said from somewhere far away.

"I don't know. But we have to get back to the ship and set sail."

"Ye think tha' bloodthirsty cullion'll come after us?"

"I *know* he will. Bloodmoon won't give up until we are all dead."

Rowan shrugged out of his coat and flung it over her shoulders, but she barely felt it. She barely felt anything as he placed an arm around her waist and rushed her back through the puddle-strewn streets, down the dock, and onto his boat.

She was thankful when the numbness reached her mind, for if what it was telling her was true, she doubted she'd feel much of anything ever again.

Chapter 14

Sweeping Morgan into his arms, Rowan jumped onto the railing of the *Reckoning* and dropped to the deck. He heard his men thump in behind him as he began spouting orders for the night watchmen to wake the crew who had remained on board and ready the ship to set sail. Confound it all! He'd have to wait until Abbot and Terrin rounded up the rest of his men from the taverns and punch houses before he could leave. He'd give them an hour. 'Twas all he could risk before Bloodmoon attempted another attack.

Sleepy-eyed men popped up from hatches, and seeing the urgency in their captain's face, began untying lines and leaping into the shrouds to unfurl sails. "Scratch!" he called the skinny man to his side. "You've been promoted to first mate. Prepare the ship. Post guards on every quarter, and alert me when the crew have arrived. I must tend to the lady."

Scratch's eyes twinkled above a gap-toothed grin as he nodded and darted off.

Though the rain had stopped, the woman moaned and shivered in his arms, staring up at him as if he were a ghost. "Lady Minx, by all that is holy, what were you doing in town?" He started for the companionway.

She made no reply.

Kerr. Rage broiled in Rowan's gut at the memory of his first mate—and friend—raising arms against him. Betraying him! But he couldn't think of that now, or he'd storm back into town, find the bedeviled muck-rake, and slit his throat. And that would only delay their exit and ensure a battle.

Navigating the narrow ladder, he headed down the companionway, kicked open the door to his cabin, and lowered Morgan into a chair, all the while wondering what magic stilled her shrewish tongue. Yet 'twas her silence that worried him most of all. Surely she should be berating him for putting her in such danger, or even demanding to see this illusive father of hers. Alack, mayhap he had finally found something that exceeded the limits of this lady's bravery. Grabbing a coverlet from his bed, he swung it over her shoulders and knelt in front of her, taking her hands in his. They were cold … so cold. Yet the woman made no complaint, didn't moan, didn't even look at him. Instead, she stared off into nothing.

When he'd first spotted her in the grip of one of Bloodmoon's henchmen, his heart had nearly exploded in his chest. The ensuing battle prevented him from going to her rescue, but 'twas his fear for her safety that had empowered his rum-dazed body to defeat such an overwhelming force. That same terror began to rise again, surprising him with its intensity … along with the affections that fed it.

Nick entered, dragging off his saturated tricorn and slapping it against his knee. "How is she?"

"Lady Minx, Lady Minx." Rowan snapped his fingers in front of her face, but still no response. Easing back the blanket, he examined her for wounds but found none. "I have no idea," he answered Nick. "'Tis like she's asleep with her eyes open."

"Real," she mumbled so softly, he barely heard it. "It's all real."

"Weel, the lass looks awake t' me, no?" Nick set down his hat and shrugged out of his wet coat, spraying drops over the deck. "'Tis ye I'm worried aboot." He gestured toward Rowan's bloody shoulder. "Farley's on his way."

Rowan barely felt the wound for the fury raging through him. After adjusting the coverlet tight around Lady Minx, he rose, lifted the satchel from his shoulder, and tossed it to the deck. "At least Bloodmoon didn't get the map."

"Och, is that what the scamp was after?"

"It had to be. He has no other argument with me. At least none that he knows …" Rowan gazed out the stern windows where lanterns reflected a golden sheen off the wet sand. "But if he knows about the map, then he also knows …."

"That ye slept wit' his wife?" Nick arched an incriminating brow.

Rowan ran a hand through his wet hair and grabbed a bottle of rum, bringing it to his lips.

Morgan groaned, her eyes finally meeting his. Terror fired across them—*real* terror. "You're real," she said before blinking and dropping her gaze again.

"I do not gainsay it, Lady Minx." He felt none of the usual annoyance at her ludicrous words. Something was terribly amiss.

"Perhaps give her some rum?" Nick offered.

Rowan poured a cup, knelt, and attempted to bring it to her lips, but she only coughed and turned her face away.

Pain throbbed in his shoulder, and he pressed a hand to his blood-saturated shirt.

Dropping into a chair, Nick wiped mud from his face and then stared in disgust at a spray of blood on his normally-pristine shirt. "'Tis Bloodmoon's map. Maybe if ye returned it, he willna continue his bloody vendetta?"

"'Tis *my* map. His wife Marianne gave it to me as a gift."

"For services rendered?"

Rowan frowned at Nick's lofty tone. "'Twas but a business exchange in which both parties were more than satisfied." But, in truth, Rowan felt rather vile at the moment as memories of Jorg, his guts spilling onto the street, assailed him.

"Poor Jorg." As usual, Nick's thoughts followed his own.

"'Tis Kerr's fault he is dead," Rowan shot back, tossing the rum he'd poured Lady Minx to the back of his throat, hoping it would numb his guilt.

Nick growled and leaned forward on his knees. "Kerr. I canna believe it. Traitorous dog! He almost got us all killed!"

Distant thunder rumbled.

Rowan lifted his baldric over his head and set the pistols on his desk, ignoring the pain searing down his arm. His gaze took in Lady Minx again, but she still stared blankly at the deck, looking like a wilted flower with her wet hair matted to her head and mud splattered on her skirts. The vision only increased his guilt. "Kerr must have overheard about the map. And also that the woman could decipher it."

"So, the rat traded us in like sacks of rice."

"The man's loyalty shifts with his greed." Rowan leaned back on the top of his desk and released a sigh. "'Tis my fault. Kerr didn't hide his lack of character. And now Jorg is dead, and I've made an enemy of one of the vilest curs on the seas."

"Shoulda thought o' tha' before ye sampled his wife, no?"

Rowan scowled and was about to offer a retort when Farley hurried in, satchel in hand, his face tight with concern. His gaze quickly sped to Rowan's shoulder, and he waddled toward him.

Edith ran in behind him and darted to Morgan. Kneeling, she grabbed her hands and peered into her face. "What have you done t' the poor child?"

"Nothing." Rowan said, putting up a hand to halt Farley, lest the man ram right into him. "Kerr brought her into town.

She saw too much bloodshed for any lady, even her." Another prick to his guilt.

"Real … this is all real." Lady Minx said to no one in particular, her tone hollow.

"Sit down, Cap'n. I need t' tend yer wound." Farley all but shoved him onto his cot. Rowan pulled off his shirt—the effort sending a hot dagger through his shoulder—and tossed the bloody cloth aside.

"It be a deep one, Cap'n. Hold still." Farley opened his satchel and sifted through the contents. Pulling out a needle and twine, he then grabbed Rowan's bottle of rum and poured it on his wound.

A fire ignited on his shoulder, but he kept his face staunch and focused on Lady Minx,

Farley inspected the wound. "This reminds me o' the time I pulled that spear out o' ole Willard. The man was so large, the fisherman thought he was a whale swimmin' in the bay an' shot him clean through!" He chuckled as he threaded the needle.

Edith helped Morgan to her feet and started for the door. "I gots to git her out of these wet clothes, or she'll catch her death."

"What ails her?" Rowan's eyes clouded from pain as Farley began his stitching.

"I dunno." Edith shook her head.

"I have an idea." Nick rubbed the back of his neck and glanced from the lady to Rowan. "The lass just figured out where and—more importantly—*when* she is."

An hour later, with his wound stitched and a half bottle of good rum wasted on its cleaning, Rowan stood on the quarterdeck, feet spread on the heaving deck, surveying their progress sailing from Charles Town harbor. He'd been forced to leave ten of his fifty men behind, but there was naught to be done for it. Any further delay would put them all in danger, for he had no idea what Bloodmoon was planning. But he was sure the devilish toad would attack hard and fast.

Sails drummed and shifted above, seeking the full force of the Trade Winds as the *Reckoning* burst from the protected port into the open sea. Rowan's hair slapped his face, and he snapped it aside and gazed at the half moon disappearing and reappearing behind the teetering foretopsail.

Shouts from the main deck brought his gaze to Scratch, his long mustache tossed by the wind as he marched across the deck, shouting orders. Rowan knew the man would make a good replacement for Kerr. The men respected him, and his many years at sea forbade him from making foolish mistakes.

Unlike Rowan.

He'd certainly mucked things up good.

"Where should we point her, Cap'n?" Nick asked from beside him.

"Petit-Goâve."

"But isna that French territory? "

"Aye, and Bloodmoon's wife is French."

"Och, have ye gone mad? Why would ye visit her?"

"Because, my dear friend, if I know Bloodmoon, his rage will need immediate release. And since we have slipped from his grasp, he'll seek out the next best thing."

"Then why go where the madman will most likely be?"

"Because he'll kill Marianne. And I'd not forgive myself if I didn't warn her."

Nick gripped the railing and stared at Rowan. "If he catches ye there, he'll kill ye too, no?"

Rowan huffed and raised a brow. "Then you best pray to that God of yours that I don't get caught."

The room spun around Morgan as she allowed Edith to pry off the layers of her wet clothing. Chill after chill wracked her damp body, even as her palms grew sweaty. Edith assured Morgan she was safe, and soon she'd be warm and dry and then Edith would go fetch some tea. But her voice sounded muffled and distant, as if Morgan were living in a dream world. But this wasn't a dream. The constant pain in her chest, her shallow breath, and the tingling in her fingers and toes told her she was having a panic attack—something all too familiar. Along with the feeling of doom that chased the thoughts around and around in her mind. Thoughts she didn't wish to land, for she feared if she acknowledged them, she'd drift off into blackness, never to return.

"It's real." She heard herself mumble.

"What's real, child?" Edith unlaced her stays and yanked off the stiff fabric.

Wood creaked, and the floor tilted as water gushed against the hull—sounds and movement which convinced her of the truth. "I'm on a pirate ship."

"Aye, and that's better than being in town, if you ask me, wit' all thems miscreant fools who jist as soon shoot you than pass you by."

Morgan's heart cinched tighter, if that were possible. She gasped for air.

"Now, now, child. You sit down righ' here." Edith led her to a chair and swept a blanket around her.

"I can't breathe. I need my meds!" Yet even as she said the words, she knew there *were* no meds. There would never be any meds. The realization caused her heart to fold in on itself until she thought it would dissolve. "My chest hurts. I'm having a heart attack." She leaned over and stared at the wooden floor, but even that blurred in her vision.

"Now, now child." Edith sat in a chair beside her and took her hands. "Nobody's attacking your heart. You's perfectly safe here. Try to breathe. Steady, now. In … out." She drew in deep breaths and blew them out slowly, and Morgan tried to do the same. But it wasn't working. She gripped her throat, wheezing. "Help me," she managed to squeak out.

Grabbing her skirts, Edith darted out the door, and for a moment, Morgan thought she'd left her to die all alone. But the woman returned and set a kitten in her lap.

Blackbeard! Just the sight of the cat helped settle her breathing. He looked up at her with his green eyes, then nuzzled his head against her arm and began to purr. "Thank you," she said as she stroked his fur and drew in air.

"Now, lemme git you some tea t' calm your nerves, an' then you can tell me what has you so riled." Edith smiled and stopped at the door. "You alright alone for a bit, child?"

Morgan nodded, even though the room was still spinning, and her heart felt like someone had dropped a bowling ball on it. Still, she tried to breathe deeply and concentrate on Blackbeard until the lady returned with two mugs of tea.

She handed one to Morgan, but it shook in her hands and spilled over the edge onto her damp chemise. Clutching it tighter with both hands, she took a sip and allowed the warm liquid to slide down her throat.

Edith sat and clasped her hands over her stomach. "Now, what's got you in sich a state, child."

Morgan stared at her, unsure what to say, unsure how to voice what she desperately didn't want to believe. "I thought all this was"—she glanced over the tiny cabin, still not believing that the wooden beams and lanterns and port hole were actually part of a real ship. A pirate ship!—"Never mind. What year is it?"

"Year?" Edith's face wrinkled. "Why it be the year of our Lord, sixteen hundred and ninety-four. What year do you think it be?"

Morgan did the simple math in her head. Three-hundred and twenty-one years. She'd skipped back in time over three hundred years.

"You wouldn't believe me if I told you." Setting down her tea, she dropped her head into her hands and resisted the urge to cry. Blackbeard began licking her chin. "I traveled through time. It doesn't make any sense. It's utterly ridiculous, actually." She pressed her palms to her temples. "I must be going crazy—lock me up, throw away the key kind of crazy."

"No one's going crazy. And no one's gonna lock you up again. Not if I have my way of it." Edith sipped her tea and set down the mug. "Now, tell me, child, why do you think you in the wrong time?"

"Because I was … I was … in San Diego attending a tall ship festival with my friends right before I ended up on this boat." She hesitated and bit her lip. "The year was 2015." She waited for Edith to barrel over laughing or finally admit that Morgan was nuts or even dismiss the topic and move on, but the slight rut that formed between the woman's eyes indicated she pondered the information. Finally, she grunted and shook her head.

"I seen many things in my life, child. I believe God can do whate'er He wants. Even send someone through time."

"God? You think God did this?" Morgan drew Blackbeard close as if the kitten were her only link to sanity. "Why? What a cruel thing to do to someone like me."

"First off, God ain't cruel. An' what d'ya mean by someone like you?"

"In case you haven't noticed, I have anxiety and OCD." Morgan noted the confusion in Edith's brown eyes. "I guess you wouldn't know what that is. But it means I'm crazy and I have cancer, and I can't be in 1694 on a pirate ship!"

Edith smiled. "Yet seems you are, child. Why are you so afraid?"

"Are you kidding me? I'm on a pirate ship three hundred years in the past!" Morgan pressed a hand on her tight chest and shook her head. "But honestly, I've been afraid of everything my entire life."

Edith placed a hand on her arm. "There's nothing to be frightened of. If God sent you here, He'll surely take care of you. Now, have some more tea. You'll feel better soon."

Strangely, Morgan *did* feel slightly better when she finished her tea, and even more calm after she drained Edith's cup too. At least her head no longer spun, and her heart had settled to a rapid staccato beat instead of a war drum. Edith busied herself preparing the small wooden bed attached to the wall with fresh blankets and a stuffed sack for a pillow.

Morgan's eyelids kept dropping. "You drug…ed…me," she said, finding no other explanation for the slumber that now lured her like a siren's song.

"I would never drag you nowheres, child. I jist gave you something to calm you down."

In a hazy blur, Morgan felt Edith help her to stand and then lower her to the bed where she drew blankets up to her chin. Blackbeard snuggled beside her.

Darkness swallowed her whole. Sweet, sweet darkness where there were no pirates or boats with tall sails or sword fights or … cancer. But the peaceful nirvana was not to last. Images flickered through her mind like an old silent film—cannons blasting, water gushing into the hold, sewage rising up her pant legs, pistols firing, swords chiming, blades thrusting, giant snakes crushing her bones, and Jorg's intestines pouring onto the muddy street.

In the middle of the night, she thought she heard someone reading Bible verses—the Psalms, if she recognized them from her many years at church. *Yea, though I walk through the valley of death, I will fear no evil, for thou art with me.*

Someone prayed for her. Morgan's mother? Could Morgan be waking from this nightmare? Ah, home sweet home, where all was ordered and safe. Smiling, she drifted off to sleep again.

Sometime later, the creak of wood, gurgle of water, and light drifting over her eyelids lured her back into the chaos. Squeezing her eyes tight, she longed for the sweet oblivion of slumber. But it was not to be. Shouts, a bell clanging, and the crack of sails yanked her unconscious mind from its hopes even as she heard the door open and Edith's cheerful humming.

More footsteps followed in after her.

"Shhh. She's still asleep," Edith whispered.

"I just need bandages, love. The cap'n's not feeling well." It was Farley's scratchy voice.

Shuffling ensued and Morgan peeked through her lashes at Farley grabbing something from a trunk and heading toward the door. He halted, cupped his wife's chin, and planted a kiss on her lips. "I missed ye last night."

"An' I you, you handsome dog." Edith swatted him on the behind. "Now, get on wit' you."

He winked and gave her a look of such love, it shocked Morgan.

No, she definitely wasn't home.

The rest of the morning went by without incident. Morgan tried to eat the porridge Edith brought, but it seemed the bowling ball that had struck her heart last night had now dropped to her stomach. She accepted the woman's apology for putting laudanum in her tea, and actually thanked her and asked her for more.

"It's not good for you. I seen many a hearty man become nothing but sniveling loobies from taking too much."

She wanted to tell the woman that she already felt like a sniveling looby, whatever that was, but thought better of it. Although Morgan realized she'd have to eventually consider the reality of her situation, she knew that in her present state, all she was capable of was to live minute by minute. For the time being, she felt safe in this tiny cabin in the bowels of this boat with this kind woman caring for her. So, she allowed Edith to dress her in more ridiculous layers of clothing, while listening to her prattle on about God's will and why Morgan shouldn't be afraid and how there's a reason for everything. In a small way, she reminded Morgan of her mother with her religious platitudes.

Only a small way, however, because Edith wasn't just repeating common Christianese, she actually seemed to believe what she was saying.

Yet none of it really mattered if God wanted Morgan dead. Which apparently He did. He was simply being creative going about it.

"But you forget, Edith, I still have cancer. Back home I would have received treatment. Now, I'm sure to die."

"Ah, go on, now, child. We's all gonna die. It's up to God to choose the time." She stopped and studied Morgan. "If anything, knowing that you ain't long for this world should take away your worries. If you's gonna die anyway, what have you got t' fear?"

Her words struck Morgan like a blast of cool air. Yet, she hadn't time to consider them when a knock on the door revealed Nick Doran's worried face. "The Captain's feverish. His wound's infected. He's asking t' see ye."

"Me?" Morgan took a step back. "I can't go to him. He's a pirate." The great Rowan Dutton, known for his brutality down through the ages. She swallowed. And she had done nothing but insult him and call him names!

Nick chuckled. "Aye, verra astute of ye t' notice. But at the moment, he's a pirate in need of ye, lass."

Morgan could not imagine why. Nor could she deny the fear spinning in her gut hearing that he was sick. She *wanted* to go to him, she did. But at the same time, the tingling returned to her feet and hands, and the room began to spin.

Edith nodded her approval. "Rowan won't hurt you, child. You know that."

Nick held out his hand and Morgan found hers suddenly inside of his as he led her out of her safe haven.

Chapter 15

Afternoon sunlight streamed through the stern windows as Morgan entered Rowan's cabin. The shifting light did nothing to chase away the gloom hovering over the room. Nor the smell of sickness. Her fear for her own predicament temporarily swept away, Morgan dashed to Rowan's bed and knelt, hesitant at first to take his hand, but then finally engulfing it in both of hers. Heat radiated from his skin, sending alarm through her as Nick dragged a chair over for her and one for himself.

Rising, she eased into it and stared at the robust pirate who now looked so weak and pale lying amongst his crumpled blankets. His eyes were closed, his breathing heavy and ragged, and sweat gleamed on his brow and across his wide chest. Blood stained a bandage wrapped around his left shoulder.

"What's wrong with him?" she asked.

"Came over him suddenly. Infection from the wound, most likely."

"But what has been done to help him? Do you have penicillin or any antibiotics?"

Nick frowned and rubbed his chin. "Don't know wha' tha' is, lass, but Farley applied a poultice of mashed onions an' honey nigh an hour ago."

So, that was the putrid stench she smelled. "Onions and honey?" she mumbled to herself. "What's next, leeches?"

"Aye, I agree. Wish we had some." His serious tone made Morgan's insides crumble, even as her heart raced. She'd been transported to the Stone Ages without benefit of electricity, indoor plumbing, deodorant, regular bathing, TV, computers, but worse of all … modern medicine. If she remembered her history correctly, many people died from simple wounds.

Like the one Rowan had.

She squeezed his hand, hoping to wake him, wanting to see his smile, terrified he'd slip away before she had a chance to … what? What did she want to say to this man who was no actor but a real pirate? A *real* pirate! The thought sent her blood spiraling. And from history's account, a violent, greedy pirate who was cruel to his crew and slept with other men's wives.

Yet … a man who had treated her better than any real pirate would.

She rubbed her temples where a headache formed. "Why is he not waking up? I thought you said he asked for me."

"He did, but 'tis best t' let him rest while he can. It'll do him good t' see yer face when he wakes."

She heard fear in Nick's tone, saw the unease in his eyes when he glanced at his friend. "You care for him."

"Like a son." He smiled. "Though I'll not own up t' being old enough t' ha' sired him."

Morgan couldn't help but return his smile. All the things this man had told her about his past—the British navy, his indentured servitude, the woman waiting for him back home in Scotland—were all true. Even his belief that God had assigned him to watch over Rowan. "A son for a pirate, eh?"

"Och, aye, but as ye can see, he's so much more than tha'." The boat leapt over a swell, and Nick adjusted his chair and studied her. "So, ye've sailed through time, eh?"

She laughed despite the tightness in her chest. "You say it as if it's a common occurrence."

Leaning back in his chair, he adjusted the tartan around his neck. "I've seen stranger things on these seas."

"Stranger than a woman transported here from 2015?"

His eyes widened and he whistled. "2015! I didna think the world would last tha' long. Things must've changed a great deal."

Morgan snorted. "You have no idea." She gazed down at Rowan as sails thundered above. "You believe me, then?"

"Of course."

She shook her head. "People in my day would think I'm crazy if I told them I'd traveled through time."

"Mayhap people in yer day ha' lost their faith, no?"

Morgan studied his eyes, so full of wisdom, and allowed his words to sink in. She supposed that was true. The Age of Enlightenment they'd called it—the start of a massive move away from faith in God to faith in ideas, individuals, and eventually science and technology. Anything outside the realm of proof was discarded as fantasy and falsehood.

Shouts filtered down from above, and Nick rose and straightened his vest. "I must be off t' my duties, lass. Will ye stay wit' him? Farley's tending a topman who fell from the yards."

She nodded her yes before she allowed herself to think on it. Did she really want to be alone with the notorious pirate Rowan Dutton? Yet, he didn't look so dangerous at the moment. Nor had he done her any harm before now. Even when she'd been cruel to him. Besides, she wanted to stay.

"Mayhap ye should pray for him?" Nick said on his way to the door.

"Prayer has never done me much good."

"Could be because ye don't believe it will."

"You sound like my mother, but none of her prayers got answered either," Morgan returned, staring at the man. "You know what I think? I think God will do what He pleases, when He pleases, regardless of our petty petitions."

Nick smiled. "He told us t' pray for a reason, no?" He shrugged. "Couldna hurt to try." And with that, he left and closed the door.

Morgan busied herself straightening Rowan's room. Yet again. The man—pirate—was the biggest slob she'd ever met. Maybe it came with the profession. Besides, putting things in order kept her nerves from exploding and sending her over the cliff of another anxiety attack.

Which wouldn't be a good thing in the middle of a pirate boat—a real one.

Order. There had to be order. When things were organized, when events were predictable, life made sense, and things worked out according to plan. Just like the code of a computer program. If A happens, then do B, else do C. Predictable. Logical. Safe.

Except when cancer suddenly appeared in one's liver.

Or a person was transported over three hundred years into the past.

Then there was no If-Then-Else clause to proceed to a desired result.

In fact, there was no desired result at all. Only chaos. The room swirled around her, and she dropped into a chair to settle herself.

I'm on a real pirate ship in the middle of the Caribbean! She took in the room, the weapons strewn about, the charts scattered across his desk, the ancient books, the nautical instruments … the rum! And she realized the movies had been pretty accurate. She dropped her head in her hands and stared at the wooden planks that made up the floor. *This can't be happening. This can't be happening. God, why are you doing this to me?*

Her hands grew numb. The floor spun, and she took in several deep breaths to keep from passing out. How was she supposed to survive this with her acute anxiety and OCD? Not to mention her cancer and no way to get treatment.

The truth was, she wouldn't survive. So she might as well make the best of it.

Get a grip, Morgan. Get a grip. She stood. The deck tilted. The ship creaked, and a bottle slid slightly out of place on the desk. Morgan set it back. But what did it matter? Her life was falling down a deep, dark pit of insanity, and keeping one room in order on a ship full of slovenly pirates certainly wasn't going to help.

And so the afternoon drifted by, evidenced by the changing angle of light penetrating the windows and finally the appearance of a sinking sun. Bright and brilliant, it kissed the sea in a rainbow of colors so beautiful, Morgan couldn't help but stare.

Rowan moaned and she sped to his side, tripping over her stupid skirts. Grabbing the cloth from his forehead, she dipped it in a basin of water, squeezed it, and dabbed his cheeks and neck before replacing it. She took his hand again, a torrent of fears racing through her mind. Most of which she couldn't deal with yet, some—as they related to this feverish man—she didn't want to.

The sun disappeared beneath the horizon, stealing what little light remained in the room. Rising, she searched for the flint and steel she'd seen Rowan use to light lanterns. Sounds alerted her to Farley and Edith entering, bringing food for Morgan, and broth and fresh bandages for Rowan. After lighting a lantern, the old butcher examined Rowan's shoulder, applied more of that appalling poultice, and bandaged it up again.

When Morgan asked how things looked, Farley's expression didn't hold much hope. "We'll see." He tried to smile. "Ye should get yer rest, Miss Morgan." He swiped hair over the top of his head.

"I want to stay with him," Morgan said. "He shouldn't be alone when he wakes."

"That's a good girl." Farley patted her shoulder and started to leave.

"I'll sit wit' ye, child," Edith offered, though dark circles swam beneath her eyes. She'd probably been the one reading the Bible and praying all last night with Morgan.

"No, go with your husband and get a good night's sleep. I'll be fine."

Nodding, Edith kissed Morgan on the cheek, wrapped her arm around Farley, and the couple left. Morgan touched her cheek and smiled. She couldn't remember the last time her mother had kissed her.

Two hours later, Nick came to check on his captain but upon finding him still unconscious, left for his own bed.

Morgan was alone again. Alone with one lantern that would soon sputter out, a tray of uneaten food, and a man whom she wanted more than anything to live. Why?

Her mother would say the pirate deserved to die and go to hell.

Maybe that was true. Maybe that was true of everyone. Still, there was good in this man. Lots of it for a pirate. She was having a hard time reconciling the man she'd come to know the last eight days with history's account. Yeah, the drinking and gambling matched, but Rowan wasn't cruel or heartless or wicked. If he was, he certainly wouldn't have put up with her crazy ramblings. He would have raped her, then passed her around the crew, and been done with her. But instead, he had barely touched her, had protected her … had saved her.

He moaned and thrashed on the pillow. Retrieving the cloth, she wrung it out and patted his chest and neck. Heat came off of him in waves, and she swallowed down a burst of dread that threatened to join her already frayed nerves. His old bloody shirt lay off to the side, the blood dried and caked, but she grabbed it and held the clean part to her nose. It smelled like him. Spicy and salty and male.

Maybe she should pray, after all. It was better than doing nothing.

She bowed her head and offered what God surely thought was a pathetic, whiny prayer, but it was all she could muster. Leaning back in the chair, she clutched Rowan's shirt to her chest and drifted off to sleep with one thought in mind. If he died, what would happen to her?

Chapter 16

Darkness as thick and heavy as ink surrounded Rowan. He couldn't see, couldn't feel, could hardly breathe. 'Twas like he'd been tossed into the hold of a giant ship lying at the bottom of the sea. Muted sounds taunted his ears. He groped forward, hoping to find a way out. But it was hot, so very hot. In the distance a flame sparked to life, and he started for it, but the closer he came, the hotter it grew until he felt his entire body would go up in smoke.

Then someone called to him … a woman … a sweet voice that breathed a prayer as light as a feather. That feather appeared before him, drifting up … up … up until it pierced the darkness, and a shaft of light spilled down upon him. With a mighty roar, the flames angrily licked the black void, while the light formed a door to Rowan's left.

He opened it and walked through.

The creak of wood, rush of water, and sound of snoring met his ears. *Snoring?* Rowan attempted to pry his eyes open, but pain rumbled through his head and stabbed his shoulder. The snoring continued, gentle, almost like the purring of a cat, and he attempted, yet again, to lift his heavy lids.

Lady Minx came into view, fuzzy at first, but then clear and … dazzling. She sat beside his bed, chin lowered to her chest, *his* shirt clutched in her arms, fast asleep. Despite his dizziness, despite the pain throbbing in his shoulder, Rowan couldn't help but smile.

Rays of light from the stern windows oscillated over her, their angle telling him it was early morn, their pointed direction telling him they'd found an object worthy of illumination. An angel in disguise sent here from another time and place by God—or the powers that be—to befriend Rowan, to show him what he'd been missing in all his empty sordid affairs. This little minx who challenged him, matched him wit for wit, annoyed him, frustrated him, brought him more trouble than any other. Yet, when he'd seen her in Charles Town about to be tossed into the midst of a fierce battle, terror like he'd never known had turned his blood to ice.

And he knew this little lady had touched a spot in his heart, a spot unbeknownst to him until now.

He could not fathom what she was doing here by his side. Alack, when last he saw her, she was babbling nonsense— not the usual nonsense, but the demented raving that bespoke of a mind long gone. He had feared the worst and felt the loss like a gaping rent in his soul.

Releasing a sigh, he rubbed his eyes and moved his shoulder. It pained him, but naught like the agony he had felt yesterday, or was it the day before? He couldn't remember much after the fever overtook him, save for the dismay in Farley's eyes as he leaned over to tend him. The old surgeon had never been good at hiding fear from his weathered face.

A sail snapped overhead, and a ray of sunshine struck Lady Minx across her closed eyes.

Her lashes fluttered over her cheeks before slowly opening. Her gaze landed on him. "You're awake." She sat up straight, blinked, then glanced down at the shirt she was holding and tossed it aside.

"So it would seem, Lady Minx."

"How are …." She gathered a cloth lying beside his head, dipped it in the basin, then leaned over him and dabbed it on his face and neck. "How are you feeling?"

Their arms touched, her chest hovered ever so close to his, and she smelled of lemon tea and woman. "Suddenly quite well." He grinned. But something in that grin must have frightened her, for she leapt to her feet and ran out the door, shouting, "I'll get Farley and Edith."

He instantly regretted his teasing but was happy to see her return with Farley and Nick. Return yes, but she remained at a distance as if he would devour her whole.

"Don't get up, Cap'n." Farley held up his hand, but Rowan had already swung his legs over the bed and sat.

"Don't coddle me, old man."

Nick smiled. "Aye, he's feeling himself again."

After Farley removed the bandage and examined the wound, the old surgeon lowered to a chair and scratched his bald head. "Well, I'll be a pickled herring. The infection be gone. I ne'er seen it flee so fast." Gathering fresh bandages, he began to wrap the wound again while Rowan noticed a knowing look pass between Nick and Morgan.

"Ye still need yer rest. An' a good meal," Farley prattled on. "I'll have Edith bring ye somethin'." He sat back to assess his work and smiled. "Warms me heart to see the color back in yer face, Cap'n. Reminds me o' the time—"

"Thank you, Farley. You do good work for a butcher." Rowan rolled his shoulder and pressed a hand on the wound.

"'Twas the lass's prayer, I'll wager, eh?" Nick glanced at Morgan, whose eyes widened. She'd backed against the bulkhead by the door as if she intended to bolt at any minute. "Ye did pray, didn't ye, lassie?"

She swallowed, then answered with a timid nod. What had happened to the brazen little minx?

Farley packed up his things and headed for the door. "Aye, prayer be a mighty thing, says I."

Rowan snorted. "Only if there's a God who answers." Yet he suddenly remembered the feather in his dream drifting upward to pierce the darkness. Shaking it off, he turned to Nick.

"How's Scratch handling the crew?"

Nick spread his feet farther apart to balance on the slanting deck. "Well enough. Ye picked the right man for the job."

"Good. How far are we from Petit-Goâve?"

"Wit' fair winds, we should be there on the morrow."

Rowan nodded and attempted to rise, but everything spiraled around him, and he gripped the back of the chair. Nick started for him but 'twas Lady Minx who made it to his side first, taking his arm and lowering him to sit.

Shouts sounded on the deck above, along with the thud of feet. Nick glanced aloft and slid on his hat. "I best see what's afoot."

"I should be at the helm," Rowan growled, blinking to clear his vision.

"Nay, ye should be resting jist like Farley said. I'll alert ye if anything urgent happens."

Edith darted in with a tray of tea and biscuits. "You're looking good, Cap'n. Praise be t' God for his mercy. 'Specially to those of us who don't deserve it." Chuckling, she winked at Morgan as she slid the repast onto Rowan's desk.

"Seems t' me ye are in good hands." Nick started for the door. "I'll report back later, Captain."

Rowan groaned in response, hating feeling weak and useless.

Edith wiped hands on her apron, her beaming smile shifting between Rowan and Morgan. "I best be going too. I gots forty hungry men t' feed."

Morgan turned to follow her out.

"Nay, don't go, Lady Minx." Rowan wasn't one to beg, but he hated the look of fear in her eyes whenever she glanced his way.

Turning, she stared at him and bit her bottom lip, but finally moved to pour him some tea.

"You prayed for me, Lady Minx?"

"Nick made me. It was a stupid prayer, anyway."

"But a prayer, nonetheless, and one I appreciate, withal."

She handed him the tea, the cup trembling in her hands.

"Why such fear of me all of a sudden?" In truth, he missed the defiant fire in her eyes, her brave retorts.

She stepped away and hugged herself. Scattered sunlight teetered over her with the movement of the ship, bringing out flames of red in her long hair that was unbound and unusually disheveled. He liked it that way—wild and free. Her green eyes met his, framed in those luscious dark lashes. "Because before I thought you were only an actor, paid to play a part."

"And now you think me a fierce pirate."

"You *are* a fierce pirate, are you not?"

He shrugged. He'd always been proud to be called such. He sipped the tea, but found it lacking and set it aside.

"Somehow, Rowan"—she sighed and shook her head—"I sound crazy for just saying this, but somehow I've traveled through time. I don't know how or why, but it terrifies me." Evidenced by the tremble that swept through her as she lowered to a chair. "I can't believe I'm even talking to you, Rowan Dutton, one of the vilest pirates ever to sail the Caribbean."

He grinned. "Is that what they say of me? Glad to know I made my mark on history."

"Not a *good* mark. And I'm being serious."

He leaned back in his chair and winced. "Have I been cruel to you, Lady Minx?"

She shook her head. "No, you've been … wonderful."

His glance took in the items on his desk, all neatly placed in order. He smiled. "So what else does history say of me?"

Wind whistled against the stern windows, drawing her gaze. "You believe me? Just like that?" She stood and picked up his backstaff from the desk. "I'm not sure I believe it myself. How can people travel through time?"

"Faith now, I know not what I believe, but you are no liar. Besides, there's much we don't know of this world. What makes the sun rise and set every day? How can something we can't even see kill a man?" He pointed to his wound. "Alack, I'll go even further to say that the most powerful things in this world are hidden from our eyes—the wind, for one, hate, greed … and love."

He watched her reaction to the last word and saw what he'd hoped most to see—a blush rise on her cheeks and her eyes lower. So, she *did* harbor some affection for him.

"From what year do you hail?" he asked.

"2015, if you can believe it." She set down the backstaff.

He raised his brows. "Egad! 'Tis amazing."

"My reaction exactly." She glanced at him, the fear appearing once more in her eyes.

He hated that fear.

So he kept her talking, trying to recover the enjoyable repartee they once had. "Now, pray tell, what of my legacy, Lady Minx? Do tell me that I left an indelible mark on this world." That he'd made his fortune, returned to lavish it upon his deserving sister, and lived out his days an honored member of society with a houseful of servants and a bevy of children.

She huffed. "You left your mark, all right. It says you were … *are* a ruthless villain, preying on any ship you crossed, no matter their allegiance. It says you tortured your victims and even some of your crew. I didn't listen to it all because you sounded horrible."

Rowan gripped the edges of his chair, his anger rising. "Bah! Lies all! Was there nothing about my sister? My place in society?"

"No, just that you died in a duel over some man's wife."

"Nay! 'Twill not happen." He clenched his fists and leaned forward on his knees. "I need but a few more prizes"—or one big one, if he had his way— "and then I will retire from this junketing about the seas and become a respectable gentleman."

She snickered as if she didn't believe that possible. "Apparently you changed your mind."

"Your history lies, Lady Minx. No doubt one of my enemies propagated spurious tales about me to all who were equipped with pen and parchment."

She eased away from him, moving to his bookcase. "It also says you were a drunk, a gambler, and a man who slept with other men's wives. Are those also lies?"

He frowned. "In good sooth, I'll own up to that, though I'll admit to not being proud of most of it." He rose and grabbed a bottle of rum to spice up his tea.

Facing him, Morgan backed against the book shelves as if they could somehow protect her from him. "I have to find a way to go back, Rowan. I'm sick and I need medicine."

"We have medicine here," he returned, sipping his tea while ignoring the sinking feeling tearing through his gut at the thought of never seeing her again.

"Not the kind I need." She pressed her side, as she so often did. Mayhap she *was* ill. He would seek out Farley and Edith's advice. Edith had once healed one of Rowan's powder boys of the ague with her herbs and potions. Surely she could help Morgan. "But if you don't know how you came to be here, then how can you go back?"

She walked to the window and stared out at the horizon teetering in and out of view. Several seconds passed before she spun around and declared, "The amulet! The amulet you thought I stole. That's when it happened." She took up a pace before the windows, stumbling over her skirts. "I was in the bottom of your boat." At what must have been a look of shock on his face, she added, "A replica of it. And I found your amulet in the old lantern. I rubbed it and that's when I woke up in this time. Where is it?" She scanned his desk, then began opening drawers and sifting through his things. "It's the key. I know it."

He grabbed her arm to still her, mainly because there were things he didn't wish her to find—the amulet suddenly chief among them. "Why do you wish to leave? Is it so horrible here?"

She jerked from his grip, gaping at him as if he'd asked her to climb to the mast tops. "What am I going to do here, Rowan? How am I to live? I'm a software engineer and computers haven't even been invented yet."

There was the old Morgan with her gibberish speech. "You have been well-fed and sheltered since your arrival. What to fear?"

"I cannot stay on a pirate ship! For one thing, my nerves wouldn't stand it. The battles, the sword fighting, the drunken parties, the cannons. Within two weeks, I'd be babbling in a straitjacket in the hold."

"I know not this straight jacket, but I do regret locking you in the hold. 'Twill not happen again, I assure you."

Frustration twisted her face, and she hugged herself again. The ship creaked and the stomp of feet brought her gaze above. When she looked at him again, horror creased her expression.

"The snake that was crushing me in the jungle. It was real!" Her breathing came heavy and he touched her elbow, lest she fall. "And those men, your crewmen on the island, they were really going to rape me! And the French boat"— she looked up at him, her eyes chilled with terror— "Those cannonballs were real! And the sword fights." She retreated from him. "And that man, Bloodmoon, that evil, evil pirate. He was real! I insulted him. I made fun of his name."

"You did?" Rowan chuckled. "Faith now, to have witnessed that! Served him right, the old impertinent bore." Though now his suspicions were confirmed that either Kerr or Morgan had told Bloodmoon about the map and Morgan's ability to decipher it. Otherwise, he would have shot her—or worse—on the spot.

"I can't believe … all of that … actually happened. I could have been killed." She leaned against the desk and raised a hand to her neck as if struggling to breathe.

"But you survived. And with more courage than I've seen in any woman."

"I'm not brave, Rowan. I'm a coward. I thought it all was fake, don't you see?"

He drew close to her, longing to touch her, longing to comfort her and take away her fear. "Nay. Courage like that comes from deep inside a person and cannot be feigned no matter the circumstances."

Ever so slowly, he raised his hand and brushed his knuckles over the silky softness of her cheek. "I wish you were not afraid of me, Lady Minx."

"I wish I was not afraid, period," she sputtered out, as her eyes drifted closed beneath his touch.

"When I woke, I saw you holding my shirt." He continued caressing her cheek.

"I was cold."

He smiled. "Are you sure that was the only reason?" He leaned in and placed his lips on hers.

Every inch of Morgan's body, every fiber of her being came alive the instant Rowan's lips touched hers. The first time he'd kissed her, she'd felt the usual warm desire, the normal sensations when a handsome man kissed her. But this time … this time it was that and so much more. It was life and hope and protection and a yearning to be with this man forever, to love him, to know him inside and out … to grow old by his side.

Reaching around her back, he pressed her close and drank her in as if he'd never kissed a woman before … as if he found her completely enchanting. No one had ever kissed her like that, and Morgan got lost in the heady sensations swirling through her, tempting her to toss her fears to the wind and fall into the wild dark unknown that was Rowan Dutton.

He ran a hand through her hair, exploring her mouth with his tongue … caressing … loving her. She fell against his wide chest, a mound of cotton pressed against rock—a rock who could crush her, but one, instead, whose arms barricaded her with steely warmth.

Safe at last. Her nerves unwound, her tight heart relaxed, even as her body grew hungrier for more of him. He trailed kisses down her neck, lingering, bringing her to life with sensations that sent heat spiraling down to her toes—feelings she'd never experienced before. A groan escaped her lips, her mind reeled.

Wait. *No!*

He knew exactly what he was doing. He was a womanizer, a pirate! An expert at seduction.

She pushed from him, fear returning to bind her chest. "I will not be another of your mistresses."

The desire sputtered from his eyes as if she'd dropped a bucket of ice on him. "Faith now, Lady Minx, I don't remember asking you to be."

She narrowed her gaze. "You think because you are tall and handsome and have"—she gestured toward his chest—"big muscles …" *And gorgeous biceps and a six-pack stomach,* she noted as she scanned him, angry that her body still thrummed from his touch. "And you carry a sword or whatever, that you can have any woman you want. Well, not this woman!" Morgan flattened her lips. Not again. She'd not be lured in again with a handsome face, studly body, and soft words, only to be dumped like a deflated doll later on. No siree. Apparently she was as stupid in 1694 as she was in 2015. At least she'd caught herself before she made another colossal mistake.

Rowan just stood there, looking all the more alluring for the charming grin on his face.

"Give me the amulet. I wish to go home now." She held out her hand.

He crossed arms over that gorgeous chest, winced slightly at the pain, and continued smiling at her.

"I know you have it. I saw you put it on your desk. Where is it?" She circled said desk and reached down to open drawers again.

But his firm grip around her wrists—both wrists—stopped her. "It pleases me you no longer fear me, Lady Minx. But once again, I don't respond well to demands."

She struggled against his grasp. "What are you doing? Give me that amulet!"

"'Tis my amulet, if you please. A sentimental gift from my mother which you tried to steal. Curse me for a rogue, but I'll not let you do it again."

"I wasn't ste—and yes, I will curse you for a rogue, a stupid rogue. What's wrong with you? I thought you'd be happy to be rid of me."

He pulled her toward him, pressing her against him once again. "Did I just kiss you like I wished to have you gone?"

His hot breath filled the air between them, her struggling useless against a strength that seemed unhindered by the fever that had just ravaged his body. "You kissed me like a man who seeks a mistress."

"If that's all I wanted, you'd already be in my bed." He released her, a flash of sorrow crossing his blue eyes.

She backed away, noting he took a stance between her and his desk. "Oh, is that so?"

Anger wiped the sorrow from his face as a frown stole his normal confident grin. What was she doing? It was one thing to anger this man when she'd thought he was an actor, but now, she knew exactly *what* he was. Still, what did she have to lose? Like Edith had told her, the cancer would steal her life soon enough.

"Please Rowan. Let me go home." She softened her tone, but his face remained steel.

"I know not whether you came through time," he said, "or whether the amulet will send you back, but I'm not willing to take the risk."

"Why? I don't understand. I've told you I will not be your mistress."

"You wound me sorely, Lady Minx, if you think that is my goal."

"Then what? Am I to be your entertainment? A partner in lively conversation?"

"'Twill be a start."

Morgan narrowed her eyes. "Don't you have other women to harass? Other men you can talk to about whatever you pirates talk about?"

He shrugged and then pressed the bandage on his arm, a pained look on his face. "Most women would find my attentions flattering, Lady Minx. The fact that you don't makes you all the more intriguing."

"So, let me get this straight. If I was swooning at your feet right now, you'd let me go home?"

"If you were swooning at my feet right now, I guarantee you wouldn't want to go home." He grinned.

"You arrogant, conceited …" Morgan fisted her hands and bit back a curse that would only add to her list of sins. "You can't keep me here! I will not be your prisoner."

"Prisoner?" He chuckled and ran a hand through his hair. "Nay, I shall be happy to set your pretty feet upon any shore you desire."

She stared at him, her fury burning, her mind sifting through the impossibility of her situation. Why, oh, why, did she always find herself at the mercy of some gorgeous man with an over-inflated ego?

"In 1694, you know as well as I do that I wouldn't last long."

"Hence, 'tis best you stay under my protection."

"You always get what you want, don't you?"

"Aye."

"Selfish pirate!" Spinning around, she stormed from the room and slammed the door in his face.

Chapter 17

"Now, you pay them no mind, child." Edith cast a glance over her shoulder at the pirates loitering about the boat, then slid her hand over Morgan's as they stood at the railing on the main deck of the *Reckoning*. A pirate ship. A *real* pirate ship. No matter how hard she tried, Morgan couldn't shake the truth from her mind. Even now, she wondered what had possessed her to come above deck in full view of men who were nothing but thieves and rapists.

But nearly a day and a half cramped below in Edith's cabin, sick to her stomach, and suffering from one panic attack after another, had convinced her to agree to Edith's suggestion to come above for fresh air. Fresh, warm, salty air that now filled her lungs, chasing away the stench from below, but reminding her that she was in the middle of the Caribbean.

Over three hundred years in the past.

Her stomach clenched as panic once again spun her mind into a tizzy and buzzed through her fingers and toes until she could no longer feel them. She wished she could no longer feel her heart either—wound so tight that it pained her. Along with her inflamed liver, which the cancer continued to devour.

Actually, she was a big hot mess—a dying, hot mess in a world of trouble at the moment. Yet, beside her, Edith closed her eyes, lifted her face to the warm sun, and began to sing a song about the faithfulness of God, His Holiness and wondrous love, as if nothing was wrong with the world. Sunlight brought a blush to her skin—the color of milk chocolate—as if the Almighty Himself were bending down to kiss her. Morgan envied the woman's peace, even as she wondered how she could be peaceful once having been a slave and now in another kind of slavery aboard a pirate ship. On the other hand, Morgan's mother, who lived in comfort and ease and spent every waking moment at church, was always bound in a knot of frustration and fear.

The boat rose and plunged over a wave, spraying Morgan. She clung to the railing, trying to keep her balance while Edith giggled in delight.

Dabbing at the moisture on her neck, Morgan gazed over the sea, a glimmering pool of turquoise diamonds in the afternoon sun. Not a speck of land or a ship was in sight. Just the wide open Caribbean and one old rickety boat that stood between them and drowning—or worse, sharks. But that wasn't her biggest problem. It was the sharks on the ship. She could feel their eyes boring into her back. One glance over her shoulder proved her right. Those not busy with their duties gaped at her as if they hadn't had a meal in months and she was a hunk of charbroiled steak. Dipped in garlic sauce.

Scratch, the new first mate, gave her a cursory glance as he bellowed orders to the men up in the sails, while Nick, standing by the tiller, smiled at her as if to assure her all was well.

But was all well? Hadn't it been Rowan, and Rowan alone, who kept his men in line and away from her? And where *was* the pirate captain anyway? She faced the sea again, her traitorous thoughts speeding to their kiss. Despite her anger toward him, despite the fact that he was a stubborn egomaniac, she could not deny his effect on her. It wasn't just physical, though that had been intense! It went much,

much deeper. She had feelings for him. Yes, if she admitted it, she actually cared for the pirate who had been kind to her and been her rescuer.

But what did that say about Morgan? What kind of demented woman continually fell for vain, arrogant, self-centered men? In fact, she seemed to be getting worse. Jason, at least, had a law-abiding profession. Rowan was a pirate! She'd bet every penny in her dwindling savings account that he would do the same thing as Jason when he learned of her cancer. He'd dump her. Only Rowan would dump her in some wicked pirate town and leave her to her own devices.

No, she wouldn't tell him. She wouldn't tell him how she felt about him either. It would only inflate his already blimpish ego.

Speaking of … she felt that blimpish ego emerge onto the deck, felt a warmth—a pleasurable warmth—run down her back when his voice resounded across the deck, issuing an order to adjust sail. As much as she desperately wanted to, she would not look his way. She would not give him the satisfaction of knowing she noticed him.

To her left, one of the pirates, a beefy man in his twenties with a missing finger on his right hand and a black scarf atop his head, pulled out a knife and began whittling a chunk of wood, his eyes glued to her. He attempted a grin she was sure he meant to be charming, but the effect was lost at the sight of teeth that looked like they'd been dipped in mud.

Shifting her gaze, she dared a glance at Rowan and found him standing beside Nick with a telescope to his eye.

The boat galloped over another wave, and Morgan's legs began to ache from the strain of remaining upright. Just how did these men manage this day after day?

"Lordy, Lordy, but it's a pretty day," Edith remarked, still smiling and gazing over the sky, "But I needs t' git t' my duties." She patted Morgan's hand. "You be all right here, child?"

"Oh, sure, yeah. Just me and two dozen lusty pirates. I'll be fine." She regretted her sarcastic tone when the woman took her hand and gave her a look of concern.

"Why you're wound tight as a furled sail. It's sich a beautiful day. What's got you so riled?"

"How can you ask me that? You know my predicament more than anyone."

"Ah." Edith waved a chubby hand through the air. "Whether you're in the future or in the past, God be wit' you, child. An' He has a plan. He won't leave you. You gotta know that, deep in there." She pointed at Morgan's heart.

Actually, Morgan didn't know that, nor did she believe it anymore. "All I really know is that this God of yours has thrust me back in time into nothing but danger *and* to a place where the cancer He gave me cannot be cured."

"He ain't given it t' you, child. But He can use it for good. 'Sides, as I said before, if you're gonna die anyway, what's left to fear?" The wind tossed her black curls about her face as she smiled at Morgan.

Perhaps the woman was right, after all. What did any of this matter? Morgan might as well enjoy the warm weather, the beautiful scenery, the attentions of a handsome pirate. Even if she *could* get back to her own time, there was no guarantee the surgery and chemo would work. In fact, her chances had been slim. If she died here in a ship battle or sword fight, maybe that would be better than enduring the pain as the cancer grew and consumed her bit by bit.

Still, Morgan was a woman who always had a plan. Everything in her life had been planned and scheduled, down to each minute. Well, everything except the cancer and her trek into the past. Which was all the more reason to form a new plan now. She would find the amulet and make every attempt to return home. But in the meantime, she would do her best to enjoy this crazy adventure. She glanced at the pirate to her left, still leering at her, then to the dozen more behind her doing the same.

What did she have to fear?

Rowan lowered the spyglass and once again found his gaze wandering to the lady. By all that was holy, what was wrong with him? He could hardly keep his eyes off her. Nor could he stop the delight that had spun through him when he'd come on deck and spotted her by the railing. It had only been a day since she'd called him selfish and marched from his cabin. But it had seemed much longer. During his convalescence, he found himself longing for her company: her strange, bold speech; her clever retorts; her spitfire charm; and those deep moss-colored eyes so full of angst, sorrow … and promise. Now, as she stood beside Edith, her maroon skirts billowing, her shoulders high and tight, and her eyes closed to the wind, he found a rare happiness filtering through him.

He rubbed his mouth. The kiss they'd shared had surprised him. First, that she'd allowed it. Second, that out of her tightly-wound body had come such passion. Alack, he'd not seen the likes of it even amongst women skilled in the arts. Nor had he felt the likes of it in his own reaction. Which worried him the most. Lovemaking had always been one of Rowan's many pleasurable pursuits, a pastime, something to satisfy his urgings and stave off boredom. But the lightning bolt that had passed through him at her kiss, as her body pressed against his, went beyond the mere physical. It touched a deeper part of him that wanted more of her. And *only* her.

And Rowan couldn't have that.

"A pretty lass, is she, no?" Nick gave him a teasing grin.

Rowan tore his gaze from her and raised his scope. "She'll do, I suppose."

"Ye havena missed her the past day?"

"Absurd." Rowan focused on the speck of land just coming into view. "She's naught but a silly woman."

"Och, of course. Then wha' are ye to do wi' this silly lass? Do ye believe her tale?"

"Rooster." Rowan turned to the new helmsman. "Alter course ten degrees south by southwest."

"Aye, Cap'n," the young lad, who got his name from his beak-like nose and lack of a chin, replied eagerly, no doubt pleased with his promotion from seaman. Sails snapped above as the lad turned the tiller.

Rowan faced Nick. "Believe her? Aye, I do. Though I feel as mad as she for saying so. As to the how or why she came to be here, I haven't a clue. As to the what to do with her, I find myself in the same state." He shook his head and glanced her way again. This time Edith laid a hand on hers and said something that seemed to lower Morgan's shoulders, and Rowan was glad for the older woman's presence on the ship.

"Well, ye canna verra well leave her on land somewhere." Nick braced as the ship careened over a swell. "She ha' no way t' provide for herself. No relations, no idea of the way things work in this time."

"I'm well aware of that." Rowan stiffened his jaw at his friend's interference.

"And ye canna keep her here."

"Why not?"

"Och now, she's no' a pet to coddle an' hide away in yer cabin."

"Do you have a better idea?"

"Aye, perhaps." Nick gave Rowan a look of reprimand—the kind that always pricked his guilt. "But isna it more that ye wish to keep the lass for yer own pleasure, eh?"

"You think me so base?"

Nick's brows arched.

"I grant you"—Rowan sighed—"I've given you cause. But I am not a man to take advantage of a woman who does not eagerly return my interest."

"But ye hope t' charm her interest t' eagerness, no?"

Wind tossed Rowan's hair in his face. He raked it aside, noting that Hunt had positioned himself within a few yards of Lady Minx. "The only thing I hope for now is to rescue Marianne Bloodmoon from certain death." He hoped his friend would take the hint and change the topic.

"Still on tha' mad quest?"

"Aye, and from the looks of it"—he handed Nick the spyglass—"We'll be at Petit-Goâve by sunset."

The quartermaster placed the scope on his eye, focused it for a second, then nodded. "'Tis a fool's errand an' ye know it."

Rowan gripped the railing and stared at the land growing in his vision. "Bloodmoon cannot be there yet. We sailed straight from New Providence."

"But his ship is smaller an', hence, faster." Nick stated what Rowan had already determined. "Wha' will happen t' yer lady should ye get yerself killed?"

Rowan chuckled. "You assume the impossible, Nick. But in the event of my demise, she will become your charge, of course."

Nick shook his head and snorted. "Jist what I need, a mad lassie t' take care of."

Hunt was even closer to the lady than before—his pretense at whittling not fooling her in the slightest as she cast anxious glances his way. In a way, Rowan missed the brave lady who would have given the lusty pirate a piece of her mind, but how could he expect any lady not to tremble on board a pirate ship?

"Now, if you don't mind"—Rowan gestured toward Morgan—"can you rescue Lady Minx from Hunt before the fiend pounces on her?"

Morgan had to admit she was relieved to see Nick's beaming face appear beside her and offer to escort her below. Every time she faced that beastly pirate pretending to whittle his wood, he was even closer to her than before. Soon he'd be standing right beside her, grinning with those muddy teeth and undressing her with his eyes. She shuddered at the thought. She had wanted to head below herself, but didn't want to run into a pirate all alone in one of the narrow corridors before she made it to Edith's cabin.

But then Nick appeared, his red hair aflame in the sunlight, his green eyes lively and twinkling mischievously. Why, she had no idea, but she imagined it was something Rowan had said.

Taking his arm, she turned and finally met the Captain's gaze. He stood on the deck above, hair waving and coat flapping in the breeze, hands gripping the railing, and staring down at her with the oddest look—a mixture of admiration, anger, and … concern.

"What is Rowan's problem now?" she asked Nick as he led her down a hatch then up another ladder. "And where are we going? Edith's cabin is below a deck."

"We're going t' Rowan's cabin, lass. An' his problem is tha' he's a blooming fool."

She halted, a hint of a smile on her face. "I agree, but I'm still not going to his cabin. Not if he wishes to … to …."

"Nay. 'Tis my idea. I need ye t' do something."

"You want *my* help? For what?"

"Come along an' I'll show ye." He continued down the dim teetering hallway that reminded Morgan of one of those slanted houses at a carnival.

Bracing herself on the walls and more curious than frightened, she followed him into the Captain's cabin, her eyes automatically snapping to the spot where she and Rowan had kissed.

A wave of heat doused her as the deck tilted, and she grabbed the back of a chair. Circling the desk, Nick rummaged through a drawer, pulled out a map, then rolled it out on the desk.

It was the map Rowan wanted her to decipher.

A weight settled in her stomach. Rowan hadn't been concerned about her safety. He only wanted her to decode his stupid map. "He put you up to this."

"Nay. 'Twas my idea."

His gaze never left the map, and she found herself believing him as she approached the desk. "So you can steal the treasure from Rowan?"

He recoiled. "Och, now, lass. Ye wound me. D'ye think me so malicious as t' betray a friend?"

Morgan huffed. "Well, you *are* a pirate."

"Privateer, but I suppose it doesna matter." He smiled.

"Then why do you want me to decode it?"

"T' save Rowan's life."

"Oh, please. So dramatic." Morgan rubbed her eyes then glanced over the desk, already a mess after she'd tidied it up. *Wait.* She smiled as a thought occurred to her. "Help me find Rowan's amulet, and I'll decode anything you want."

Nick frowned. "The one ye stole?"

"I didn't ..." Morgan growled. "Never mind. Yes, that one."

"What d'ye need it for, lass?"

Circling the desk, she began opening drawers. "I know this sounds crazy but I think it might have some power or something. I think it's what brought me here."

"An' ye hope 'twill send ye back."

"Exactly."

He grabbed her wrist, holding it fast. "I dinna think Rowan will want ye looking through his things. Why no' jist ask him t' see the amulet?"

"I did. He won't let me."

Nick's brow wrinkled. "Why no'?"

"He wants to keep me here for some reason." To feed his ego. To charm her into his bed. She really had no idea.

Nick's mouth twisted as he seemed to ponder this information. Finally, he released her. "Verra well, I'll help ye."

But Morgan's excitement was soon squelched when, after they'd searched every inch and nook of the desk, no amulet presented itself.

She stepped back and sighed. "Great. He's hidden it somewhere."

"Sorry, lass, but I still need yer help wit' the map."

"I've already told Rowan that I'll decode it when he brings me home, which, I guess now means when he lets me try the amulet."

Nick frowned and tugged on the tartan at his throat. "Lass, ye don't understand." His gaze met hers, unusual fear sparking within it. "If ye don't interpret this map now, Rowan may no' be able t' help ye wit' anything—ever again."

"What are you talking about?"

"Because he's going t' get himself killed. He's going t' rescue Bloodmoon's wife before the vile cur ha' a chance t' kill her."

"Bloodmoon would kill his own wife? For what?"

"For entertaining Rowan."

"Entertain … oh." Heat swamped her face. "You mean …" A burning sensation tore through her chest, one she knew all too well—jealousy. "So he actually *did* sleep with her like Bloodmoon suspected. And now he has to go clean up his own mess. Great." She moved away from the desk, suddenly feeling nauseous. "How is that my problem?"

"Because I know ye care for him."

"Don't be ridiculous." She looked away, unsettled by his perception.

"An' because 'twas yer doing Bloodmoon found out." Wind whistled against the windows and Nick shifted his stance.

"How do you figure?"

"Are ye no' the one who told him?"

Morgan settled into a chair, the hideous scene in the tavern playing out in her mind. "I suppose I did tell him about the map ... I even described it. And that's when he went ballistic." She trembled at the remembrance, though she'd thought it an act at the time. Guilt washed over her. Quickly replaced by anger. Or was it jealousy? The thought made her more angry. "Nevertheless, it wasn't me who slept with the man's wife! And how will decoding this map help anyway?"

Nick planted hands on the desk and leaned over to study the chart. "Rowan's been seeking Brasiliano's treasure for years. I'm thinking if he knows exactly where it is, he might forsake his noble quest t' save Marianne an' retrieve it."

"You would have him seek treasure over saving a life? I thought you were a God-fearing man."

"He'll no' save her life, lass. 'Tis already forfeit. The lady sealed her fate the minute she allowed Rowan in her bed."

Why did that thought disturb Morgan more than anything? She knew who Rowan was ... *what* he was. She'd read his history. Which reminded her ... she stood and gave a victorious grin. "You don't have to worry about Rowan. I happen to know for a fact that he doesn't die until 1714 in a duel with a jealous husband. Apparently he never learns to stay away from married women." She snorted as another pain sliced her heart.

Nick raised a brow. "But ye ha' changed things, eh, lassie?"

Morgan could only stare at him as the boat's creaks and groans etched truth in her mind. If she *had* changed history, if she had changed Rowan's course, then … anything was possible.

Fear curdled in her stomach.

"It falls t' ye, lass. Ye are the only one who can save Rowan from the grave."

Chapter 18

"I'll need paper, parchment, or whatever you call it, something to write with, a ruler, and two hours," Morgan said with the same authority she often used as project leader at Qualcomm Industries.

Nick's grin couldn't be wider as he hurried to gather her supplies. "Rowan will be busy aloft directing the ship to anchor near Petit-Goâve, lass. Tha' should give ye plenty of time. I'll leave ye t' it." And off he went, his bootsteps fading down the hallway.

Morgan sighed, still not believing she was going to help a notorious pirate find buried treasure. If you had told her that a month ago, she'd have laughed herself to tears. If anyone had told her she'd be in 1694, she would have called the men in the white coats.

Plopping down in Rowan's chair, she leaned her elbows on the desk and dropped her chin in her hands. Her life used to be so ordered, so planned. Everything in its place and her future mapped out to the minutest detail. Just like this ridiculous treasure map before her. Only like this treasure map, someone had come along and not only distorted, but encrypted all her plans until nothing made sense anymore.

The boat seesawed to the left, sending the quill pen Nick had given her tumbling across the map. Snagging it, she felt the familiar tightening in her body as if someone were playing tug of war with her nerves. What she wouldn't give for a couple of Xanax right now. And some Vicodin for the pain in her side from the cancer. But she had neither. It was best not to think of it—of where she was and, more importantly, *when*. Instead, she would focus on saving Rowan.

Not that he deserved it.

Blackbeard leapt on top of the map and began batting another quill pen.

Happy to see him, Morgan scooped him up and nuzzled his cheek, relishing his gentle purr, which always calmed her down. "Where did you come from, little one?" He looked at her with those slanted green eyes as if he completely understood her predicament before licking her nose with his sandpaper tongue. Giggling, she kissed him and set him on the floor. "I best get to work, Blackbeard. We haven't much time."

It only took her half an hour to decipher the code—a simple transpositional cipher—but the hardest part was reconfiguring the sizes of the land masses on the map and then redrawing them in the correct proportions on the blank paper. Getting used to the quill pen was part of the problem. Having to dip it in ink every few seconds drove her insane. Not to mention she now had ink all over her fingers. It didn't help that Blackbeard thought the feathers on the pen were attached to a bird and fair game for his hunting prowess. More than once she had to scold him and put him on the floor. More than once he decided that lying down right where she needed to draw was as good a spot as any.

During all of this, the boat slowed, turned, then slowed again. Sailors' feet pounded above as shouts ricocheted like lightning. Outside the windows, the sun finally lowered to the horizon, and she set down her pen and turned to watch it spill crimson, coral, gold, and saffron over the water like paints from a tipped bottle. She stood in awe, never remembering sunsets so beautiful in San Diego.

Or maybe she just hadn't scheduled time to enjoy them.

Sails flapped above as the ever-present sound of water against the hull dulled to a gurgle. More shouts, including one she recognized as Rowan's voice, echoed through the boat, reminding her she hadn't much time left to finish the map. Turning, she picked up the pen and ruler and started calculating the final measurement when the door swept open and in marched Rowan, eyes widening when he saw her.

Nick followed him, along with Farley, his flabby face folded in worry.

"Ah, there ye are!" Farley released a sigh. "Edith was worried about ye, miss. When she didn't find ye in our cabin, she asked me t' check up on ye."

Rowan marched toward her, all man and muscle and smelling of the wind and sea. His gaze narrowed on the map and her scribblings beside it. "Alack, what are you doing with my map?"

His loud shout frightened Blackbeard, sleeping on the edge of the desk, and sent him dashing across the papers, knocking over a bottle of rum and spilling the amber liquid all over the original map.

"Bedeviled beast!" Rowan cursed and started for the cat, but he dove under the bed. "'Tis perfectly good rum you spilled. And all over my map!"

"You didn't have to shout so loudly." Lady Minx scolded, and he spun to find her sopping up the rum with one of his shirts.

He plucked it from her hand. "Faith now! 'Tis my shirt!"

"Well, if you wouldn't leave them lying all over the floor, I wouldn't have grabbed it." Her tone was all spunk and fire—just like the old Lady Minx—but her eyes held fear as she backed away from him.

Taking a minute to settle his temper, he tossed his shirt in the corner and drew a deep breath. Ink splotches blurred in a puddle of rum on the top half of the map. He fisted his hands and forced back a growl that would no doubt send everyone scurrying from the cabin. 'Twas only the sight of the new map beside it that stayed him.

Farley chuckled. "That kitten reminds me o'—"

Rowan dismissed him with a snap, sending the old man darting from the room, but not before Rowan noted the mischievous grin on Nick's face.

"You put her up to this?" he asked his friend.

Nick rubbed his chin and nodded toward the map. "Och, now, dinna ye want the infernal thing deciphered?"

"Devils Blood! Play not the innocent with me, Nick. Besides, 'twas to no avail. 'Tis obvious from these scribblings"—he gestured toward nonsensical numbers and letters strewn across a new piece of parchment—"that she found the code too difficult."

"Maybe you should ask me before you jump to your numbskull conclusions."

Her impudent tone brought his eyes to hers. *Numbskull?* Hmm. Rowan was sure he'd just been insulted, but his angry retort fell flat on his lips when the lady spread out the new map beside the first, a look of smug satisfaction on her lovely face.

"Looks t' be a near-perfect depiction of the Spanish Main!" Nick proclaimed as he eased beside him.

And indeed it did, crudely drawn, but Rowan recognized the islands and land masses, and they seemed to be in the correct positions.

Lady Minx pointed to the string of letters atop the old map. "A transpositional cipher, a Scytale actually, used by the Ancient Greeks." Her tone bore an excitement he'd never heard in her before. "Quite simple in its design, really. Anyone with knowledge of code could crack it. You just take these letters and wrap them around the right size rod." She picked up a roll of parchment. "Only took four tries to find the right diameter."

Rowan scratched his head. He had no idea what she was talking about—as usual. "What of these numbers and the strange shape of these islands?" He gestured toward rows of numbers at the center of one of the land masses on the old map.

"They are also code. They reveal the exact dimensions of the real island and the distance in all directions from the land masses that surround it." She pointed to her new map. "So all I had to do was translate them and then draw their actual shape here."

She went on to describe how once she had the correct measurements and distances between each piece of land, she was able to place everything in the correct proportions on the new map.

The infernal cat slunk out from under the bed and eyed Rowan with smug disdain. He'd chase the beastie out of his cabin if he wasn't so interested in what the lady was saying.

She leaned over the map, one curl dangling from the scarf—his scarf—binding her hair atop her head in a rather alluring style that revealed her slender, creamy neck. A neck that led down to creamy curves peeking above her bodice. Rowan swallowed and shifted his thoughts to the matter at hand—the treasure. "Where is the hidden treasure?"

"See this word here?" She pointed to the original map where a nonsensical word was written on a large island. "That says treasure."

He shifted his gaze to the map she had drawn, seeking the true location of the island.

She beat him to it with the tip of her slender finger. "Here. This tiny dot. As far as I can tell, it's a very small island just off the coast of St. Thomas."

"I know the place!" Nick slapped Rowan on the back. "'Tis tha' speck of dirt where we sought refuge from tha' squall last year. Though it wasna much of a haven, if I remember. Too small an' no real harbor for anchorage."

"Aye, but it had a series of underwater caves inland," Rowan added with a grin. "The perfect place to hide treasure."

"Yup. That's where it is." Lady Minx smiled and lowered into his chair, rather pleased with herself. The cat leapt in her lap as if there were no place it would rather be.

Rowan couldn't blame him.

"Good work," he finally said, reaching for his rum, but finding the bottle empty. Growling, he glared at the cat nestling against Lady Minx's soft curves. He could swear the mangy critter grinned at him.

"How about a reward, Captain?" Morgan cocked her head. "The amulet? Surely I've earned the right to at least hold it?"

"Seems fair to me." Nick rubbed his hands together. "When do we set sail, Captain?"

Ignoring them both, Rowan strode to his cabinet and began selecting the weapons he needed—a long knife to join the sword at his side, an axe, and two pistols. "I will consider it, Lady Minx. After I return. *If* your map leads us to the treasure, that is."

"After you return?" she asked, the exuberance in her voice dripping out with each word.

"I must make haste to save Marianne before 'tis too late." He slipped his baldric over his head.

Nick groaned.

"You're *still* going?" Morgan said. "I can't believe you're still going!"

Stuffing pistols into his baldric, Rowan turned, shifting his gaze between Nick and Morgan. "Ah, so that's why you deciphered the map, to distract me from my mission."

"Which should ha' worked since ye've wanted nothing more than this particular treasure for as long as I can remember."

"You surprise me, my friend. Should I allow a chestful of jewels and doubloons keep me from saving a life?"

"'Tis your life I'm trying to save," Nick muttered with a scowl as he plunked on the edge of the desk.

Rowan chuckled. "Begad, what madness is this? You play the selfish rogue and I, the saint?"

"Och, now. I wish that were true." Nick snorted.

Lady Minx rose, the cat still in her arms. "Can't you see we are just trying to save your life?"

He dared to cup her cheek in his hand. "Your care has not escaped my notice, Lady Minx." Instead of jerking away, she leaned into his touch. A speck of affection appeared beside the angst in her eyes, giving him hope she truly cared for him. Even if she had translated the map in order to get the amulet.

"Never fear, I will return. Alas, by your own account, I am not to die for another twenty years."

She moved from his touch. "But my presence here may have changed that."

"Pshaw! You worry overmuch. When I return, we shall embark on an adventure. Boatloads of treasure await us, Lady Minx—more than you could ever imagine, even in your time."

"I don't care about the treasure. I care …" She slammed her mouth shut then raised angry eyes his way. "I can't believe you slept with another man's wife. Especially *that* man. Total yuk."

"His wife is much prettier than he."

"Very funny." She released a sigh. "If you don't die by his sword now, you'll die from another jealous husband's later on."

He closed the distance between them. "Yet, I have discovered I might be persuaded against such a course."

Her expression softened. "But not this course. Not this night. Promise me you'll return. I demand it, in fact."

"I'm wholly at your feet." He swept a bow before her.

"I doubt you're holy anywhere," she retorted, causing him to laugh.

He ran a finger over her cheek. "On that point, I'll agree."

"Obstinate, stubborn, pigheaded …" She flattened her lips, jaw working and eyes flaring. "I won't be a part of this. If you want to get yourself killed, go right ahead." And with that, she and the beastie in her arms stormed out the door. Halfway down the companionway, Rowan heard her stumble over her skirts and growl.

"Ye are a fool is wha' ye are," Nick said after she left.

"And this fool shall return anon." Rowan circled his desk. "You will keep an eye out for her. And on the impossibility that I should not return—"

"I dinna wan' t' hear it." Nick held up a hand.

"You *will* hear it, and you'll obey me should your God seek an audience with me before the night's end."

"Ye best pray He doesn't, Captain. For I am no' sure ye are ready t' meet Him."

Morgan alternated between sitting on the window ledge in Rowan's cabin and pacing before it. Only blackness gaped at her through the salt-encrusted panes, but somehow, keeping vigil for Rowan made her feel she was at least doing something useful. The fool had brought along only one man, Terrin—a big fellow who was apparently an "expert shot with both pistol and fist" according to Nick. Also according to Nick—because Morgan had not been on deck when Rowan departed—Rowan had said he should return within four hours. If not, then something had gone amiss, and Nick was to follow through with his instructions. What those were,

Morgan had no idea and Nick wouldn't say. No doubt he didn't want to cause her alarm.

Yet at the moment, all she felt was alarm.

The boat rolled over an incoming wave, swinging the lantern hanging on the ceiling and casting bands of light and shadow over the room. Blackbeard nudged her arm, seeking pets. But even the cat couldn't soothe Morgan tonight.

At first she'd thought her fears stemmed from the fact that losing Rowan would mean losing her protector, her provider, and the one constant that linked her back to her own time. But she soon realized it was much more than that. She feared for his safety, she feared for his life. She feared she'd never see him again. Never see those charming quirks of his, never witness his unique larger-than-life personality, how one side of his lips curved in a roguish grin at the sight of her, his commanding presence, his intelligence and wit, how his men respected him and leapt to do his bidding with but one command … and the way he looked at her as if she were that chest of gold he'd been seeking for so long.

The thought of losing him cut her deep to her core.

Yup, her man-picker was most definitely broken. For some demented reason she had a thing for bad boys—the ruggedly handsome, devil-may-care types who made girls swoon and parents have nightmares. The Harley-riding, hell-raising, smooth as glass, confident men who could charm their way into a nun's bedroom. Yup. Morgan had fallen for a bad boy who put all the bad boys in her time to shame. A pirate!

If her mother could see her now. The thought brought a giggle to her lips as she stood and took up a pace again. Though there were no clocks on this stupid boat, surely four hours had passed.

And still no Rowan.

Her stomach cramped and she pressed a hand over it when the door opened, and Edith entered with a tray.

"I thought you might like some tea, child. To help wit' the waiting."

"That's kind of you, Edith. Thank you."

She set down the tray and poured Morgan a steaming cup. "No sense in worrying yourself crazy over him. If I knows anything 'bout the captain, he can take care of hisself."

Lifting the cup, Morgan took a sip. "I hope you're right."

"I *am* right." Edith poured her own cup then sat down in one of the chairs and glanced around the room. "I never been in here wit'out the captain. He isn't the most tidy man, is he?"

Morgan couldn't help but smile as she took in his clothes on the floor, his crumpled bed, and messy desk. She had started to put things in order, but even that did not unfrazzle her nerves. "Aren't you worried what will happen to you and Farley if Rowan … dies?" She could barely eke out that last word.

"Course not. God knows what will happen an' He's already gots a plan."

Morgan's mother had spouted the same Christian cliché on more than one occasion. The only difference was, when things went nuts, Morgan's mom went nuts. Whereas when uncertainty surrounded this kind lady before her, she grew even more peaceful. If that were possible.

Edith took another sip and slid her cup on the desk. "Why don't we pray for him?"

Morgan laughed. "God doesn't honor prayers for pirates."

"God hears all prayers, child. He loves all His children, 'specially pirates." She winked.

Shouts echoed from outside, along with the sound of something banging against the hull. Footsteps scampered, and Morgan exchanged a smile with Edith. "Thank God. He's back."

Only it wasn't Rowan who marched through the open door in that confident swagger of his. It was Nick, followed by three men, one of them a brawny man whose clothes dripped water all over the floor.

Her heart caved in on itself.

"Where's Rowan?" She peered around Nick down the shadowy hall, refusing to accept the truth.

The brawny pirate cursed and wrung water from his coat into a puddle on the floor. "I barely escaped wit' me life. That dung-souled cockerel!" Only then did Morgan see blood staining his shirt.

Nick forced the man to remove his coat and sit. "Edith, go get Farley."

The woman darted off.

"Where's Rowan?" Morgan asked again, this time her voice sounded hollow.

The beefy man gazed up at her and snarled. "Captured, by that son of a maggot, Bloodmoon."

Morgan's legs gave out. Thankfully there was a chair nearby. Toppling into it, she raised a hand to her pulsing throat. "He'll kill him. We must rescue him!"

"Nay." Nick faced the other two pirates. "Once the boat is in its cradle, raise anchor, unfurl all sails, an' tell Scratch t' set course for Jamaica."

Morgan couldn't believe her ears. "Leaving? We can't leave him here!"

Farley rushed in with his medical satchel in hand and Edith on his heels. As he knelt to work on the bleeding man, Nick swung to face her. The terror streaking across his eyes did nothing to calm her nerves. "Upon his capture, Rowan ordered me no' t' attempt a rescue, lass. Petit-Goâve is a French town, an enemy city, an' word is Bloodmoon ha' a small army guarding his house."

"I can attest t' that," the wounded pirate said, wincing as Farley peeled off his shirt. "'Sides, he's not stayin' there fer long. Sailin' out first thing in the mornin', is what we heard.

To join wit' two other ships and capture that Spanish fleet sailin' from Nombre de Dios."

"Good," Morgan said, hope rising. "Less men to battle when we rescue Rowan."

"Bloodmoon will take him." Nick stared out the window, rubbing his chin.

Terror drove Morgan to her feet. "To kill him!"

"Nay, lass. Rowan still ha' the map Bloodmoon seeks, no? He won't kill him until he has it in his greedy hands."

"Oh, great. He'll just torture him to death."

Nick's silence confirmed her fears, and she leaned against the desk. Taking her arm, Edith led her back to the chair. "Now, now, child. It'll be all right. You'll see."

"Ouch!" The pirate shouted as Farley poured rum on his wound.

"What about Marianne?" Morgan asked. "Did you find her?"

"Aye, murdered in her bed, she was," the pirate said. "Just a hour or so afore we got there by the looks o' her."

Oddly, Morgan felt sorry for the lady. Her only crime was falling for Rowan, something Morgan could well understand. "So it was a useless mission just like you said, Nick."

"We was about to leave, we was ... but two o' Bloodmoon's men came upon us. We fought them off but the noise musta brought the others. Ouch, careful ye old sawbones!" the pirate shouted at Farley.

"D'ye want yer insides spillin' out? Stay still so I can stitch ye up."

Morgan stared at Nick, who was still looking out the window. "Then we must go after him. He'll be easier to rescue on a boat, right?"

"Ship and aye." He spun around. "But we'll need help."

"I don't understand."

"'Twas Rowan's orders. Head to Kingston and find his sister and her husband, The Pirate Earl."

The Redemption

Chapter 19

Morgan had now been on a boat—ship—for twelve days, and had come to know the various hums and creaks of wood, jerks and cants of decks, and flutter and thump of sails to indicate that they were turning, speeding up, or slowing. At the moment they were slowing … considerably, and turning slightly, and she wondered if they'd arrived at Kingston.

She hadn't left Edith's cabin for two days, too afraid to wander about the ship without Rowan in charge, too afraid to do much of anything but sit with Blackbeard and plead with God for Rowan's life. But as usual, heaven was silent.

She would probably die of cancer in a few months, but did she have to ruin Rowan's life in the process? If not for her, he wouldn't be a prisoner on Bloodmoon's ship and suffering God-only-knew-what tortures. How was she supposed to live out the rest of her agonizing life knowing that? She dropped her head in her hands. *Why, why did You send me back in time, God?*

But she was done crying and praying. It did no good anyway. Not for her tight nerves, nor for her predicament. Blackbeard circled her feet and meowed. Scooping him up, she rose and paced the small cabin again. Two feet in one direction, two feet back, with an occasional glance out the porthole—if she stood on her tiptoes—to remind herself she hadn't been buried in a four-foot-cube coffin and left for dead.

Edith did much to remind her of that glorious fact, as the woman constantly checked on Morgan, brought her food, and tended to her needs. Morgan apologized profusely for intruding on her space and evicting her husband to sleep with the other men in the gun room, but Edith was her usual kind self, waving her hand through the air and declaring a little separation now and then was good for a marriage. What a kind, unselfish woman. She even took time out of her duties to bring Morgan ginger tea for her upset stomach, a rather nasty herbal concoction for her cancer, and biscuits and dried beef for supper. Not to mention the fish soaked in coconut milk for Blackbeard.

Such a lovely lady deserved more than a depressed, panic-stricken, sobbing roommate, and Morgan had determined to do her best to cheer up.

After all, a pinprick of hope remained. She'd not missed the glimmer in Nick's eyes when he said they were going to find Rowan's sister and some pirate Earl. Surely Rowan wouldn't have ordered such a thing unless he knew they would help him.

Edith burst into the room, rubbing her apron and smelling of fish and flour. "Come above, child. You'll want to see Kingston harbor an' what's left o' Port Royal."

"I don't know." Morgan sighed. "Is it safe?"

"O' course! Come along, now." Edith all but dragged her out the door and up a ladder, through a hatch, and onto the main deck. Sunlight blinded her. Wind slapped her, flapping her dress and sending her hair into a tailspin as she stumbled behind the older woman who took her up another ladder to another deck where Nick stood beside the helmsman.

He smiled at her, but continued spouting orders to the crew to lower sail and turn the tiller. Edith dragged her to the railing. On the main deck, pirates pulled thick, heavy ropes, while above among the sails, others lined the beams and gathered loose sail cloth.

"Look!" Edith pointed. "There's Port Royal!"

Shielding her eyes from the sun, Morgan gazed off the front of the boat where a strip of land reached into the sea like a long pointy finger.

"Haul taut! Furl mainsail and spanker! Two points to starboard!" Nick shouted, and Scratch repeated the order from the main deck.

The boat tilted and Morgan clung to the railing as they slowed even further and headed for an opening between the strip and the mainland.

Edith grew silent, her sorrowful stare upon what appeared to be broken-down buildings lining the shore of the peninsula. The *Reckoning* glided past a fort that extended out from the land, guarding the harbor with guns poking through turrets and men marching on top of its walls. Though some of the structure's bricks had crumbled, most of it was intact. Which is more than Morgan could say for the buildings in the city behind it. A few stood upright, including a church with a tall white steeple, but otherwise, only ruins extended as far as the eye could see.

"*This* was your home?" Morgan asked.

Edith remained staring at the sight, an unusual sorrow clouding her expression. "I only seen it once since the quake. So much is missing, down at the bottom of the sea."

Morgan swung an arm around Edith's shoulder and drew her close. "I'm sorry."

"So many people died. They's only now starting to build it up again." She gestured to the men assembled around various buildings hauling planks of wood and wagon-loads of bricks.

"It will return to its former glory, I'm sure."

"No, I doubts it. The sea has reclaimed most o' the land. An' the people have moved to Kingston across the harbor." She tilted her head toward the mainland as they passed Port

Royal and sailed into the most beautiful bay Morgan had ever seen.

Swaths of glittering turquoise and emerald filled a natural harbor sheltered from the sea by the peninsula of Port Royal—a giant pool of calm, crystalline waters that stretched toward the mainland, where a golden shore gave way to blue mountains beyond.

Several ships anchored in the harbor, most congregated toward the mainland, and a vision crossed Morgan's mind of cruise ships and people jet-skiing and parasailing, reminding her once again that she was no longer in the twenty-first century. She closed her eyes, listening to the sound of seagulls and the water humming over the hull as the ship slid through the warm bay. How had her life become so out of control? All her plans and schedules ripped from her—everything that made her feel secure and safe. Now, she had no idea what was coming in the next minute, let alone the next day.

As if sensing her discomfort, Edith laid a hand on Morgan's arm. "Don't worry, child. It'll be alright, you'll see."

Morgan opened her eyes to the woman's reassuring smile. Her mother had said the same thing on so many occasions, Morgan no longer believed it.

"All hands, bring ship to anchor!" Nick bellowed across the deck before he appeared beside Morgan and gazed toward the mainland. Other than a few wooden buildings, most of the city of Kingston was comprised of tents, which surprised Morgan since she'd heard the earthquake had happened two years ago. But she supposed without machinery or easy access to building materials, things in this century didn't happen fast.

They slid past several tall ships rocking in the bay.

Nick slammed his hand on the railing. "Och, aye. God is indeed wi' us!" His exuberance caused Morgan to follow his gaze to two ships anchored closer to the city.

Edith squinted toward the vessels.

"Why? Who is it?" Morgan asked.

"The *Ransom* is here like Rowan said. Tha's his sister's ship." He gestured toward a ship with only two masts anchored close to another one of similar size. "An' there is another surprise as well," Nick exclaimed. "See tha' other ship beside it. That's the *Redemption*."

Morgan guessed the name was supposed to produce some reaction. It did in Edith, who offered a "Praise be to God!"

Nick laughed and scratched his beard. "You really are no' from our time, lassie, eh? Tha's the great pirate-missionary's ship, the famous Captain Edmund Merrick."

Clank! Alexander Hyde, Lord Munthrope, met his mother's blade high and to the right. He hadn't expected such a swift move for one so old, but as usual, the lady surprised him. Spinning away from him, she slashed toward his legs, but he met her thrust and leapt out of the way. Sweat formed on his forehead. Afternoon sun showed no mercy to those foolish enough to swordplay above deck. But how could he resist his mother's challenge?

She grinned at him as she whipped her blade through the air. "Had enough, my son?"

Alex dabbed the sweat from his brow, wondering why his mother never appeared to perspire, but only to glisten in the sunlight. In truth, the lady appeared far younger than her over-fifty age—the exact number she would not divulge. Mayhap 'twas the breeches, boots, shirt, and doublet which made her look more like a boy than a woman, Mayhap 'twas the bounty of golden curls—in which only a few streaks of gray appeared—that defied her every attempt to restrain with pin and clip.

Or mayhap 'twas the way she now twirled her blade and challenged him with her sparkling blue eyes.

Lud, but he had missed her during the five years he'd lived in Port Royal. He swung his blade to her left. Their swords met with a chime that echoed in the still air and brought a clap from Rusty, the helmsman standing watch on the quarterdeck. White teeth beamed from within a freckled face haloed by a bush of flaming hair tamed by a black bandanna.

"Ye show him, milady!" he shouted.

Lady Hyde cocked her head and gave her son a sly look. "Pray tell, don't go easy on me, Alex. I need the practice."

"Easy? Pshaw!" He lunged toward her midsection. She shoved his blade aside and leapt onto the bulwarks before he could swoop down on her again. "I give you my all, milady." Though, in truth, he *did* hold back slightly. Forsooth, she was a woman, after all.

"Alack, 'tis unfair you've been practicing with Father," he added.

"Whilst you have grown fat and sluggish in your newly-married life, my son? What has happened to the great pirate earl?" She laughed, jumped down from the bulwarks, and rushed him again. Sunlight glimmered off their blades as they collided and rang through the humid air.

Alex gently shoved her back and cut in to her left, but she sprang with the agility and speed of a cat and caught his chest with the tip of her blade. She held it there, a superior grin playing on her lips. "Do you forfeit, Pirate Earl?"

Boot steps preceded an authoritative voice, "What's this, woman? Are you to kill my only son?" Captain Edmund Merrick emerged from the companionway of the *Redemption*, strode toward them, and planted fists on his waist, eyeing them both with an alarm that failed to reach his smile.

Alex's mother lowered her blade, her chest heaving. "Nay, my lord, I'm only trying to rid him of his spongy muscles for our upcoming adventure." She sauntered to her husband and slid her arm through his.

"Spongy?" Alex gave an indignant chuckle and sheathed his blade. "Then, I must confess that, indeed, I *was* holding back, Mother." But she was no longer paying him any mind. Her full attention was on her husband. Shifting his stance over an incoming wavelet, Alex stared at the way his parents looked at each other after nearly thirty years of marriage—as if they'd just met and fallen in love. He only hoped for the same lifelong affection for he and Julianna, though it had certainly proven true for the two years since their wedding.

Ripping his gaze from Charlisse, Merrick faced Alex and gripped his shoulder. "Don't let her win, it only goes to her head. She fancies herself a pirate, this lady. Ever since she commanded my ship all those years ago."

"And I have more than proven it, milord, *through* all those years since." She rose on tiptoes and kissed his cheek, making Alex suddenly sad he hadn't been allowed on their many adventures when he'd been a child. In truth, he'd seen more of his parents these past two years than in all his years growing up. Mayhap, not quite. Still, he was more than thankful to God for the time they had now, spreading God's love throughout the West Indies.

However, he found himself all the more ashamed of his wasted years of dissipation and pirating at Port Royal. If not for Juliana and God's mercy, he'd be at the bottom of the bay with so many of Port Royal's pirates. Yet, for some unknown reason, God had saved him—saved him and forgiven him and given him new life.

"Alex," the sound of his wife's voice brought his gaze to Jackson, his father's first mate, helping her through the hatch from below. The large bald Negro had sailed with Merrick ever since Alex could remember, and though he had slowed down a bit, his powerful frame still invoked fear from the hardiest of pirates.

He'd taken to Juliana immediately. Of course. She had that effect on everyone—sweet, generous Juliana.

She thanked Jackson and wobbled toward Alex, her face beaming.

Alex's mother stopped her. "You should be resting in your condition, Juliana. Especially during the heat of the day."

"I know, Lady Hyde, but—"

"When are you going to call me mother?" One brow arched on Charlisse's face.

Juliana laid a hand on her arm and the two ladies exchanged such a loving glance, it made Alex swallow. He knew how much Juliana longed for a mother's love after her own had died five years ago. "Forgive me, *Mother*. I heard the chime of swords, and I grow so bored below."

Merrick swept a hand through his coal black hair, frosted in gray, and snorted. "Ah, don't tell me we have another lady pirate in the family?"

"Do allow her to bear my son first." Alex swung an arm around his wife and drew her close.

"Son, is it?" Merrick smiled and winked at Charlisse.

Alex placed his hand over his wife's swollen belly. "Has to be. No female kicks this hard."

"And *all* night," Juliana added with dismay. "He's causing me nearly as much trouble as your son did while we were courting—dancing and twirling around in there like some foppish jester."

Merrick smiled at Alex. "Let us pray he doesn't emerge covered in satin and lace with white paste on his face."

Alex chuckled. His father referred to Alex's triune persona as the town buffoon, Lord Munthrope, and the feared

Pirate Earl—a deception he'd managed to pull off for many years.

They all laughed, and a glimmer caught Alex's gaze from his ship, the *Ransom*, anchored just a few yards off the *Redemption*'s starboard beam. Jonas, his first mate, hovered over one of the cannons, directing the crew to polish the brass, amongst other things, in preparation to sail on the morrow.

"You expect news of Reena tonight, Father?" Alex asked.

Concern tightened Merrick's stubbled jaw as he stared toward shore. "Aye. The man I sent to investigate arrives soon. His ship was sighted off the eastern shore this morning."

Alex's mother grabbed a lock of her hair, her eyes moistening. "Foolish, foolish girl."

"We will find her, my love." Merrick raised her hand to his lips for a kiss. "God will be with us as He always is."

Jackson marched to the railing and pointed aloft. "Captain, a ship approaches."

They all snapped their gazes in that direction, but it was Juliana who screeched in delight and pushed past Alex.

"'Tis my brother's ship. *The Esther's Dowry*. Or whatever he calls it now. I'd know it anywhere. Rowan has come home!"

Chapter 20

Morgan once again found herself climbing a rope ladder on the side of a pirate ship. This time, instead of Rowan, Nick followed beneath her, both to catch her should she fall and to keep prying eyes from peeking up her billowing skirts.

Nerves even tighter than usual, she had no idea what sort of people she would meet once she got on deck. Pirate missionaries? Quite an oxymoron, if you asked her. You were either one or the other, but how could you be both? Still, if they were willing to help save Rowan, she wouldn't care if they were flying monkeys. In fact, despite her racing heart, she'd insisted on accompanying Nick and his men, not wanting to leave Rowan's fate up to anyone else. Even though Nick seemed a decent enough guy, he *was* a pirate after all. And pirates liked to mutiny, didn't they? As Kerr had already proven.

A thick, tanned arm extended down to her, and she gripped it and allowed the owner to hoist her on board. Attempting to swing her legs with as much modesty as possible over the railing, she landed on the wooden planks, released the man's hand, and gazed up to thank him. Wowza, but the man was handsome … in a dark, rough I'm-*not*-the-boy-next-door sort of way. His grin was even more proof she definitely had a weakness for the wrong type.

Nick leapt behind her, along with Terrin and Scratch.

"Where's Rowan?" A pregnant woman darted up to them. "Where's my brother?"

Nick shook his head. "No' here, lass. I'm sorry."

The lady shrank back as if she'd been slugged and snapped her gaze to the *Reckoning* as if—in defiance of Nick's words—she hoped to find Rowan walking across the deck. Morgan could relate.

"But where? Why? …" She gripped her belly, and the handsome man who'd pulled Morgan on board moved to take the woman's arm for support. So this was Rowan's sister, though Morgan could have probably guessed from her appearance. Same light hair—though Rowan's was a bit darker—same blue eyes, same good looks.

"You must be Captain Merrick," Nick said with a bow toward an older man who stood in the middle of the deck, dressed in black leather, strapped with weapons, and wearing a suspicious scowl. Age lined a tanned but handsome face, while gray slashed his otherwise jet black hair. Morgan glanced between him and the man who'd helped her aboard, realizing they had to be father and son.

"I *am* Merrick," the man replied. "And you best have a good reason for sailing on Captain Dutton's ship without benefit of the Captain himself."

"I do. That's why we've come."

An older woman, dressed in men's clothing stepped forward. "Then answer Juliana's question. Where is her brother?" Her tone bore authority, her blue eyes narrowed upon Nick, while her hand hovered over a sword strapped to her hip.

There were lady pirates too? Hey, what sort of missionaries wore swords? The sun set behind Morgan, but its departure did not relieve the sweat trickling down her back. Why had the wind suddenly halted? She gasped for air beneath her stays, regretting coming aboard with these volatile people.

"He's been captured an' in need of our help," Nick said. "I'm his quartermaster, Nick Doran. This is Scratch, the first mate, an' Terrin." He thumbed to the two men behind him. "An' this is Miss Morgan Shaw."

Merrick and the woman glanced her way but returned their gazes to Nick. "Captured by whom?"

Tired of all this chitchat, Morgan swallowed her fears and forced her way forward. "By Bloodmoon. And he's going to kill him if we don't save him right now. We don't have time for this. He said you would help."

Rowan's sister swung a pointed gaze to Morgan as if just now seeing her. More curiosity than anger tainted her expression.

"Bloodmoon? William Bloodmoon?" Merrick's face twisted in disgust.

"The same," Nick answered.

"Please, you must help him!" Morgan urged. Her nerves were getting the best of her, causing the clouds to spin and her legs to wobble, but she had to speak up. Had to make these people see the seriousness of the situation.

"Who are you?" Rowan's sister asked.

Morgan blew out a sigh. "Nobody. Just a friend."

"A friend of my brother? He has no women friends." She laughed then moved toward Morgan and touched her arm. "You don't look well, Miss Shaw."

"William Bloodmoon. Are you sure?" the handsome man, who must be her husband, asked as he stomped to the railing and gripped it with force.

"Aye."

He shared a look of horror with his father.

"Ye know him?" Nick asked.

"Unfortunately."

"I've had dealings with him as well." Merrick scrubbed a hand over his tight jaw.

"What does Bloodmoon want with him?" the older lady asked.

Nick released a sigh, heavy with shame. "He crossed him, slept wi' his wife, stole a treasure map. 'Tis a long story."

Merrick frowned.

"Oh, Rowan, will you never learn?" Releasing Morgan, Rowan's sister seemed to wither before their eyes. Her husband led her to sit on a nearby barrel.

"What does it matter why?" Morgan's pulse raced out of control. "His life is at stake."

Rowan's sister gazed up at Merrick. "I know he probably deserves what he's getting. But he's my brother."

"Never fear, Juliana." The older man who was all leather and roughness finally smiled, and in that smile, Morgan saw more kindness than she thought possible from such a man. "Of course we will help him. He's family now. Besides, none of us are getting what we deserve."

A tiny wavelet of relief eased through Morgan. Not enough to stop the sky from twirling, but it was a start. "We should leave right away. God knows what Bloodmoon is doing to him as we speak."

"Aye, God does know, but we'll leave first thing in the morning." Merrick's tone carried such finality that no one dared question him.

It was the older woman's turn to approach Morgan. "Dear, you don't look well. Come sit." Though touched by the lady's obvious concern, Morgan resisted her pull. "We can't wait until morning. We have to go now."

"Jackson," Merrick called over his shoulder. "Escort Miss Shaw below. Put her in Macon's cabin."

But Morgan didn't want to go below. She didn't know these people. She wanted to go back to Rowan's boat with Nick. Drat! What had she done?

A black monstrosity emerged from behind Merrick—the biggest man Morgan had ever seen. Even bigger than the

WBA heavyweight fighters Jason had watched on TV. Why, her thigh was as big as his arm! Three gold earrings shimmered from his right ear as he leaned over her, his bald head swirling in her vision.

Her heart near to blasted through her chest. *No!* She couldn't breathe. A buzzing rang through her head.

"She's a wee bit skittish," was the last thing she heard Nick say before the world grew fuzzy and dark.

Something cool touched Morgan's forehead and eased down her cheeks. A whispered prayer misted around her, and for a moment she thought she was home again, a little girl sick in bed while her mother kept watch over her. Good memories from a time before her father left and her mother had wigged out and all was right with the world.

But the gentle sound of wood creaking and the slight sway of her bed jarred her senses back to the present—or the past. Crud. A person could get a headache trying to figure it all out. Wait, she *did* have a headache. A bad one.

She peeled her heavy eyelids open to find the older pirate woman kneeling beside her, holding Morgan's hand and praying, while Rowan's sister sat on the other side, dabbing Morgan with a wet cloth. Such kindness among pirates. Maybe they *were* missionaries, after all. She scanned the room—another closet-size cabin—lit by a single candle on the table and a lantern hanging above.

"There you are," the older woman said upon seeing Morgan awake. "We were worried about you."

Worried about me? Morgan drew a deep breath and tried to sit. "I'm fine. It's just the heat and all these ridiculous tight clothes." And the fact that she needed her meds, and Rowan was being tortured as they spoke, and she'd traveled back through time. But she refrained from freaking them out by saying all those things.

Both women stared at her oddly. She was getting used to that. The older woman helped her sit and handed her a mug of water.

Morgan sipped it hesitantly, waiting for the bitter stale taste she'd grown accustomed to in the water aboard these old boats, but it was sweet and fresh and flavored. Her expression must have given away her surprise for the older lady said, "Ginger for your stomach, peppermint for your headache, and a bit of rum for your nerves."

Morgan stared at her. "How could you possibly have known all …."

"I'm Charlisse," she said. Although, she was probably as old, if not older, than Morgan's mother, there was a youthfulness about her, a liveliness, and a beauty that would last through the ages. A few lines and sags marred an otherwise angelic face framed by golden curls streaked in silver. But it was her eyes that spoke of life. As blue and sparkling as the sea at noonday, they exuded a joy and peace Morgan could only dream of.

"Nice to meet you," was all she could mumble in return. She gulped down more of the sweet water.

"This is my daughter-in-law, Juliana."

Morgan smiled at the other woman, who now circled the cot, wrung out the cloth in a basin on a table, and struggled to lower her pregnant body beside Morgan. She took Morgan's hand and placed the damp cloth against her wrist. "This will help with the heat."

The door opened and another lady entered, another blond beauty, making Morgan feel rather drab in comparison to these three.

"This is Gabrielle, my daughter." Charlisse gestured for the lady to join them. "Come meet Miss Shaw."

"You poor dear." Gabrielle approached, her skirts brushing against the only table in the tiny cabin. "'Tis this horrid Caribbean heat. I don't know how people stand it. I do hope you're feeling better."

The lady leaned over to study Morgan with the kindest smile she'd ever seen. Though taller and thinner, she was just as stunning as her mother, the same sweet face and mass of golden curls, but with dark eyes instead of blue.

The deck rose over a wave, sending the lantern swaying above them.

"Thank you. I'm feeling better now." Morgan was not used to being coddled. Whenever she'd been sick back home, her roommate Tiffany left her alone, and whatever guy she was seeing gave her a wide berth, not wanting to catch anything. "I'm sorry to be any trouble."

"Trouble, Pshaw." Charlisse rose from her knees and lowered into one of the chairs. The pirate outfit she wore clung to a physique that was anything but old. "We all need help now and then."

"Oh my, you're trembling," Juliana remarked, still holding Morgan's hand.

Morgan snatched it back. "It's nothing. Just nerves."

"It must have been frightening for you on board Captain Dutton's ship with all those pirates." Within Charlisse's tone was an empathy that made it seem she knew *exactly* how that felt.

"Especially my brother," Juliana added with a laugh, causing the others to smile, but then she faced Morgan with alarm. "He didn't hurt you, did he?"

Morgan huffed. "You mean did he lure me to his bed?"

Silence enveloped the room, except for the creak of wood and thump of footsteps overhead. Gabrielle gasped. Juliana looked away, and Charlisse smiled. All three blushed. *Drat.* Morgan had forgotten they probably didn't discuss things so openly in this time.

"He was actually very kind to me." She placed a hand over her aching side. "Well, except for locking me in the hold."

"Mercy me!" Juliana took Morgan's hand again. "I'm so sorry."

"He thought I was … it's a long story."

"However did you end up on his ship?" Gabrielle asked.

Morgan swallowed and set her empty mug down, wondering what to tell them. "I was a stowaway. It was an accident really. I … I was looking for a place to hide … and fell asleep … And the next thing I knew, we were at sea." Good. She hadn't lied.

Julianna dabbed Morgan's wrist again with the cool cloth. "What folly possessed you to board a pirate ship in the first place?"

"I didn't know it was a pirate ship." Actually she didn't. Not a real one, anyway.

There came that odd look again from all three women as if they couldn't imagine anyone stupid enough to not recognize a pirate ship.

"Horrifying." Gabrielle fidgeted with her hands in her lap.

Morgan looked up to find Charlisse's steady gaze fixed upon her as if she were poking and prying beneath the surface of Morgan's skin, seeking her secrets. Shifting beneath her knowing eyes, Morgan glanced down at the floorboards.

"Well, 'tis a good thing you are here with us now," Gabrielle declared, raising her chin in the air. "God be praised for bringing you to us safe. A pirate ship is no place for a lady."

Charlisse glanced at her daughter and smiled. "You forget, daughter, 'twas on a pirate ship where I fell in love with your father."

Gabrielle waved the thought aside. "That's different, Mother."

"How is my brother?" Julianna took the cloth and rose.

"Well, strong. A good captain." Morgan surprised herself at the void she felt inside just talking about him. "His men respect him."

Sadness lingered in Juliana's smile. "I wish … I pray he would quit this ludicrous freebooting and come home. I miss him."

"He mentioned to me that he needs to pay you back for something." Morgan drew a deep breath, feeling her nerves already loosen. Was it the rum or the company of these ladies?

"For what?"

Morgan shrugged. "He says he won't come home until he has enough money to pay off his debt and settle you both in luxury."

"Daft man!" Juliana tossed the cloth in the basin, splashing water over the edge.

Charlisse rose and wrapped an arm around her. "Never fear. He will come to his senses soon."

A bell clanged above, echoing through the ship, and drawing the gazes of the women.

"Time to prepare for supper, girls." Charlisse smiled at Morgan. "We have guests tonight."

And with that, both Juliana and Gabrielle made their exit, telling Morgan they'd see her soon.

Her nerves returned. "Where is Nick?" she asked Charlisse.

"You'll see him at dinner." Charlisse opened the doors to a tall cabinet, revealing additional clothing and underthings.

"Here's a fresh gown, and there's some water and clean cloths." She gestured to the basin where Juliana had tossed the rag. Two small towels lay beside it, along with a hair brush, hand mirror and some pins. "I'll leave you to your toilet and will return to escort you to dinner in an hour."

Toilet? Morgan didn't want to tell the lady she hadn't seen a real toilet in thirteen days, but she was sure she meant something else entirely. "Thank you, but I'm not very hungry."

"Of course you are. You're as thin as a ship's mouse."

Morgan frowned and attempted to rise. "Please, we need to go find Rowan. I'm worried for him."

"We will. Have faith." That faith seemed to beam from the lady's eyes as she left, closing the door behind her.

Faith? Morgan couldn't remember the last time she'd had faith in much of anything.

Morgan had been on these old boats long enough to not expect much in the way of dinner. But when she entered the captain's cabin, the sight that met her eyes not only surprised her but caused her mouth to water—something that hadn't happened in quite some time.

A long table took up the center of the room, covered in white linen that shimmered in the light of several candles in silver holders placed down the middle. Around them, platters of food gave off steamy scents of roasted meat, buttery rice, fresh biscuits, and corn. And she suddenly wished she had more of an appetite.

Gabrielle and Juliana were already seated beside Juliana's handsome husband, Alex, while Captain Merrick sat at the head of the table. Also in attendance, another man with short brown hair and thick sideburns whom Morgan had not met. Thankfully Nick was also there, offering her a warm smile. All the men stood when she and Charlisse entered, making Morgan feel even more like a lady than she did in all the layers of frilly skirts she wore.

Even Charlisse had taken off her pirate garb and put on a lovely emerald gown with embroidered lace at the hem and neckline.

Merrick's face lit at the sight of his wife, and he went to escort her, then pulled out her chair as if she were made of precious china. Morgan blinked at the sight. How long had they been married?

Behind him, stern windows like the ones on Rowan's boat, revealed Kingston harbor dappled in moonlight.

"May I introduce Jonas Nash, Miss Shaw." Alex gestured toward the man she didn't know. "My quartermaster and ship's surgeon."

Jonas dipped his head. "A pleasure, Miss."

Morgan smiled and sat beside Nick.

"Normally Jackson would join us, but we didn't want you fainting on us again, Miss Shaw." Merrick chuckled and took his seat.

Crud. The huge black guy. "I'm sorry, Captain. It wasn't him. I was feeling faint before I even saw him." Though the sight of such an enormous man hadn't helped.

"Don't let them bother you, Miss Shaw." Juliana smiled, her golden curls glittering about her neck in the candlelight. "I must admit he frightened me at first as well. But he's truly a kitten beneath all that armor."

At her mention of kittens, Morgan wondered how Blackbeard was faring, but no doubt Edith was taking good care of him.

"Let us pray," Merrick said, and everyone bowed their heads. All except Morgan. She wanted to see for herself whether it was possible these pirates were pious. But everyone *did* actually bow and close their eyes, and the prayer Merrick uttered was short, sincere, and heartfelt. Afterward, everyone said "Amen" exuberantly before they started passing the platters of food.

Though it smelled delicious, Morgan took very little. Her nausea had returned, along with the pain in her side. A constant reminder that her time on earth was coming to an end—a painful, drastic end. Still, if she wasn't able to get back to her time for treatment, she might as well do one good deed before she died—save Rowan Dutton. Despite the fact he was a pirate, he'd been kind to her, saved her, and watched out for her, even when he got nothing in return. Which was more than she could say for the men she'd dated back home.

Nervousness stirred her already agitated stomach. She must bring up the topic of leaving soon to save him. But she was a guest and didn't want to seem rude or ungrateful. Besides, the glass-doored cabinet against the far wall was filled with swords, guns, and other murderous weapons—not to mention the cannon perched at the foot of the bed—all reminders that she was dealing with pirates. *Real* pirates. Missionaries or not.

Nick spooned a heaping pile of meat onto his plate and passed it to her. "We havena been back to Port Royal since soon after the quake. It appears they are attempting t' rebuild the city."

"Aye, but the size of the land has been so drastically reduced"—Alex poured Juliana a glass of wine, his voice filled with sorrow—"'tis unlikely it will ever be the city it once was."

"Sad in a way," Nick returned, "though 'twas a vile den of the worst sorts, no?"

Merrick lifted a fork of roast pig to his mouth and nodded, but Morgan sensed a sorrow about him. "I met God in that city," he said after he swallowed. "'Twas there that Reverend Buchan found me bleeding and drunk in his church." He smiled at his wife. "And 'twas there this pretty young thing walked into the *Drunken Skunk* all by herself and demanded Edward the Terror—the most vicious pirate on the Caribbean—release me!"

Charlisse laughed and shared a knowing smile with Juliana. "What a lady won't do for her man."

Alex snorted and glanced lovingly at his wife. "Lud! For a man? This lady dared to venture unescorted into the most depraved places merely on some minor errand of mercy."

"But if I had not, I would have never met you, for there you were among the most nefarious of cullions," she retorted, grabbing a biscuit off a passing plate.

"Surely, you mean if not for me *saving* you, Sweetums, we wouldn't have met."

"I protest, milord Pirate, I was doing quite well on my own. Almost out the door unscathed I might add."

"Unscathed, bah!" Alex gazed at his wife, a mischievous twinkle in his eye.

Gabrielle threw a hand to her chest and sighed. "I still thrill at hearing how God saved you both. Got you out of the city and onto the *Ransom* before the quake hit."

"Yes, and the orphans and Isaac and Eunice, too," Juliana said.

"You forget Jonas, my good friend." Alex glanced at the brown-haired man, but Jonas' eyes were on Gabrielle. The lady noticed and returned his smile before she shyly looked away.

"I could never forget Jonas," Juliana said with a fond glance toward the man. "He's the only one who kept dragging you back from debauchery to the straight and narrow."

"And a difficult task it was, if I do say so!" Jonas lifted his glass in the air, and Alex saluted him with his.

The boat teetered over a wave, shifting a bowl of guavas and rocking the wine in Morgan's glass. She nibbled her biscuit, hoping it would stay down, but finding the discussion among these pirate-missionaries more than fascinating.

Charlisse glanced fondly at her son. "Reverend Buchan is surely smiling down at you from heaven, seeing how you saved his precious orphans."

Juliana swallowed her mouthful and looked up at Merrick. "Thank you, Me—Father, for helping us relocate them to Barbados. And setting up Eunice and Isaac in a home where they can care for them."

"And sending them monies for support each month," Alex added.

Merrick smiled. "As you did for years with the stipend I sent you."

Alex shook his head. "'Twas the only decent thing I did while in Port Royal."

"You *did* make quite a name for yourself, son," Charlisse said with a teasing glance. "Just not the name your father and I had hoped you would."

Merrick and Jonas laughed.

Merrick ran a hand through his hair, his piercing gaze shifting between Alex and Gabrielle. "We could have been better parents. We left you and your sisters alone far too long. Foolish on our part. We were so zealous in doing God's work, that we neglected the most important work He had given us."

"Not your fault," Alex said. "I was a grown man who made my own choices."

Merrick grimaced. "Not unlike my foolish choices when I was your age. Must children always follow in their parents' footsteps?"

Juliana laid a hand on her husband's. "If they end up where you have ended up, 'tis a good thing. Besides, God has forgiven us all."

Looking embarrassed, Gabrielle shifted her eyes toward Nick and Morgan. "Must we air our family past before our guests?"

Jonas turned toward Morgan with a warm smile. "You'll soon find that Merrick and Charlisse treat everyone, even strangers, as if they were part of their family. 'Tis what makes them such good witnesses for God. All of them." His gaze drifted to Gabrielle again, and she lowered her lashes above a smile.

"So, you are really missionaries?" Morgan finally asked. "And pirates?" she added with a laugh.

"'Tis more like missionaries *to* the pirates," Merrick said. "Though I'll admit to doing some pirating in my past."

"Not to mention the occasional letter of marque which allows you to privateer." Alex plucked another piece of meat from the tray.

Morgan sipped her wine, finding it the only thing that settled her stomach. "I don't understand how you can convert pirates. Aren't they pretty much set in their ways?"

At their odd looks, she added. "Evil, thieves, wicked people who don't care about God and being good."

Alex's eyes—so piercing like his father's—shot to her. "Mayhap, miss. But we don't tell them they have to be good."

"Then what kind of missionaries are you?"

Charlisse shared a glance with her husband. "We tell them they are loved. We tell them they have a good Father, a loving Father, the Creator of all things, who made them and loves them so much that He died for them."

Morgan withheld a cynical snort. "And that works?"

"Everyone wants to be loved and valued." Merrick took his wife's hand in his. "Once they truly believe that God loves them despite all their wickedness, it changes them."

"Love never fails," Charlisse said.

"It casts out all fear," Gabrielle added.

"Amen," Nick and Jonas said together then shared a smile.

Morgan stared down at her uneaten food, feeling like a stranger among these people. They spoke about God as if He were in the next room, as if they really knew Him. If she were honest, after everything that had happened, she didn't believe God loved her. But what did it matter? She still went to church, read her Bible, prayed and did everything right. Well … almost everything.

"When are we going to rescue Rowan," she blurted out. "I can hardly eat for fear of what he suffers."

Merrick kissed his wife's hand then leaned back in his chair. "Tomorrow. At sunrise. Do we know where Bloodmoon is heading?"

"Aye." Nick swallowed the food in his mouth and washed it down with wine. "Something aboot a Spanish treasure fleet sailing from Nombre de Dios."

Merrick nodded and glanced at his son. "We've heard of it. There's more than one pirate headed to plunder them."

Candlelight twinkled in Alex's blue eyes. "Then we'll have to find Bloodmoon before he joins them."

Morgan's breathing returned to normal. Thank God they intended to do something.

A knock on the door startled her. After Merrick's "Enter", a short chubby man entered bearing a paper in his hand and an anxious look on his face. He gave it to Merrick, who broke the wax seal and held it to the candlelight.

Charlisse slowly rose, her face tight and lips pursed.

"Is it about Reena? Pray tell, Merrick, what does it say?"

Alex and Juliana also rose.

"It is as we feared. She has run after Freddy, trying to save him."

"But how can she?" Charlisse's voice cracked. "Pray tell, what ship?"

"HMS *Viper*, apparently."

Alex snatched the letter and perused it. "Do Kent and Isabel know?"

"Nay." Merrick turned and stared out the window. "They were to meet us here in a fortnight. I will leave word where we have gone."

Charlisse sank back to her seat and raised a hand to her throat. "We must find her. We have to save our baby."

Nick leaned toward Morgan. "Reena is their other daughter. I heard them speak of her before."

Alarm prickled over Morgan, even as her stomach sank. Surely they would go after their own daughter first before rescuing a pirate who caused his own predicament?

Chapter 21

Morgan stood at bow of the *Redemption*, gripping the railing with both hands while balancing her feet on the heaving deck, suddenly rethinking her decision to come above as the ship set sail. But she'd had a horrid night filled with nightmares of Rowan dying a torturous death, calling out for her to save him. Several times when she'd woken in a cold sweat, she thought she saw shadowy creatures hovering above her bed. She would have written them off as tricks played by moonlight coming in through the window. Except there was no window. So, she'd cowered beneath her covers all night, longing for day to arrive. As soon as it did, she left the spooky cabin and came above.

Now, closing her eyes, she took in a deep breath of fresh Caribbean air, spiced with tropical flowers and life, as she listened to Captain Merrick bellow orders behind her.

"Let fall main and fore topsails! Haul aft the sheet!"

Footsteps pounded and men shouted further orders as some scrambled across the deck while others leapt into the rope ladders leading above. The boat jumped, seawater misted over her, and she opened her eyes just as the *Redemption* emerged from Kingston Bay into the open sea. Ahead of them—with sails looking like pregnant bellies against the rising sun—the *Reckoning* plowed through the sea, while one glance over her shoulder revealed the *Ransom* following in their wake. Three mighty bo—ships, two captained by former pirates turned missionaries, and one whose captain still roamed the seas in search of treasure.

Despite her tight nerves and upset stomach, Morgan wanted to remember this magnificent moment—the glorious feel of the wind and spray on her face, the heaving of the ship beneath her feet, the sight of majestic ships parting the foamy water, and the way the wind flapped her long flowing skirts and fingered through her hair like a long lost lover.

If she was going to die, better to have lived this adventure during her last days than slowly shrivel away in a hospital bed while people visited with pitying looks and flower arrangements sporting silly balloons that vainly wished her well.

Charlisse, back in her pirate garb, appeared beside her, startling her from her morbid thoughts.

"Thank you for going to save Rowan first," Morgan shouted over the wind. "Nick told me that Reena is your daughter, and she's in some kind of trouble."

A momentary shadow crossed Charlisse's expression, but then it was gone. Turning, she closed her eyes to the rising sun as it scattered gold and peach jewels over the turquoise sea.

"Rowan is in trouble too," she finally said. "And much closer. God is with Reena until we get there."

Sounded like something Morgan's mother would say. "I'm sorry she's in trouble. I know my mother totally freaks when she hasn't heard from me in a while." Speaking of her poor mother, the woman had probably checked into the funny farm by now not knowing what happened to Morgan.

Wind flipped Charlisse's curls into her face, but she shoved them away and studied Morgan curiously. "Where is your mother?"

"San … home. Probably worried."

"You should send word to her."

Morgan wished she could. She nearly laughed at the contents of such a letter.

Mom,

Don't freak, but I've been transported back in time to the year 1694. I'm on a pirate ship sailing to the rescue of the notorious pirate, Rowan Dutton, who's been captured by the vile and evil pirate William Bloodmoon, who is torturing him because Rowan slept with his wife and stole a treasure map leading to a great fortune buried on an island.

Her mother would have a conniption fit, down several pills, and call her church for emergency prayer.

Maybe it was better Morgan couldn't send a letter.

Smiling, she faced forward. Rowan's ship started to turn. Wind dribbled from its sails, causing the canvas to flap violently like the mouths of hungry birds seeking sustenance for the day. Finally, they caught the wind and bloated. "I should have gone back to the *Reckoning* with Nick." She had wanted to, longed to be near memories of Rowan, but everyone seemed of a different opinion.

"On a ship full of pirates? 'Tis no place for a lady."

"Nick would protect me."

"He would try, to be sure, but with the captain gone, the men may not be so willing to follow the code they signed." The ship rolled over a swell, but Charlisse barely shifted her boots for balance. She smiled at Morgan. "Besides, Gabrielle and I are thrilled to have another lady on board."

"You've been very kind. Thank you."

"I would love to get to know you better, Miss Shaw. From whence do you hail? Who are your parents? What dire straits led you to stow away on a pirate ship?"

"My story is not that interesting, I promise." More like unbelievable.

Charlisse nodded and gazed over the sparkling water. "I came to these seas searching for something as well, and I ended up on a pirate ship just like you. Captain Merrick's actually. A lady all alone on a ship full"—she lowered her voice and gripped the hilt of her cutlass—"of lusty, cutthroat pirates."

Morgan chuckled at her pirate accent. "But you survived."

"Yes."

"And fell in love."

Charlisse glanced over her shoulder at her husband, standing on the quarterdeck, feet spread apart, wind flapping his shirt and hair. "Indeed."

"And it's been smooth sailing ever since?" Morgan asked, curious as to what kept them so happy together.

Charlisse laughed. "With Merrick? Nay! We've had our share of troublesome times. Every marriage does."

Some more than others, apparently. "What is your secret?"

Charlisse cocked her head and studied Morgan. "Love God with all your heart, keep Him at the center of your marriage, and find a good man."

Morgan couldn't help but grin at the simplicity of her advice, naive though it may be. Her parents had both been Christians, and she was sure her mom thought her dad was a good man when she married him.

"So, Miss Shaw, what *did* you come to the Caribbean in search of?"

Morgan stared out to sea. "Nothing. I'm not looking for anything." Truthfully, she wasn't, hadn't been when she boarded Rowan's ship. She'd just wanted to hide—from Jason, from her life, from her cancer.

The ship creaked over a wave, misting them with cool water. Charlisse put her hand on top of Morgan's. "Sometimes we may not even know we are searching for something."

Morgan had no idea what that meant.

"Helm ten degrees to starboard! Ease sheets and braces!" Merrick bellowed and Jackson repeated, adding, "Let go fore tack!"

The *Redemption* veered to the right, following the *Reckoning*, white foam spewing off its stern.

Morgan gripped the railing tighter. "Did you find what you were looking for? I mean, besides Merrick?"

"Yes, and much more," Charlisse said. "I'll tell you all about it sometime. But first, you must answer me one question."

"Sure."

"By all that is Holy, how did you ever fall in love with Rowan Dutton?"

Morgan's heart stopped beating. She tore her eyes away from Charlisse's taunting grin and faced forward again.

She didn't answer. Mainly because she didn't even know if she *had* fallen in love with him. Sure, she cared about him, but love? Crud. Was it that obvious? Foolish, foolish girl! She rubbed her temples where an ache came to life. Begging off with a headache, she excused herself and headed below, hoping to take a nap, willing to face her haunted cabin rather than confront her feelings for Rowan. But instead, the rolling of the ship and the roiling of her stomach prevented rest. So, she paced, stared in the small mirror hanging above the dresser, brushed her hair, practiced lighting the candle with flint and steel—never getting the hang of it—and paced again. Like a caged cat, she felt more anxious than she'd ever been, more desperate for escape. Why? She was safer than she'd been since she'd arrived in this time. But something was terribly wrong, an evil foreboding she'd felt since she'd come aboard the *Redemption*, a restlessness that went beyond her normal jitters.

Gabrielle came to take her to dinner, but Morgan insisted she wasn't feeling well. The sweet lady lit a lantern and said she'd have some tea sent down right away. But instead of just tea, Charlisse knocked on her door a few hours later and carried in a tray of food. From the darkness out in the hallway, Morgan assumed night had fallen.

A chill followed Charlisse into the room, and Morgan hugged herself and thanked the woman for thinking of her. Leaving the door open, Charlisse set down the tray and urged Morgan to sit and eat.

"I'm not hungry."

Back in her gown, Charlisse pushed down her skirts and sat on the cot, patting the spot beside her. Happy for the company, Morgan lowered to sit, but as the moments passed, she felt more and more uncomfortable in this lady's presence. There was something in the way Charlisse was looking at her—as if she were once again prying into Morgan's deepest secrets.

"You're ill." Charlisse broke the awkward silence between them.

Morgan bit her lip. "Yes, as I said. My stomach is upset."

Charlisse took her hand in hers. "You're so tight, so nervous. Bound up in fear and anxiety."

Morgan's heart thumped out of control. "How do you know that?" She always tried her best not to act like a nervous nelly in front of others. In fact, most of her friends were surprised to find out she was on anti-anxiety meds.

"I sense spirits on you."

"Spirits?" Morgan jerked her hand back and scooted away. "You aren't some kind of witch doctor?"

"Of course not. Evil spirits, Morgan. I sensed them on you when I first saw you."

"She has the gift." A deep male voice resounded from the door, and Morgan looked up to see Merrick entering, lantern in hand. He shut the door behind him, set the lantern on the table, and took a seat.

Panic sifted through all rational thought. "Are you both nuts? What are you talking about?" Morgan scanned the tiny cabin and saw no way of escape. "This isn't some kind of intervention, is it?"

Merrick rubbed the stubble on his jaw. "I don't know what that is, Miss. We've only come to help. You see, God has given my lovely wife the gift of discerning spirits."

Morgan swallowed, her pulse racing as she searched her memory for where she'd heard that before. Yes, in church. The gifts of the Holy Spirit from Corinthians, if she remembered. Her pastor had only mentioned them in passing, not giving them much credence.

The ship creaked. Water pounded against the hull. Morgan shifted uncomfortably on the seat and hugged herself.

"What is your relationship with God?" Charlisse asked.

So that's what this was about. Morgan lowered her shoulders and released a breath. "You don't have to evangelize me. I'm a Christian. I believe in Jesus and all. Geez, you really *are* missionaries." She gave a half-hearted smile.

Charlisse returned her smile and took Morgan's hand again. "Anxiety and fear are strong in you. Like snakes, they have coiled around you, suffocating you, robbing you of the life God wants you to live."

Visions of the huge snake that nearly crushed Morgan flashed before her. "Wait. If you're talking about demons, Christians can't have demons." She repeated something her pastor had said.

The deck tilted, and Merrick leaned forward, elbows on his knees. "They can't possess a child of God completely, but they can inhabit and torment if a person allows."

"Well, there you go." Morgan flipped her hair over her shoulder. "I never allowed them. In fact, I've been trying to get rid of them for years."

Not that it had done her much good. Not that she believed in demons, anyway. "Besides, they aren't demons. I'm just a nervous person. I got it from my mom."

Charlisse cocked her head. "'Tis true. Not everything is demonic. But some things are." She squeezed her hand. "And you must believe me, I sense them on you." She continued to hold Morgan's hand tight while she closed her eyes. "There's another spirit here. A spirit of sickness, disease, death."

Morgan's gut knotted. Her palms grew sweaty. She tried to yank her hand back, but Charlisse held it tight.

"Cancer." Charlisse opened her eyes.

"How do you know that?" Morgan jumped to her feet. Had Edith told her? But no, they'd never met.

"Right here." Charlisse raised her hand to hover over Morgan's right side.

Okay, this was getting a little too freaky. Hugging herself, Morgan backed against the wall. "There's no way you could know that." She bent over, trying to catch her breath. "My heart. I feel like it's going to explode!"

"They know their time is short. They are only trying to frighten you." Morgan felt Charlisse's hand on her arm again.

"They're succeeding." She managed to cough out.

"We want to pray for you, Morgan." The sound of Merrick's boot steps filled the air. "God wants to deliver you from these oppressors. He wants to set you free."

"Can you even do this?" A cyclone of needles sped through Morgan, crimping her with pain. She looked up to see Merrick standing behind Charlisse, his eyes flooded with concern, care, even love. "I mean, Jesus dealt with demons, but that was a long time ago, and He was God."

"God never changes, Miss Shaw," Merrick said. "And Jesus told us we would do even greater things than He did."

Charlisse tightened her grip on Morgan. "Do you want them gone?"

"Of course." Morgan flattened against the wall, feeling the knotty wood press into her stays. "Have you done this before? Is my head going to spin around? Am I going to spew green vomit? Don't we need a priest?"

What was she thinking? This was nuts! These people were nuts! Although at the moment they looked at her as if *she* were nuts.

"I've cast out many demons and never seen that." Charlisse smiled. "They must go when we command them in the name of Jesus. There is naught to fear."

Easy for her to say. A buzzing filled Morgan's head, filtering through her body until every nerve was ready to explode.

Charlisse led her to sit on the cot again.

Morgan dropped her head in her hands and squeezed her temples. "I still don't know what to believe. I've never seen this or heard of it in our church." Though there'd been rumors of some charismatic crazies casting out demons in the church down the street.

A throb rose where the cancer consumed her body. Morgan pressed a hand over it and groaned. It felt hot to the touch. What was going on? She lifted her gaze, but her head was as heavy as a bowling ball. A breeze fluttered the flame in the lantern on the table, casting ghoulish shadows over the ceiling. A breeze? From where? Charlisse and Merrick felt it too, for they both glanced around. Cold. It was so cold. How did it become so cold all of a sudden? Morgan hugged herself, her breath coming fast and misty.

Charlisse and Merrick exchanged a knowing glance before they both laid hands on Morgan.

"Spirit of anxiety, spirit of fear, spirit of cancer, we command you to depart this woman and never return in the name of Jesus."

For a moment nothing happened. The ship moaned as wind and wave whistled against the hull. Morgan was about to shrug off all this silliness when an uncontrollable breath rose in her throat, begging for release. She expelled it. Then another rose and another as if she'd just run a marathon and was heaving for air. Her body trembled. She shoved out one final breath with a deep-throated groan that didn't sound like her voice at all. The ship bolted and the roar of water against the hull increased. She glanced up. Shadows vague and dark appeared in the air behind Charlisse and Merrick, drifting up … up …

And then they were gone.

Kneeling before her, Merrick laid a hand on Morgan's side and nodded to reassure her of his actions. "Cancer, in the name of Jesus, I command you to shrivel up and die."

The ever-present, torturous pain released its claw-like grip on Morgan's right side and … simply … vanished. Her heart slowed, her breathing settled, her nerves unwound. And the air warmed once again.

She blinked, stunned. Just a coincidence, right? Or maybe she was dreaming.

Charlisse joined her husband kneeling on the floor before Morgan, both of them taking her hands, both of them uttering the most beautiful prayers for peace, joy, courage, and life to flood Morgan and for the Lord to keep her on the right path, to protect her, to show her how to walk in freedom. Then with a kiss to her forehead, Charlisse rose, and she and Merrick left as quickly as they had come as if they did this sort of thing every night.

But the room was different. The sense of foreboding was gone—the fear, the anxiety, the dread. And Morgan felt so very tired. Unsure what to think or believe, she laid back on the cot and fell into the deepest sleep she'd had in years.

Once again, Rowan yanked the irons that bound his hands. Despite the pain searing his wrists, it was the only thing he could do to try and escape. Mayhap the iron had rusted through and would soon break beneath his efforts. But it remained as strong and formidable as his present dismal lot.

He had no idea what day—or night—it was. The time passed in nightmarish episodes of excruciating torture, followed by mind-numbing hours of darkness, stench, and sweat locked in the hold. He'd awoken just an hour ago, chained within an iron prison, sitting in the soggy bilge that soaked through his breeches and seeped up his shirt, sending a chill through him, despite the heat.

His body had long since ceased seeking relief from pain, his stomach had long since forgotten the feel of food, and his mind had long since given up hope of rescue. Even if Nick managed to find his sister and brother-in-law, why would they bother to risk their lives for the likes of him?

Nay, this was his fate—to be tortured and eventually murdered at the hand of this madman, Bloodmoon.

Trouble was, Rowan knew he deserved it.

He was not a man prone to regrets. But when he'd seen sweet Marianne lying stiff and cold in her bed, her auburn curls a halo around a face whose last expression was one of horror, and a neck covered in bruises where her husband had strangled her, Rowan had felt his first stab of agonizing shame. And it had not left him since.

Not when Bloodmoon had tied him to the top mast for a day, nor when he had given him thirty lashes with the cat-o-nine, nor when he'd unleashed five of his strongest men to "give Rowan a beatin' he'd not soon forget". He deserved it all and more for all the men's wives he'd taken to bed with nary a thought for the pain it might cause them. Nay, Rowan's only thought had always been for his own pleasure.

The sea pounded against the hull, accompanied by the squeal of rats and creaking of crates and barrels. A light appeared in the distance, sliding down a ladder like a waterfall of hope before a pair of boots followed. Then another, and another.

Rowan braced himself for the coming pain.

"Have ye thought about me offer?" Bloodmoon's pockmarked face appeared before the iron bars, made all the more hideous in the lantern light.

Kerr appeared beside him, grinning like the traitorous snake he was, while a third man held another lantern.

"As I have informed you, I do not have the map to which you refer. Aye, I admit to having it once, but it was stolen from me at Charles Town."

"A plague on yer thievin' head!" Bloodmoon gestured for the man behind him to unlock the gate. It swung open with screeches of pain that mimicked the ones blaring through Rowan. Bloodmoon and Kerr stomped inside and stood before him.

Rowan attempted to look up at them, but one of his eyes was swollen shut, and the men's distorted images blurred in the other. "Forgive me if I don't get up, gentlemen. If you're looking for the map, mayhap you should ask Kerr here. He's the one who spread the news of its existence through Charles Town."

"'Twas not me, but your pretty little whore who told Bloodmoon about the map." Kerr stooped, his lips slanting in a victorious grin.

Even knowing he couldn't reach him, Rowan lunged in his direction. The coward shot back, making it worth the pain throbbing up Rowan's arms. "You know what they say about traitors, Kerr. The Kraken swallows them whole and slowly digests them over months and months, then spits out their bones at the bottom of the sea where no one will find them."

The smirk on Kerr's face defied his nervous swallow. "They say the same for adulterers, I'm told."

"Then I shall meet you there," Rowan ground out.

"Enough!" Bloodmoon's bellow echoed through the hold. "For the last time, where is me map?"

"Lud man, I have no idea. Acquit me or kill me and be done with it. I grow weary of your mawkish dalliance."

A sneer followed Bloodmoon's huff. "Let us not rush the inevitable. First ye'll pay for stealin' me wife."

Rowan tried to focus his one eye on the man, but saw only a seething mass of hatred. "With a husband like you, 'tis no wonder she ran into my arms."

The strike came swift and hard and shoved Rowan's face so far to the left, he thought his neck had broken. But no, he was still breathing. Unfortunately.

Bloodmoon's face swelled like a puffer fish, his eyes spikes of fury. "A storm approaches. When it's passed, I'll keelhaul ye until there be no speck o' skin left on yer body."

Rowan returned his glare. "Any man who murders his own wife in her bed deserves hellfire."

Which was exactly where Rowan was going as well.

The next blow drove Rowan back toward blissful unconsciousness.

Chapter 22

Rising before dawn, Morgan slipped from her cabin and made her way down the narrow hallway to the ladder that led above. She wanted some time alone to gaze at the moonlit sea and thank God for her newfound freedom. *True* freedom, for she'd never felt so good. All her life it was as if giant chains had been wrapped around her body, tightened each day by some unknown force, restricting her breathing, squeezing her heart, and jumbling her thoughts. But now, just like that, the chains had fallen off, blown away in the wind as if they were but dust.

She emerged onto the deck and drew in a deep breath. Had anything ever smelled so fresh and alive? The briny air filled her lungs, danced through her hair, and fluttered her skirts as if happy to see her. Halting, she took in the scene. Darkness hovered over the ship—a pirate ship, by all accounts. Yet, for the first time in her life she felt no fear, no nervousness, no depression! She hadn't even tidied up her room before she left—hadn't felt a trace of the overpowering compulsion to put everything in order.

Had God truly delivered her? Had all of her anxieties and depressions been the result of demons? She knew that wasn't true of everyone with these problems, but for her … well, she'd seen them leave with her own eyes, felt the grip of their claws loosen on her soul.

And now … she was a new person. *God, You're real!* Morgan shook her head, realizing she'd never truly believed. She had wanted to believe—desperately wanted everything she read in the Bible to be true. But deep down, where her insecurities brewed and the rejection burned and the cancer had sprouted … deep down, she hadn't been sure. Now, she not only knew He existed, but she knew He loved her! *Her?* Mousy, nerdy, geeky, wimpy Morgan. He loved *her*.

She started for the railing. The ship leapt over a wave, and she tripped on her skirts and tumbled to the side. Strong hands gripped her arm and steadied her waist. A prick of alarm sped through her as she peered through the darkness at the shadowy figure.

"Never fear, Miss Morgan, 'tis me, Merrick." The deep voice scattered her fears as he led her to the railing. "One would think you'd have your sea legs by now."

"It's these ridiculous skirts. I'm not used to wear—" She gripped the wooden rail. "Thank you."

He moved to stand beside her, a dark shadow of power and strength … and something else. A sobering reflection of courage and—dare she say—holiness, goodness. She didn't know whether to be afraid of him or fall at his feet. Yet no one deserved that kind of worship but God. Captain Merrick was a man like any other. Still, from what she'd heard, he was also a missionary who inspired more respect from heathens than the pope himself.

"How do you fare after last night?" he asked.

"I feel free." Morgan smiled. "Thanks to you and your wife."

A cloud moved, streaking his black hair in silver moonlight. His smile crinkled the corners of his dark eyes. "Don't thank us. 'Twas all the Father's doing."

The *Father*. Morgan sighed and glanced over the black sea, swathed in milky light. "Why do you call Him that?"

"Because He *is* my father." Merrick crossed arms over his chest. "I came to these waters years ago running away from my earthly father. What I found was my real Father. The One who will always love me and never leave me."

"I'm nothing more than a nuisance to my earthly father."

"As was I." Merrick chuckled. "Though we mended our relationship later in life." He released a deep sigh. "Fathers … so important to a child's upbringing, yet so many of them fail. So many of *us* fail." His jaw stiffened and Morgan remembered the conversation at dinner and laid a hand on his arm.

"We are only human."

"Indeed." He nodded. "Speaking of bad fathers, did you know that Charlisse's father was Edward the Terror, once the cruelest pirate on the Caribbean? He even tried to kill her."

Morgan laughed. "Okay, she wins in the bad father department." The deck canted, and Merrick placed a hand on her back to steady her. The chivalrous gesture warmed her, and she could see why Charlisse loved this man. Just being near him made Morgan feel safe and cherished. Odd quality for a pirate. "You were a pirate once, too," she stated more than asked.

"Aye. A pretty good one, if I'll admit to it. One of the most successful in the Caribbean. *And* the most feared." He winked at her.

Part of Morgan found that hard to believe, but standing next to this man, who exuded power and authority, she found herself easily picturing him in the role. "But you gave it up for God."

"'Twas nothing to give up but emptiness and vanity, Miss Morgan. And in return I received a life of adventure and purpose I never dreamed of and an eternity in a place far better than this."

Tears burned in Morgan's eyes. "I've gone to church my entire life and never met people like you."

"Never saw pirates in church, eh?" His eyes twinkled with mischief.

Morgan laughed. "That too." She lowered her gaze to watch the foamy sea clawing up the hull. "Most people don't speak about God like you do, as if you really know Him. Like He truly loves you. All I ever heard in church was what a sinner I was and how, because Jesus died for me, I had to try real hard to follow all God's rules to be a good Christian."

"I suppose many people believe that. 'Tis a shame really because Jesus came to set us free from trying to earn our way into heaven. He came to give us new life." Lifting his head to the starlit sky, he smiled as if he were smiling at God Himself. "He offers us new abundant life where we are fully loved as sons and daughters. That is incredible in itself, but He also empowers us with His Spirit to battle the enemy of this world and open people's eyes to the truth."

Rumbling in the distance brought Morgan's gaze to the horizon, where clouds obscured the first glow of dawn. "I feel like my eyes were closed for so many years. I always thought being a Christian was boring. You have shown me what an adventure it is."

Dawn's glimmer settled on Merrick's face, highlighting his strong, stubbled jaw and piercing eyes as he stared over the sea, deep in thought.

Minutes passed before Morgan commented, "People in my church never do what you did last night."

He glanced her way. "Cast out demons?"

"Yeah. Nobody talks about them. Nobody has your wife's gift of discernment. At least no one I know."

The *Redemption* plowed through a wave, showering them with mist. "I find no surprise at the revelation," he said.

Morgan wiped moisture from her arms. "Then how did you come to understand it all?"

"I read the Bible. Another thing most believers don't do. Or are told they *shouldn't* do because they haven't the mind to grasp its meaning. Bah!" He huffed. "God makes His Word plain to those who wish to understand it."

A breeze wafted around Morgan, carrying the spicy scent of rain as men began to crawl up on deck from below, yawning and stretching.

Merrick cleared his throat and raised a questioning brow. "Do tell, Miss Morgan. What is this I hear about you harboring affections for that rapscallion, Rowan Dutton?"

Morgan flattened the traitorous smile that instantly lifted her lips. "I don't know what you're talking about."

"Indeed?" He leaned closer to study her with those imperious eyes of his. "Your expression betrays you."

Even as he said it, heat burst on her cheeks, and she looked away. "How could I love a man who steals for a living?"

Merrick faced the sea, arms over his chest again. "I'm in agreement on that. Especially a proper lady as yourself. Stealing, raping, pillaging, drunkenness, whoring, and other unmentionable wicked acts. Not things which endear a feminine heart."

Morgan cringed at the hideous list. "You're wrong. Rowan isn't like that."

"Rowan, is it?" One eyebrow rose. "So familiar?"

"He may be a pirate, but he doesn't do all those things. Besides, he's been good to me ... protected me ... taken care of me. Even when I was mean to him."

"Ah, defending a pirate, Miss Morgan? What will be next? Marrying one?"

She cut off her quick retort when she saw his smile. "You're teasing me."

"Nay." He shrugged. "Mayhap a bit." He grew serious. "My concern is for your safety, Miss. Having been a pirate— a rather depraved one, I might add—I know how they think. A comely lady as yourself, naive and chaste, would make great sport."

"Sport?" She huffed.

"Prey. The chase of such a prize, along with the capture, brings far more thrills then, if you'll beg my pardon, bedding any trollop."

"But he has never tried anything. He's been a complete gentleman." Except for kissing her.

"He's an unregenerate pirate, and by all his sister's accounts, a man accustomed to charming his way into ladies' beds."

"I know all about that. He's different with me." Was he? Or was he only playing a game. No. Morgan would not believe it. Rowan was a good man. And despite Merrick's warning and all good sense and reason, Morgan loved him. She knew that now.

As if confirming her thoughts, the sun peered above the horizon, an inverted yellow smile, instantly warming her with its golden tendrils.

Merrick's lips grew tight, and he let out a huff of frustration. "You remind me of Charlisse when she was young. So naive, so trusting. Good qualities"—he leaned toward her—"unless you find yourself on a pirate ship."

Golden light drifted over his face, accentuating both the lines and the strength. Yet, the more she looked, the more she saw a softness appear, a concern. "You really *do* care about me."

He shifted his shoulders as if shrugging off her compliment. "I hate seeing a woman taken advantage of. 'Tis my duty to defend them."

"Thank you. That means a lot." She dared to touch his arm. "I promise to be careful."

He nodded and grinned. "Another quality you share with my wife—stubbornness." Then, squinting toward the rising sun, he scanned the horizon. Sailing in front of them, the *Reckoning* materialized in the first rays of light, while one glance over the stern revealed the *Ransom* kept pace behind.

Morgan also noticed a cluster of dark clouds brewing to the east. Merrick saw it too and frowned.

"All hands wear ship!" he shouted over his shoulder. "In mizzen, up main, down foresail!" He faced Morgan again. "A storm approaches."

"It won't stop us from reaching Rowan, will it?"

"Nay, but it might slow us down. Go below. 'Twill get rough on deck." And off he went, braying orders across the deck.

Facing the sea, Morgan closed her eyes to a blast of wind and did the one thing she'd been dying to do since she came on deck. She prayed. Sure, she'd prayed a lot in her life, but it had always felt like talking into the air. This time, even before she spoke a word, she felt God's presence surround her, fill her, embrace her.

She prayed for their safety through the storm and for the *Reckoning* and the *Ransom*. She prayed for her mother and what she must be suffering in Morgan's absence. But most of all, she prayed for Rowan. For his protection, for God to open his eyes to see Him, and for their success in rescuing him without incident.

When she opened her eyes, the waves swelled around the ship, the sky had darkened once again, and the wind whipped around her. But she felt peace inside. More peace than she'd ever known. Looking at the black clouds broiling on the horizon, she whispered into the wind, "Rowan, hang in there. We're coming to get you."

An overwhelming feeling of loss and desperation filled her, and she realized that she truly did love him. That somehow in this mixed-up crazy time-travel adventure, she'd fallen in love with a pirate.

She lowered her gaze and gripped the railing. "Please God, don't let him die."

"That's him. That's Bloodmoon's ensign—a red moon in the shape of a skull." Morgan heard Captain Merrick announce to his first mate, Jackson. Slamming his telescope shut, he stuffed it in his belt and issued a string of orders that sent the man across the deck bellowing to the crew.

Morgan peered through the morning mist but could only make out a dot on the horizon. Still, just the thought that Rowan was near made her heart skip.

She'd spent a long day and night below in her cabin while the storm wreaked havoc upon the seas, feeling much like an old sock tumbling around in a dryer. Charlisse and Gabrielle had kept her company until they retired for the evening. How they could sleep was beyond Morgan, but she used the time to pray—to thank God for delivering her from her anxieties and OCD and probably a host of other problems she wasn't aware of. She wasn't even nauseous anymore, though the ship was bucking like a wild stallion.

As to whether God had healed her from cancer, she didn't know. What she did know was that He loved her, and she trusted in that love. Whatever happened, it would all work out according to His plan. The sea finally settled late into the night, and she caught a couple hours of sleep before she rose, washed up as best she could, and came above.

Now that Bloodmoon had been sighted, she could think of nothing else but saving Rowan. But where were the *Ransom* and the *Reckoning*? She scanned the horizon. Nowhere in sight. Had something happened to them during the storm?

Merrick slid beside her and leaned one elbow on the railing. His graying dark hair was tied behind him, though one loose strand leapt across his stubbled jaw. Leather straps crisscrossed his chest, stuffed with pistols, while a sword hung at his side. Age had not drained him of a vitality and strength of presence that must have been overpowering in his youth. "You should go below, Miss Morgan. We'll be upon them in under an hour, and if I know this raucous cur, he'll put up a fight."

"What happened to the other ships?"

He gazed out to sea. "Thrown off course during the storm. They'll join us soon."

"I'd like to stay here, if you don't mind," Morgan said as if she had a choice. "I want to see Rowan as soon as possible. Maybe I can help?" As soon as the request left her lips, she knew it was ridiculous. What could she possibly do during a ship battle?

Merrick's left eyebrow arched significantly as Charlisse—back in breeches and shirt and strapped with weapons—popped up from below.

"Miss Morgan, unless you are skilled in the art of naval warfare, I highly—" Merrick began but was interrupted by his wife's embrace.

"Charlisse is staying above," Morgan protested. "Isn't she?"

Merrick gave his wife one of those looks Morgan could only dream of—a look of intimacy born from years of love and understanding. "I have tried my best to get my wife to stay below during a skirmish, but alas, 'tis one battle I consistently lose."

"Finally you admit defeat, milord." Charlisse grinned.

"Only temporary surrender." He kissed her forehead.

Emotion burned in Morgan's throat as she watched the loving exchange. She could not remember a single time her parents had looked at each other with such unconditional devotion. Ever. Morgan had given up believing that such romance existed in the world. Apparently, over the years, she had given up believing in a lot of things.

Merrick tore his gaze from his wife. "I must insist you go below, Miss Morgan."

"Let her stay, Merrick." Charlisse put her hands on her hips. "If she's anything like me, which I think she is"—she winked at Morgan—"she'll sneak up here anyway."

Morgan liked this woman more and more by the minute.

Raising hands in the air, Merrick shook his head, kissed Charlisse on the cheek, and headed back to the tiller. Charlisse then gave Morgan strict instructions about where to stand and what to hold onto during battle.

Surprisingly, Morgan felt more excitement than fear as she took up a position clinging to a post beneath what Charlisse called the quarterdeck.

An hour later, as promised, with the *Ransom* and the *Reckoning* still not in sight, the *Redemption* sailed within a mile off Bloodmoon's stern. Two ships had joined the monster—no doubt more pirates. Undeterred, Captain Merrick continued to sail full speed toward them.

"Prepare and run out the guns!" His shout ricocheted above her.

The ship leapt and plunged, sending foamy squalls sweeping over the deck and pouring through holes back to sea. Morgan's arms and legs ached from trying to keep balance, but she wouldn't miss this for the world.

Groups of men hovered over cannons perched at the bow, while one glance over the side revealed the muzzles of more guns punching through the hull.

Oddly, Morgan felt no fear.

One sailor took handfuls of sand from a sack and sprinkled it over the deck. Another group of men spread nets above their heads. Young boys no older than fifteen carried pouches and burning sticks to the sailors manning the guns.

Still Morgan felt no fear.

But when a sword of flaming yellow shot from the stern of Bloodmoon's ship, and Merrick shouted, "Hit the deck!" terror finally flooded her.

Chapter 23

Boom! Boom! A thunderous explosion jarred Rowan from his semi-conscious agony. The ship trembled, timbers moaned, and the sludge by his feet quivered. He opened his good eye, grabbed onto one of the rusty iron bars and attempted to pull himself up.

Regardless of the reason, the cannon fire boded well for Rowan's predicament. Whether Bloodmoon was attacking or being attacked, the encounter would keep him occupied and his thoughts from devising Rowan's next torture. He didn't relish being keelhauled, despite it being the torturous ending he deserved.

A distant cannon boomed and the ship veered to larboard. Rowan flew across his cell, striking bars along the way. Pain seared through muscle and bone. Finally, he wedged himself in the corner as water roared against the hull and the ship canted high in the tack. The bilge sloshed across the deck, rats floating atop on debris. The single lantern hanging on a hook outside his cell sputtered out, leaving him in darkness. Just as well. He didn't wish to see the shot bursting through the hull, the sea's claws gushing in to drag him to the depths.

He only hoped Bloodmoon was as good at battle as he was at torture.

Or did he? Maybe 'twould be better to die now, to sink to Davy Jones' locker, a fitting, honorable death for a Brethren of the Coast.

The ship completed its turn and settled once again. The sea pounded entrance against the hull. *Boom! Boom! Boom! Boom!* Guns exploded in rapid succession. The ship trembled and jerked to starboard. Despite his condition, Rowan itched to go above. There was nothing worse for a pirate captain than to be locked below decks during battle. Besides, he wished to see who they were fighting. If the Spanish, he'd be in no better straits in their hands. If another pirate, he might fare slightly better, but—dare he hope—mayhap 'twas his sister come to the rescue?

Nay. That hope was soon squashed beneath the sound of wood splitting and an ear-piercing explosion.

Rowan covered his head and ducked.

Morgan's ears hurt, as if dozens of people were beating on her ear drums, muffling all other sounds and causing an ache to fill her head. She covered them and crouched against the wall that led up to the quarterdeck as another volley belched from the *Redemption*'s cannons. The ship trembled. Footsteps pounded. Men shouted. While all through the mayhem, Captain Merrick's steady tone invoked nothing but courage and assurance.

"Steady now, men. Braces ease, trim your sheets, trim the bowlines! Watch your luff, Rusty!"

Acrid smoke covered the deck. Holding her breath, Morgan batted it away, rising and trying to peer through the haze at their enemy. To her right, Bloodmoon's ship made a sharp turn away from them, angry foam jetting off its stern and smoke puffing from a hole high on its side. They'd hit her! *Good.* Or was it? Rowan was on board!

"The other ship's comin' straight at us, Cap'n!" one man yelled up to Merrick, and Morgan—tripping on her skirts as usual—sped to the railing and squinted into the distance where men hovered around two cannons perched at the oncoming ship's bow. Two ships against one. No, three. She glanced over the other side of the *Redemption*, where the third pirate ship had turned coming to Bloodmoon's aid. How were they going to fight three pirate ships? Her breath hooked in her throat, and she struggled to release it, lifting up a quick prayer.

The *Redemption* lurched, nearly toppling her as sails flapped and sought the wind above.

Charlisse's voice—a huskier version of it—turned Morgan around to see the lady marching across the main deck, curls tossed in the breeze, hand on the hilt of her sword. "Stand fast, men! Courage! God is with us." Then facing a skinny, soot-faced man beside her, she added, "Load the langrel, Mr. Krane. Aim for her rigging and fire upon my order." The man tipped his hat and rushed off just as her eyes—burning with intensity—met Morgan's.

"What about Rowan?" Morgan shouted above the din. "We don't want to hit him!"

"Never fear. He's below decks," Charlisse replied with assurance before she gave Morgan a motherly you-better-do-what-I-say look and gestured for her to return to her spot by the quarterdeck.

Morgan happily complied, stunned at the sight of the woman commanding these men in battle, while also wondering what it would have been like having a mother like her.

The thought made Morgan smile.

The thunder of cannons turned it into a frown.

Heart racing, Morgan covered her head and braced for impact. The zip and whine of speeding metal filled the air. A splash sounded, followed by the eerie twine of rope snapping. One glance upward told her the shot had ripped through a sail.

Jackson shouted something she couldn't make out, and men scrambled up to fix the damage.

Morgan backed against the wall, mind reeling with the reality of where she was and what she was doing. Yet instead of terror that would have debilitated her, she felt a natural fear, but more excitement than she dared to admit. And she wasn't even medicated!

To her right, Bloodmoon's ship was still making a turn while the other pirate sailed swiftly in their direction, foam curling like a villain's mustache up its bow. To her left, the ship that fired on them was lowering some of their sails and easing closer.

"Should we lower main and course?" Jackson asked.

"Nay," came Merrick's reply. "We'll speed right past their shots, then make a swift tack to starboard. Have the men ready at sail and tiller. Charlisse, my love," he shouted down to the lady who turned and shielded her eyes to look up at him. "Do try and hit their rigging this time." His tone taunted.

Sweeping off her hat, Charlisse bowed before him.

Were these people kidding? Didn't they know they were outnumbered? Morgan wiped sweat from her brow and watched as Charlisse issued further orders to the crew. Perhaps it was their faith that made them so brave. Like David facing Goliath or Daniel in the lions' den, they confronted danger not knowing the outcome, nor knowing whether God would deliver them. Yet trusting Him with the result. In fact, from what she'd seen and heard these past few days, these people lived their entire lives that way, with no worries for today and no plans for tomorrow.

Yes, Morgan had been delivered of her anxiety and fear—thanks be to God—but she doubted she could ever live her life so vicariously. She just wasn't wired that way. There was comfort in plans and schedules, and she was sure God agreed.

Right now, however, a pirate ship sped toward them, intent on sinking them to the depths. A small ship, much like the *Redemption*, it sported a red flag with a black hourglass on it. As it slowed, gun ports popped open on its hull, and ten harbingers of death poked their charred heads through the holes.

Morgan was suddenly glad she'd made peace with God.

Charlisse stood at the head of the companionway as calm as if she were attending church, her gaze fierce upon their enemy, her focus intent. "Fire on the upsweep, Gentlemen!"

Morgan had no idea what that meant, but within seconds the air reverberated with the roar of several cannons. Again smoke suffocated her. Coughing, she covered her face with her arms as Merrick bellowed a string of orders—something about raising tacks and sheets and helm's a lee.

The *Redemption* tilted so far to the right, seawater rushed onto the deck, and it took all of Morgan's dwindling strength to not tumble back out to sea along with it.

Distant guns pounded the air. Morgan tensed, her breath coming hard and fast. The foreboding whiz of cannonballs chimed, then the jarring crunch of wood, the stomp of feet and shouts of fear. The ship staggered beneath the blow. Terror buzzed through her as thoughts of sinking into the sea—or worse, being captured by Bloodmoon—wrangled her mind. But she heard no water gushing and finally dared to peek through the haze. Merrick leapt down from the quarterdeck and joined Charlisse.

"What damage?" he yelled as he leaned over the railing to inspect for himself.

"Larboard timbers crushed at the water line, Cap'n," a sailor replied, "and bulwarks smashed on the foredeck."

Morgan hoped that wasn't a bad thing. Even so, it seemed their enemy had fared much worse. One of their masts was broken, and ropes and sails had fallen to the deck. Merrick's men cheered at the sight as their enemy turned and slowly sailed away.

"Blake, Surk, take some men and get below to patch that hole," Merrick ordered.

"Aye, Cap'n."

As they sped off, Morgan made her way to the railing and peered over the side. Smoke sizzled from a blackened hole the size of her head about three yards down. The only problem was that each time the ship rocked, seawater poured through it into the hold.

"She's sluggish." Charlisse gazed up at the sails.

"Aye," Merrick said. "We lost the foretops and now with this rent in the hull."

Jackson marched across the deck toward them, the three earrings in his ear glittering in the bright sun. "Orders, Cap'n?"

Charlisse plucked the scope from her husband's belt and held it to her eye. But Morgan didn't need it to see that the two other pirate ships were heading straight for them. Bloodmoon's was slightly behind the other one, which had three masts and was much larger than the *Redemption*.

"Load musket shot in the bow swivels and rake them as she approaches." Merrick ran a hand through his hair, jaw tight. "Then veer to port. We'll take on Bloodmoon. He's the one we want." He surveyed the horizon. "Egad, where is Alex?"

Jackson nodded and marched away. "Stations for wearing ship! Clear away head bowlines!"

Morgan inched up beside Merrick, hesitant to disturb him in the middle of a battle. "But we have to be careful, right? Rowan's on board."

Without looking her way, Merrick nodded, but Charlisse smiled, instantly transforming from warrior to mother. "My husband knows what he's doing. My, but you're a brave little thing to stay above."

Brave? No one had ever called Morgan that. And for some reason coming from this woman, it meant the world to her.

Merrick instantly stiffened, and Morgan followed his gaze to the pirate ship that was now only thirty yards off their bow. A flame shot from one of her cannons. Charlisse forced Morgan to the deck.

"All hands down!" Merrick shouted, though he remained standing.

The shot splashed into the sea just feet from them, and Morgan returned to her spot, allowing Merrick and Charlisse to do their work. She wanted to pray but couldn't form a coherent thought, much less the right words. Besides, God knew their situation. And He was here. She could feel Him— like she never had before.

Tension strung tight across the *Redemption* as sailors darted this way and that, obeying their captain and his lady's orders. Above, men adjusted sails as the thick canvas fluttered and then caught the wind in a loud snap. A flash of blond hair drew Morgan's gaze to the foredeck where Charlisse stood behind a group of men manning two cannons.

"FIRE!" Her voice boomeranged and a volcano spewed from the iron beasts.

Whatever damage the shots did to the approaching ship, it wasn't enough to stop their reply as another ear-piercing boom echoed across the sky. Sweat slid beneath Morgan's gown as she waited for the impact, praying to God it didn't land on her and blow her guts all over the place. Not exactly a great visual. Or the way she wanted to end up. But the cannonball whipped past just feet from where she stood and crashed into the left railing before plummeting into the sea.

She expelled a ragged breath and stared at the smoking spikes of wood that could have been her bones. Far too close for comfort.

Morgan didn't have to be a sailor to know that if that shot had hit one of the masts or crashed into the hull below the waterline, they'd be done for.

Merrick bowed his head, lips moving, before he lifted his gaze and shouted orders that brought the *Redemption* into a sharp turn. Bracing herself, Morgan held onto the post as the deck slanted high and seawater gorged over the side.

The pirate ship followed them in relentless pursuit. Men stood on her decks growling and spitting and raising weapons in the air. Morgan swallowed. Not exactly a friendly bunch, were they? They fired another cannon from their bow, missing the *Redemption* by inches. Morgan gazed ahead. Bloodmoon's ship had turned and was coming straight for them. They would be trapped between two enemy ships like meat sandwiched between cannon bread. Ridiculous analogy.

A metallic taste filled her mouth, an old familiar friend she knew quite well—terror. But she instantly doused it with three little words. *I trust You.*

The boom of several cannons rumbled behind them. Merrick pressed the telescope to his eye and scanned the horizon just as the pursuing pirate ship staggered beneath the blows. Whose blows? They hadn't fired at them. An ominous snap and crack split the air, and the top half of one of her masts toppled to the deck. Smoke billowed from a fire below decks.

"Huzzah! Huzzah!" Merrick's crew shouted, fists in the air, and smiles on their faces.

"Who is it?" Charlisse sped to her husband's side.

"'Tis the *Reckoning*!"

Morgan slouched against the wall. *Thank you, God.*

"Praise be to God!" Charlisse shouted as Merrick swerved the scope in Bloodmoon's direction.

"Straight for her, Rusty," he ordered. "Sharpshooters to the tops!"

"Ready the larboard guns!" Charlisse shouted.

Sails flapped above as the *Redemption* completed its turn and sped toward Bloodmoon's ship. Minutes later, they were within thirty yards, bow to bow and closing fast. Cannon blasts drew Morgan's gaze behind them to the *Reckoning* engaged in a fierce battle with the other pirate ship. And winning from the looks of things. *Way to go, Nick!*

A thunderous roar snapped her attention forward. Smoke coiled from two cannons mounted on Bloodmoon's bow. She didn't move, didn't duck, didn't cover her head. If the shots were going to hit her, it really didn't matter anyway.

But they both splashed powerlessly into the sea on either side of the *Redemption*. Morgan released her breath as Charlisse's bellowing order sent their quick reply. Merrick's cannons hit their mark, firing spikes of wood over the railings of Bloodmoon's ship and setting the foremast ablaze. Men scattered like ants, returning in seconds with buckets of water to put out the fire while Bloodmoon strutted across the deck, face red, spitting curses Morgan could hear from where she stood.

Merrick took the tiller from Rusty and maneuvered the ship closer to Bloodmoon's. Gunfire popped in the air like firecrackers. Dashing to Morgan, Charlisse forced her to the deck, then covered her with her body as Jackson ordered the sailors above them to return fire. Deadly bullets rained down upon Bloodmoon's men from the *Redemption's* tops.

Screams and shouts filled the air. The ships collided with a jarring crunch, and Merrick's men tossed roped hooks over the railing and lashed the ships together.

Charlisse rose and grabbed the hilt of her sword. Morgan stood by her side, heart thumping as Merrick's men swarmed the deck, shouting and growling and armed to the teeth. Was she now to be in the middle of hand-to-hand combat?

Bloodmoon stormed toward the intruders, sword in hand, leading his men toward the railing. But one shot in the air from Merrick's pistol, followed by the eerie cock of dozens of guns coming from the twenty men on the main deck and the thirty in the *Redemption*'s tops, stopped them cold.

Merrick planted a boot on the railing, cutlass in hand. "Good quarter will be granted provided you lay down your arms, open your hatches, and haul down your sails. Or my men will be forced to shoot you where you stand."

Chapter 24

Rowan had been at sea long enough, had been in enough of his own battles, to recognize from the shouts filtering down from above, the sounds penetrating the hull's thick wood, and the movement of the ship, that Bloodmoon had been defeated—the inept snok. Whether that was a good thing for Rowan, he had no idea. Regardless, he could do naught but remain chained in irons and await his fate.

Shouts ricocheted back and forth above deck, along with the pounding of feet and the crack of a pistol. He could make out the muffled voice of the victor demanding they lay down their arms. The accent was British and the words and their threat sounded like something a pirate would say, though he did not recognize the voice. Not good news, for he'd made his share of enemies among his fellow freebooters.

The *clank* and *clink* of weapons being tossed into a pile indicated the yellow-livered bloater had indeed surrendered. Rowan's nose itched, and he reached up to scratch it, but the irons jerked his hands back and shot pain through his arms. Something dripped down his forehead. Blood or sweat, he didn't know. A rat began gnawing on his foot and he kicked it away. He reeked like a pile of feces, hadn't eaten in days, and his body felt like it had been trampled by a herd of wild pigs. But a spark of hope ignited at the thought that, if the victors *were* pirates, the first place they'd look for treasure would be the hold, and upon finding Rowan, they'd have to bring him above for their captain to decide his fate. Which meant that before he died, Rowan would at least breathe fresh air, feel the sun on his face, and view the glittering Caribbean one last time.

Voices, the sound of footsteps, and the ray of light trickling down the ladder told him he was right. Two sailors descended, holding lanterns and guns before them, while a third man followed, the silver buckles on his boots revealing that he was the man in charge. Rowan braced himself, trying to make out details in the gloom with his one good eye. He was ill-prepared for the sight of the man who leapt down the final rung of the ladder and glanced around, hands on his hips.

Captain Edmund Merrick, the legend, right here in the hold of Bloodmoon's ship.

Though Rowan had never met the man, he'd seen him at a distance once. And Rowan had run in the opposite direction. He hadn't known whether the great pirate-turned-missionary would preach to him or lock him up, but neither had been a pleasant prospect.

Now, as the legend approached, his eyes glinting in intensity, Rowan felt unusual shame flood him in the man's presence.

He stopped before Rowan's cage and grinned. "You must be Juliana's wayward brother."

For a moment, Rowan couldn't speak, could only blink and stare at the man he both respected and feared. Finally, he returned the legend's smile. "In the flesh, milord. Or what's left of it. Now, pray tell, have you come to preach or punish?"

"Neither." He gestured for one of the men to unlock the cage. "I've come to set you free."

A few minutes later, Rowan emerged onto the deck behind Merrick to a blast of wind, a flash of bright sun, and a feminine shout of glee. The last sound caused him to peer into the glare, his eyes watering, to find the source, but all he saw was a blur of green skirts leaping over the bulwarks and growing larger in his vision.

The lady bounded into him, wrapped her arms around him, and squeezed until every fiber of his body screamed in pain.

Morgan. Her unique sweet scent filled his nose, making him almost not care about the pain. Yet when he cupped her chin and brought her joyous tear-filled face to his, all thoughts of pain vanished beneath the love pouring from her eyes.

"I was so worried about you," she said, her concern turning to horror as she studied him. "What did he do to you?" She wiggled from his embrace. "Drat! I've hurt you. You must be in pain."

"Not anymore." Rowan eased a lock of her hair behind her ear, still not believing she was here, that she cared enough to come for him.

"How touching." Bloodmoon spit onto the deck. "An' whose wife be this, ye craven cockroach?"

Rowan glanced up to see the villainous maggot and several of his men locked within a prison of muskets and pistols aimed their way. On the foredeck, more of his men were bound with ropes and guarded by Merrick's men. A ship was grappled beside them—the *Redemption*, if he was correct—while another ship he'd recognize anywhere sailed toward them. The *Reckoning*! What a grand sight she was with her snowy canvas, trim lines, and foam spraying off her bow. He never thought he'd see her again, or this precious woman beside him, and it took him several minutes to adjust to the idea that he wasn't going to die.

At least not today.

"I shoulda keelhauled ye when I had the chance," Bloodmoon continued his insulting tirade.

"Alas, but you didn't," Merrick returned, approaching the man with an assurance born of years of victories at sea. "Sorry to deprive you of your devilish tortures, Captain."

Now that Rowan saw Merrick in the sunlight, he was surprised to find a man of his age looking so virile. Though the years had banded his black hair in gray and lined his sun-bronzed face, his body appeared firm and robust beneath his attire, his eyes sharp and piercing, and his demeanor one of wisdom and strength. His wife—the woman whom legend said captained a crew of forty bloodthirsty pirates to go in search of her husband—stood beside him, a rare example of aging beauty and vitality.

"So, ye be the great Captain Merrick?" Bloodmoon snorted his disdain and crossed beefy arms over his chest. "Heard ye turned yellow and became a sanctimonious sod, an *old* sanctimonious sod, by the looks of ye."

"And yet this *old* sanctimonious sod defeated you upon the seas."

"Aye, but wit' help from yer friend there." Bloodmoon thumbed toward the approaching *Reckoning*.

"With help from God," Merrick retorted with aplomb.

"God, bah! That be the difference 'tween us. I serve no God or man."

"Indeed, I fear you are correct. You serve only Satan." Wind blasted Merrick's hair behind him. "'Tis one or the other."

Bloodmoon let out a loud belch and his men chuckled. "So what are 'ye to do wit' me now, Preacher? Turn me in or hang me from yer yardarm fer crimes committed upon the seas?"

Rowan grinned. Aye, give the man his just punishment. Despite Merrick's religion, Rowan had heard he was not a man to be crossed.

"Nay." Merrick braced as the ship pitched over a wave. "But the price of your freedom is thus—consider your life, consider the path you've taken, and ponder where it will lead."

Rowan couldn't believe his ears. One of his legs buckled beneath him, and Morgan swung an arm around him for support. "Let me take you to the *Redemption*," she whispered, but he gently shook his head and kissed her forehead. He wanted to hear what transpired between his arch-nemesis and this Godly pirate.

"Me path leads to treasure and women, where it always do." Bloodmoon gave a brown-toothed grin and glanced over his crew, eliciting their chuckles.

Charlisse moved closer to the villain, studying him intently, her long curls blowing in the wind, her boots firm upon the rolling deck. "Bloodmoon, no matter what evil you've done. No matter what atrocities you've committed, God loves you like a Father loves an only son. And He wants you to turn to Him and receive His free gift of forgiveness through His son, Jesus Christ."

"God agin, is it?" He cursed. "Yer a fine lookin' woman, but ye've got ballast fer brains."

Catcalls and whistles preceded laughter from Bloodmoon's men. Rowan suppressed his own chuckle. Were they really trying to convert this dark-hearted knave?

"On the contrary, I speak the truth," Charlisse said loudly for all the men to hear. "The only truth that leads to life eternal. You do want to live forever, do you not?"

Bloodmoon huffed. "No one lives forever."

"Everyone lives forever." Merrick shared a smile with his wife. "But 'tis God who grants you the freedom to choose where you'll spend your eternity, heaven or hell."

"Then I choose hell." Bloodmoon announced with pride, glancing over his men for their approval. "Where I will rule an' choose me own fate."

"You'll do neither, I assure you, for you'll be subject to a monster worse than yourself."

Merrick's authoritative statement caused a slight hesitation, a flicker of fear in Bloodmoon's eyes. Or so, Rowan thought. But then it was gone, and the pirate spat on the deck.

Merrick gripped the hilt of his cutlass. "I have it in mind to give you one more chance, William Bloodmoon. Why? Because someone gave me a chance once. But mark my words, if I catch you pirating again, I will be compelled to turn you and your men over to the authorities. Consider this your last chance to redeem yourself and be the honorable man God wants you to be."

Rowan stumbled toward Merrick. "You can't let him go! He's a thief and a murderer! He killed his own wife in her bed."

Bloodmoon shrugged. "She was a lyin' whore that deserved her fate. As do ye."

Merrick arched an incriminating brow toward Rowan. "All of us deserve hellfire." Both his tone and the look in his eyes stopped Rowan from further protests. He knew the man was right.

With one order from their captain, Merrick's men lowered their weapons and started back for the *Redemption*. Accepting Morgan's help, Rowan hobbled across the deck, casting one final seething glance at Bloodmoon. But the man wasn't looking his way. Instead, his eyes, filled with curiosity and shock, were still on Merrick, who had leapt on the bulwarks and turned to face him.

"Now off with you, Bloodmoon," the pirate missionary said. "And sin no more."

Unable to believe what he'd just witnessed and in too much pain to care, Rowan clambered over the railing and leapt onto the deck of the infamous *Redemption* as Merrick's crew cut the grapnels holding the two ships together.

Morgan, still clinging to his arm, as if she feared he'd disappear, led him toward the companionway to go below. "Nay, love. I wish to stay above." He smiled her way and she nodded and led him to sit on the bulwarks.

"I'll get you some water." She sped off, dropped down a hatch, and reappeared within moments, a ladle in her hands.

Rowan accepted it, greedily gulping down the fluid that tasted sweet as honey, all the while smiling at her, noting a new sparkle in her eyes. He didn't think it possible the little minx could become more appealing, but there was a fresh glow to her face and an innocence and vulnerability as if she'd shed a layer of armor.

That armor returned in her tone. And in the sting of her slap on his arm. "You stupid, stupid man. What were you thinking? You almost got yourself killed!"

"Ouch." He rubbed his arm, thankful he didn't have to answer the minx when Charlisse interrupted them. "A pleasure to finally make your acquaintance, Mr. Dutton. Juliana has told us much about you."

Rowan frowned. "I apologize for what you've heard, milady."

To her credit, the lady didn't deny the bad reports, but merely smiled and extended her arm. "We should get you below where our ship's surgeon can tend to your wounds."

"Where's my sister?"

Charlisse scanned the horizon. "We were separated in a storm. But I have no doubt the *Ransom* will be here soon."

Which meant he needed to set sail immediately. As much as he wanted to see Juliana, he wasn't ready yet. Especially not in this condition. How many times had he dragged himself back to their home in Port Royal, besotted and bruised due to some ruckus he'd started at the gaming tables. Nay. The next time he saw his sister, he wanted to be dressed in the finest Flemish silk with a pouch full of money hanging at this waist.

"Stand by to make sail! Set royals and flying jib!" Merrick bellowed across the ship, then nodded at a large Negro before he approached Rowan.

Over his shoulder, Rowan saw Bloodmoon raise what sails he had left and speed away. "Faith, I can't believe you allowed that madman to go free," Rowan addressed Merrick.

The infamous captain gave a half smile. "Precisely for the reason of faith, Captain Dutton. Besides, I saw something in his eyes. Methinks God was speaking to him."

Rowan withheld a snort of disbelief. "Regardless, I thank you for saving me. I owe you my life."

"'Twas upon this little lady's insistence." Merrick gestured to Morgan. "She and your first mate, Mr. Doran, were quite relentless in their efforts to free you."

A woman Rowan had never seen before—a rather attractive blonde—crept tentatively on deck from the companionway, glancing this way and that.

"Ah, precious." Merrick extended a hand. "May I present my daughter, Lady Gabrielle Hyde."

"A pleasure, milady." Rowan nodded.

"Oh, dear sir." She placed a hand on her mouth as her gaze wondered over him. "You are sorely wounded. Father, delay no longer and allow this man to see Mr. Henshaw below."

"Indeed, I insist," Merrick said.

"Not to seem ungrateful, but I'd rather return to my ship." Rowan's gaze landed on the mighty vessel heaving-to just yards from the *Redemption*.

"If you wish. Of course. We have business to attend to as well." Merrick shared a concerned glance with his wife.

Morgan gripped Rowan's arm, causing another burst of pain. "But shouldn't you wait until your sister arrives? She was so worried about you."

Gabrielle glanced over the horizon. "Indeed. She will be devastated not to see you."

"I will see her soon enough. I have something I must do first." Against every aching muscle and bone, he struggled to rise. Morgan's aid brought his glance her way again, and for the first time, he wondered whether she would go with him. But why would she? If she was to stay in this time, she'd be much safer with these missionaries.

The thought did more than sadden him. It nearly crushed what was left of his heart as shouts of greeting hailed him from his ship. He glanced in their direction and saw Nick waving his hat before climbing over the railing into a lowered boat.

"I wish you would stay awhile and let us tend your wounds and rendezvous with your sister," Charlisse urged.

"Thank you for your kindness, milady." Rowan searched their faces and was nearly brought to tears by the genuine concern in their eyes.

These people were not at all what he expected.

"You're family, Rowan." Merrick flicked hair from his face and gripped Rowan's forearm. "You can call upon us for anything."

Family? The only real family Rowan had left was Juliana. And he'd done naught but disappoint her. He wanted to tell this honorable man to rethink the offer, for Rowan would bring naught but shame to this family, but instead he nodded and swallowed a burst of emotion.

Nick hailed him again, and Rowan waved at the boat that was almost at the *Redemption*. He turned to Morgan, feeling as though his heart teetered on the edge of a cliff. "I assume you will stay here." He tried to smile but found he couldn't.

Her brow wrinkled as she glanced over Gabrielle, Charlisse, and Merrick with more affection than he thought possible for having known them for so short a time. His heart started to crumble.

But then she turned to him with that sassy look of hers. "You're not getting rid of me that easily, *pirate.*"

He found his smile again.

The boat thudded against the hull, and one of Merrick's men tossed a rope ladder over the side.

"We will miss you." Charlisse and Gabrielle took Morgan's hands.

She leaned toward them and whispered, "Rowan needs me." But the wind carried her words to him. Instead of stabbing his pride, as they would have done to most men who bragged of needing no woman's help, they nestled deep into his heart.

Charlisse gave her an understanding look and leaned to whisper something in her ear that made Morgan laugh. Then she clutched Morgan's shoulders. "Remember what God has done for you."

God? Lud. Had these people befuddled Morgan's brain with their pious nonsense?

"How could I ever forget? Thank you for everything." Morgan hugged the lady.

"We will meet again. I know it." Tears moistened all three ladies' eyes while Merrick assisted Rowan onto the railing.

"Back to pirating?" he asked.

"If I say yes, will you clap me in irons?"

Merrick helped Morgan step up beside him. "You heard what I said to Bloodmoon."

A bunch of gibberish about God and love and forgiveness? Aye, he'd heard. "I did." He clutched Morgan's waist. "Thank you for saving my life." He glanced over all of them. "Thank you for risking your lives for me."

"Make us proud we have done so." Merrick stepped back and crossed arms over his chest.

Rowan was not a man to cower before another, but the honesty and concern in the man's eyes flooded him with a rare conviction. The sooner he got away from these people the better. The next thing he knew, Rowan would be heralding the same God gibberish—or worse, joining a monastery. Gripping Morgan's waist, he assisted her down the ladder, shaking off the odd, annoying feeling that he would never be the same after his encounter with Lady Hyde and Captain Edmund Merrick.

Chapter 25

Morgan settled into a chair in Rowan's cabin, petting Blackbeard while battling extreme emotions of joy that Rowan was alive and terror that his injuries were too severe. God only knew what sort of barbaric surgery they performed in this time. If there was internal bleeding or any of Rowan's organs were damaged … well, she didn't want to think about what they would do.

The ship had long since set sail as evidenced by the rush of water against the hull and teetertottering of the deck. Lanterns flickered from various positions about the room as Edith assisted Farley, handing him archaic-looking instruments while he hovered over Rowan's bare chest, poking and prodding.

Morgan had opted to stay during the examination—as long as Rowan kept his pants on, a request to which he'd winked and made no promises. Yet despite her horror at the sight of the deep lacerations covering his back and the dark bruises and cuts marring his magnificent chest, she was glad she had remained. Despite his pain, Rowan's gaze kept searching her out as if she were his only anchor in the storm of agony he suffered.

Every time his blue eyes met hers—exhausted eyes, searing in pain—something passed between them. Some unknown band of affection, of understanding, that invisible bond that ties people together who have experienced the same tragedy, the same fears and heartache. She really couldn't explain it except to say it moved her, made her want to run to him and promise to be by his side forever.

Farley dabbed some foul-smelling elixir on Rowan's back, and he groaned and grabbed his knees. "Lud, man, are you trying to kill me?"

"Not today." Farley chuckled.

Edith took a rag and dipped it in a basin of water. "Now, yous stay still, Captain. This salve will keep out infection."

"It will keep out the devil himself," Rowan growled, glancing up at Morgan.

"Good." Morgan replied curtly. "We don't need him here anymore anyway."

To which he growled again.

After applying the salve, Farley bandaged his back and then did the same to the wounds on his chest and arms. Next, he poured rum on the cut angling across Rowan's cheek to the side of his head, but Rowan snatched the bottle before he could finish and took a heavy swig.

"This one'll need stichin', Cap'n," the portly man announced, digging through his satchel for the necessary tools, while Edith dabbed Rowan's swollen eye with the rag.

"Once I met a man wit' wounds equal if not worse than yers, Cap'n." Farley retrieved a needle and twine. "Tortured fer days by the King's men at Marshallsea fer not disclosin' the whereabouts o' what he stole. When he was near death, they—"

"Acquit me, woman." Rowan gently nudged Edith away, while effectively silencing Farley. "Such bedeviled fretting makes me wish for the privacy of my cell on Bloodmoon's ship."

"Don't listen to him." Morgan rose and set the cat on her chair, sashaying towards him. "He's being a grouch. I know he's grateful for your help, aren't you Rowan?"

"I have no idea what is this *grouch*." He winced as Farley drove in the first stitch. "But I'll admit to being thankful."

Edith set down the cloth and approached Morgan. "I missed you, child. It's so good to see you."

"Aye," Farley added, not looking up from his work. "She was crazed wit' worry durin' the battle."

"You?" Morgan smiled at Edith. "Worry? I can't picture it."

"Let's jist say I did a lot of praying, child." She stuffed an ebony curl into her bun and then leaned closer to peer in Morgan's eyes. "There's something different 'bout you. I dunno. A lightness, a sparkle …"

"I have much to tell you, Edith." Morgan glanced at Rowan, then whispered, "Later."

"No doubt those blasted missionaries have filled her brain with mush." Rowan seethed out in a painful groan.

"Oh, I do hope so!" Edith clapped her hands together, her face bright with joy. "But lemme tell you, Farley was worried for you too, an' Mr. Doran. We's all prayed hard."

Rowan shifted in his seat. "Faith now, was anyone worried about me?"

Morgan suppressed a giggle as Edith waved a hand in the air. "We's always praying for your sorry soul, Cap'n." She chuckled. "Well, I best go git you some tea an' something to eat." And off she went.

Minutes passed as Farley stitched the side of Rowan's head. Every time he slid the needle through Rowan's skin, Morgan could swear she felt the pain herself. Even Blackbeard strolled over to Rowan and circled his feet as if sensing he was in need of comfort.

Finally, Farley stepped way, washed his hands in the basin, and grabbed a towel.

Rowan sat back in his chair, looking more pale than she'd ever seen him. Sweat glistened over his bloodied and bruised chest as he struggled to breathe. With his free hand, he reached down and scooped Blackbeard into his lap and began stroking the kitty.

Now she knew he was sick.

"Ye've got a broken rib, a skull fracture, lots of cuts and bruisin' but nothin' too serious from what I kin tell. O' course I can't see inside ye, so we'll have t' wait."

Rowan took a gulp of rum. "Thank you, Farley. I'm quite all right. Just tired."

"Aye, ye need yer rest, Cap'n. Infection could set in on yer wounds, 'specially on yer back, so's we needs t' keep an eye on 'em."

Edith entered, tray in hand, and set it on the desk. Nick followed behind her and smiled at Morgan, before he addressed his captain. "Och, now, ye look as if ye'd been keelhauled."

Rowan huffed and reached for a biscuit off the tray, the action causing him to wince. "I *feel* like I've been keelhauled. But, thanks to you, my friend. And you, Morgan"—he glanced her way—"I would have been on the morrow."

"My pleasure." Nick scratched the red whiskers on his chin. "Though I canna say I'll always be there when ye act like a fish-brained fool."

Rowan cocked a grin. "In good sooth, I hope so, for my past dictates there'll be more fish-brained foolery in the future."

Nick chuckled. "I canna argue with that."

Farley gathered his things and gestured for his wife to follow him out. "We leave ye t' yer rest, Cap'n."

"I will as well," Nick said. "Jist tell me where t' point the *Reckoning*."

"Need you ask? Toward the island where Brasiliano buried his treasure." Rowan pressed a hand on his side.

"You can't be serious?" Morgan snapped. "You're still going after the treasure? After all this?"

"Why wouldn't I, Lady Minx? Have I not suffered enough to keep its location secret?"

Nick snorted. "So old Bloodmoon didna make ye talk?"

"What do *you* think?" Rowan attempted a pompous grin, but it fell flat beneath a cringe of pain.

Nick shoved his hat atop his head. "T' the island as ye wish, Captain. Now, get yer rest." He faced Morgan and gestured toward Rowan.

"I'll look after him, Nick."

A hint of mischief sparkled in his eyes before he strode from the room and shut the door.

And just like that, she found herself alone with this stubborn, battered hunk-of-a-pirate who'd been tortured by a madman and barely escaped with his life. The CIA had nothing on these pirates. Waterboarding would have been child's play compared to what Rowan had endured, and still he had not revealed the location of the treasure.

Unusually nervous in his presence, she folded her hands in front of her and stared out the stern windows, where darkness painted sea and sky with inky black before scattering silver jewels over both. So beautiful, this Caribbean, always changing, always new, so unlike her organized, predictable life.

She felt his eyes upon her and shifted her gaze to his cluttered desk, then to the stained and knotted deck, then at the wrinkled folds of her skirts, anything but at the man's bare chest with those gorgeous muscles all bandaged and bruised. And Blackbeard nestled in his lap. Was there anything more appealing than a tough, bad boy petting a kitten?

"I hope you're proud of yourself." She finally broke the silence.

"I am. But for what great feat do you refer?"

She finally looked up at him. "The great feat of nearly getting yourself killed on some fool's errand."

"Ah, that." He grinned and grabbed a piece of fish from the tray, plopping it in his mouth. "But I *didn't* die."

"You play so free with your life, Rowan. As if it means nothing to you."

The ship creaked over a wave, and she stumbled.

"Why should it?" He shrugged, leaned over to grab the rum and took another gulp.

"Because you are God's creation."

His lips slanted. "If so, I imagine he's recast the mold since his error." Setting Blackbeard on the floor, he struggled to rise.

Morgan darted to his side. "Here, let me help."

"Lud, woman. I'm not feeble."

"I know that, you big oaf, but everyone needs help now and then." Positioning her shoulder beneath his arm, she hugged his waist and led him to his cot. He smelled of sweat and stink and blood, but she didn't care as she nudged him to lie back on the pillow.

He stretched one hand behind his head and gazed at her with that look of his that never failed to melt her insides—desire, longing and admiration all bundled together. "I'm feeling a bit chilled, Lady Minx. Why not join me and keep me warm." He patted the blanket beside him.

"I'd slap you if you weren't in so much pain."

He smiled and took her hand. "It's good to see you, Lady Minx. In good sooth, I've never received such an affectionate greeting as when you flew into my arms earlier today."

"Don't let it go to your head."

"Alas, but it has already gone to my heart." He caressed her fingers, the cuts and callouses on his hands scratching her skin. "Why did you come back with me?"

It was a question she kept asking herself. Since she had no idea whether the amulet would work or if Rowan would even let her try to go back to her time, every logical intuition, every rational thought told her that remaining with missionaries was the best choice, the safest choice. But another part of her, a voice deep inside, had urged her to follow this pirate into the unknown, had told her that she was done playing it safe. "Because obviously you need someone to knock some sense into you."

He moved his hand up to lightly brush her cheek. Her body reacted to his touch, and she hated herself for it. "If you must know, I'm here to take care of you," she added nervously.

"Indeed? In that case, I fear I'm in great pain, Lady Minx, and in need of your immediate attention. This, for instance"—he lifted his hand where a gash sliced his thumb—"'tis excruciating."

Smiling, Morgan placed a kiss upon it.

"And this, I fear." He pointed to a bandage on his arm.

She kissed it.

He flattened his lips and sighed. "And here as well." He gestured toward a red mark on his chest.

Leaning over, she pressed her lips on the spot, gazing up at him playfully.

"And here." He lifted his jaw where a dark bruise formed, and she placed several kisses across the spot, feeling her blood spin being so close to him.

He tapped his lips before they curved seductively. "And here."

"You are a cad, you know," she said before she pressed her lips to his. She tried to be gentle, not wanting to pain him, but she felt his passion rise and his arm circle her, pulling her close. He tasted of blood and rum and desire, and she lost herself in the way he hungrily, yet delicately caressed her mouth, so gentle for a man all roughness and steel. Heat swamped her—pleasurable heat that made her yearn for more. Her thoughts whirled, her body ignited, but a shred of reason forced her back.

She pushed from him, only then remembering the wounds on his chest. But he gave no indication of pain, his look one of complete adoration.

He eased a lock of her hair behind her ear. "You intrigue me, Lady Minx. You enchant me like no other woman."

His words sent a thrill through her. She lowered her gaze but did not move from him, did not want to give up this closeness with him yet. "That's just the rum talking."

"Nay. I've had my share of rum through the years, and it's never spoken thus."

She smiled. "You are a charmer, Rowan, I'll give you that."

His blue eyes searched hers, intent, needy, dare she say— vulnerable. "Pray tell, will you be this charmer's lady?"

It was a question she longed to hear, an admittance of his affection for her—one she never thought to hear from such a man. But it was a question she couldn't answer. At least not yet. Not with the crazy thoughts spinning her mind into confusion. Not the least of which was that she was three hundred years in the past. And this man was a pirate, a thief who lived by violence and dissipation. Besides, what exactly did he mean by *being his lady*?

Blackbeard leapt onto the bed and snuggled beside Rowan.

"At least someone will share my bed." Rowan stroked the cat then studied Morgan, his expression serious. "Tell me you won't leave me and go back to your time."

"So, you finally believe?" She backed away and moved a chair close to sit down.

"Aye, but you didn't answer my question." His eyes fluttered closed for a second. He struggled to open them, but they shut again. He mumbled something she couldn't make out, and then drifted off to sleep.

Thank God, because she didn't know the answer to his question. Something *had* changed between them, at least for her. She knew that she loved him—that she *really* loved him. But she had no idea how he felt in return. Something in his eyes told her he felt the same way, but she'd been fooled by a handsome face before—*many* of them. He could simply be charming her for some reason. Besides, "be his lady" was not exactly a marriage proposal.

Marriage? What was she thinking? She must still have a spirit of stupidness plaguing her.

How could she forget this man was a womanizer, a Don Juan of the seas, a man who preferred other men's wives and used them for his own pleasure? And did she mention he was a pirate? One still intent on getting his ill-gotten treasure. How could she ever trust a man like that?

Still, as she watched him sleep, she could not deny the overwhelming draw he had on her, her intense yearning to make him happy. She dropped her face in her hands. *Oh, God ... Father, I have no idea why You brought me to this time—* well, in truth, she could guess it might have had something to do with delivering her of those demons and getting her to see God for who He was, which she was extremely thankful for—*but why make me fall in love with this man? Please help me know what to do.*

Chapter 26

Morgan stood at the starboard railing—yes, she had finally learned some of the ship terms—the next morning, face to the wind, feeling better than she had in years. Her energy had returned, as had her appetite, and she was sleeping soundly. The pain in her side was gone, too. Along with most of her worries—at least the things she used to fret over. She had no idea what tomorrow would bring, or the day after, and although it did unsettle her a bit, she knew God had a plan.

In fact, if she remembered correctly from Scripture, God was a lot like her in that He always had a plan. Though she wished He'd share some of it with her at the moment.

Nick, who had greeted her earlier, leapt down from the quarterdeck and slipped beside her. "Surprised t' see ye here on deck, lass, wi'out benefit of escort." The wind fingered his short red hair as his eyes met hers.

The ship tilted and Morgan braced her shoes on the deck. "You mean why am I not terrified to be alone with all these pirates?"

He grinned. "Weel, if ye put it tha' way, aye."

Behind them, Scratch shouted orders for the crew to adjust sail, sending men clambering up ropes and speeding to the tops.

Morgan's gaze followed them, still amazed they could leap so fast without fear. "Something happened to me on board the *Redemption*. Merrick and Charlisse … well, they showed me how wrong I've been about God."

Nick's smile couldn't have been brighter. "Pleases me t' hear tha', lass. 'Twas wha' Edith an' I were praying for. If anyone could get ye t' see God, 'tis those two."

"You? Prayed for me?" The ship lurched over a wave as she studied the man. When Morgan had told Edith what had happened last night, the woman mentioned praying for her. But Morgan hadn't considered that anyone else would care enough to pray. She swallowed a lump of emotion at this pirate's concern.

"An' for Rowan," he continued. "An' for all involved. Powerful stuff, tha' prayer, eh?" His eyes twinkled.

"I guess … I mean, yes, it is. Charlisse sensed evil spirits on me and commanded them away in Jesus' name. It was … incredible."

"Ah, demons, was it?" He squinted toward the sea, no shock found on his expression.

"Why does everyone in this time know so much more about spiritual stuff than people in my day?"

He shrugged. "No' everyone here. Jist those of' us who've ha' experiences, is my guess." He rubbed his bearded chin. "Ye tend t' encounter the enemy more when ye are encroaching on his territory, if ye know wha' I mean."

She didn't. Until now. But that made sense. Like being on the front lines in a war. If you're pushing back the enemy, you're in the line of fire. Still, she couldn't imagine how she'd ever been a threat to Satan. Why had he attacked *her*?

"I still get scared sometimes, like during the battle and when I knew Rowan was being tortured."

"Aye, 'tis the natural fear God gives us t' keep from being foolish."

She nodded. "And it doesn't feel controlling like it did before."

He glanced up at the sails and then shouted over his shoulder to Scratch, "Braces ease, trim your sheets!" before he returned his attention to her. "Now if we can only convince Rowan tha' God loves him, so he'll give up this cutlass-slashing, ship-thieving, wife-stealing life he's chosen an' settle down."

Morgan smiled, even as sorrow shrouded her. "I doubt a man like him will ever settle down."

"Nay? Mayhap not. But the way he looks at ye, I think he'd be willing t' try, no?" He winked.

She wanted to say that no, she doubted it, but his words warmed her anyway. Shielding her eyes, she scanned the horizon where sea and sky met in a marriage of gorgeous blues tainted with pink and gold.

"Bloodmoon is still out there," she said, "and I doubt he's going to give up searching for Rowan and his treasure map."

"I quite agree, lass. 'Tis wha' concerns me most of all."

Farley popped on deck, the wind instantly flipping his stringy hair off his bald spot.

"Miss, the cap'n's askin' fer ye."

"How is he today, Farley?"

"Well enough. Still sore o' course, but ornery as ever." He chuckled. "Which be a good sign, I s'pose."

But Rowan wasn't ornery at all when she entered his cabin moments later. He sat on the window ledge, gazing upon the sea. Though still barechested and looking like he'd fought a horde of storm troopers, his color had returned, his skin was free of dirt, and he'd put on fresh pants. At the tap of her shoes on the deck, he turned and the delight that swept over his face nearly sank her to her knees.

"Lady Minx, you came."

"You're the captain, and you summoned me." She gave him a coy look, feeling suddenly nervous.

"You've never listened to me before."

She merely smiled and stepped further into the room. "Is there something I can do for you?"

To this, his smile grew even bigger, spiced with desire.

She arched a brow.

"I wish your company, if you'll oblige me. Nick and Farley have conspired to keep me below until I'm recovered."

"Ah, you poor thing. To have such friends who care about you."

He winced as he rose from the ledge, pressing a hand to his chest.

Morgan was at his side in a flash, wrapping an arm around his waist. The scent of lye and musk and Rowan filled her nose, and she fought back the heady sensation of him.

He drew her close, leaning slightly on her as she helped him to one of the chairs. "I feel better already." His voice was strong again.

She backed away, narrowing her eyes. "You did that on purpose, so I'd come help you."

"How else to bring you close?" Rays of sunlight combed the cabin, glimmering off his earring and brightening his playful grin.

"If you think I'm going to kiss you all over your body again …" The words left her mouth before she realized the impact they would have on the color of her face, which she now felt heating like a stove.

Rowan only grinned wider. "I will offer no protest should the desire come upon you."

She lowered into a chair, desperate to change the topic. "I met your sister."

He shifted his gaze away, all playfulness draining from his expression. "Juliana." He spoke her name with such fondness, such reverence. "How is she?"

"Pregnant."

His eyes lit up. "Indeed? How marvelous. So, she is happy?"

"Very. Her husband is … well, he's a good man. She will have the baby soon. A month is my guess." The ship creaked and groaned over a swell. "She loves you, Rowan. She wants to see you so badly."

"Badly?"

She huffed. "Desperately, I mean. Whatever happened between you … whatever you think you owe her, she doesn't care. She just wants *you*."

Pressing his chest again, Rowan leaned forward on his knees and stared at the floor. His hair hung around his face, so she couldn't make out his expression, but she sensed his sorrow.

"Please, Rowan. Give up this crazy quest. Return to the family who loves you. Merrick and Charlisse are now your family, too. I'd give anything to have parents like that … *anything*." Her thoughts drifted to her own parents and all the bickering and fighting, drugs, alcohol, and love of money she'd grown up with.

He gave a snort of disgust. "They got to you. With all their pious pomposity and moral codes."

"They showed me the truth, Rowan. About God. How loving He is. How forgiving. And they helped free me from the bondage of fear."

He growled, rose before she could help him, and shuffled to his desk. "I don't wish to argue with you, Lady Minx." Opening a drawer, he pulled out a sack and brought it to her, smiling as if he held a great secret.

"What's this?" She loosened the tie and peeked inside, her excitement rising. "Oh my." She blinked, not believing her eyes. Paint brushes, at least five of different sizes, and what looked like paint in a dozen tiny jars.

She glanced up at Rowan, breathless. "How did you …?"

"I purchased them at Charles Town." He took his seat again. "Alas, in all the ensuing mayhem, I forgot about them."

Stunned, she could only stare at him. "You remembered that I loved to paint?"

He smiled. "You approve, Lady Minx?"

Rising, she spilled the items from the sack across his desk. "Very much! Thank you, Rowan."

"There is but one caveat," he said.

Placing a hand on her hip, she waited for some salacious request.

"Paint something for me. From this cabin so I can watch. The sea, the sky, the desk, anything."

"How about you?" No sooner had the words left Morgan's mouth then the painting of Rowan she'd seen back in her time filled her vision until she could see nothing else. But no … couldn't be. The signature had been LM, not MS. She glanced at him again, only now connecting the jagged cut on his cheek with the one in the painting. Her thoughts spun insensibly.

"A grand idea, Lady Minx! What is the matter? You look as if you've seen the devil himself."

She glanced back at the paints and brushes and attempted to steady her galloping heart. "But I don't have a canvas."

"I'll have one of the crew cut and stretch a piece of sailcloth."

"Very well, I agree. On one condition." She raised a brow. "Put on a shirt."

As promised, Rowan ordered Hendrix, the purser, to stretch a piece of sailcloth over a wooden frame then prop it on a small tripod. It wasn't perfect, but it would do. Besides, Morgan couldn't believe how wonderful it felt to hold brushes again, to mix paint on the makeshift wooden palette, to blend colors and apply them in various shades and textures to the canvas.

But when she looked up to see Rowan in his white shirt, leather jerkin strapped with a silver-buckled baldric, his hair tied behind him, and the earring winking at her from his right ear, she felt an overwhelming sense of déjà-vu. Like she'd been here before. In this place, at this time. Or maybe it was that, somehow, this singular moment, this painting, was one of those defining events in history that had to happen in order for things to proceed as planned.

What that plan was, she had no idea. But she was thrilled to have the perfect excuse to study every detail about Rowan in an attempt to transfer the essence of this fascinating man onto canvas. Besides, the hours they spent together gave her a chance to know him better. They talked about life and music and food, how he came to be a pirate, and what his childhood was like—his loving, generous mother taken too early from him and his cruel, abusive father who never believed Rowan was worth anything.

"So, I poured myself into gambling, drinking, and wenching to prove him right." Rowan gave a cynical laugh. "Lost the entire family fortune during a time when my dear sister was desperately trying to run the business by herself."

Morgan dipped her brush into the paint. "I'm sorry, Rowan. Having a loving father is so important. Mine wasn't cruel like yours, but he was absent, making his fortune and having little time for me and Mom."

He frowned. "Seems parents haven't improved much over the years."

"It's humanity that hasn't improved much." She finished the last of the under-shading then looked up at him. "I've discovered God is a far better father than any earthly one. He always loves you no matter what. He never disapproves of you, or leaves you, or is too busy for you."

Rowan looked away. "Tell me what it is like in your time."

"Look back my way, Rowan." He did and she commenced her painting, disappointed that he never wanted to talk about God—the answer to all Rowan's heartache and needs.

Blackbeard raced into the room and leapt on top of Rowan's desk, scattering papers. They both laughed as the ship bounced over a wave. Morgan waited for it to settle before she applied the paint, gaining a new appreciation for how easy it was to paint on solid land.

As she worked, she attempted to explain the twenty-first century to a man from the seventeenth. No easy task, mind you. More than once, his face twisted so much in confusion or maybe disgust—the former mainly at the technology—that she had to order him back to his normal expression.

"I can hardly credit such fanciful tales, Lady Minx. These devilish … what did you call them, computers and tables?"

"Tablets."

"And phones? Objects that speak to you and show moving pictures. 'Tis the devil's work, I tell you."

She laughed. "Some would agree with you."

"However, I find the lack of female attire quite to my liking." He grinned.

She wanted to throw a pillow at him but couldn't find one handy. Instead, she peeked at him over the canvas. "You're the type of guy women in my day call dogs."

"I've been called worse."

"I bet."

"Pray, are there no pirates in your time?"

Morgan mixed a new color on her palette, having trouble with these odd paints. "Some, but far away near Africa."

"Hmm. Methinks I prefer to stay in my time." Blackbeard leapt into his lap, and Rowan stroked his fur. Morgan couldn't help but smile at the sight.

"You'd definitely be a duck out of water in my time. Though the ladies would love you."

"I may be a dog, but I am no duck, Lady Minx. And the ladies love me here."

"True. Thanks for the reminder." She needed to remember just what type of man he was and not get caught up in the way he was looking at her, the way he continually looked at her. Like he could look at no other woman. It was doing funny things to her insides …

And she didn't like it one bit.

In fact, as the afternoon passed and she learned more about him, that tingling sensation grew only stronger. She discovered his favorite food was lamb pie and something called Applecream—boiled apples in wine and cream sauce—but when he asked about hers, she had difficulty describing a cheeseburger and fast food and finally gave up. As a child, his favorite thing to do was play a form of hide and go seek with his sister. He chuckled as he relayed the story of how Juliana got stuck hiding in one of their father's trunks, and the entire house went up in arms when she could not be found for hours. In the end, they discovered her sound asleep, drooling on their father's best silk shirt.

He gazed out the window, a smile on his face at the memory. At that moment, she imagined he looked just as he had back then—a mischievous little boy. She smiled and continued to ask him questions as she applied the paint. She discovered he enjoyed a good orchestra, the music compositions of Giovanni Coprario, whoever that was, and he liked to dance. That last thing surprised her the most. She could not picture the muscular pirate waltzing across a ballroom floor, or whatever dances they did in this time. In fact, she was surprised at the depth of his education and culture. For a pirate.

The next morning they shared a small breakfast of coffee, hard biscuits, and overripe bananas before she took up her brushes again. Thankfully, the whale oil she'd left them soaking in had kept them supple. The day passed once again in pleasant conversation, and she found herself enjoying more and more their long hours together devoid of any pretense or sexual innuendos. The painting was coming along nicely, and she hoped to finish it by the next day. Which was perfect timing since they'd be arriving at the treasure island by then.

She had longed for an opening in the conversation where she could convince Rowan once again to give up his quest for treasure and return to his family, but it never came, or perhaps she didn't want to rile him and disturb their developing friendship.

On the third day, Morgan found Rowan on the quarterdeck talking with Nick. She took a minute while balancing on the heaving deck to watch him as he scanned the horizon with his telescope and then shouted orders to the crew, his jaw strong, his wild hair blowing in the wind, his boots firmly planted on the deck. Only a slight hesitation in his step and his grip of the railing here and there when the ship bucked gave any indication of his injuries.

A shiver coursed down Morgan's back, and she swung to find a dozen pirates gaping at her, malicious intent dripping from their eyes. Would they attempt something now that their captain was injured? No. She glanced back at Rowan. They would have done so already. Still, it reminded her that natural fear was a gift from God and something she should pay attention to.

Nick pointed her out to Rowan, and he eased down the ladder onto the main deck, only a slight wince indicating his pain.

"You should be below resting," she said, shoving hair from her face.

"Are you my mother now?" He smiled.

"No, not that you don't need one."

He placed her hand in the crook of his elbow, and together they strolled around the ship, enjoying the morning breeze, the sparkling sea, and even the hot sun on their faces. Morgan got the feeling Rowan had an ulterior motive for the morning walk—one of reinforcing his health and vigor to the crew, along with his possession of her—for he seemed to make special effort to show no weakness, no stumbling, no evidence of pain on his expression, as well as staring down those men who dared to glance her way. None of Morgan's boyfriends had ever protected her. In fact, one of them had left her all alone in a bar in a seedy part of town after they'd had an argument. She realized now that it was by the grace of God she hadn't been attacked as she walked home in the dark.

How odd that it was a pirate who made her feel cherished and protected. Curling her fingers around his bicep, she relished in his strength. He smiled down at her, and she tripped on her skirts, causing them both to laugh, even as her heart soared. She was living a dream—every woman's romantic fantasy—like some cheesy romance novel. But unless she could convince Rowan to turn from piracy, this particular story wouldn't have a happy ending.

Maybe this was why God had sent her back, not only to heal her, but to save Rowan from an untimely death.

After several trips around the ship, she finally begged him to go below so she could finish the painting. Once he settled back in his chair, she found him staring at her oddly.

"What?"

"You look different. Fresher. You let down your hair instead of tying it behind your head. Your eyes carry a new sparkle, your face glows from the sun, and something else." He glanced over the room. "Lud, you haven't tried to put my cabin in order! Even after that infernal cat caused havoc on my desk. You aren't ill, are you?"

"Quite the contrary." Morgan smiled. "I am healed … delivered. I was bound up in fear and anxiety, but God set me free."

He groaned. "Sorry I asked."

"It's true, whether you choose to believe it or not." Morgan wiped paint from one of her brushes, then dipped it in a new color. "It will never be enough, you know."

"Of what do you speak?"

"The treasure. All the gold in the world will not dull the ache in your soul."

He frowned. But Morgan finally saw her opening and couldn't quit now.

"Sure, you can steal this treasure, repay your sister, buy a fancy house and expensive clothes, and gain the fickle respect of other rich, important people, but you'll still be empty inside. You'll always be that little boy whose father rejected him."

Rowan rose and stormed toward the stern windows. "Is that what you think of me?"

Morgan's heart plummeted. "Of course not. But I believe that's what you think of yourself." She stared at the painting. Just a few more touches here and there, and it would be done. Did that mean her time with Rowan was coming to an end? She set down her brush and stood as sorrow overwhelmed her. "Please, Rowan. Turn from this thieving life, get a respectable occupation, and trust God. Then you'll have self-respect as well as the respect of others. If you continue, you'll die before your time."

"Everyone dies. 'Tis how one lives that matters." He crossed arms over his chest and continued staring out the window.

"Exactly."

Silence, except for the rush of water and creak of wood, strung tight through the cabin. Finally, Rowan waved a hand over his shoulder toward her as if she were an annoying insect. "Enough of this religious prattle. I grow weary of it. Begone!"

Morgan's pulse leapt at his harsh tone, even as her stomach soured. Only moments before he'd been gazing at her as if she were the answer to all his dreams. Now, he dismissed her as if she'd been just a temporary diversion, an entertainment that had outlived its fun.

Raising a hand to her throat, she fled out the door and into the companionway, unavoidable tears spilling down her cheeks.

She shouldn't be here. Not on a pirate ship, nor in the seventeenth century. She'd gotten caught up in the adventure, the romance. But Rowan was a pirate through and through. A capricious, thieving, womanizing pirate. And she'd been a fool to think she could change him.

No, she must find a way back home—back to her own time and her own life.

Chapter 27

Rowan cursed himself for a foolish rogue. Despite the pain of his injuries, the last three days with Morgan had been the best of his life. He'd never met anyone like this intriguing lady. Ofttimes, he grew bored in his conversations with women—the few he'd tried to talk to, anyway—but he could never predict what Morgan would say. Not once. Her stories were witty and interesting, her descriptions fun and lively, her interests akin to many of his own. Her laughter was an elixir to his soul, and her smile never failed to make his heart swell.

In truth, he could spend a lifetime looking at that smile.

So why had he become so enraged and dismissed her so rudely? Over what? God? The God who had ignored Rowan his entire life? Let Morgan—and his sister and those sissies, Charlisse and Merrick—believe what they would, but Rowan would not allow a distant God to interfere with his courtship of this enchanting lady.

Which is why he'd planned a special supper just for her. He'd ordered Edith to cook up a batch of turtle stew, complete with yams, pickled onions, and mango soaked in rum for dessert. One of the crew had polished the silver and candlesticks, while another had found the cleanest scrap of sailcloth to be used as a tablecloth. Now as Rowan stared at the table, steam rising from the food housed in pewter bowls and plates, candlelight sparkling over the silverware, he grew unusually nervous.

What if she didn't come? He'd sent Nick to invite her a few minutes ago, but it seemed like hours had passed as he waited for a peek at her coming down the companionway. He straightened the lace at the cuffs of his finest cambric shirt, then brushed invisible dust from his best doublet, trimmed in gold braid. With his hair pulled back and his jaw as clean shaven as he could get it with his knife, he awaited his fate, nearly laughing at all this ridiculous behavior for one woman.

His glance took in the ruby amulet lying atop his desk. A knot formed in his stomach. He resisted the urge to quickly shove it into his desk drawer. Instead, he slipped it in his pocket as a reminder that he'd determined to ask Lady Minx a question tonight. But it was her answer that terrified him more than anything. Forcing down his fears, he gazed out the stern windows at a night that was as black and restless as his spirit.

Voices met his ears, spinning him around to see Nick, a victorious grin on his face, step inside the cabin and give a mock bow. "Miss Morgan Shaw," he announced the lady with all the aplomb of a courtier.

The lady, decked in her usual green skirts and cream-colored bodice, halted at the doorway, her expression hesitant as those lustrous moss-colored eyes met his.

He extended his hand. "Miss Shaw, thank you for accepting my invitation."

His smile seemed to disarm her as she entered further, her gaze scanning the candlelit table, surprise brightening her expression.

"I'll leave ye t' yer supper." Nick bowed out and Rowan thanked him as he shut the door and faced her.

"I hope you'll accept my apology for my atrocious behavior earlier today."

She eyed him suspiciously. "You clean up well, Rowan. If I had known, I would have dressed for the occasion." She turned away, but not before pain burned in her eyes. "What is it you want? Are you trying to bribe me?"

"Lud, woman." He ran a hand through his hair, loosening strands from his tie. "You use me monstrously yet again. How can I assure you of my sincerity?"

She sashayed to the table, still not meeting his gaze. "I was only thinking of your happiness, Rowan. Maybe I overstepped my place, but I just want you to have the joy and peace I've found in God."

He approached and held out a chair for her to sit. "I do not fault you for it, Lady Minx. I only ask that we not discuss religion tonight."

"Deal." She smiled up at him and took a seat.

Their meal passed in pleasant conversation. And though Rowan found his appetite had abandoned him, he took great pleasure in watching Morgan enjoy her food. Why, the lady even finished an entire glass of wine!

He pushed back from his plate and sipped his rum, relishing the way candlelight glinted in her eyes, transformed her skin into translucent silk, and set aglimmer strands of red amongst her brown hair—hair that flowed around her face and down her back like a satiny waterfall. "I've never seen you eat so much."

"Oh my." She giggled and placed a hand over her mouth. "I'm such a pig. I'm so sorry." She washed down her food with another sip of wine. "I don't know why I'm so hungry."

"Please continue. I'm glad you are enjoying it."

She sat back and pressed a hand over her stomach. "I've had too much already. But thank you. For all of this."—she waved a hand over the candlelit table—"I didn't figure you for the romantic type."

Rowan lifted his brows. "'Tis unclear what you mean, Lady Minx, but I will admit to knowing what pleases a lady."

Suspicion swept away the playful interest on her face, and he reached his hand across the table for hers, hoping to bring it back. Hesitantly … reluctantly, she took it. He caressed her fingers, seeking the right words to express feelings he couldn't even understand himself. "I vow to spend all my days devising ways to bring you pleasure. If you'll allow me."

She studied him, her eyes flickering between his. He knew he affected her. He knew she desired him, for her chest rose and fell, and her skin warmed beneath his touch. But did her affections go beyond the physical—something he had never sought from a woman before.

"Whatever you wish," he said. "Ask and I will grant it."

Tender yearning filled her eyes, and for a moment he thought she'd surely come to him and fall into his arms. Instead, she jerked her hand away and stood.

"I wish to finish the painting."

Not exactly what he had in mind. He groaned inwardly. "I'm not in the correct attire."

"I have only a few more strokes." She hurried to stand behind the canvas, skirts swishing. "Just sit in your same spot and look my way."

He happily obliged. He would never forget these past three days, watching her as she painted him. The way her lips twisted as she concentrated on the canvas, the slight wrinkle above her pert little nose, and the intensity of her gaze upon him—as if he were important … valuable. Something he'd never felt before. He loved hearing the sound of her voice as she shared stories of her life—strange but beguiling tales of a distant land in a distant time. Yet, stories that contained everything that made Morgan, Morgan. And he had lived for her every word.

Now, however, it only took her a few minutes, a few dips in paint and splashes on the canvas, and she rose, beaming at him as if she'd just found buried treasure.

"Are you going to show me, Lady Minx?" Though in defiance of his promise, he'd stolen a peek at the canvas after the first day, but he'd not seen it since.

She laid a hand on her stomach. "I don't know why I'm so nervous." Then gripping the tripod by the base, she slowly turned it around, all the while studying his reaction.

Rowan saw himself staring back at him. A pirate. A gentleman. A man scarred by life. A perfect portrait, exquisitely shaded and vibrantly colored. But it was so much more than that. She'd captured something in him, in his eyes, that he'd never seen in himself, that he didn't know could exist within him. *Hope* … and *love*.

"You hate it." Her disappointed tone brought his eyes to hers.

He rose, shaking his head. "Nay. 'Tis exquisite. 'Tis … utterly and completely perfect. You have great talent, Lady Minx."

Candlelight glittered off her smile. "You think so? Really?"

"But you haven't signed it." He pointed toward the bottom. "You must sign it so everyone will know 'twas the great artist Lady Minx who created such a masterpiece."

An odd look came over her face as she shifted her gaze between him and the painting as if she just remembered something important. Then picking up a brush, she leaned and painted in small letters on the bottom right, LM. "Lady Minx." Laughing, she stood back to admire her work. "It's been Lady Minx all along. I'm the famous pirate painter!" She shook her head.

He had no idea what she was talking about—as usual—but he came to stand beside her and dared to wrap an arm about her waist. Instead of moving away from him, she put down the brush and turned into his embrace.

"Oh, Rowan. What is it about you, you crazy pirate?" She glanced up at him and smiled, her eyes moistening.

He brushed his hand over her cheek. "Thank you for forgiving me."

"Who says I did?" She cocked her head.

"Your eyes."

"And what else do my eyes tell you?"

"That you love me."

She pushed back from him playfully. "Oh, they do, do they? A bit full of yourself, aren't you?"

"If that means what I think it means, then aye." He pulled her back and wrapped his arms around her once again. "And I can prove it." He lowered his lips to hers, gently, softly at first, then upon feeling her passion rise, he cupped her cheeks in his hands and went deeper, relishing in the intimacy of the moment and her tiny moans of pleasure. He wanted more of her, not just physically, but in every way.

And the realization scared him to death.

Withdrawing from the kiss, she leaned her head on his chest.

He stroked her hair. "Say you'll stay with me, Morgan."

"As what? Your mistress?" Her voice, still husky with desire, was laced with despair.

"I prefer the term lady companion."

She stepped away from him, leaving him cold. "And just what would that entail? Sleeping with you, I suppose?"

"One of the many benefits." He grinned, but she wasn't smiling anymore. 'Twas as if a shadow had encompassed her. She lowered her chin.

He brought it back up with a touch of his finger. "I'm not the type of man to commit to lifelong marriage. I live my life on the whim of what comes each day. 'Twould be cruel to promise you any more than that."

"Or cowardly?" She huffed. "Besides, who said anything about marriage?" She moved to his desk and fingered some of the trinkets. "Think about what are you offering me, Rowan." She spun to face him. "To live on this pirate ship with you? At risk daily of being raped by one of your men or blown up in one of your raids?" Anger burned in her eyes. "You think you have so much to offer a woman because you're handsome and charming and you might be good in bed. That may suffice for other men's wives or loose women looking for a good time. But it isn't enough for me." She lifted her chin and stared staunchly into his eyes. "I am God's princess and worthy of an honorable, good man who will commit to me for a lifetime. I will be no man's mistress, nor will I give myself or my body away to someone who can toss me aside when they grow tired of me."

Rowan felt like he'd been blasted by a broadside. He'd never had a woman speak to him thus. He'd never allowed it. Nor had he ever considered any woman worthy of a lifelong commitment.

Not until he'd met Morgan Shaw.

Her anger fled, and she lowered her gaze, black lashes fanning her cheeks like felled trees in a forest. One tear broke through and slid down her face. "I love you, Rowan. I know I'm crazy to feel that way, but I can't help it."

She loved him! He started toward her. "Then stay with me. I will make you happy, I promise."

She held up a hand to stop him. "Don't go for the treasure tomorrow, Rowan. Give up that quest and return home. Give me some reason to believe you'll change."

"You ask the impossible. I cannot return to my sister with nothing."

She hugged herself as another tear spilled down her cheek. He wanted to wipe it away. He wanted to tell her he'd quit pirating, become a pauper, a monk … whatever it took, just so she'd stay with him.

Instead, he reached in his pocket and pulled out the amulet.

Her eyes widened.

"I've never felt this way about anyone," he said. "Nor have I asked any woman to be my lady. There is something special between us, something most people never experience. I cannot promise you I will change, but I can promise you that I love you. So I leave the choice up to you. To choose me or choose to go back to your time and leave me forever."

Clank! Clank! Clank! The sound of a massive chain rattled through Morgan's sleepy mind. Muffled shouts ensued, followed by the thump of feet, and finally a mighty splash. She reached up to rub eyes that felt caked in mud. Hadn't she just fallen asleep? It couldn't be morning already. She glanced over to look for Edith, but she was gone and the bedding on her cot neatly made.

Morgan closed her eyes again beneath a rising headache. Purring rumbled beside her, and she absently reached to pet Blackbeard who'd been her only comfort throughout the long night. She hoped she hadn't kept Edith up with her endless pacing, but how was she to sleep after Rowan's ultimatum? The amulet had been right there in his hand—possibly her only way home. All she had to do was grab it, and if it worked, all this craziness would end. She could return to her family and friends and her normal, safe life. But she couldn't bring herself to do it. Not with the love and desperation pouring from Rowan's eyes. And not with the way her heart nearly disintegrated at the thought of never seeing him again.

So, she'd given him an ultimatum in return. Give up his quest for treasure, just this one time, and prove to her he was willing to change. If he could do that, she'd stay away from the amulet. Regardless of whether it could send her home or not, she'd remain with Rowan and help him become the man God wanted him to be.

Sitting, she swung her legs over the edge of the hard bunk and dropped her head in her hands. More shouts echoed from above, and she tried to decipher the voices, seeking the one that made her feel more alive than ever before … yet all the while listening for the sounds of a boat being lowered and Rowan departing—final proof that he loved his treasure more than her.

She would not face him until she knew—had told him as much. And so she sat, listening as the ship teetered and creaked and the water lapped against the hull—all sounds that told her they had stopped and were anchored somewhere.

Blackbeard nudged her before squeezing between her arms to plop on her lap.

"You wouldn't go after the treasure and leave me, would you, little one?" She stroked his fur. "Even if you are named after a mean ol' pirate."

He stretched and rolled on his back so she could rub his belly. She happily complied for several minutes before he leapt back onto her cot and snuggled among the blankets.

An unpleasant smell rose from the dress she'd been wearing for a week, so she passed the time trying to clean it as best she could—along with herself—with the water Edith had left in the basin. Her kingdom for a bar of soap, deodorant, or some perfume. But that wasn't going to happen. So she did her best to make herself presentable. Not that it mattered because the noises drifting down from above confirmed her worst fears.

Forcing back tears, she lowered back onto the cot and waited for the sound of the boat pushing off from the hull. There it was—the thud of oars striking wood. Her heart turned to sand. Rising, she drew a deep breath, opened the door, and headed to Rowan's cabin.

As she entered, dawn's light curled fingers of gold through the stern windows, shimmering over the remnants of their romantic dinner last night, reminding her of the special time they'd shared, eating, talking, laughing … kissing. She touched her lips, her heart soaring at the memory. To her right, the painting stared at her—with that look of complete adoration she'd captured in his eyes. The one she'd first seen on the replica of this ship back in San Diego. She hadn't been completely sure it was the same painting until yesterday when she'd put the final touches on it. Then when the realization hit her that she'd signed it LM for Lady Minx, her head had spun with shock. Apparently she had a future in painting pirates if she remembered what the silly tour guide had said on the replica. Which meant she was supposed to stay, wasn't she? Groaning, she rubbed her temples. Impossible!

But God was a God of the impossible, wasn't He?

She drew a deep breath. The cabin smelled like Rowan, spice and man, and she hoped it would steady her nerves, but it only caused her heart to sink. Not ready to leave this time quite yet, she moved to the window where a white sandy beach surrounded by lush greenery oscillated in and out of view. The Caribbean was so beautiful. Particularly in its natural state before commercialism took over and resorts rose on every shore. She would miss it.

She would miss Rowan most of all.

"Father, I don't know why this happened to me, but I know You are making all things work out for the best. Please give me strength to do what I must." What she had sworn to do if Rowan continued his quest for the treasure, proving he would never change and she could never trust him.

Wiping away a tear, she spun to face the desk and opened the top right drawer where Rowan said he would place the amulet for her to decide. On the off chance it didn't work, she would insist he deposit her at the next port, or, better yet, take her to Kingston, where she would eventually run across Charlisse and Merrick. Surely they would help her get on her feet. Either way, she was in God's capable hands.

She reached into the drawer.

It wasn't there. She sifted through the contents, then searched the other drawers, and finally scanned the top of the desk.

She stomped her foot. "Liar! Beast!"

"Och now, ye wouldna by chance be referring t' Rowan?"

Morgan looked up to see Nick leaning against the door post.

"He lied to me!"

Nick cocked a brow. "And tha' surprises ye, lass?"

Morgan circled the desk, feeling more betrayed than she expected. "Yes, it does. I thought we had an understanding … I thought …"

"Tha' he loves ye?"

She frowned at the man's uncanny way of reading her mind. "He said he'd leave the amulet here for me to decide whether I would stay with him or not. I told him that if he went for the treasure, I would leave."

"Ah, tha's why he seemed so unsure of himself this morn," Nick said. "No' like him at all."

"Still, he left."

"Aye. A man's lifelong dream is a hard one t' turn yer back on, even if 'tis the wrong dream."

"Why are you here, Nick? I thought he'd bring you along to help."

"Nay. My orders are t' protect ye, lass. When I didna find ye in Edith's cabin, I knew ye'd be here."

Morgan released a heavy sigh. She supposed she should be comforted that Rowan thought of her, but her anger forbade any nice thoughts about the man at the moment.

"How long will he—"

"A sail! A sail!" A shout blared down the companionway, spinning Nick around. He turned back only long enough to grab her hand and pull her along behind him, up a ladder, and onto the quarterdeck to a blast of wind and the firing rays of a rising sun.

She came to a halt beside Rooster at the helm and Scratch with telescope to his eye, studying something in the distance. He handed it to Nick.

"Where away?" Nick asked.

"A point off the stern quarter."

Morgan followed the direction of Scratch's finger and peered into the morning haze. Something flickered on the horizon. Or at least she thought she saw something. There it was again.

Nick groaned.

"What is it?" she asked.

He lowered the scope and slapped it in the palm of his hand. "'Tis Bloodmoon's ship. The ignorant carp musta followed us. Devil's blood! I shoulda known."

"Bloodmoon?" Sweat broke out on Morgan's palms.

"Aye. He'll be here within an hour."

Morgan stared at the ship now forming on the horizon. "He's going after the treasure. He'll find Rowan and kill him."

Nick's jaw tightened. "Aye, tha' would be his plan."

"Then we have no choice. We have to warn him!"

~ ~

The Reckoning

Chapter 28

Rowan thrust his sword through a mass of thick vines blocking the trail. In front of him, Abbot and Terrin did the same, while behind him, Hendrix and three more of his crew marched in single file. Not wanting to leave the *Reckoning* undefended, he'd brought just enough men to haul the treasure back to the ship. Unless there was more gold than the rumors bespoke, which would be fine by Rowan. They had plenty of time to make several trips.

Birds of all sizes and colors leapt from branch to branch above him, warbling their happy tunes, while insects hovered in a misty cloud about his sweaty face and neck. But he and his men would be there soon. He could already hear the water gushing over the cliff into the pond, that—according to the map—hid the chest full of treasure within the arms of its silty bed.

Rowan had been to this island once before. He and his crew had sought shelter from a storm, but had ended up staying several days when they discovered fruit and fresh water. Lud, he'd even swum in that same pond where just a short distance beneath his feet had lain enough wealth to make all his dreams come true.

If there was a God, He definitely had a sense of humor.

A humor that seemed to have escaped Rowan at the moment, for despite the good fortune about to come his way, he found his spirits low and his feet barely able to slog through the mud. 'Twas that infuriating, self-righteous woman! She had bewitched him. 'Twas the only explanation why his thoughts sped more to her than to the impending fortune that would solve all his problems.

He slashed the branch of a large fern and trudged forward, fingering the amulet in his pocket. Guilt swamped him, weighing him down more than the humidity saturating the air. He hadn't planned on taking it, but the very thought that she'd be gone when he returned to the ship was unbearable—unconscionable, in fact—and had nearly kept him from going. This way, at least he'd have another chance to speak with her, to convince her of his love, that treasure or no, he couldn't live without her. Of course it wouldn't hurt that he would already have the fortune in his possession.

Still, though he could hear the water clearly now and his men were beginning to chatter excitedly, he found no joy bubbling within him. Quite the contrary. What in hellfire was wrong with him? More than once, he'd even entertained the thought of turning back, forsaking the treasure, and marrying the lady. Faith, wouldn't that be a mad turn of events! The great pirate Rowan Dutton giving up his freedom, his treasure, for the likes of a woman of no name, property, or fortune.

Swatting a bug, Rowan brushed aside a thicket of greenery and emerged onto the shore of a sparkling pond. Abbot and Terrin were already kneeling and splashing water over their faces and necks and bringing handfuls to their mouths. The rest of his men soon followed, cursing and dabbing the sweat on their necks with bandannas.

"Hotter than Hades, says I," one of them proclaimed as he tugged off his boots and waded into the water.

"Hendrix, Terrin, strip down," Rowan ordered, raking a hand through his sweaty hair. They were his best swimmers, and he would need their help hauling the chest to shore.

Flinging his baldric and pistols over his head, he laid them aside and removed his shirt, not allowing the pain still emanating from his wounds to show on his face. He fished in his pouch for the map and held it up to the light. Falls, aye. Morgan's interpretation of the code was scrawled right in the middle of the island beside the picture of a waterfall. Which could only mean one thing. Brasiliano had hidden his gold behind the waterfall or beneath it. Exactly where Rowan would have hidden it as well.

He glanced to his left, where water cascaded over a twenty foot drop into a rippling pond that smoothed to near glass as it extended toward the opposite shore. Treetops and blue sky reflected in the water like a painting, while nothing but a maze of green lined the sand in all directions. Good. They were alone.

"Hendrix, Terrin, with me. The rest of you keep watch." Rowan sat on a rock to remove his boots when the sound of footsteps and leaves shuffling intruded on the peaceful rush of water. Grabbing his cutlass, he leapt to his feet and faced the jungle. His men did the same, cocking pistols and hefting swords.

Leaves moved and Abbot cocked his pistol. Rowan grabbed his wrist, staying the shot just as Nick burst into the clearing.

"What the devil are you—"

Green skirts flashed between the branches, and Morgan followed behind him, her breath heavy, her hair full of twigs and leaves, her skin glistening with sweat. And despite his anger at the interruption, he'd never seen her look so beautiful.

"'Tis Bloodmoon," Nick panted out as his stern gaze met Rowan's. "He's here. Anchored offshore by now."

Rowan fisted his hands, cursing himself. "He followed us. Of course."

Morgan rushed to him. "You have to leave. He'll kill you."

He wanted to take her in his arms and tell her he loved her. Instead he turned to Nick in anger. "Are you daft? What possessed you to bring her? Especially with Bloodmoon on the way."

Nick shrugged. "Have ye ever tried t' order her aboot?"

Rowan growled, glanced over at Terrin and Hendrix all ready for a swim, then over at the falls where the wealth he'd sought his entire life lay within his grasp.

"How close is he?"

"Close enough." Nick gave him that look Rowan knew all too well—a look that bespoke of the seriousness of the situation.

Morgan tugged on him. "You don't have time, Rowan. Please come back with us."

Rowan glanced over his men. "Give us a moment." Then taking Morgan's hand, he led her through a mass of greenery to a more private spot where he spun her to face him.

"Lud, woman, do you know the danger you've put yourself in? Bloodmoon may kill me, but what he'll do to you will be worse than death."

"Exactly. All the more reason we should go now." She pulled him, but he remained in place, staring at her, at the fear and desperation in her eyes. "Listen, Rowan. I came because I knew I'd have a better chance than Nick of persuading you to come back."

The shock of her words spun his thoughts into bewilderment. "You could die. I'm not worth it."

Her expression softened as she reached to caress his jaw. "That's what love does, Rowan."

Something shifted in his heart. A change so palpable, he could swear he felt it grow in his chest. He stared at her, through her shimmering green eyes, and straight down to her heart that was so full of love for him.

And he realized that all the treasure in the world could never compare to her.

Morgan saw something flicker in Rowan's blue eyes, as if a light went on, scattering the darkness. He pulled her against his sweaty body, but she didn't care. It felt incredible to be in his arms again—it felt right. He gently stroked her hair as a deep rumble began in his chest, growing louder and louder, and eventually spilling from his lips. Was he laughing at *her*, mocking her love for him?

She stepped back. "What's so funny?" But the look in his eyes was anything but taunting. It was affection, admiration, and joy all bundled together.

His lips curved as he rubbed the stubble on his chin. "I must be going mad, but I've a mind to ask you to be my wife."

She didn't know whether to laugh, cry, or leap for joy. The sincerity in his eyes caused her to do all three. Yet still … she finally sobered and studied him intently. Had she heard him right? "I have to admit that's not quite the way I pictured a man proposing to me."

"My apologies, Lady Minx. Allow me to correct my bumbling attempt." He knelt in the mud, took her hand in his, then gazed up at her, a serious but unusually vulnerable look on his face. With his bare chest glistening, hair hanging to his shoulders, a day's stubble on his jaw, and a cutlass strapped to his side, he appeared a pirate by all accounts—the existential bad-boy charmer she should run away from as fast as she could.

But love wasn't always safe. Life wasn't always safe. And Morgan had learned that the control she'd thought she had over everything was all a delusion. Only by resting in God did she find peace.

"Miss Morgan Shaw, will you do me the honor of becoming my wife?" Rowan felt through his pockets with his free hand. "Alas, I have no ring, but I promise to purchase you the most beautiful one in all of the Caribbean."

He was serious. He was *actually* proposing. Shock sped through her, followed by unbelief, and then a joy that tentatively crept out from hiding, making sure the way was clear from danger, from heartbreak. But was it? "With whose treasure?" she asked him, her hopes teetering on his response.

"Not this treasure." He nodded toward the pond behind him. "Not if gaining it means losing you, Lady Minx." He caressed her hand again. "I never thought I'd say this, but you mean more to me than a ship-full of treasure."

Morgan's vision clouded. "What changed your mind?"

He continued kneeling in the mud, the steely pirate brought to his knees, still gazing at her as if she were made of gold. "The thought of you leaving me forever," he said. "And knowing you'd risk your life for mine. I suppose I never truly believed you could love a blackguard like me."

The sound of a throat clearing followed by Nick's voice filtered over them. "It would be better if we left sooner rather than later, Captain."

Rowan kissed her hand. "Torture me no longer. What say you, Lady Minx?"

She lowered to kneel beside him, smiling. "I say yes!"

He showered her face with kiss after kiss, then wiped her tears with his thumb. "Why are you crying?"

"For joy, my love. For joy!" A sparkle caught her eye, and she glanced down to see a gold object by his knee. A piece of jewelry of some sort? "What is this?" She picked it up and turned it around.

A heart shaped ruby embedded in engraved gold stared up at her. *The amulet.*

Her heart stopped. Her insides screamed *NO!*

She gazed up at Rowan in horror. His eyes—equally filled with terror—shifted between her and the amulet.

Yet moments passed and she remained. Expelling a huge breath, she held the precious amulet to her chest. "It doesn't work. Thank God, It doesn't work!"

Rowan helped her to stand, his own breath heavy with relief. "'Tis best we leave."

"I'm so happy, Rowan," she said as he put his arm around her and led her through the bushes. Another tear spilled down her cheek. She stared down at the amulet, admiring the gold crosses on either side of the beautiful ruby, reinforcing even more that God had saved her.

The tear fell from her jaw, drifted through the air as if it weighed no more than a feather.

Rowan gasped, and in her blurry vision she saw his hand reach for the amulet.

Horrified, but unable to move, she watched, as if in a dream, her tear—a glittering pearl shimmering in a ray of sunshine—falling down … down … down…

Rowan grabbed the amulet.

Her tear struck.

Water engulfed Morgan. She gulped for air. The sea flooded her lungs. Blurred shapes and shadows surrounded her. She kicked her feet, but they got hopelessly tangled in her gown. Her arms felt weighted with lead. Above her, streams of light twisted beyond the surface. She moved her hands and flapped her legs, trying to swim, but her dress and underthings were like an anchor. She sank further and further into the darkness. Her mind reeled with shock. How did she get here? Where was she? *God, help me. Please …*

A splash sounded above her. Arms grabbed her, pulling her through the liquid death, hoisting her into the sun. Her lungs screamed for air. She landed on something hard. Faces twirled around her. A mouth landed on hers.

"Breathe! Breathe!" someone shouted.

Air tried to force its way through the water in her lungs. Pain. All she felt was pain.

A mouth encompassed hers again. More air.

She coughed, turned her head, and spewed a lungful of water.

Clapping and cheering sounded. A siren blared.

She gasped for more air.

"You're going to be all right now, Miss." The accent was British.

"What happened to her?" Men in uniform surrounded her.

"No idea. She just appeared in the water."

Morgan felt herself being lifted and placed on a gurney.

"Thank you," she managed to mumble to the man who had saved her, before the ambulance doors slammed shut.

Chapter 29

Muted sounds, distant and strange, tiptoed through Morgan's mind. Not the creak and groan of a ship, not the jarring flap of sail or the rush of water against the hull, but odd beeps and bells and phones ringing and people talking and shoes shuffling over tiled floors. Along with the incessant drone of electricity.

The smell of antiseptic and sickness stung her nose, and she nearly gagged, searching for the soothing scent of oak, tar, and the sea. And the musky, spicy smell that was only Rowan.

"Rowan … Rowan." The name dragged her further from her unconscious bliss. But then the pain started—her heart an empty shell, a black hole sucking her life into emptiness. "Rowan." She'd lost Rowan. *No!* She retreated into oblivion.

"Darling, you're awake." The familiar voice dragged her back. "Morgan. I'm here, darling."

Against everything within her, Morgan pried one eye open. Her mother sat by her side, holding her hand and looking more tired than Morgan remembered. Short brown hair curled around a face that bore more lines and sags than her fifty years should warrant. Still her drug-hazed eyes held genuine love and concern.

"Mother."

The woman tried to smile, though fear peeked from the corners of her lips. "What on earth happened, dear? How did you end up in the bay?"

Morgan opened her other eye, knowing before she did what she would find. A hospital room, complete with beeping monitors, trays on wheels, blue privacy curtains on a track around her bed, an old TV set hanging on the wall, and that sickly sterile smell that made her stomach lurch.

So, the amulet had worked after all. Her breath clogged in her throat and she raised her hands—empty hands. "Where's the amulet?"

"What amulet?"

"I was holding an amulet." Her heart plummeted. She must have dropped it in the water.

"Are you all right, dear? You look so pale."

"How long?" The words drizzled from Morgan's lips, from a mind that was growing more dazed by the minute.

At her mother's curious look, Morgan added, "How long have I been gone?"

Her mother shook her head. "You went to the Royal Tall Ship Festival just this morning. Why were you dressed in that old gown? And how did you end up in the water? I hope you weren't drinking at one of those pubs downtown."

Morgan blinked, trying to collect her thoughts. Just a moment in time. She'd only been gone a moment in time. Yet her entire life—her very eternity—had been saved in that single moment.

"I was on Rowan's shi—" Where had the replica of his ship gone? She breathed out a sigh, trying to steady her racing pulse. "It's a long story, Mom." A very long story. One that her current state of shock prevented her from telling.

"I told you not to go to that festival. Especially with *that* friend of yours. No doubt this is all her fault." Her mother scowled. "Besides, you are sick, Morgan. You must remember that."

The cancer. Would it have returned now that Morgan was back? Yet, aside from the trauma of being home again, she still felt different—strong and healthy on the outside and free and renewed on the inside. *God, what is going on? Please?*

His presence remained.

"Why are you crying?" Her mother squeezed her hand. "You're safe now."

A nurse peeked around the corner, and upon seeing Morgan awake, sped to her bedside, smiled and checked various instruments. "You'll be fine now, Miss. Just a wee bit of water in your lungs, but you're breathing well on your own."

Why did she have a British accent? Morgan studied the tag on the woman's uniform. Above her name, Emily something, the words "Queen Arabella Mercy Hospital" stood out in stark black letters.

"Where am I?"

"In hospital, Miss," the nurse replied. "You fell into the bay. Don't you remember?"

"What city?"

"San Diego, of course." Her mother shot an embarrassed look toward the nurse.

Morgan rubbed her forehead. "I've never heard of Queen Arabella Hospital."

"Nonsense. It's the largest hospital in town." Her mother gave a nervous chuckle. "She's disoriented is all."

"Nearly drowning will do that." The nurse smiled and checked Morgan's pulse, then shoved a thermometer in her mouth while she squeezed her arm with one of those blood pressure machines. When she finished, she turned to leave, announcing the doctor would be there soon to release her.

Morgan tried to gather her thoughts yet again, but they spun out of control. "Mom … something incredible happened." Should she tell her? Would she even believe her?

"Now, don't you worry about your father," her mother replied as if Morgan hadn't said anything. "He called and sends his love. He'll drop by our flat tomorrow. You know how busy he is." She gazed out the window as sorrow darkened her face.

Flat? "Mom, I'm cured of cancer. God healed me."

Her mother's plucked eyebrows collided. She opened her mouth to say something when Tiffany bounded into the room. At least Morgan thought it was Tiffany. Bright purple hair, cut in a spiky bob, replaced her normal platinum blond. Gobs of sparkling—and way too bright—makeup was plastered over her face, and her low cut blouse and short skirt were even too risqué for her.

"What are *you* doing here?" Morgan's mother snipped.

"She's my friend, Mom."

Ignoring Morgan's mother, Tiffany leaned on the edge of the bed. "What the hell happened, girl? When I left you on that bench to go get a drink, I didn't expect you to jump in the bay!"

"You wouldn't believe me if I told you. Last thing I remember was you and Brad on the replica ship, the *Reckoning*." Just saying the name drove a nail through Morgan's heart.

"The *Reckoning*? I don't remember a ship called that. And who is Brad?"

Morgan stared at her friend, more confused than ever. Either Morgan was dreaming or she'd gone completely crazy. Maybe that's why she was here in the hospital, and no one was telling her this was the mental ward.

"Never mind. What's with the accent? And this …" Morgan fingered Tiffany's hair. "When did you dye your hair?"

"It's been this color for months now, silly." Tiffany chomped on her gum.

Morgan scanned her friend's attire. "Going out clubbing so early in the day?"

Tiffany cast a glance toward Morgan's mother, who had turned to stare out the window again, then leaned toward Morgan and whispered. "I have a date."

Her mother snorted. "Is that what you call it?"

Morgan knew that tone—that self-righteous judgmental tone of her mother's that made everyone around her feel like dirt. Morgan would have none of it. "Tiffany's not a prostitute, Mom. She's my friend and my roommate."

Frowning, Tiffany looked away, but Morgan's squeeze on her hand brought her gaze back.

"You've always been a good friend, Morgan. I wish we *were* flatmates, but you live with your mum."

What in the heck was going on? Morgan's heart ran a marathon in her chest. She rubbed her eyes. "Maybe I just need rest."

Tiffany kissed her cheek and whispered in her ear, "I best go before your mum has a heart attack. I'll phone you later."

Morgan nodded and struggled to sit. "Where are my clothes?" The sooner she got out of here, the sooner she could discover what had happened. And more importantly how she could get back to Rowan. The thought brought renewed tears to her eyes, but she batted them away.

"I brought some from home." Her mother handed her a paper bagged stuffed with a pair of jeans, panties and bra, a shirt, and sandals.

"Thanks, Mom"

"But really, dear. You still haven't told me why you were in the bay. And in that silly old dress?"

"I don't know. I guess I just fell in." No sense in telling the woman what Morgan was having a hard time believing herself.

"Of all the …." Her mother's thin lips twisted in that familiar castigating frown. "First you stop going to church with me. Then you make friends with that"—she glanced out the door where Tiffany had just left as if the devil himself had paid them a visit—"*person*. And now you embarrass me to death by these silly antics."

Morgan sighed. Well, at least some things hadn't changed.

She slipped behind the curtain to dress. How weird it felt to have jeans on again … almost uncomfortable. How many days had she longed for her jeans on board Rowan's ship, despising the constraining and cumbersome clothing she'd been forced to wear? Only somewhere along the way, she'd gotten used to it, had actually enjoyed the way it made her feel pretty and feminine. She nearly laughed at the thought, but then started to cry again. *Why is this happening, Lord? I want to go back to Rowan. Dear God, I want to go back.* She nearly crumpled to the floor when she heard the doctor enter.

Quickly drying her eyes, she went out to meet him, but he was already talking with her mother.

"She doesn't have cancer, Mrs. Shaw. At least none we can find with our preliminary blood tests."

Her mother blinked and glanced at Morgan, who only smiled in return.

"That's impossible. She was diagnosed with Stage 3 just a few weeks ago."

"We'll take another blood sample before she leaves, and if we see anything, I'll schedule an MRI, but it looks like she's cancer free."

Just when things couldn't get any weirder, the ride home blew Morgan's mind. Were there such things as parallel universes? If so—and she'd believe anything was possible after what she'd been through—God must have sent her back to the wrong one. For one thing, the steering wheel in her mother's car had moved to the passenger side. Morgan had slipped behind it, ready for the drive home, only to have her mother exclaim, "I never let you drive my car, dear!" before ushering her to the driver's side. As if that wasn't strange enough, her mother proceeded to drive on the left side of the road. Morgan nearly wrestled the steering wheel out of her hands before she noticed everyone was driving on that side.

However, all that was forgotten when Morgan glanced out the windows. She barely recognized the city of her birth. Shopping centers, restaurants and high-rise buildings she'd known all her life had been replaced by strange, almost European-style architecture—offices, pubs, tea houses, taverns, restaurants boasting the "Best fish and chips in the Kingdom", department stores and supermarkets with names she'd never heard of. A coffee shop called Costa had replaced the Starbucks near her house. Even the billboards were different. One pictured a king and queen waving in front of a palace. Another boasted of the city's cricket team, ironically named the Pirates.

By the time they reached the apartment she supposedly shared with her mother, a massive knot had formed in Morgan's chest. What had happened to America? Why was everything suddenly so British?

A million questions screamed in her mind as her mother ushered her inside the sparsely decorated living room—or lounge as she called it. But Morgan could voice none of them. All she could think about was Rowan. Where was he? What had happened to him after she'd disappeared?

She sank onto a stained couch and tried to steady her breathing. Maybe she was having a nightmare. A very horrible nightmare.

Her mother's worried face blasted into her vision. "I'm going to put on a pot of tea, dear, and bring you some biscuits. You'll feel better in no time." She patted Morgan on the back and sped off to the kitchen.

Tea? When had her mother ever drank tea? It was always coffee. Starbucks was her home away from home. Morgan dropped her head in her hands and gripped her hair. *Think. Think. Think.* What was happening? She'd obviously come back to the present. But not the present she knew.

She jumped to her feet. "Where's my iPad? Which one is my room?"

Her mother rushed from the kitchen, dish towel in her hand. "What's an iPad?"

Only then did Morgan see the boxy TV set in the middle of the living room, not the digital HD flat screen her mother owned that took up half a wall. Dazed, Morgan headed down the hall, peeking in doors to find her bedroom, feeling as though she moved through a dream. There, the room with everything perfectly in place and her paintings covering the walls. Flinging open her closet doors, she rifled through her clothes, then pulled out her dresser drawers and rummaged through her neatly stacked underthings and t-shirts.

"What are you looking for?" Her mother entered behind her.

"A tablet, mother. An electronic table. And have you seen my iPhone?"

"I don't know what you are talking about, dear. Please sit down, you're worrying me."

No iPad presented itself, no iPhone, no laptop, just some weird round gizmo with a curved screen and a tiny movable ball at the bottom.

"What is this?" Morgan turned it over, looking for an on-switch.

"It's your Electronic Slip. You know that, Morgan." Snagging it, her mother pressed a button on the side and handed it back to Morgan. "You must have hit your head when you fell in the bay. Oh my, I knew they shouldn't have released you from the hospital so soon."

The round screen lit up with the name EdinCorp scrawled in white letters on a blue background. Morgan tapped it. Nothing happened. No icons appeared. "How does this work?" She sank onto the bed, pressing her fingers all over screen.

Easing beside her, her mother laid the pad aside and took Morgan's hands. "Never mind that. You need your rest now."

"Where am I? What has happened to me?" Tears filled Morgan's eyes.

"Don't go barmy on me, dear. I couldn't take it." Plucking a bottle of pills from a pocket in her apron, her mother slammed two to the back of her throat.

Morgan gathered herself. She had to be strong. She always had to be the strong one. "Just answer me one question, Mom. And don't freak."

Too late. Her mother's expression twisted in apprehension.

"What country is this?"

Terror streaked across her mother's glassy eyes. "Why do you ask such a thing? Are you trying to give me a nervous breakdown?"

"Just please answer me."

"The UBE, of course."

"United ...." Morgan started.

"British Empire," her mother finished and laid the back of her hand on Morgan's forehead.

Morgan's stomach tangled in a knot, forcing bile into her throat. She had changed history. She'd done something that had stopped the United States from being born. The implication struck her like a tornado, nearly knocking her from the bed. Leaping to her feet, she pressed a hand over her thrashing heart. "What have I done? What have I done?"

Her mother merely stared at her. "Morgan, please calm down. Remember your health." She handed Morgan her bottle of pills. "Here, take some of these."

"I don't want your pills, and I don't have cancer."

"Sweetheart, I don't want to frighten you, but that was only one test. They could have been wrong."

Grabbing the weird pad, Morgan tapped the screen again. Nothing. Finally, she tried spinning the round ball at the bottom. The name EdinCorp instantly faded, replaced by a long menu of items listed in an outline. "How do I get to the Internet? I need to look something up."

"The what? You're not making any sense, Morgan. Please."

Of course. An American invented the Internet. And without Steve Jobs and Bill Gates, there was no Microsoft and Apple. Even if they were alive, there may have been no opportunity to create their technology. "What do you use this pad … I mean slip for?"

"Writing, keeping track of things, lists to remember, calculator, games, things like that. I don't really use mine."

"Can I look up information, like in a library?"

"You mean the EELib?"

Morgan nodded, though she had no idea what that was.

"We can't afford the subscription, Morgan. You know that." Her mother swallowed nervously and stared at the bottle of pills in her hand.

Morgan gripped her wrist before she managed to open it and take more. "You don't need those. I'm okay. Really." Tossing the slip to the bed, she moved to her window and looked out on a world she no longer knew. "Oh, Mom, you wouldn't believe what happened to me if I told you. I hardly believe it myself. But one thing I've learned, God is in control. He loves us and we don't have to fear anymore. We don't have to worry all the time. He *does* answer prayer and He will never leave us." She faced her mother, but the poor woman's lip quivered.

"I know that dear. Of course I know that."

But did she really?

Replacing her pills in her pocket, her mother sniffed and drew out a handkerchief. "There's a computer at the library."

Without the Internet it wouldn't do Morgan any good. But a library might. "Where's the closest one?"

"You know, the San Diego Park Library."

Morgan knelt before her. "It's going to be all right, Mom. With God's help I'm going to fix things."

Yet even as she said it, even as she borrowed some weird British money with the image of a queen on it for a bus, and headed out the door … even as she walked through the ornate wooden doors of the library, she wondered if God could change history. Of course He could. He could do anything, right? He'd transported her through time, and He could do it again.

Even though she'd lost the amulet.

But *would* He send her back? Would He want her to fix things? And if so, why had He brought her back here in the first place? Her mind cycloned with too many thoughts, too many questions, too many unknowns.

God, I know I was a control freak before, but taking all control away? Really?

And how am I supposed to live without Rowan?

That last thought drained her remaining strength, and she grabbed onto the edge of table to keep from falling. She must keep the tears from falling too, or they'd kick her out for making a spectacle of herself. Brits were notoriously stodgy that way. Or so she'd heard.

She made her way to the history section, desperate to discover why the American British colonies had failed in their revolution. It only took three good reference books and one hour to find out that the British army and navy had quickly squashed the "impertinent rebellion of colonial savages" as one book had put it. "A disorderly, uneducated breed of farmers and tradesmen who knew no more about military discipline and strategy than a brothel full of trollops."

Still, Morgan could not find the exact reason they were defeated. Especially when real history proved that these *uneducated savages* had outwitted and outmaneuvered the most powerful army on earth at the time.

Leaning back in her chair, she blew out a sigh and rubbed her eyes. Maybe she would never know. That upset her the most. Especially when she continued to read and discovered that, without the United States' help in World War II, the Nazis had overrun Europe and were now in a war with a Muslim Caliphate over land in the Middle East.

The room began to spin and she laid her head on the table. The world was in chaos. And all because of her. What could she have done to change things so drastically? She'd only been in 1694 twenty-one days, had only spoken to a handful of people.

Father, please help me.

The word "Rowan" whispered in her ear. A palatable pain severed her heart. *What are You trying to tell me?* The old Morgan would have assumed God was torturing her for some sin. The new Morgan knew better. Rising, she perused the volumes of history books lining the shelves. But there was no book about Rowan Dutton, the great pirate, and no mention of him in the larger volumes listing famous pirates.

Finally, in the index of one of the older books, she spotted his name, *Dutton, Rowan, pirate.* Her lungs turned to stone. Did she really want to know? She carried the volume back to the table and sat, caressing the worn cover for several minutes as she attempted to stop her heart from bursting through her chest. What if he'd died a horrible death? What if she'd had no effect on his life at all? What if he married a beautiful princess and had forgotten all about her?

She chided herself for the last selfish thought. Of course she'd want him to be happy.

Either way, was there anything she could do to change a history that had already happened?

But she had to know. There had to be a reason God had sent her back in time. She flipped to the page and ran a finger down the script.

Rowan Dutton (1671-1694)

Her breath fled her.

Captain Rowan Dutton had an unremarkable and short career as a pirate on the Caribbean from 1692-1694 and was finally killed by William Bloodmoon in a fight over treasure on Little St. James Island. He is buried there to this day.

Chapter 30

Morgan dreamed of cannon fire, glittering turquoise seas, and tall sails flapping in the wind. Rowan's handsome face appeared before her. Those stark blue eyes of his looking at her as if she were the most precious thing in the world. He smiled and reached for her, beckoning her to come … to come back to him.

Rowan ... Rowan ...

A tear spilled from her eye, jarring her from her sleep. A stack of books blurred in her vision as she listened for familiar sounds—wood creaking and rushing water and shouts from above, longing to hear that singular voice of the man she loved.

Oh, God, please let this have been a nightmare! Please!

But all that met her ears was the sound of traffic outside the window.

She tried to lift her head, but her face appeared to be stuck to something. Placing her hands on the desk, she carefully pried it from—ah, yes, she looked down—from the atlas she'd been studying. A map of the Caribbean. The map showing the location of Little St. James Island. The same island where Brasiliano had buried his treasure.

The same island where Rowan had proposed to her.

She rubbed her eyes before the tears came. She'd spent way too much time crying last night, crying and praying, then pleading with God and crying some more.

The whistle of a tea kettle rang down the hall. Morgan looked at her clock. 6:30 a.m. When had her mother ever been up this early? She must really be worried about Morgan. Which is why Morgan had purposely checked out the books she needed and came home early last night.

But it had been a long, agonizing night as the realization of her situation finally found root in her mind. Rowan had gone for the treasure anyway. Had he done so because Morgan had disappeared, or had that been his plan all along? Hadn't she had any effect on him whatsoever? Maybe that's why God had sent her back in time in the first place—to try and save Rowan. But when God knew Rowan would go for the treasure anyway, He plucked Morgan back to her own time. To protect her. To protect her heart. Her head spun trying to figure it all out.

But one thing was clear. She had not only lost Rowan, but the world had been turned upside down.

All the good that America had done for the world and for her own people—the freedom she offered, the technology, the innovation, the charity, the missionaries, the wars she joined in the fight against tyranny—all of that had been ripped away as if thousands of pages had been torn from a history book.

Not to mention that for some reason her good friend Tiffany was now a prostitute!

And Rowan had died twenty years younger than he would have.

And it was all her fault.

How did one live with that?

One didn't. One went mad. Which is what Morgan felt like she was doing, a slow descent into insanity. Yet at the moment, it sounded more appealing than living beneath the weight of her guilt. Had she failed God? Was there something she was supposed to have done back in 1694 that she hadn't?

It was all too much to consider.

So, she prayed and prayed … and prayed.

And despite her agony, despite her tears, she felt God's presence. She felt Him smiling down on her. Most of all, she'd felt His peace. As if all this craziness was part of some master plan and she had only to trust Him.

Trust. Not something she did very well. No, that's not true. She'd trusted in structure, order, plans, and schedules—everything in its place and time.

But now everything was out of place and time!

She rubbed her eyes again and slowly stood, gazing once more at the map on her desk. During the long hours of the night, she had heard one thing from God. Or so she'd thought. Maybe it was just her own desire, her need for closure. But the urging had grown stronger and now overpowered her with the first rays of the sun.

She must go to Little St. James Island. She must see Rowan's grave for herself. She must sit by his gravestone—if there even was one—and tell him how much she loved him, how much she missed him, and how sorry she was.

She had to say goodbye.

Her research had told her that Little St. James was now a resort for the rich and famous, but they had reserved a small section on the western coast of the island as an historical landmark containing a small fort and graveyard, where Rowan was purportedly buried. But how to get there? It would take money and connections she didn't have.

"Breakfast is ready, dear!" her mother called down the hall.

Morgan smiled. She knew just what to do.

"But you can't leave." Morgan's mother pressed down the folds of her flowery dress and slid into a chair in their living room. Complete with stockings, pumps and a pearl necklace, she was all ready to go to church. The Anglican church, apparently, was alive and well in the UBE, though Morgan couldn't swear to the "well" part, since her mother seemed no closer to God than when she'd attended the nondenominational church in the American San Diego.

"You're not well," she added. "You shouldn't be traveling." She fumbled with her purse and scowled. "I knew I shouldn't have allowed you to call your father."

"Mom, I'm twenty-four. You can hardly send me to my room. Besides, as I keep trying to tell you, I'm not sick anymore. I'm only going to Little St. James for a few days. It's a British colony, anyway. No harm will come to me."

In fact, Morgan had discovered that Britain owned most of the Caribbean and much of Mexico too. Another odd turn of events. Still, she hated appealing to her father for money. But how else could she afford to travel there, let alone pay the exorbitant fee required to even land on the island. She didn't even want to stay at their stupid resort, but the travel agent said anyone setting foot on the island must pay for a week's stay.

Her father had definitely choked at the price. But in the end, it was her cancer that made him agree, saying she needed the rest before she started chemo. Though she hesitated to correct him at the risk of losing his generous gift, a twinge of conviction made her confess that God had healed her of the cancer. To which he laughed and insisted all the more that she needed rest. Before she'd hung up, she'd told him that she loved him, and that God loved him too, and she prayed those words would sink deep into his soul one day.

Now, as her mother fidgeted on her chair, searching her purse for her pills, Morgan felt compelled to try to convince her again of the reality of God. She glanced at the clock on the wall and bit her lip. She had to leave or she'd miss her plane.

"Mom." Morgan knelt on the carpet before her mother's chair. "God loves you. You don't have to do anything to gain

His love. He'll always love you the same, no matter what. He just wants a relationship with you. He wants you to talk to Him like a real person."

Confusion churned in her mother's eyes.

"He's like Jesus, Mom. He does miracles—healing, casting out demons, raising people from the dead. He hasn't changed."

"Honey, everyone knows all that stopped with the apostles."

"My health is living proof that isn't true, Mom. Why do you put God in a box when He has so much more to give you? Peace, for one thing. Freedom from worry and fear."

Her mother cupped Morgan's jaw and smiled. "I don't know what happened to you, Morgan, but I'm glad to hear you speak of God."

Morgan took one more glance at the clock, stood, and grabbed her suitcase. "I love you, Mom. I'll see you when I get back." She leaned down and kissed her mother's cheek then hurried out the door before her mother made a scene.

After a six-hour grueling flight—during which Morgan questioned her sanity more than once—she landed on St. Thomas. From there she would take a charter boat to Little Saint James, just a few miles offshore. Exhausted, she gathered her things from the overhead, and filed out behind tourists giddy with excitement—and alcohol. Each of them traveled with lovers, friends, or family.

Morgan was alone.

Alone, yet braver than she ever remembered being, for she would have never made this trip by herself before. Yet, what did she truly hope to accomplish—other than further heartache—by visiting Rowan's grave? If she could even find it.

As soon as she began descending the steps onto the tarmac, a breeze ripe with tropical flowers and brine whisked away all her dour thoughts. She drew it in like a heady balm and glanced over the waving palms and ficus, the lush mountains rising to meet a cerulean sky, the turquoise water of the bay, and she smiled.

She was home.

People behind her cleared their throats. "Miss?" She continued down the stairs, excitement trembling through every nerve. That excitement only grew as she took a cab to the docks where she'd chartered passage on a boat. A yacht was more like it. Filled with people who reeked of wealth and privilege. Not that Morgan had anything against being rich. People who worked hard to earn their money deserved to enjoy it. She just despised the way some of them flaunted it and looked at her ragged jeans and t-shirt as if they would ask her to serve them drinks at any moment.

By the time those drinks *were* served—not by her, thankfully—and the boat took off, the sun kissed the horizon, causing it to blush in crimsons and corals. Morgan kept to herself by the starboard railing, gazing with delight over the sparkling sea she'd come to love so much. Gripping the wooden rail, she closed her eyes and listened to the sound of the water gushing against the hull, relished in the rise and fall of the boat over the waves, and tried desperately to pretend she was back on the *Reckoning*.

But the roar of the motor, clank of ice cubes, and mindless chatter of her fellow travelers forbade her even one moment of fantasy.

Just as well. It would only cause her more pain. And she didn't need more pain. Especially when Little St. James came into view. Memories, fresh from only two days ago, pierced her already-wounded heart—the crescent moon-shaped emerald bay, crystal shores, and rising jungles beyond. She could even picture Rowan's ship at anchor, teetering back and forth as wavelets came in from the sea.

But instead of the magnificent *Reckoning*, there were expensive sailboats and yachts bigger than houses and a fancy wharf that stretched from the water to several small buildings onshore and then beyond them to a large white one that resembled a palace. As the sun sank into the sea, men wearing shorts and flowery shirts scrambled out to light torches lining the walkway. Lights winked at them from the buildings, and a band began to play as the boat came to a halt and the crew helped the now-inebriated passengers onto the dock.

Against her every attempt to stop them, tears clouded her eyes.

"Are you all right, miss?" one nice man dressed in a hotel uniform asked her.

"Yes, thank you. Can you tell me where the historic fort is?"

He took her suitcase and walked her down the wharf. "About thirty or so meters down the road toward the west, Miss. But you can't go there at night. They've already closed up shop, I expect."

But Morgan did not let that stop her. She *could* not let it stop her. There was no way she could sleep tonight, knowing Rowan's grave was so close. She checked her suitcase at the hotel's concierge and headed down the paved road, grateful when the music and laughter behind her began to fade. Not so grateful when the pavement turned to gravel and the darkness grew as thick as the jungle lining the road. But a light ahead gave her hope, revealing a locked gate, beyond which she could only make out shadows.

Gripping the steel bars, she hoisted herself up and over the fence with ease and dropped to the dirt on the other side. Her heart thumped like the pounding of the waves in the distance. She could *feel* Rowan on this island, could almost smell his unique manly scent, hear the smoothness of his voice, see his confident swagger.

What was she doing? He was dead.

And she was a fool.

She started forward. Stone walls rose from the shadows, thick and aged. A small fort, no bigger than a large house perched on the edge of a cliff, materialized out of the darkness. Two cannons poked through openings in the wall, pointing their now closed muzzles toward the sea.

With only the light of a half-moon to guide her, she inched around the fort, seeking the graveyard. A mist rose from the Caribbean, curling over the edge of the cliff and swirling about her ankles. An icy chill chiseled up her back. Hugging herself, she navigated the rocky ground, stubbing her toe more than once and peering into the shadows. From what she'd read, Rowan's grave was clearly marked and just meters from the fort.

Then she saw it. A rounded stone grave marker rose from the ground like a hand reaching from the underworld. It had to be. Her fingers tingled. Blood rushed to her head. She drew a deep breath and started for it, tears already burning behind her eyes. Mist curled over the stone, and Morgan dropped to her knees and swatted it away.

Rowan Dutton
1671-1694
Pirate and Friend

Despite her tears, she couldn't help but smile. Only Nick would have taken the time to carve *Friend* into the stone. Closing her eyes, she leaned her palms on top of Rowan's grave

"Oh, Rowan, I miss you so. I'm sorry I left you."

She finally gave her tears release, and they came pouring down her cheeks with abandon. Sobs waved through her like a summer squall, and she gripped her stomach and leaned her forehead on the dirt. She didn't know how long she lay there, but long enough for the mist to cover her like an icy blanket and mud to cake her cheek.

She pushed herself up and stared once again at the stone, running her fingers over the words—the last remnant of the man she loved. Waves pounded in the distance, crickets chirped, and a night bird sang a mournful song. Rowan's only companions for centuries.

"What a lonely place to be laid to rest," she whispered.

An aged male voice sounded, sending her heart into her throat. "No, he's not been lonely."

She leapt to her feet, batting tears from her face, ready to fight or run if need be. "Who's there? What do you want?"

A man appeared out of the mist. An old man by the way the moonlight formed crevices on his face. He wore dirty jeans and a plain cotton shirt, and held a cane in his hand. He stared at her and smiled.

"I've been waiting for you for a long, long time."

Chapter 31

"What are you talking about?" Morgan backed away from the strange man. "Who are you?

"My name is Caleb Niles. But that isn't important." He kept staring at her as if she were a ghost—a delightful, magnificent ghost.

"Listen, I'm sorry," Morgan said. "I'm trespassing. I get it. But I came a long way to see this grave."

"I know you did, Miss Shaw." He kept smiling at her.

Morgan took another step back. "How do you know my name?"

He held up a wrinkled hand. "I'm not going to hurt you. Far from it." He sighed and leaned on his cane. "I came to help you." He glanced down at Rowan's grave. "Who do you think's been caring for this grave all these years?"

Fog slinked around her legs, shooting icicles through her and spinning her thoughts into chaos. "How do you know about Rowan Dutton?"

"He's my great-great-great-great, well, too many greats to count." He chuckled. "Let's just say I'm his grandson by eight generations or so."

At first such delight swept over her that she nearly ran to hug him. But then confusion—along with reason—wrestled her joy away. "Wait. He died the day I ... he died without having children."

The man's lips slanted. "That's one version of it, I suppose."

A cloud moved, freeing the moon to coat him in silvery light, allowing Morgan to search for any sign of insanity. But she found only clarity in his eyes. He knew her name, but he could have gotten that from her father. Still, she'd told no one about Rowan. "Did my father send you?"

He shook his head and smiled again.

"What do you want?"

Waves thundered and a salty breeze fingered his thin, gray hair.

"It's what *I* can give you that's important."

Yup. The man had to be crazy. He'd probably been the caretaker for this historic site for decades and had succumbed to delusions of being related to Rowan. And besides, who smiles like a giddy schoolboy at someone they've never met?

"Listen, I just want to be left alone. If you don't mind." She glanced at the grave. "I promise I'll leave soon."

"He told me you'd come. The message passed down through the centuries, of course. But he told me you would." He began fishing in the pocket of his jeans. Morgan prepared to run should he pull out a weapon. "And when you did, he said to give you this." He withdrew an object, a piece of jewelry from the way the moonlight glimmered on it, and held it out to her.

The amulet.

Morgan's legs gave out. He caught her elbow before she fell to the dirt. "How … what?" she mumbled as a buzzing filled her head and traversed down her body.

She grabbed the trinket, studied it, caressed it, made sure it was the same one. It was. Then holding it to her chest, she stared at the man in wonder, unable to speak.

He was still smiling. "He passed it to his son who passed it to his daughter who … well you get the idea. Instructions were passed along with it for the offspring who would be alive in this time. Then it came to me." He waved his cane over the scene where moonlight dripped like milk from trees and frosted the mist that waltzed over the ground. "It hasn't been a bad assignment, really. Great place to spend my retirement, especially since my wife died two years past."

"I'm sorry," Morgan managed to mutter, still clutching the amulet. "What instructions? Why give it to me now?"

His gray brows rose. "Because you must go back to Rowan. If you don't, I'll never be born."

"But you're obviously here."

"In one reality, yes."

Morgan squeezed the bridge of her nose and groaned. "None of this makes sense."

"Rowan wasn't supposed to die when he did," the man said matter-of-factly. "He was supposed to marry you and have eight children and be happy and turn away from piracy."

Eight? Morgan gaped at him. "But you don't know that. How can you know that?"

"Because I'm here talking to you now."

"But he's buried right here." Morgan stared at the grave then back up at him. "But you're here too. How can that be?"

He shrugged. "All I know is I'm supposed to tell you that you must go back. You're the only one who can save him."

"Then why did God send me back to this time in the first place?" Morgan groaned. "I don't get it." She rubbed the amulet, trying to conjure up tears. Of all the times to not be able to cry!

"It's your tears that make it work," he said.

"I know." She had figured as much after the last time the infernal trinket had hurled her through time. Tears of sorrow had sent her to the past, tears of joy to the present. What sort of tears would work now? Even so, was it really possible to go back? A thrill sped through her. "I still can't believe it."

"After all you've seen, *this* you don't believe?" He laughed, but then his laughter faded. "But there's just one problem."

Her gut clenched. Of course.

"There's no guarantee what time you'll end up in. You have a three-year window. You could arrive long after Rowan's been killed, or you could end up at the same time you left. I hope for my sake, it's the latter."

"But when I returned here, it was as if no time had elapsed."

"That's how it *should* work. But there's no guarantee."

"You mean I could end up in 1696 with Rowan dead, no friends, no family, no means to make a living?"

He nodded. "And once you go, you can never return. It's a huge risk." He rubbed his jaw like Rowan used to do, and she blinked at the similarity.

Morgan's palms began to sweat. "But the fact that *you're* here proves it will work … right?"

"In one reality, I suppose."

"Stop saying that!" Morgan ground her teeth together, frustrated, confused, unsure.

"However"—he raised a finger in the air—"That's in God's hands, isn't it?"

She drew a deep breath and gazed toward the sea. "Yes. I've learned that everything is in God's hands."

"So why not trust Him?"

The words sounded so simple. But the reality of what God was asking her to do shook every foundation she'd ever laid, everything she'd ever known and relied on. In this time, she had family, a home, employment, friends, and—though it wasn't the same world she left—familiar things around her. If she crossed time again, she would be completely and utterly alone. Everything would be stripped from her, everything she could cling to for help and support.

Everything but Me.

The voice inside her was strong and sure. But … how could she do it? It was like leaping over a cliff and expecting someone to catch her.

She raised her gaze to the old man again. "Can you tell me one thing, Mr. Niles? What happened to America? Do you know?"

He tapped his cane in the dirt as a salty breeze spun his gray hair. "I do. Though only by the Almighty telling me. He said you'd ask and that I should tell you that your great-granddaughter saved a man named George Washington from being killed. I'm not sure who he is, or was, but I'm guessing someone important."

Morgan's lungs turned to stone. She gasped for air.

He chuckled. "From the look on your face, I'd say you have another reason to go back. Not sure what this nation America was like, but I'm guessing it was a good place."

"It was," she mumbled, still trying to absorb the fact that her great-granddaughter played such a huge role in the country's beginning. Now, she had to go back. Or at least try.

But how could she? *Oh God, help.* It was one thing to be swept back in time without her permission, but quite another to do it on purpose, to jump into that black hole with no idea where she would land or if she'd even make it in one piece. And if the timing was off, Rowan would still be dead and America would still not be born.

"I don't get why God sent me back to this time in the first place. Maybe He doesn't want Rowan to live. Maybe He doesn't want America to be a nation." But that couldn't be. Could it? She closed her eyes, trying to collect her thoughts.

Caleb touched her elbow, steadying her. "Maybe God just wants you to trust Him."

Opening her eyes, Morgan nodded and drew back her shoulders. She had no idea why all this was happening, all this back and forth through time. But she had learned one important truth—God was real, He loved her, and He was intimately involved in her life. Like an adoring Father to an only child, He wanted the best for her, He wanted to teach her and help her grow to maturity, but He also had a plan for her life. And it wasn't always going to be easy.

But more than anything, He wanted her to trust Him.

Easy to say. Hard to do.

Yet, what else could she do?

"You're right." She smiled at Caleb and moved to give him a hug.

He embraced her tightly as one would a long-lost relative. "I've waited a long time for that hug." He wiped moisture from his eyes.

"Pleased to meet you, my dear great great-great-great … grandson." She laughed. "Feels weird saying that. Thank you for believing. For doing what Rowan asked. Thank you for bringing this to me." She held out the amulet.

"My pleasure." He smiled. "You might say my life depended on it."

Morgan took a step back. She had no need to conjure up tears, they were already streaming down her face.

"How will I know what day it is when I get there?"

"You'll end up right here on this spot. Just look for Rowan's grave. If it's here, you're too late."

I believe this is what You want me to do, Father. I'm trusting You. Heart thumping like a wildcat, Morgan held the amulet beneath her chin and allowed one of her tears to spill onto it.

An unknown force shoved her to her knees. Bright light forced her eyes closed. Heat swamped her. The crash of waves grew louder. Birds chirped. A gentle breeze brought the scent of salt and earth to her nose. She breathed deeply of it and tried to gather her nerves.

Now, the moment of truth.

Trembling shook every bone in her body. She opened her eyes, squinted in the sunlight, squeezed them again, then swung her gaze to the grave.

It was still there.

No! No! No! Morgan blinked, rubbed her eyes, and stared at the grave again. She collapsed to the ground in a heap, crumbling into dust, crumbling alongside all her dreams and hopes.

"Rowan!" she screamed and leaned her head onto the mound of dirt. Freshly turned dirt, not the packed, weed infested dirt that had been there before. She peered up through eyes flooded with tears to see the stone, not aged and worn, but newly carved.

Yet it said the same thing … portended the same doom for Morgan.

God, why, why? She convulsed with sobs as she dropped her face into the dirt again. *Now, what am I to do?* How would she live? Where would she go? *I trusted You.*

But worst of all, she would forever be without Rowan.

And America would never be.

"I don't understand, Father." She gasped beneath a sob. "Why send me back if it won't change things?"

Trust. The word whispered on the ocean breeze, stirring her hair like a lover's caress.

Still, she sobbed and sobbed, gripping handfuls of dirt, tempted to claw her way to Rowan lying beneath. But that was insane.

Maybe she was insane, after all.

Hours passed as she lay on top of Rowan's grave. Her tears finally spent, her body stopped convulsing, her mind drifting into a numbed state in which everything around her seemed but a dream. If only that were true and she could drift away, up into the clouds, up to where God resided and all was happy and safe.

You still have work to do.

The voice came from inside her, but it wasn't her. If she had any energy left, she'd laugh. What could she possibly do in this time, in this place, on this tiny island?

A deserted island. The realization blasted over her. She had no food, no way to get off the island except for the occasional pirate who came to bury treasure or scrape that gunk off his boat—ship, she corrected herself and nearly laughed again.

Father, if I have work to do, You're going to have to get me off this island. It was more of a statement than a prayer, for she really had no desire to do so. She would be perfectly content to lie here on Rowan's grave until her body shriveled away and set her spirit free.

A pelican landed in the grass a couple yards away. He flapped his wings and lifted his long pointy beak toward the sky, gulping down a fish.

She watched him with an odd—almost detached— fascination as he turned to face her, staring at her curiously with tiny marble-like eyes on either side of his small head.

She didn't want to be stared at. She wanted to be left alone. "Shoo! Get Lost!" she managed to shout at the bird.

Whistling met her ears. Not a bird's whistle, but a person's. "Penelope!" A man's voice sent Morgan's heart crashing into her ribs. Pushing off the ground, she struggled to rise, squinting into the sun now hanging low in the sky. The fort was no longer there, of course. What *was* there was a man in sailor's clothing walking her way. *Pirate.*

She turned to run. The stupid pelican flew after her, flapping its wings like some deranged bat before landing in her path.

"Get out of my way!" Morgan wove around the annoying bird.

"Miss! Miss! Are ye all right? Don't be sceered. I won't be hurtin' ye none."

The pelican leapt in her path again just as the man touched her arm. "Are ye all right?" he asked again, his eyes widening when he saw her jeans and t-shirt.

Small ribbons of gray etched through the man's long dark hair that was tied behind him. Short, but built like a sailor, his eyes crinkled in kindness.

"Yes. I'm fine."

"Are ye lost, Miss? Scads what are ye doin' out here all alone?" Dragging off his hat, he turned to the bird. "Penelope, back to the ship, ye flap-eared dolt!"

Only then did Morgan see the tips of two masts over the bluff. She glanced back at the bird, who waddled off like a chastised child. "You have a pet pelican?"

He scratched his bristly chin and chuckled. "Odd ain't it? She sort o' took to me an' me wife when we anchored at Bridgetown. Can't get rid o' her. The bird, not me wife, I mean." He laughed at his own joke. "She stays wit' the ship and helps catch fish fer the crew. Proof positive God has a sense of humor, says I."

His mention of God helped settle Morgan's nerves. "Then you're not a pirate?"

At this, he slapped his floppy hat over his pants and leaned over chuckling. "Nay, nay, Miss. Jist merchants. Me and me wife, an' our meager crew, o' course. Naw, nothin' to fear from us."

He shook his head and gazed back toward his ship. "Oddest thing, though. We had plenty o' water on board fer our trip, but when I sent ole Baker down to git a barrel, it had all leaked out. Ne'er saw the likes o' it. So, we were forced to stop here to get more." He scratched his head again and looked at her with suspicion. "Odds fish, an' here ye be."

And here she was, just having prayed—well, sort of prayed—for God to get her off the island.

"God works in mysterious ways, don't He?" the man added.

She would agree if she weren't so angry with Him at the moment.

"I don't suppose you could give me a ride to Kingston?"

Chapter 32

As it turned out, the merchant, whose name was Eli Wane, was on his way to Kingston. Coincidence or God? Eli said it was all God. Morgan had to agree. Who else could orchestrate events with such precision? What she didn't understand was why God hadn't used that precision to bring her back to the same time she'd left, for from the looks of the grave, she'd only missed Rowan by a month at most.

Just a month! What was that to God?

Still, she felt His presence and knew He was watching out for her. Knew He must have a plan. Even though her heart felt as though it had sunk to the bottom of the sea.

Though Morgan was tentative at first about boarding the merchant ship, Eli's wife Alice made her feel right at home. She placed her in a cozy cabin away from the crew, gave her a gown and underthings to wear, and spent hours talking to her, constantly exclaiming how lovely it was to have another woman on board.

Good grief, the woman could talk! But Morgan didn't mind. It kept her thoughts from both her grief over Rowan and her dire predicament. And it enabled her to avoid any prying questions to which she had no answer, or ones which her answers would label her crazy.

They fed her well, and other than conversing with Alice and spending restless nights teetering in a hammock, Morgan most enjoyed her strolls above deck where the stiff breeze galloped through her skirts and the sky spread an azure bowl over a sea glittering like sapphires. The sounds of water sloshing and planks creaking and sailors shouting brought her a sense of comfort, made her feel closer to Rowan, even though she knew she'd never hear his voice again or see him marching across the deck in that confident strut of his.

At times—well, many times—tears would fill her eyes, but the wind dried them quickly, keeping her agony a secret. Yet, even in the midst of an unknown future, Morgan found solace in recounting the many miracles God had performed in her life. It gave her hope that He still had more to come. She came to realize why He'd sent her back to her own time. It was a test. A test of her faith. Did she really trust Him? Was she really willing to give up all control and fling herself into His arms? She had. And now the rest was up to Him. He had a plan for her back in this time. And if it wasn't to marry Rowan, then it was something equally important. Maybe she was supposed to become the famous pirate painter LM, after all. The thought brought a smile to her lips and courage to her heart.

However, when they arrived at Kingston a week later, that courage seemed to drop to the depths along with the merchant ship's anchor. After saying goodbye and thanking the Wanes profusely for their kindness, she clutched her skirts, took a deep breath, and started down the sandy street of a town that appeared to be made up of nothing but tent-like structures, horses, wild pigs and chickens, and several disreputable-looking men wearing knifes, swords, and pistols.

She swallowed hard as some of those men's eyes honed in on her like sharks to a minnow. Only a few women strolled the streets, mostly blacks, some who looked like Indians, and just one or two white women on the arms of gentlemen.

Which is what she needed—one gentleman's arm in particular, or a particular pirate's strong arm would do. But that would never happen again. Women traveling alone were considered loose in this time, so she did her best to keep her head down and not appear wanton in any way.

Bells rang, horses neighed, and somewhere a fiddle played a sad tune. Across the bay a dozen or so tall ships floated at rest, their masts bare, their crews on shore for drink and women, while boats scurried back and forth from the closer ones, carrying goods. She searched for the *Redemption* or the *Ransom* or, even better, the *Reckoning*, but couldn't tell one from another.

Stepping over a pile of horse droppings, she headed toward one of few buildings in town, hoping to find a kind face, someone to ask about Charlisse and Merrick. The kind face belonged to Mable, the madam at a brothel, whose face lit up at the mention of Merrick.

"They set sail months ago. Ain't seen 'em since."

"What about Captain Dutton's ship, The *Reckoning*?"

The lady's painted face scrunched. "His anchorage weren't ever here, so I never met him. Heard he got killed, though."

Morgan swallowed a burst of sorrow. "I don't suppose you know the Pirate Earl and his wife?"

"Aye, thems I know. They're buildin' a home jist down the street a ways, through the jungle a bit, on a hill overlookin' the sea."

Morgan blinked and stared at the woman, too shocked at the good news to believe what she heard. But the words finally settled in what was left of her rational mind. Grabbing her skirts, she sped off in the direction the woman pointed, yelling "Thank you, thank you!" over her shoulder.

"If ye ever need a job, Miss, you come back and talk to ol' Mable."

Leaving the town behind, Morgan slowed as the street narrowed and ascended up a hill. A wagon passed, loaded with what looked like sugar cane, and the driver tipped his hat at her and continued onward. Just when she thought she'd gotten lost and was about to turn around, a wooden gate carved out a section of the jungle to her right. Over the top stretched an iron rod bearing a sign that said *Paradise Gained.*

Yup. That sounded like them. Unlatching the gate, Morgan slipped inside and started down a wide dirt path that soon opened to a field of grass dancing in the ocean breeze.

In the distance, a small brick house with a wide wooden front porch stood before the foundation of a much larger house set on a cliff overlooking the sea. Palms and flowering cassia trees offered shade to the structures and beauty to the scene, along with clusters of wild orchids, hibiscus, and begonias.

The mighty Caribbean stretched to the horizon in ribbons of glittering jewels in the noonday sun. Morgan stopped for a minute to take in the beauty, excitement spinning through her at her upcoming reunion with Juliana and Alex.

Movement tugged her gaze to the right where a man stood near the edge of the cliff, gazing out to sea.

Must be Alex. She started toward him, but the closer she came, the less the man looked like the infamous Pirate Earl. And the more he looked like …

Heart leaping into her throat, she stopped and stared … blinked, rubbed her eyes, and stared some more. The man's light brown hair, streaked in gold, blew unfettered behind him. Tight black pants were tucked inside knee-high boots. His white shirt fluttered in the wind beneath a very familiar vest fringed in silver, while a gold earring gleamed from his right ear. But it was the way he was standing … the particular stiff line of his shoulders, the slight tilt of his hips, the way he crossed arms over his chest and stared off into the distance as if he bore the weight of a thousand agonizing hearts.

Morgan inched closer … and closer … and closer … her mind not believing what her eyes confirmed with each step.

He heard her then. Glanced over his shoulder … eyes locked on hers … brows bent together. He stared, turned around. Stared some more. A black cat nestled in his arms. He took a step. The misery shadowing his features slowly lifted.

Rowan!

Morgan didn't know how. Didn't know why.

And didn't care.

She ran to him.

Setting down the cat, he engulfed her in his arms, picked her up and swung her around, laughing, crying, and laughing again, his voice breaking in sobbing ecstasy.

She wrapped her arms around his neck and showered his cheek with kisses. "Rowan, Rowan, I love you so much, Rowan!"

Setting her down, he stared at her, his chest heaving, his eyes filled with disbelief. "Morgan. You're here!"

She nodded, tears spilling down her cheeks.

He cupped her face and studied every inch of her. "Oh, God. Thank you!" He drew her close. "I thought I'd lost you forever."

Morgan leaned her head on his chest and drew in a deep breath of him, savoring his strength that surrounded her like a shield, protecting her from every bad thing, every tragedy, every heartache.

She was home.

"Hey, you're supposed to be dead! I just came from your grave." She pushed from him and playfully slapped his arm. "You went for Brasiliano's treasure! Even after you promised me!"

He gave her that delicious, mischievous grin of his. "Nay, Lady Minx. That was Abbot." He took her hands and glanced down as if trying to contain his emotions. "After you disappeared …" He hesitated. "After I lost you, I couldn't do anything, couldn't breathe, couldn't move. 'Twas Nick who brought me back to the ship. Abbot defied my orders and went after the treasure himself, he and three of my crew. Bloodmoon killed him in a sword fight, and Nick thought—"

"It would be a good idea to say it was you buried on the island." Morgan finished as the realization struck her.

"Since my pirating days were over, 'twas best my enemies thought me dead."

"But surely Bloodmoon would have told everyone it wasn't you."

"Nay, he and his entire crew sank to the depths in a storm a week later." He shook his head, frowning. "Providential for me. Not so much for him."

Finally overcome by the excitement, Morgan's head grew light. She stumbled, and Rowan helped her to sit on the grassy knoll and knelt beside her, elbows on his knees. "Rowan, I thought you were gone. You scared me to death."

He brushed a lock of hair from her face. "'Twas you who scared me to death! I thought I'd never see you again."

Blackbeard leapt into her lap, nudging her with his head and uttering a happy *merowww*. "Blackbeard!" Scooping up the cat, Morgan nestled him close, tears filling her eyes. "You kept him. I can't believe you kept him."

"He was all I had left of you. Him and this." Rowan produced the amulet from his pocket. The ruby winked at her in the sunlight as if they shared a grand secret. Hadn't she just held it in 2015? She reached for it like an old friend.

"Ah, ah, ah." Rowan snagged it back and dropped it in his pocket. "Do you take me for a fool, Lady Minx? I forbid you to touch it ever again. In truth, though it was my mother's, I fear I must rid myself of the dastardly thing post haste."

She touched his arm. "No. You can't. You must save it. Give it to your son with a message."

"A message?" He rubbed his jaw, but then his eyes widened with a twinkle. "Son?"

"Yes. I'll tell you later." She lowered her lashes, suddenly shy.

He brushed a curl from her forehead. "Alack, so you *did* go back to your time?"

Closing her eyes beneath his caress, she leaned into his palm and nodded.

"But here you are. How?"

"A long story." She gazed up at him, rubbed the stubble on his jaw then gripped his arm as if to reassure herself he was real. Strong and firm, like always. The scar across his cheek had healed and faded, along with the wounds on his chest she could see through his flapping shirt. His baldric and pistols were missing, as was the sword at his side, but a long knife was housed tightly in his belt. "Did I hear correctly?" She teased. "Did the great pirate Rowan Dutton forsake his buccaneer ways?"

He grinned. "Aye. You changed me, Lady Minx." Wind tossed hair in her face, and he lovingly eased a strand behind her ear. "You and your God. *My* God now."

Another burst of happiness exploded within her. "Really? That's the best news I've had in a long time! I'm so happy, Rowan."

"He forgives me," Rowan said. "And He's given me a new start."

"He's given *us* a new start." She smiled. "What about your wealth, your status?"

He shrugged and glanced out to sea. "In truth, they have lost their appeal. I'm a son of God now. How can you achieve more status or fortune than that?"

"Are you ever going to kiss me, you crazy pirate?"

"With pleasure." Pulling her up toward him, he pressed his lips on hers and drank deeply, gently, and eventually passionately. His stubble scratched her cheek, his breath warmed her neck, his love flooded her body, warming and exciting, transporting her through time, into an eternity where they would always be together.

Pulling back, he leaned his forehead on hers, breathing hard.

Someone cleared their throat in the distance.

Rowan glanced over his shoulder. "Come, I want you to meet someone." His eyes sparkled as he helped her up and led her toward the house, where Alex stood on the porch holding something in his arms.

"Where's your crew, your ship?" she asked Rowan as Blackbeard sped off in pursuit of a lizard.

"In the bay. Getting ready to set sail. Alex and I plan on aiding Captain Merrick in rescuing his daughter." He squeezed her hand. "Nick and Edith will be so pleased to see you."

"Me too." She smiled.

If Alex was shocked at seeing her, he didn't show it, only grinned as his glance shifted from her to Rowan. "God is indeed a God of miracles," he stated before nodding to Morgan. "Good to see you again, Miss Morgan. Seems you have arrived just in time. I do believe Rowan would have withered away from grief if you hadn't."

She exchanged a loving glance with Rowan as they mounted the steps and her gaze landed on the swaddled bundle in Alex's arms. She squealed with glee. "I see I'm not the only happy arrival."

"Meet Miss Esther Hyde."

Long lashes feathered flawless skin in an angelic face that was as small as Morgan's fist. "A girl. She's beautiful, Alex. Congratulations."

"Morgan!" Juliana burst onto the porch and dashed into Morgan's arms. "You're here! We thought you were gone forever."

"God had other plans." Morgan nearly choked in the woman's tight grasp.

Juliana gave her brother a sly smile. "I told you things would work out for the best."

"That you did, sister dear." He smiled.

"Esther is beautiful," Morgan said. "Just beautiful!"

Both ladies wiped tears from their faces. "She is, isn't she?"

"And you are well?" Morgan asked. "The delivery went well?"

Juliana nodded, gazing up at her husband. "If only my husband would allow me to hold my daughter once in a while. I can hardly pull her from his arms."

"You'll have plenty of time whilst I am away, Sweetums." Alex replied in mock severity.

"Away?" Juliana snorted. "You're not going anywhere without me, husband."

"Indeed?" Alex's brows rose.

As the couple began to argue playfully, Morgan slid back to stand beside Rowan. He swung an arm around her waist, staring at her as if she would disappear if he dared look away. She leaned to whisper in his ear, "Speaking of children … I have it on good authority that we are supposed to have a bunch of them. Eight, I believe was the number I heard. And at least one of them is extremely important for history. After we are married, of course."

He turned her to face him, took both her hands in his, and raised them to his lips for a kiss. "Then we best not delay another moment, Lady Minx."

If you enjoyed this book, you might enjoy the other books in the series, ***The Redemption***, ***The Reliance***, ***The Restitution***, ***The Ransom***, ***The Reckoning***, ***The Reckless***.

Author's Note

To all my beloved readers, this is purely a work of fiction told from the point of view of a young American woman. References to the greatness of the United States and the country's value in world history are in no way meant to disparage any other country or their accomplishments. Having never been to England, I did my best to envision what America (or at least San Diego) would be like if it had always been under British control. I also did my best to envision a world in which America had never been. Since I have no basis on which to gauge what type of world that would be, I can only go by what history tells me. It is not my intention to insult Britain, its people, its innovation and technology, or its incredible value to our world.

In addition, I do not hold the view that every ailment, including cancer, anxiety, depression, or OCD is a result of demonic oppression. This was the case with the heroine, but I do not believe that is always true.

About the Author

AWARD WINNING AND BEST-SELLING AUTHOR, MARYLU TYNDALL dreamt of pirates and sea-faring adventures during her childhood days on Florida's Coast. With more than fifteen books published, she makes no excuses for the deep spiritual themes embedded within her romantic adventures. Her hope is that readers will not only be entertained but will be brought closer to the Creator who loves them beyond measure. In a culture that accepts the occult, wizards, zombies, and vampires without batting an eye, MaryLu hopes to show the awesome present and powerful acts of God in a dying world. A Christy award nominee, MaryLu makes her home with her husband, six children, four grandchildren, and several stray cats on the California coast.

If you enjoyed this book, one of the nicest ways to say "thank you" to an author and help them be able to continue writing is to leave a favorable review on Amazon! Barnes and Noble, GoodReads, Bookbub (And elsewhere, too!) I would appreciate it if you would take a moment to do so. Thanks so much!

Comments? Questions? I love hearing from my readers, so feel free to contact me via my website:
https://www.marylutyndall.com/
Or email me at: marylu_tyndall@yahoo.com

Follow me on:
BLOG https://crossandcutlass.blogspot.com/
PINTEREST: http://www.pinterest.com/mltyndall/
BOOKBUB:https://www.bookbub.com/authors/marylu-tyndall
AMAZON: https://www.amazon.com/MaryLu-Tyndall/e/B002BOG7JG
Instagram: https://www.instagram.com/marylu_tyndall/

To hear news about special prices and new releases sign up for my newsletter on my website Or follow me on Bookbub!
https://crossandcutlass.blogspot.com/p/newsletter-signup.html
https://www.bookbub.com/authors/marylu-tyndall

To hear news about special prices and new releases that only my subscribers receive, sign up for my newsletter on my website or blog

Check out my **Reckoning Pinterest Board** as you read!

Other Books by MaryLu Tyndall

THE REDEMPTION
THE RELIANCE
THE RESTITUTION
THE RANSOM
THE RECKONING
THE RECKLESS
THE FALCON AND THE SPARROW
THE RED SIREN
THE BLUE ENCHANTRESS
THE RAVEN SAINT
CHARITY'S CROSS
SURRENDER THE HEART
SURRENDER THE NIGHT
SURRENDER THE DAWN
FORSAKEN DREAMS
ELUSIVE HOPE
ABANDONED MEMORIES
SHE WALKS IN POWER
SHE WALKS IN LOVE
SHE WALKS IN MAJESTY
WHEN ANGELS CRY
WHEN ANGELS BATTLE
WHEN ANGELS REJOICE
TEARS OF THE SEA
TIMELESS TREASURE
WRITING FROM THE TRENCHES

~ 391 ~

9 780990 872351